RISE OF THE HEROES

A Novel By

Sedona Capellaro

ISBN-10:1502876329
ISBN-13:9781502876324

For

Auntie Nee, who loved to read.

&

Auntie Janice, who never lost her imagination.

ACKNOWLEDGMENTS

I would like to thank my family and friends for their support, helpful tips and inspiration for the completion of *Rise of the Heroes*. I could not have done this without you. Thank you to my friends for being understanding while I locked myself in my room like a hermit to write and be my creative loner self.

Thanks to my mom, for her advice, love and scolding's when I get all doom and gloom about things that piss me off. Thanks to both my parents for their amazing support during and after this book's creation. Thanks to my dad, for giving a work of *teen fiction* a chance (and liking it) thanks for always giving me full support and helping me choose a title.

Thank you to my loving husband, who took the time to feed into my insanity by not laughing at me when I asked random off the wall questions and helping me figure out how to translate into words the sword fighting scenes and hand-to-hand combat scenes... even though I broke things with our fake swords...sorry babe, no more sword fighting in the house.

Thank you to my little brother Taylor, who inspired me to do something I love and run with it, no matter how scary I think it might be.

Thank you to my best friend Amanda, who always tells me the truth, even if I don't like it and who I can always count on for anything even if my request seems impossible...or crazy.

Also, to those wonderful people who helped me edit...giving this book sort of better grammar and okayish spelling, I couldn't have done it without you.

Thank you to my Uncle Greg, who kept in touch with his theater teacher, so that one day I could ask for advice on how to begin this process.

Thanks to Ted Bacino, who gave me the right direction to take, so I could get this book (and the next…however many) to print, so I could share it with the world.

Thank you to those perfect strangers who told me they were excited for me and excited to read *Rise of the Heroes*. You helped me push myself to finish it so I wouldn't let you down.

Thank you to my childhood friend, *My Zach*, who taught me how to value true friendship, taught me what love is and of course, how to properly make a fort, you're my hero and I will always remember everything you taught me.

Without any of you I would not have been able to do this. Your support and love kept me moving forward and made me proud of myself for the first time, so thank you, for everything.

If I forgot anybody, it's because I'm a jerk-face, so I'm sorry about that…sort of.

Chapter One

I am running. My heart slams into my ribs as if it can outrun my feet. I am running as fast as my legs can carry me. The uneven ground slows me down. I dodge tree limbs and stumps as cool night air burns fire through my lungs. I must run faster. It is too close. I can hear its feet pounding into the earth behind me. Fear turns my blood to ice as it pumps too fast through my veins. It is getting closer. I can smell it as it gains on me. The sickly sweet scent of rot and sulfur assaults my nose mixed with the scent of the forest. I burst from the trees to a clearing, a large almost perfect circle in the middle of the thick trees. The harsh light of the moon hurts my eyes making them water. I hear a river just beyond the clearing. My senses tell me the river is close. If I could get to it and jump in the rushing water, the thing could not follow. I do not know how I know this, but it is my only chance. I am at the tree line leaving the clearing behind me. I pump my burning legs. My hair whips violently behind me in the wind, as I push myself harder. The back of my neck tingles and I know the thing is behind me. It lets out a growl that rattles my bones. It is right there, closing in. I cannot stop, I cannot look. I have to keep moving. Do not look Skye, do not turn and look. I have to look.

I woke up covered in sweat, breathing way too heavy to be considered normal. My black comforter lay in a heap on the hardwood floor and my sheets were tangled around my legs. I looked bleary eyed around my small room, gasping for air as I untangled myself from my sheet web. It was nearly sunrise based on the dull blue light coming through the large window above my messy desk. A chuckle from the dark corner of my room makes me scream and scramble back up the wall behind my bed.

"Well…that was very entertaining, I think you could have done without the drool though." he said as he got up from my squashy armchair, stretching to his full height. *Damn him to hell.* I thought trying to regain my composure.

I let out a breath, beginning to calm down again as he plopped himself down on the bed with me. I flipped on my bedside lamp casting light onto his face. His eyes shone bright green in the light of the lamp. Each day his bright eyes seemed to range from hazel to green to blue, depending on his mood. His short sandy brown hair stuck up in the back, making him look carelessly handsome. A lopsided grin crept up his thin face, telling me he was about to say something sarcastic. Before he could open his mouth I made sure to hit him hard with the pillow I was clutching. He tumbled off the end of the bed. *Good, serves him right.* I thought feeling triumphant for finally getting one over on him.

"What the *hell* Zach! You could have woken me up or something!" I said hoping my voice sounded more menacing to him than the squeaky sounds I was hearing. He came up laughing and crawled back onto the bed throwing the pillow at me. I dodged it and glared at him, wrapping my arms around my knees still feeling shaken from the nightmare.

"When I first got here, it was still too early and you were doing fine, all curled up like a little mouse in a nest. I figured you should keep sleeping. Then you started thrashing around and throwing your blankets… same nightmare again?" Zach asked, his voice turning serious with a hint of concern.

I had been having the same nightmare ever since we moved to Washington. Every single morning right before the sun came up I woke up in a full freak out; sweaty, short of breath and rattled to the core. The *thing* that chased me through the woods was always the same, you would think I'd be used to it by now. I always looked back in the dream and caught sight of it. It looks human but there's something very, just *wrong* about it. The flesh on its arms and face is grey, like gross wet concrete grey, with weird symbols burned black into it. It always wears some kind of dark pants and a dark t-shirt. Its eye sockets are dark holes with no eyes but with deep red and orange hellfire flickering in the empty space. Its mouth is always gaping, as if the jaw had been broken open, with jagged teeth like a sharks, covered in bloody yuckness from something it probably ripped apart. It always moves at an ungodly speed and smells like sulfur and rotten flesh. I shuddered remembering the details of the thing.

"Yeah, that thing is so gross and when I wake up I swear I can still smell it…and no…I know what you're going to say… I'm not the one that stinks." I said knowing he would have a witty comment to that. A smile threatened to take over his face, but he managed to hold it down.

"You sure little mouse? Cuz your morning breath is kickin." he said still trying to be serious. I hit him again.

This was how our morning routine went every day. He ended up in my room before the nightmare kicked in and then he seemed to make it better. It's totally against the Academy Dorm Rules but we don't care. He's my rock and I am his. Besides, our relationship is just *not* like that. He is my family. I grinned at him and flipped him off. This made him roll his eyes at me.

"Classy Skye, *real* classy." he said shoving me off my own bed. I landed on my covers in a heap on the floor. I glared up at him, causing him to smirk at me.

"Okay little mouse, classes start in a little over an hour and I want to actually *experience* breakfast today. Time to get up and moving… and *please* for the love of god, go brush your teeth and take a shower." he said grinning down at me. I stuck out my tongue as I stood up. I glared at him as I grabbed my outfit for the day from my tiny closet and headed for my bathroom. He grabbed my remote from my bedside table and flicked on the TV. I smiled to myself looking at his long form spread out on my messy bed. He scratched the thick blonde goatee on his chin, which sprouted out as soon as we moved here. I giggled at him as he absently chewed on the string from his black hoodie. He made a point to turn to glare at me which usually means I have ten seconds before I get attacked. I love pushing his buttons.

"Okay, okay, I'm going!" I said throwing up my hands and shutting the door.

The dark grey tile floor chilled my bare feet as I turned on the shower to full heat. I stripped off my sweats and tank top and hopped in the stone shower. I let the hot water run down my face washing away the nightmare. I couldn't seem to shake it off this time. Putting my hands and forehead on the rough stone wall, I took a few calming breaths. The walls chilled my head and hands as I let my thoughts wander aimlessly.

The stone walls of this place make everything feel freezing all the time. The school is an actual *Castle*. The Castle had been built by some rich guy back in the day who thought he was a king or God. He apparently died of some kind of weird mental freak out before it was fully finished and it fell into disrepair. The Chambers family bought it about 100 years ago and remodeled the Castle. At first it was a summer home for the Chambers family, later they decided to turn it into a private school for children of the rich elites of the world. The Castle was remodeled again and they added four, three story dorms and one large-scale gym across a massive courtyard. The whole school and grounds felt very medieval.

The main Castle holds classrooms, the Library, the kitchens, a Dining Hall or *Ballroom*, along with the Infirmary and staff offices.

The grounds are a large-scale rectangle with a big, highly manicured, grassy courtyard in the middle, complete with stone benches and statues of Greek Gods all over the place. The Gym houses the staff members on the second and third floors in their own apartments. The Gym and Castle face each other with the two three-story dorms on each side. Over the past five years the Chambers family added horse stables, riding arenas, a massive indoor combat arena, green houses, grazing pastures and a slaughter house, all behind the dorms on one side of the grounds while the dense woods loom behind the other two dorms. If I had to guess, I would say there was at least 200 acres of grounds for the school. The builders like to use lots and lots of grey rocks, as if they want to blend in with the constant grey skies, it felt dreary. The only part I'm a fan of, is the cathedral style ceilings, making every room feel bigger. My dorm room is pretty small, but with the tall ceilings it didn't feel like a little box. I'm just glad to have a bathroom I don't have to share with anyone.

Chambers Academy in Washington State's Cascade Foothills, has been my new home since late June. The summer was crappy and cool and now that it's October, it's even colder. It rains excessively here and I can't stand it sometimes. I'm from a small town in Arizona where we actually saw the sun more than once a year. Zach and I were the only two that go to Chambers without having rich parents. Both our mothers landed jobs as Professors. Professor's kids get a full free ride education; the downfall is we get to be at the bottom of the social ladder.

My mom got a job offer to teach Natural Science. Since the job market is such a mess, she took it without hesitation. Zach and I grew up next door to each other and his mom got the same offer, but for her skills in Geology. Zach and I thought it was really weird that both of our mothers were offered positions at the same time to the same place, but neither of us could complain, because we were going to be together. I would have probably died if I had to leave him behind and come to Washington alone. As annoying as the weather is, I was happy my mom finally got a decent job that didn't involve waiting tables until three in the morning.

In 2008, the world economy started to fall apart. The housing market collapsed, followed by banks and car companies. The US Government tried to give everyone a hand by giving out free money. That failed because the money just ran out. Nobody could seem to use it to make a comeback, or create new jobs for the working middle class. Even the super rich started to lose money, not much, but enough for them to make a stink about it. The middle class soon fell into poverty.

Now, jobs are near impossible to find and the people are suffering in silence. Nobody can talk about how much it pisses them off or how bad things are without being thrown in prison for treason, all thanks to the Silence Act. That's the fun of it, everyone has to pretend everything is all sunshine and daisies. You are not allowed to mention any of it in public at all. The Silence Act was created to stop free speech so the masses in the US didn't revolt against the Government like they did in Egypt and Ukraine in 2013. The People, even the Media, can't talk about politics or the wars or how your constitutional rights are violated all the time.

Wars with other countries were erupting all over the place off and on again. Syria, Afghanistan, Russia, Ukraine, Japan, Israel and even China are fighting with each other. The USA, England and France are trying to keep it under control. WWIII has finally started. The threats of open war and bombings constantly haunt the people of America, everyone is afraid. Nearly all of our armed forces are aiding in every country but this one, to help stop the fighting. Most of our population, male and female aged 18 to 25, is overseas fighting and dying to try to get the world right again.

Since Government had reinstated the draft, Zach and I had gotten our draft letters right before we moved, at the beginning of June. That gave us one year to finish high school, pretend to be wild and reckless and then get kicked into the armed forces. As soon as we graduate we get shipped off to boot camp. We both try not to think about where we will end up.

The US Government recently required all students over 16 were trained in combat, just in case of an outbreak of war on homeland soil, since most of our soldiers were out of the country. The Government wanted everyone 'combat ready' as a failsafe. This was thanks to the recently passed Combat Act. We spent the summer practicing our hand-to-hand combat skills with the weapons master Joe. It gave us something to do and a head start on our combat training classes. Sadly it also prepped us for when we head into the military after graduation. It's scary to think about the wars raging right now while we are hidden, pretending to live in times of peace, in the middle of nowhere.

So, Zach and I came to the grey state with no kicking or screaming. Now that we were settled, we felt that complaining about the weather helped pass the time. The tans we had from all the years of living in the sun, were already gone. It's like the grey skies of this state just sucked out any life you might have had.

After brushing my teeth, I glanced up at the tacky mahogany framed mirror and studied my reflection. I still looked like the same person I was in Arizona. Same copper colored hair framed my face and fell down in waves to my butt. Same small nose with freckles sprinkled across it and over my high cheekbones, same orange colored eyes and dark lashes. Crazy eyes, I know…my eyes are the color of flames, orange with flecks of gold. I probably got them from my MIA father because my mom is all blue-sky eyes and sandy blonde hair. With a tan on my skin, the fire and copper worked for me. Call me shallow or vain but, I really thought I was somewhat pretty with tan skin. Now, thanks to the lack of sun, I just looked like another pale gothic teenager with freaky eyes. If I weren't so short, it probably wouldn't matter what my face looked like. I'm on the low side of five foot three. I wouldn't say I'm super thin or anything, I definitely have some curves going on, but I'm short, so I'm invisible to everyone but Zach, which is ironic because he stands a little over six feet tall. We are very odd looking when we stand side by side. He usually rests his elbow on my head just to piss me off. A hard knock on the door disturbed my nitpicking of my reflection.

"Dude, Skye, you're going to make me miss breakfast *again*!" Zach said in an irritated tone yelling through the door. I knew not to test him this early with an empty tummy, so I quickly finished my minimal amount of makeup, pulled up my dark blue jeans and threw on my heavy black sweater. I ran into my room and threw on my cowboy boots, scarf and wool coat and grabbed my bag. Wearing layers is very popular in this state with the weather being confused all the time. *Damn Washington weather to hell.* I thought as I wrapped my scarf around my neck.

Zach and I raced down the side steps to the bottom floor and out the small hidden stone door to the grounds. This awesome hidden side door is how Zach was able to sneak in so easy. The side stairs took you out a side door, which was supposed to be locked from the outside, but we did a little tinkering with the lock and a best friend entrance was made! The door came out between my dorm and his, so it made it really easy for him to get to my room. We walked quickly across the massive courtyard with a fine mist coming down from the always-grey sky. We made it to the dining hall with 30 minutes to eat and then haul butt to class.

Chapter Two

I always feel awed walking through the Main Castle doors. The entrance to the Castle is just plain *huge*. It has two jumbo-sized doors smack dab in the middle of two towers that dominate the front of the Castle. The doors alone are at least 10 feet tall each and heavy as hell. Once inside, a giant grand staircase made of grey marble and wrought iron handrails occupies the center of the grand entrance.

Our school has a weird set up for a school cafeteria. I guess this is how super rich kids eat, because this place is *really* formal. The Dining Hall sits inside the front tower on the left of the staircase. The school tries to keep it cozy though, there's about ten deep chocolate brown squashy armchairs facing the massive stone fireplace. There's floor to ceiling windows on one whole side of the room with large doors that open to a patio made of stone, for outdoor eating or dancing when we have a Ball. This place has a *Ball* for freaking everything; Harvest, Thanksgiving, Winter Solstice, Christmas, New Years, you name it and Chambers Academy has a Ball for it. Regular round tables fill the sides and center of the Dining Hall decked out with red linens and gold vases, complete white roses. Crystal and cast iron chandeliers hang from the ceiling trusses casting a warm glow over the tables and seating area. The food is always on nice tables, set up like a buffet, on the back wall where the massive kitchens are hidden behind two giant mahogany doors.

A *servant's staircase* sits along the back wall next to the kitchen. In a thick spiral the servant stairs go all the way up to the sixth floor, staying well hidden, but still large enough for five people to go up side by side.

All our food is fresh and grown here on the grounds in the green houses. This school is very much *off the grid*. Solar panels power everything, which is weird considering I had seen blue skies maybe once since moving here. The water comes from a huge underground spring and we use our food scraps as compost. But, on the flip side, we have state of the art technology for everything too. Everyone has smart phones and tablets and the internet here is faster than you could blink. Rich kids have to keep up with social media and all that socialite crap on the outside.

On the other side of the grand staircase is the wide-open Library and of course, a second massive fireplace to match the one in the Dining Hall. The Library reminds me of what rich people in movies have in their houses. There's no beady-eyed librarian and it's hardly ever quiet. Study cubes are randomly placed all over, with lots of couches and chairs to make us all comfy. Book shelves line every freaking wall and go all the way up the six story tower. Two black iron spiral staircases lead up to the skywalks, which reach the walls of books and lead to each floor of the main part of the Castle.

"I *told* you we would make it today. I keep my promises." I said loading my plate with eggs and lots of bacon from the buffet table. Zach snorted and shook his head.

"Yeah, except it's been over two weeks! You're lucky I haven't shriveled up and died!" he said as he loaded his plate and followed me to sit down.

"Always the dramatic one." I said under my breath, rolling my eyes. We sat in our favorite spot in front of the fireplace in the biggest squishy chairs closest to the heat of the fire. Zach and I preferred to face the fireplace and eat with our plates in our laps so we didn't have to sit too close to the kids sitting at the tables. They were children of super rich important people and Zach and I were poor nobodies, we were better off staying away from them. I felt a headache coming on, I had forgotten how noisy it is in the Dining Hall in the morning. Phones made beeping sounds and laughter carried around over the general murmur of too many people talking at once.

I started eating my bacon with my fingers, staring at the flames in the fire, when a pair of designer jeans and knee high black boots blocked my view. I looked up at a girl I had never seen before. Her eyes were striking, like big emerald jewels, lined with thick black lashes. She had lovely fair skin and full red lips. Everyone here seemed to have overly bright crazy colored eyes, this chick was no exception. Her blonde hair was braided to the side with hot pink dyed artfully into her long braid.

I glanced over at Zach and almost choked on the bacon I was still chewing. His fork of eggs was half way to his mouth, which was hanging open and his eyes were wide unblinking as he stared at her. He looked hilarious. She spoke up, dragging my attention back to her.

"May I sit with you guys?" she asked. For a second of madness, I wanted to be a total jerk and tell her to go away, but I held my tongue. I had never seen her before now; I'm willing to give people a chance. I looked her over again. She might be dressed in fancy rich kid jeans and boots, but her artfully torn up black and pink t-shirt and leather jacket made me feel like she could be normal. Most kids here wear super expensive overly fancy outfits, like what you see in magazines or those stupid polo shirts and slacks. I glanced at Zach again. He was still there, egg and fork still in place. I recovered from the shock of her first, trying not to laugh at Zach's display of gawking.

"Uh…sure, I guess. That's Zach." I nodded in his direction and he promptly dropped his fork onto his plate with a clatter. I fought down a laugh again. "And I'm Skyelaa, but you can call me Skye. Are you… new here?" I asked looking up at her wondering if she was here to check out Zach. I'll give people a chance but I am naturally untrusting of females. They think by pretending to be *my* friend I will hook them up with Zach and that is *sooooo* not the case. He's my best friend and too many girls have hurt me because he didn't want them. It's a messed up system. One girl, at our old school, put gum in my hair because Zach shot her down for the Homecoming dance and went with me instead. That alone made me a little petty about other girls.

"I'm Miles, well…it's really *Elmirah* Crane, but who the *hell* names their daughter that? Anyway, I'm from Seattle and just started here, today is my first day of classes and I was actually wondering if you guys would mind showing me around? The Dean assigned Lindsay Cambell to show me around yesterday but she…well, she's a bitch and just took off when I asked to see the stables… she said horses and dirt is for *poor people*? Anyways, you two look normal, so what do you think? Would that be cool?" she asked as she sat in the chair next to me. That brought a smile to my face.

Well… this one's a keeper. I thought to myself. Lindsay Cambell is a *bitch*. Lindsay is your typical mean girl; she's a rockin five foot eleven, with a body of perfection. Her fiery red, gently curled hair and flawless skin are *always* in perfect order. She has crazy beautiful electric blue eyes with white flecks like feathers that make guys drool. I envy her looks, but nothing else because her personality just plain sucks. She's rude, spoiled, petty and goes out of her way to make people feel like they are beneath her. From day one she hated me, called me names, spread nasty rumors about me and treated Zach and I like the plague. All because she found out, we were here tuition free and our mothers weren't rich socialites. I smiled over at Zach who had come back from his fit of awkward.

"Course you can Miles. Come join the Poverty club." he said and she chuckled. Her laugh was like the way she talked, like soft chimes. It was kind of delightful...*ugh delightful? What the hell is wrong with me?* I thought noticing instantly, Miles brings out the girly side of me a little too much for my liking.

"What classes you got?" I asked shaking off the feeling. She dug into her hot pink messenger bag and pulled out a piece of paper handing it over. Miles was either a genius or her parents were determined to get her into a top of the line college. All her classes were AP classes and we had AP History and AP Natural Science together. Those of course were the only thing I was smart in, as this school didn't think Painting and Creative Writing were AP worthy.

"Okay, so you're super smart like Zach here... all AP classes?" I asked. Miles shrugged and a little blush colored her cheeks. "You have Nat Sci with me first and History with both of us second. Then English with Zach and Latin with him too. After that is lunch, then you have Trig with Zach and Geology with him too and...oh Painting with me. And Combat training for an hour after dinner." I said. She nodded looking excited.

"This is my first time having to do combat training; I just turned 17 last week and with me switching schools there was no point in starting it at my old school...heck I was only there for three weeks anyways. I hate why we have to do it, but... I'm kind of excited to learn to be trained in combat. But I don't get to start it officially until the end of the week though." She said. At least we were the same age, Miles looked much younger than 17 to me.

Zach and I are literally one month and five days apart in age and both turned 17 over the summer. Thanks to Joe and training here during the summer, I was pretty good at fighting now. Zach and I are both trained up enough to hold our own. We both can shoot a gun pretty well, but enjoy the specialty weapons more. Zach is great at sword fighting and using the crossbow. I'm great at knife fighting and using the long bow. We are both good at hand-to-hand but for some reason, I'm better at it than he is, which shocked me because of my size. Zach told me it's because all dangerous things come in small packages, like rattle snakes, poisonous spiders and little mice like me.

"Well that's great, at least you won't ever get lost here because you will always be with one of us. I guess you're kind of stuck with us for good now. I hope we don't end up irritating the crap out of you too fast." I said with a smile. I more hoped she didn't end up irritating me. I'm easy to irritate…I think it's from the lack of sleep or sun. The bell chimed signaling that it was very much time to go learn stuff. I sighed and looked down at my cold bacon. I grabbed up my stuff, tossing the food in the compost bin in the corner and the three of us began the hike up the servant steps to the sixth floor of the Castle.

As usual we barely made it on time. My mother wouldn't appreciate me being late again. I sat at my usual lab table in the back with Miles keeping close behind me looking slightly nervous. In public schools if you were new, you had to do the whole 'Hi I'm the new kid speech' but at private schools, we got to avoid that embarrassment. Miles didn't strike me as the type to care much about doing that, but I could tell she was relieved.

She sat down like a hot mess, dropping all her crap on the table by mine. People had been staring at both of us and whispered behind their hands. Lindsay was the only one not really whispering, making sure her voice carried back to us.

"I heard she's the Deans niece and her father had to *beg* to even get her in here. I guess she comes from a *blue collar* kind of family. Yuck… I heard has a criminal record in Seattle too… something about breaking the Silence Act. I personally think it's a bunch of bull letting trash like her attend this school. I also heard she's here on a *scholarship*…so she's as pathetic as they come. It looks like she found someone who's as low class as her, I saw her hanging with the

Poverty Twins this morning." Lindsay said to her friends. Lindsay's little clique of bitches all giggled. God I hated them sometimes.

This bitch clique consists of the overly pretty crew of; Maddie Sims; a short, slightly homely looking brunette, with a round face and deep purple hued eyes, Kayla Crew; a dark skinned slender beauty with yellow cat-like eyes and Carla La'vue; a curvy beauty from France with long caramel hair and sea green eyes. See, it's the eye thing here, like it's a requirement for admission or something.

I snorted and rolled my eyes. I'm used to being bullied by pretty girls; it happened a lot in our old school. Between Zach's slew of followers and my weird colored eyes, I learned to let insults roll off my back, well… mostly. By the time I got here and school started, I had a pretty thick skin when it came to Lindsay's onslaught of insults. Miles looked like she wasn't as used to it as I was. Color was rising to her cheeks and her hands were clenched into fists. I reached out and patted her arm.

"Don't listen to them Miles, Zach and I don't care about who you're related to or not or whatever. We don't care about how much money you have or what social group you run with. We don't judge people." I said reassuringly as I patted her arm. She looked over at me with tears in her eyes. That shocked me. This girl needed to be a *little* tougher than that or they would eat her alive here.

"How did they *know*? I never said anything to Lindsay about that." she whispered to me. I looked at her feeling really confused now.

"*What* are you talking about? You…were released from prison or something?" I asked feeling a little impressed because Miles didn't strike me as the type to commit any kind of crime.

"No, I was arrested in the U-District in Seattle for standing by a group of people who were planning on protesting the Silence Act downtown the next day. I spent all of ten minutes in a holding cell when my dad posted bail and talked the cops out of pressing charges. I was literally just *standing* there with my friend talking about other crap and next thing I know I'm thrown to the ground, hand cuffed and tossed in the back of a cop car. I am not a criminal, just wrong place wrong time kinda thing. But I mean, whatever about them knowing that, how did they know that Dean Jacobs is my uncle? That was not supposed to get out to anyone but the staff." she said her voice shaky. I couldn't figure out why that even mattered. Everyone knew Professor Warren was Zach's mom and Professor Miller was mine. But hey, if it upset her it must be pretty bad. I tried to sympathize with her.

"Miles, its *fine*, Lindsay has her ways of getting all the info she needs to make everyone feel like crap. She's a pro, could be an investigative reporter for a gossip rag mag if she wanted to. Don't worry too much; she's just a board rich girl with nothing better to do. If it makes you feel better, I got here in June while everyone was gone for the summer and somehow Lindsay knew my mom was Professor Miller and that I'm here tuition free, before classes even started. Same with Zach, his mom is Professor Warren. She made fun of me more than she did him because he's cute and whatever. She called me names, spread a bunch of rumors and *even* tried to trip me down the main stairs once. I take the back stairs to avoid her and her crew. They like to hang out on the landing of the second floor and tease people. It's as if she's a combo-pack of all the mean bitches from my old school in Arizona. If you avoid her, she will back off a little. So don't sweat it. If she sees it getting under your skin she will just keep it going." I said.

Wow, I'm not much for a monologue but I just kind of rolled with that one. I felt like I needed to protect this girl from the world at all costs, weird, I only really ever cared for three people my whole life; my mom, Zach and Mom Two (aka, Melinda Warren, Zach's mom). *What the hell is happening to me, I'm with this girl for less than an hour and all of a sudden, I'm all bleeding heart for her?* I thought to myself.

"Thanks Skye, I know I'm being a baby about it, but he asked me to keep it to myself, so that people wouldn't think he was showing favoritism or something. I even came here using my mom's last name so nobody would know…It's cool though I'm sure it would have come out eventually. And, she can kiss my ass about having a problem with us being friends; I'm not ashamed to be in the Poverty Club…sounds, like Robin Hood. Like we are fighting the rich kids here and keeping it real with the rest of the world. These kids are the elite, they don't know what it's really like out there, but we do and that's how we're different." she said as my mom walked in and did her signature whistle calling for quiet. *Club? When did Zach and I become the leaders of an actual Poverty Club? I thought when we called ourselves that we were totally joking.* I thought feeling amused at the idea.

I sat there mulling that over in my head. These kids in this school really were the elite brats of the century. Miles was totally right. They had no idea what it was like to feel hungry or to have to sew your own clothes so you can keep wearing them. They didn't have to work on the outside like I did. Well, I didn't consider it work. I painted landscapes of the Red Rock formations around our town and sold them to rich tourists.

Our old hometown still got tourists but only the rich and super rich went there now-a-days. My mom sold handmade jewelry and worked at a diner at night while teaching Natural Science at the Community College twice a week. We made it work, but living in an Airstream and never eating more than one meal a day and washing our clothes in the stream wasn't a picnic. If Zach's camper hadn't been parked next to mine when we first got there when I was two I probably would have really known what it's like to feel poor and lonely. We had great times building forts, playing in the creek that ran along our campground and catching tarantulas. Yeah, we did catch giant spiders, gross, I know.

"Skyelaa? Are you with us back there?" my mom's voice made me jump. A few people snickered. *Of course, my face would turn red at this moment…perfect.* I thought trying not to feel stupid.

"Uh, sorry ma…uh Professor, I spaced out for a second there. What was the question?" I asked trying to will the blush away.

"You need to learn to focus Skyelaa… anyways, I was asking why the Scientific Community now requires Plutonium and Uranium on the Periodic Table?" My mom asked as her cobalt eyes bored into my soul. Damn her. I couldn't remember which one was naturally occurring and which one was manmade. I did what I always do. I tried to guess, I figured 50/50 odds weren't that bad.

"Because Plutonium is a naturally occurring substance of the Earth and Uranium is man made from the partial deconstruction of the Plutonium cells. Uranium is now on the table because it's as commonplace in the world as Plutonium. This of course is due to the creation of large-scale bombs, nuclear power plants and use of Plutonium and Uranium for medical equipment. The Plutonium is dangerous to the world when its molecules are messed with and broken down too much to reach the Uranium. Which in the sense of things is probably not a good thing because man has officially altered the balance of the natural world by messing with something so toxic…right?" I said my voice finishing strong and determined. *Nailed it!* I thought while my mom looked stunned. *Uh oh…did I screw up and break the Silence Act?* I thought as my feeling of triumph faded out like water vapor. She cleared her throat and quickly recovered.

"Well, yeah your right. Man messed with naturally occurring Plutonium, which contains, when broken down some Uranium isotopes. Only when the isotopes are altered are they even more damaging to the world around us. In a sense, Skyelaa is right, the balance of nature is thrown off and in order to restore it, the uses of all radioactive substances need to end. If not soon, the natural world will revolt and try to right the imbalance." my mom's face looked flushed as if she was out of breath. I swear I could hear a pin drop. In the two months of classes, she had never gained absolute silence. Shock shone in her eyes as she looked around at all of us. Miles's hand shot into the air. My mom blinked a few times and cleared her throat as she nodded at Miles.

"Miles ma'am." Miles said as she lowered her hand. My mom nodded again and made a note on her hand held tablet. "So you have a question Miles?" my mom asked.

"Yeah, let's say the theory is correct with the radioactive material now affecting the natural world, hypothetically speaking what could the side effects be to the world and mankind?" she asked. *Oh boy, this is a hell of a can of worms.* I thought feeling guilty. This could land my mother in hot water with the Government if someone reported her. The Silence Act covered things like these. When they say Silence on all political issues, they mean it. Saying out loud to a classroom full of potential voters, that mans creation of radioactive material is bad, is like pointing a fat finger in the Governments face. This is a big No-No. I now felt like a huge ass for even mentioning that at the end of my long-winded response to her question. I glanced over at Miles and back at my mom.

"Well, hypothetically speaking? As in just a random guess based on my scientific background and experience, and not my personal opinion?" my mom asked.

"Yes ma'am. I am just curious, perhaps I'll write my final paper on the hypothesis of the uses of Plutonium and Uranium and what factual science has to offer as answers." Miles said calmly.

Yup I now had a girl crush on this chick. She just saved my mom from getting into any trouble. Lindsay would probably be the first to report a violation of the Silence Act on my mom because she hates me. I let out a breath.

In school, the teachers and professors are allowed to use their working knowledge and super bon-bon degrees to give us knowledge, but their personal opinions on anything Government related must be left out. I'm not saying that the Government is all insane and can listen to every classroom in America; they don't really have the time to spend doing that. They have the technology for sure, but not the people to compile the reports and waste time listening to random chatter in a classroom. There are bigger things like wars and terrorist attacks going on. People only really were arrested when they were not being careful or some jerk reported them to the local police. Now even if some jerk like Lindsay reported my mom, Miles had her covered.

"Well Miles, think of it this way, your body has everything in it off the Periodic Table that is found and natural made from the Earth. Let's say you ingest some manmade poison such as Uranium. Your body will react with all the firepower it has in steps, saving the 'big guns' for last. Your body will first try to expel the toxin. You will sweat, urinate and maybe vomit. If this doesn't work you will get a fever, the fever is an indication that white blood cells have taken over to try to fight and kill the toxin. If they cannot, your fever will get higher and higher. When the fever reaches its peak trying to burn out the toxin, your body will start to drop your temperature rapidly, cooling your core. Next come seizures, because of the heat from your fever and your body beginning to dehydrate. You will continue to vomit and sweat expelling the toxin. If you cannot get rid of it you will die as your body shuts down slowly organ by organ." My mom paused and looked around at all of us. She had everyone's full attention so she continued looking happy at our focus.

"Now think of the Earth as a large scale version of the human body, only much harder to kill and less likely to give up the fight for life. Earthquakes, floods, tsunamis, volcanic eruptions, hurricanes, major storms and atmospheric disturbances are trying to fight off the toxin. Think of these events as large-scale white blood cells and the

Earth trying to expel the toxin. That's just on the Earth's surface itself. The Earth's core could super heat or super cool to try to expel the toxin, which in this case the toxin is the radioactive materials.

Plants and animals will die off or evolve too quickly, or even end up with deformities. Humans, as part of the animal kingdom are the same. We could end up with more diseases and health issues. We could also end up with deformities or new or worsened abilities. Scientists believe, based on the facts gathered, that humans will suffer the greatest changes along with the changes of the Earth.

So, something to research for yourselves, look up what has already changed on the Earth, in the last 100 years. I want a two page paper to be handed in Friday based on this discussion with your scientific findings. I had other plans for homework but this topic seems to have your undivided attention, so we will go with this for the week. Did I answer your question Miles?" my mom asked. She had been pacing along the white screen flashing photos of nature. The screen was directly connected to her mini tablet in her hand. She probably had a lesson planned similar to this and the photos worked perfectly for it.

"Yes ma'am, I think it makes perfect sense, the Earth is just like us in many ways. Thank you professor." Miles said politely.

I couldn't help it, I was smiling like a fool. Miles was not only super smart on the book side of things, but she also knew how to keep my mom from losing her job. Lindsay had been trying since classes first started to get my mom to share an opinion on anything to do with the Government so the school would fire my mom and throw her in jail for breaking the Silence Act. Two points for Miles and me then.

Chapter Three

The bell signaled the end of class and Miles and I headed off to the fifth floor for history with Zach. We both chatted about nothing in particular on the way to class. I led Miles to the back table where Zach was already seated. He was reading some pages in his drafting book and sketching in his notebook. The boy could make a stick figure look like real life. He's such a talented artist it makes me sick sometimes. I can paint okay but I'm a little jealous of his ability to sketch anything. My paintings are often *messy* versions of the landscapes I enjoyed painting so much. Zach looked up at us and smiled.

"These seats taken? Me and my friend here thought we should introduce ourselves and see if you're single." I said managing to keep my face serious. Zach chuckled and shook his head.

"Sit down weirdo, class is about to start and I don't really want to get yelled at again for you being a distraction." he said as Miles and I sat on either side of him. The table we always sat at had room for four. *We just need one more person now to make it seem like we have more friends.* I thought looking at Zach and Miles as they talked about drawing. I guess I thought that too soon, because about a second later, a guy I had never seen, in a lime green hoodie and black jeans, plopped down in the seat next to me.

He looked like a model for surfboards. Shaggy blonde messy

hair grew in waves just to the middle of his ears; his face was really tan, so tan that I felt insanely jealous. He had a bit of a baby face with no facial hair and light eye lashes. He met my eyes and smiled, his teeth were so white it was blinding. I checked out his eyes because I knew I would see some crazy wild color. I was right, brilliant silver, like melted down bars of the brightest silver known to mankind. They were freaking cool looking. I smiled at him. *Two new people in one day is really weird.* I thought, trying to brush off the feeling that I already knew both of them somehow.

"Hi, I'm Cameron Williams, I go by Cam though, is it cool if I sit with you guys…like forever?" he asked. His voice was low and gentle, I liked it. I turned and looked at Zach and Miles they both nodded, Miles letting out a giggle. *Great, one more addition to the Poverty Club. Poor kid probably has no idea what hanging with us would do to his social life.* I thought almost feeling sorry for Miles and Cam.

"Hi Cam, I'm Skye, that's Zach, and Miles is next to him. You sure you want to risk your social status by sitting with us"? I said after pointing to my friends. Cam laughed, as if I had said something really funny.

"Dude, I really don't care about that crap. I just want to be me and be around people who are real, not fake. I don't think you guys would make me pretend to be something I'm not, like the spoiled brats that go here. I'm from Spokane, my dad's a truck driver and my mom is a vet assistant. We're a very *blue collar* family. I'm here because I was recruited by the school for a free ride scholarship for my metalwork; I like to weld stuff in my spare time, like scrap sculptures and stuff. The first person I met for a tour of the place, besides the Dean, was your mom Skye." he said looking me in the eyes with a half smile teasing his lips. Well, that was news to me. *Why didn't she say anything to me after class this morning about sending the new kids to Zach and me?* I wondered feeling oddly connected to these two new students.

"Professor Miller told me to find you. She said I would feel more comfortable with you and your friends because you guys were more down to earth, like me. It was nice of her to be all cool like that." he said as he looked at all of us with those crazy eyes. Zach chuckled and reached across me to shake Cam's hand.

"Welcome to Chambers Cam." he said. I smiled at Cam and Zach's exchange. Well this meant we needed to have a movie night then and break the 10pm lights out and no co-eds in the dorms rules.

"Alright, so as your official initiation to The Poverty Club, I say… this weekend, we watch a crap horror movie in my room and pig out on candy. After lights out Friday night, it's on kids." I said. That earned me three smiles and lots of nodding.

Turns out Cam had the same schedule as Zach, Miles and me. We all had classes together at one point or another. Zach and Cam both had Computer Design and Architecture together. He had Italian and Creative Writing with me, and Trig and Geology with Miles and Zach. The only classes I was on my own in were Geometry and Archeology. That suited me just fine for Archeology, because I had a great time in that class. Archeology is something I actually love to learn about. I'm a bit of a nerd and love rocks and minerals, ancient ruins are pretty cool too. I'm stuck in Geometry because I'm *terrible* at math and couldn't figure out Trigonometry like the rest of them. Cam even ended up with Agriculture on Mondays and Wednesdays with us and the after dinner Combat Training.

All students have two days a week that we have to help maintain the food we grow in the greenhouses. It's how the school provides enough food for all of us and we provide labor to earn our meals. Most of the kids here hate it, I really don't mind because it makes perfect sense to me. 'You want to eat, you have to earn it' is the way the world works anyways.

****

By Friday, I'd gotten a really good sense of who Miles and Cam are as people and we get along pretty darn well. For Zach and I to make any friends outside of ourselves is a huge feat.

Miles is a city girl to her core, having grown up in Seattle living on Queen Ann Hill with her dad. Her dad is some big wig at the FBI and makes huge money running anti-terrorist tactical units. He doesn't care much about the money though. Since her mom had left her and her dad before she was two, it was just the two of them. He taught her how to sail, ride a horse and even fly a helicopter, which I thought was freaking cool as hell.

He also took her to plays in theaters all over the world and on trips to ancient buildings and monuments. All around he seemed like a great dad who was always there for her. He even made her do chores; he said it was his way of making her earn her keep in the world. I thought that made him a real stand up guy. I guess even though the Dean was her uncle on her dad's side and her dad could pay the tuition, she came here on a scholarship. The school had sought her out like they had done for Cam about 2 weeks ago. They said the school told them it was something to do with her having special abilities that the school needed in students. Miles thought it was just because the school wanted to up the student population so they could brag about high graduation percentages so they could up the tuition costs. Either way, I was glad she was here now.

Cam is more of a country boy. His family has a full-blown farm over in Spokane Valley Washington. He helped his parents by taking care of the land while they were gone at work. At night, because he went to school part time and worked the rest of the day on the farm, he would weld his sculptures or got to go out riding. I had been wrong. He wasn't a surfer; he was an outright adrenaline junkie. He rode dirt bikes, rock climbed, white water rafted, base-jumped, snowboarded and did free style motocross at fairs in the summer for cash winnings. He said his favorite thing in the whole world was anything that could possibly kill him. He wants to squirrel suit off the cliffs up by the mountain and parachute into the valley below us. I wanted to join him on that one, only because I am terrified of heights and that would be an extreme adrenaline rush.

Zach and I had been kind of the loaners of the student body for the past two months. Even though he is good looking and easy to get along with, everyone knows we are only here because our moms are professors. The rich elite kids are really hard to get to know and become friends with. They have really high standards about how much money or power your family has and what socialite group you're in with. Zach and I have none of that to share, so a lot of the student body doesn't accept us. People either pitied us for being poor, or hated us for being allowed to taint the campus with our free hand out of education.

One thing kept bugging me though. Why didn't they have brothers and sisters? I know why Zach and I didn't…maybe it made sense for Miles's situation too. But Cam's parents were still together. I just found it a little strange that we were four *only children* all hanging out together. Not to mention we are all here because the School wants us to be. That alone is a little bit creepy. I didn't dwell on it for long as I wandered in to the class I hated most and none of my friends were in, Geometry. *Ugh sometimes I wish that I could opt out of this class because whatever I get stuck doing in life I won't need this crap.* I thought as I headed past everyone to the back of the room.

I sat in the back like I always do and watched all the others file in. Kayla Crew from Lindsay's mean girl clique was in this class too. Apparently, she is just as bad at math as I am. None of the rest of her friends are in this class either. That always makes me smile a little. The smile was always short lived because she still belonged with the elite kids, so no matter what, she had someone to sit next to and gossip with in here. This time she snagged her claws into some guy named, Jake...or Josh... eh who cares what his name is. They were talking looking at something funny on her smart phone. *Probably funny cat pictures or some stupid gossip about who's sleeping with someone's boyfriend.* I thought already annoyed at the giggling and whispers.

Suddenly Jake, or Josh whatever, turned at looked pointedly at me. His eyes bored into me as if he could hear my inner trash talking. It was hard to tell what color eyes he had from the back of the class, they looked like...well, the sun. I couldn't tell if they were white, orange or yellow. He turned back and said something else to Kayla before I could even decide to glare at him or flip him off. I had a feeling they had been talking about me or something that involved me and I didn't like it at all. I just wanted to be left the hell alone. I had a year and then I would be graduating and far away from here probably dying in the war. My thoughts drifted to what bigger problems I had after graduation. *I think I would join the Air Force, learn to fly and steal a jet so Zach and I could run away from the war and go live on an island alone.* I thought. My future seemed to be set and short lived based on what was to come with getting drafted. I sighed and tried to think of something more positive.

The professor walked in and cleared his throat loudly, which he did every day to make us be quiet. Everyone paid him *most* of their attention. The professor is fun to stare at. He looks like an old wolf, with a long nose, poufy grey hair, a long beard and deep green eyes that seem to always find his prey. The man *had* to be old as dirt, but didn't have a line of age on his face to show for it. He began his lecture and sought out his prey with those knowing eyes to answer his questions. Today the prey was Kayla. *Oh this should be good.* I thought feeling happy it wasn't my turn today. He asked her to answer every question in his lecture and I enjoyed watching her squirm through the entire class period.

I practically skipped into Painting class after an unusually dull Archeology class. The professor's heart didn't seem into the lesson on obsidian rocks today. She seemed highly distracted. I brushed the concern of her distraction aside as I drug my easel over near the window to my usual spot. I was working on painting the forest right out the window and the perfect view of the massive inactive volcano they called Mt. Rainier that peeked over the treetops.

The great thing about painting class is the professor doesn't care what you paint, just as long as it's your own and you show proper use of your tools. Different brushes, pallet knives, oil colors, acrylics and watercolors. As long as we paid attention during the Wednesday lecture of historical art and proper use of tools, we were free to be artists.

The professor always says, *"Do what feels right today, let the brush guide your thoughts into a direction and stick with it."* I love Professor Kirra; she is younger than all the others are and let us call her Kirra, instead of the formal title, Professor Williamson. Kirra is an artist to her core, with tattoos all down her arms of flowing symbols and colors and probably all over her body too. She has long raven hair, always braided down her back with streaks of blue and purple artfully dyed into it. Thin and tall, like probably six feet tall at least, with eyes the color of teal waters in a tropical paradise. Kirra is a little bit my hero. She's so free; I've never seen her angry or even frown. She always seems to have the ghost of a smile on her lips.

I was setting up my color pallet when Miles drug her easel next to mine. She had a blank canvas in her hands as she plopped down on her stool next to me.

"I like the detail in the trees, you have an eye for the small individuality of each branch." she said looking over at my canvas. I smiled at her. I had been working on this piece since classes started in

September.

"Thanks, I love doing paintings of landscapes and nature. What kind of work do you favor?" I asked. I had watched Miles start a painting and then trash it, looking unsatisfied every day all week long. I had a feeling she was feeling pretty stuck with where to start. Starting a painting is the hardest part.

"I'm big into everything I guess. Sometimes I paint people, other times its animals or nature. Just whatever I think of, or sometimes what I dream too." said Miles as she set up her pallet.

"Your dreams?" I asked, thinking of my haunting reoccurring nightmare, making me shudder.

"Yeah, it helps me understand them sometimes…especially nightmares. It makes for scary looking paintings sometimes, but it makes the dreams make more sense or at least me less afraid of them." she said. Well that sounded a little depressing. I didn't *ever* want to paint that monster in my own nightmare. *Especially the eyes, they would follow me around haunting me while I'm awake…no thanks.* I thought as we fell into a comfortable silence as we worked. I enjoy her company. I usually glued myself to the window all by myself, which usually suited me, but it's nice having her next to me. We didn't need to talk, each of us totally absorbed in the canvas. It was like coming out of a daze when Professor Kirra came over and shook my shoulder.

"Hey, it's lookin good Skye. Class is over now and you two are going to be late if you don't haul outta here." she said with a smile. I looked over at Miles who looked as dazed as I felt. That always seemed to happen to me when I painted. We hastily packed up our stuff and put it in our individual supply closets. I caught sight of what Miles was working on. I stopped in my tracks, as a chill ran up my spine. It was a rough beginning to a wooded meadow, a meadow which formed almost a perfect circle with a figure running through the middle of it. It was very rough, like most paintings are before you begin the process of details. *It couldn't be the same as my nightmare.* I thought fighting back a panic attack. Miles looked up at me concerned.

"Skye? Are you all right? What's wrong?" she asked as she turned her easel towards the wall next to mine.

"What…is that going to be?" I asked trying to hold it together.

"I'm not really sure yet. It's from a dream, like a nightmare I guess. But, it was really bleary during the whole dream. That grey thing there in the middle of the painting…I think it's a monster or zombie… it scared me to death when I first had the dream. Like I said, I paint my dreams to try to overcome or understand them… I know it's weird." she said a blush creeping up her cheeks. I was *not* going to tell her about my own dream. So, I shrugged it off. *Maybe we both have seen the same movie and this is the result?* I thought to myself. I think I liked that idea best. I threw on a reassuring smile and walked out of class with her.

"I'm good, it just looked a little familiar to me, I think it will turn out great though…a little creepy but great." I said. She smiled back at me as we headed down the servants stairs.

We didn't have Agriculture, so we headed straight to the girls dorm to go dump our stuff in our rooms. As it turns out, Miles ended up in the empty room next door to me. That's great, because when you have a six-foot tall best friend who happens to be a boy, sneaking into your room all the time, it's good to know your neighbors. My room is at the very end of the hall so, it's a dream come true. Miles is on my right and the side staircase is on my left. Perfect.

The rest of the rooms up on my floor were empty, because the school didn't have as many students as they did rooms. The other girl's dorm across the courtyard from mine was full while, only the first and part of the second floors are full in my dorm. I'll admit, I'm a bit spoiled and I like having my own floor.

Zach's dorm is full; he's in the boy's dorm next to mine. The boy's dorm across the courtyard is nearly empty with only one floor full. If my floor filled up, I would probably hike up to the attic and stake out a room up there. Growing up in a camper made me really appreciate space and silence.

I set my school bag on my messy bed and wandered over to Miles's room. It was unlocked and I probably should have knocked, but I have really crappy manners sometimes. Miles was putting her things neatly on her desk in her spotless room. She jumped a foot in the air and squealed when I shut the door behind me.

"Sorry! I should have knocked! Miles, I'm sorry, I have terrible manners!" I said, though I was trying not to laugh. She was facing me now, clutching her chest like her heart had popped out.

"God Skye! I think I had a mini heart attack! Geeze… you don't need to knock if it's unlocked. Only cops and teachers knock anyways, my rule of thumb is that none of my friends have to knock when they pop by. You must have the same rule of life then?" she asked, a smile tugging the corners of her mouth. I shrugged looking around at all her paintings and photos of her and her dad doing stuff.

"Yup, sorry I scared you though, guess I sprung the 'not a knocker' thing on you a little soon here." I said. She nodded as she opened her closet pulling out a red scarf.

I wanted to jump into her closet and roll around in it. *She has amazing clothes!* I thought. We were about the same size and all the colors I was seeing were the same that I loved. Blacks, reds, oranges, charcoals and even some electric neon colors too.

"You have amazing clothes! I'm so jealous right now…all my

favorite colors too!" I said chuckling to myself. She smiled and pulled out a bag I hadn't noticed, from the very top corner shelf.

"Here, we wear the same size even though I think you're a little shorter…no offense… anyways, this is all stuff I don't wear anymore that I was going to get rid of before I came here. But, my dad said to bring it just in case I needed them still. He gets a little paranoid and said we could be snowed in up here for a while and extra clothes could come in handy. I think you'll wear them more than me and if I happen to need them, I know where you sleep." she said laughing as she tossed the bag to me. It was *packed* with jeans, shirts, tank-tops, a couple dresses, and a couple jackets including a beautiful real brown leather one that fit like a glove. There was also one pair of knee high, amazing, real leather, brown boots, with thick rubber soles and a chunky heel. I almost cried. The jacket and boots matched perfectly. My cowboy boots are on their last leg of life and I'm running out of leather patches and shoe goo to fix all the holes and tears. A new pair of cute boots literally made my day.

"Are you sure? I mean, these are *all* name brand and high quality things in here. These boots alone are, I dunno, almost three hundred dollars?" I asked for the hundredth time. Miles rolled her eyes again as I finished playing dress up in the bag of clothes and left on the boots and jacket.

"Skye, take all of it now, or I'll throw it out my window. I told you I don't need it. Think of it as me paying you back for all the help." she said. I looked at her, confused.

"What help?" I asked. She sat down on the bed as I neatly folded everything and put it back in my bag of goodies.

"Combat training. You've been here in the class for a couple months and I know I will need your help. I'm *dead clumsy* and will probably need extra training on the side. I got out of it this whole week, but my uncle said I have to start today. My dad kept saying it was more important than anything else here, I think he knows something is going to happen soon…you know, like with the *stuff we can't talk about?* I just got a letter from him saying that I had to get on it as soon as I was settled. He said in his letter, that I would need it, but couldn't say much more about it yet." she said looking down at her hands. I nodded, her father had some power out there in the world and maybe something was coming. I felt a little pull in my gut when I looked at Miles, sitting on her bed looking all sad and slightly pathetic. I wouldn't let anything happen to her. *No way. I have to protect her at all costs… I feel very protective of her…weird.* I thought to myself.

"Miles, you're going to be fine at it. And yeah, maybe something is coming, hopefully not, but with what's been happening with the wars and stuff; I knew it would only be a matter of time. So why don't all of us, Cam too if he wants, throw in extra practice on the weekends. Zach and I took some extra training over the summer with the weapons master, Joe. She is a real hard-ass but she knows her stuff, I can ask her for help if you want? I'll owe her a favor but it would be worth it if your dad is right. You know, Zach and I got our draft letters this summer. We have until June, before we ship out and for us to make it out there, extra training might be good." I said. Joe would be the only one I would want training us anyways. She wouldn't tease Miles for being clumsy like some of the other professors or the other kids will.

"That would be great, thanks Skye. I'm so sorry you were drafted already. That's…well its awful. I don't know what to even say." she said pity crawling over her face. I shrugged, swallowing hard. My own mother didn't know about the letter yet. I've been too scared to tell her. I did what I do best; I put on my brave face and changed the subject.

"No biggie, well its dinner time, we should probably go meet up with the guys or something?" I said as I grabbed up my stuff and we headed out of her room over to mine. I threw my new goodie bag on my bed, lead her to the side steps and out my secret door. As soon as we opened it to come out, Zach and Cam were right there waiting for us.

"Let's eat, I'm starving and I know you are." I said looking up at Zach and hooking his arm. He chuckled as Miles hooked Cams arm.

We strolled over to the Castle together talking about the movie night we had planned for after training. It was perfectly planned. Zach and Cam's rooms are next door to each other. They planned to finish their homework after training and heading over to my room at lights out at 10pm. I'm the only one who has a 60" Flat screen TV mounted on the wall. Zach and I found it in the back of my closet hidden behind a false wall. Weird thing to hide in a wall, but he fixed it up and mounted it in my room. It made for perfect movie nights, like being in a theater. I kept snacks and soda in the false wall now, thanks to my mother who gave me the mini fridge from the camper. My excitement grew at the thought of having a movie night with my new friends.

Chapter Four

Dinner was nice with the four of us enjoying each other's company in front of the fireplace. We were laughing, joking and having such a great time we were almost late to our 6pm combat training. The massive Training Arena, sat behind the horse stables and horse riding arena. We had to run through the falling rain to make it on time to change into our training gear. We hurried past the green houses and stables, jetting into the locker rooms though the side doors, with only a few minutes to get changed into our gear. I knew we had to hurry when the rest of the girls were already dressed and heading to the arena.

We all have our own locker, with three sets of training clothes, which were black cargo pants and black t-shirts. The uniforms also require a utility belt to hold a standard nine millimeter handgun with two extra clips, two throwing knives and a hand held radio and a small med pack in a waterproof zip pouch. We don't get real bullets for the guns unless we are target shooting during training. The guns and clips are full of blanks until our trainer issues live rounds. We have to wear thick black tube socks under the standard issue military black combat boots. They gave each of us more socks than we knew what to do with. Foot care is very important to the military; we had to get our feet checked once a month for fungus or blisters. Gross.

I quickly showed Miles what to put on for the training. It was

Friday, which meant hand-to-hand sparring. Therefore, the utility belt needed to be empty of all weapons with only the med kit. They did this to teach us to be used to the weight of the belt with and without weapons. We finished dressing and headed to the weapons cage to get the rest of Miles's gear so she could put it in her locker.

Joe was the lady in the cage that cleaned and cared for all of our gear. She's a mean looking woman with a hard chiseled face and built like a lineman. Joe's brown hair was buzzed short, military style, which didn't fit her girly overly bright, lilac eye color.

"Hi Joe, could you get me a nine with three full clips of blanks and two blades? And can I ask you a favor?" I whispered to her as she dug out the gun and blades for me. Joe and I have an understanding and a pretty good friendship.

Zach and I are the only ones that seemed to show her any attention or who are nice to her. The way I saw it when I first met her, is that she is in control of all my weapons and that's the last person I would want to be mad at me. So, I found out she has a sweet tooth and always bring her candy from my stash when I can. We became fairly close over the summer when she was teaching Zach and me to fight. She usually hooks me up with extra stuff, like knives, I have a little collection of them now in my false wall. She handmade some of them and they are really awesome blades.

Joe leaned closer to me, the iron bars of the cage splitting her features and nodded to Miles with suspicion. Miles was red in the face and looked nervous as hell.

"She's cool; these are for her to keep in her locker." I said and sent Miles to go put them away. "I need to ask if Zach and I can use the Arena and training weapons every Saturday night for a while? After 7pm? We need to help Miles with the training and work on it ourselves. There will be four of us total, Zach, me, Miles and Cam. You already know about Zach and my situation with the draft and now, I have it on good authority that something big may be happening soon. You want in on this? Maybe teach us a thing or two?" I asked. Joe's eyes lit up a little. She had been confined to the Cage after the new trainer came in September. Before that, she was preparing to teach classes during the summer, Zach and I had become her only students. The new trainer is above her rank from the US Army and had been assigned to take over her training courses. It had come as a shock to Joe; she had been really excited to teach.

"Only if you get me some of those chocolate chip cookies your mom makes. Don't be late. I expect all of you here at 6:45 sharp every Saturday. I will be training you. You know a lot Skye, but I would rather do the teaching. You will stay until lights out at 10pm and speak of this to no one, you get me? In addition, I want all the information the little one over there has on what is happening on the outside. My *commanding officer* said right now the status is *need to know* and I guess I don't get to know. I happen to know who the little one's uncle and father are. I need information on the status of the latest terrorist threats, to be reported to me each week. So we have a deal?" she said her voice low and rough. *Cookies? No problem.* I thought feeling a little excited. My mom made the best chocolate chip cookies in the west. I looked to Miles and she nodded, I reached through the bar and shook Joe's meaty hand.

"It's a deal boss; I'll have the goods and the gang with me tomorrow at 6:45 sharp. Thank you for doing this. It means a lot to me Joe. If anyone asks, we got in trouble and have detention with you cleaning weapons." I said as Joe nodded in approval. Miles tried to smile at Joe as we headed off to training but it looked more like a grimace. I could tell she was sweating and shaky as we walked out of the corridor into the arena. The rest of the class was warming up on the mats. Lindsay caught my eye from across the room and glared at me. I glared back, turned my back and ignored her. I had to focus on Miles. I glanced over at Miles who was looking around, looking impressed and slightly overwhelmed.

The Training Arena, like everything here, is huge. It's really a giant dome, with everything anyone could ask for. An indoor running track runs along the entire outer wall of the structure. In the middle are 20 large mats for sparring. There's a boxing ring, a 3-story rock wall, a wall full of practice knives, daggers and swords. Climbing ropes that reached up to the roof and catwalks six stories high in the rafters. In the catwalks, is all the equipment needed for repelling down to the floor as well as aerial assaults, like swinging down from tree tops to shock an enemy. At the back of the dome, a sound proof bulletproof glass wall houses the indoor shooting range, next to that room, is the archery range. The Olympic size pool sits in the basement, along with the weight room and a sauna. This place has it all.

Zach and Cam were already on a mat stretching and warming up. Miles and I sat down next to them and started to stretch. I was coaching Miles on focusing on her legs for strength instead of upper body, when Sergeant Scott called the class to order. Our trainer, a tall burley man, with a shaved head, is all business. He has a hardcore military mindset and hardly ever smiles. Sergeant Scott is one of the only people here with just plain brown eyes, no crazy color, just a nice smooth brown.

"It's Friday, so we will be sparring hand-to-hand with each other. I want you to keep it clean. No cheap shots and absolutely no weapons. *You* are the weapon. Use the takedown methods we have been working on. Once you get this down, you may move to kicks and blocks. Monday we have free train on anything you want to improve. The rest of next week, we start back on knives. Now partner up and get to it!" he shouted as we scrambled to the edge of our mat.

I grabbed Miles's hand. There was no way we would not be partners. Everyone knew she was new and would try to destroy her. The rumor about her uncle being the Dean had done its business and pissed off all the rich kids. In their eyes, she was like Zach and me, here because of favoritism and not because of money or power. I normally tried to be partnered with Lindsay, so I could show everyone what a sissy she really is, but not this time. Miles gripped my hand back in a death grip. Nobody even approached us to partner up so the four of us had a mat to ourselves. I had Zach and Cam go first. Sergeant Scott was there to coach us today, two new kids, one with no training at all, meant he had to supervise and teach them some moves. Miles and I sat down and kept stretching out our muscles as we watched the boys go at it with Sgt. Scott assisting.

"I hope I can figure this stuff out Skye. I don't wanna look like a total fool out there. And with my dad saying how much of a big deal it is, I don't want to disappoint him." said Miles. I glanced over at the boys. I could see Cam had some training already as he blocked Zach's hits easily.

"Miles, I got it covered. Joe is the best; she will make us work harder than we do in here. Zach and I did some of the basics in the summer with Joe and learned a hell of a lot. But, you have to keep us in the loop on what your dad knows. That's the catch and when you strike a deal with Joe, you never go back on it. This is serious, I'm not saying Joe is a mob boss or something, but she is in control of our weapons, we usually get the good stuff. If we end up on her bad side…well we could get crap gear, or no gear. I'll get her the cookies, you gotta get her the news she wants from your dad as soon as possible." I said quietly, as to not be overheard. Miles smirked at me.

"Cookies? She was serious? That's a new one… I can tell Joe whatever my dad knows, that he will pass on to me. My dad and I don't keep secrets, *Silence Act* be damned, and I'll write him and let you know what he says. Are we starting tomorrow night?" she asked. I nodded as Cam and Zach plopped down beside us. I quickly told Zach and Cam we have *Joe training* every Saturday. Zach nodded and started telling Cam what *Joe Training* meant. Sgt. Scott headed our way and signaled for me to get up.

Miles and I stood up and faced each other on the mat. Sgt. Scott gave her a run down on how to hold your hands and arms, and then showed her the proper stance. He came over to talk to me, his voice low and quiet.

"Skye, go easy on her, slow down your attacks so she can see them coming and let her instincts do the blocking. I have to go check on Josh. He's my best fighter and finding him a worthy opponent has been a hell of a challenge. I'm the only one that is a challenge to him. Do me a favor and coach her while you go half speed okay?" he said. As he turned to walk away, I had an idea.

"Yes sir, I'll keep it down…and sir?"I said as he turned back to me.

"Let me try and face off with Josh. Maybe it's time we do co-ed sparring sir? It would be good for me to learn right? Mostly because there's no guarantee I will only face another female in a combat situation." I said. Then I blushed like a road flare. *I cannot believe I just said that.* I thought feeling stupid. He shocked me when he started laughing. I made him not only smile but freaking laugh! I think I should get a gold star for that.

"I said he was my *best* fighter. Your good but I think he would take you. He has been training privately for five years on top of his other… achievements. You have trained for what, three months? Your good kid, one of my best, but he's better. Co-ed fighting begins after Halloween, just for your information." he said and walked over to another mat.

I didn't know if I should feel insulted or complimented. Damn him to Hell. I faced Miles again; she had a mocking grin plastered on her face.

"Wow, Mister Tough Guy over here…trying to fight boys now

huh?" she said laughing. I rolled my eyes willing myself to stop blushing and got into my stance. Miles stopped laughing and mirrored my stance. I walked her though her stance, hands, arms and awareness. Key to being a good defense was awareness and reaction. The key to offense, is knowing your body, action and reaction. There are little signs an opponent gives away right before they attack, being able to see those signs can give you the upper hand.

I lunged at her from the right, but faking that punch and connecting with a sneaky left hook. Good thing it was half speed. She dropped to the mat like a stone. I sighed and helped her back up.

"Ow, that was your half speed? Let's do *no speed* from now on." she said rubbing the red mark on her cheekbone. Zach jumped up as if his butt was on fire and raced over to her side. *Uh, okay that's weird.* I thought watching him coddle her.

"Are you okay?" he asked touching the spot on her cheek. You would think I sucker punched her at the mall, with the way he was acting. I cleared my throat loudly. Cam was chuckling over on the edge of the mat. Zach's face turned pink.

"Okay…are you good Miles? Not going to die on us?" I said hotly, feeling irritated at his overreaction. Zach smiled sheepishly at me and went back to sit with Cam who was trying to keep a straight face. I shook my head and looked back at Miles, she was smiling slightly. Oh dear, I knew where this was going to go. I just wasn't sure if I liked it yet. I went back into fight mode and gave her the rundown of her mistakes.

"Your first mistake was that you were only focused on one side of me. You have to watch the opponent's *whole* body. If you focus on *all* of my body as I move, you will know what side I will attack from. Every time someone attacks, they show a sign a split second before they move. You can see it if your focused on *all* of your opponent. You would have blocked my punch but your arm came up just a little too late. Let's go again with the same move but I won't tell you what side the hit will come from. Either left or right. For now, I'll leave out kicks okay." I said, getting my stance again. Miles did too.

After our hour was up, she was sweaty, covered in red marks on her face and arms, but had successfully blocked my last five punches. She even snuck up on me and almost landed a hit of her own on my face. I felt proud of her. We got changed, said goodbye to Joe, who gave us a wink and headed to the dorms. We both decided we needed showers.

When I came out of my bathroom Zach was perched up in my window, good thing he took off his boots, because you have to step up on my desk to get up there and I didn't need mud on my homework. The only light in the room was from my little lamp by my bed, casting his face into shadow. I turned on my corner lamp too. Zach looked down at me looking slightly sad.

"What's wrong?" I asked pulling on my sweat pants and sweatshirt… it wasn't the first time he had seen me in my underwear.

"I dunno, I was just thinking how weird it is that we have these two other people that actually like being around us. *And* I like being around them. Are you mad at me for letting them sit with us? It's been just the two of us for so long, I don't want the way we are to change." he said looking out my window. I sighed and climbed up my desk and sat across from him on the large ledge, hugging my knees.

"We will never change. It's always going to be just us. Besides, I like them both, they're really great people. I'm not mad at all, I think Miles is great and Cam is very cool. Are you really worried about them hanging out with us as friends, or worried that I'll get mad because you think Miles is cute?" I asked. Zach smiled sheepishly as a little blush crept over his cheeks. I knew him too well, this was his roundabout way of asking if I thought it was a good idea for him to ask Miles out.

"Well…yeah okay. I thought she was cute the moment I saw her." he said.

"I know… I saw the whole mouth open and drool thing." I said laughing. He blushed and put his head in his hands like he was embarrassed to look at me.

"Shut up! Okay… so I looked like a fool when we first met her, fine… rub it in. I'm just saying, you're my number one and I don't want anything to change because one of us starts dating someone else." he said looking serious.

"Zach, you're my number one too okay. Plus… whoever I might date or fall for, will just have to accept that. Same with you though. The girl you fall for will have to be cool. If you start dating a drama queen control freak, I'll kill her and then kick your ass. Miles is cool. I like what I'm seeing so far with her and it's only been a week. That right there is saying something. Nevertheless, take your time; let's really *know* her first, before you jump into a dating thing. We have lots of time to make sure she is worth it and won't turn into a *crazy*. Besides, you might be stuck with me anyways, because she *might* end up falling for Cam for all we know." I said.

"Well, if that happens I'm cool with it, Cam's a good guy. Hey… maybe you should date him and distract him!" he said excitedly.

"Nice you jerk! I'm not some kind of hooker! So rude…yeah, I think Cam is cute, but I don't think he's my type. You're going to have to do this the old fashioned way… time and lots of showing off." I said, squealing, as Zach grabbed me and tickled my sides. I thrashed and squirmed almost taking us both off the ledge and crashing onto my desk. Eventually we calmed down. I sat curled in a ball in his lap with my head on his chest looking out into the dark woods. I didn't want the moment to end or turn dark but I couldn't help myself.

"We can't forget our letters though. This might be our last year together Zach. I will try my best to go wherever you go, but the Government might separate us. I don't know what I'll do without you." I said feeling tears heat up the back of my eyes. Zach sighed into my hair.

"Skye, I love you more than anything. You've always been with me, through everything. Wherever we end up, I *know* it will be together. I would die for you. We made a promise when we got our letters that we would find a way to join up with whatever armed forces we could that would take us as a team. I plan to keep that promise. And I know you will too. I just wish we had more time to fall in love or be young and reckless...Maybe we should make another promise?" He asked quietly. I looked up at him, seeing that his eyes were stormy blue grey and sad.

"What did you have in mind?" I asked in a thick voice, I still felt like I was going to get hysterical as more hot tears crept down my cheeks. I had to look away from him before I cried harder, I always felt weepy and girly when we talked about the draft letters. I laid my head against his chest again trying to calm myself down. When the time came and we told our mothers, I knew I would fall apart because that meant it would be real. Right now, it was starting to feel real again. Damn the draft to hell.

"Promise me, that this whole school year, until the day we ship off, we are reckless and act like teenagers. We break the rules, have fun and maybe fall in love with someone? Promise that we don't talk about this until we have to tell Mom and Mom two." he said into my hair. I sat up and turned to face him, again with tears leaking out of my eyes now. Crying was not my thing but with him it never mattered, he never judged me.

"I promise. Consider it my pleasure to be a bad influence on you, like always and keep you young. However, my only stipulation is we make sure we *never* get Mom and Mom two in trouble with us. We can't be caught. They will have enough to worry about once we tell them… they cannot lose their jobs too…promise?" I asked. He nodded and we did our pinky swear from when we were kids, sealed with a kiss on our closed fists. I settled back into my spot against his chest and watched the clouds roll angrily around the full moon. We sat like that in comfortable silence for a while.

We got down off the ledge once the bell rang signaling lights out. I pulled out my false wall and grabbed four root beers, in the glass bottles, which made the beer taste even better and set them on my desk. I pulled out my box of DVD's, soon Zach and I had two movies for us to choose from. An original horror flick from the 1970's and a modern slasher film with lots of gore. I was pulling out a bag of cheesy poufs from my stash when the door opened and Miles and Cam strolled in both wearing sweat pants and hoodies. Miles had a box under her arm.

"Oh, what's in the box?" I asked as she sat on the edge of my bed next to Zach, who was already starting to blush. She popped the lid on the brown box.

"Care package from my dad. Couldn't have planned it better, it was in front of my door when we got in. Look… his homemade pumpkin spice cookies, beef jerky and bags of chips." she said tossing me a cookie. I took a bite and they were delicious, as if autumn was doing a happy dance in my mouth.

Cam pulled my squashy armchair over to the center of the room and plopped down in it with a root beer in hand. I passed the others root beers and we debated over which movie to watch. After joking and squabbling, we decided on the modern slasher, deciding to save the 70's throw back for after the Halloween Ball next week. Miles and Zach awkwardly snuggled up against my pillow and each other on my bed, both trying not to touch each other. I looked over at Cam taking up my chair. *Well, this is the best way to help Zach with Miles right?* I thought and leapt onto Cam's lap.

"Ow! Easy Skye! Geeze, you about smashed my manhood!" Cam yelled. He had caught me just in time to avoid any 'manhood smashing'. I giggled and snuggled in next to him with my legs over his knees.

"Sorry, guess I didn't think that one through Cam... Zach? Play film?" I said looking over at Zach as him and Miles laughed at us smashed together in my chair. The movie started and we all settled in.

About twenty minutes into the films gory killing spree, a loud knock at my door startled me out of Cam's lap. We all looked wide-eyed at each other. The boys leapt up and both bee lined into my bathroom and shut the door. Miles looked around in a panic, kicked both their shoes under my bed and we both plopped down on my bed trying to look casual.

"Come in." I said trying to slow my breathing. Zach and I had made our promise to be reckless but, two boys and two girls in my room would look *really* bad and would land us all in hot water. Miles and I appearing to be alone and breaking the lights out rule was a much better option.

My door opened slowly and none other than Professor Kirra stood silhouetted against the hallway light pouring into my room. She didn't say a word, her hair was a mess and covering one whole side of her face, so I couldn't even really see her. She wore her training gear, similar to the gear we wore in combat training, but her gear came with thigh holsters for guns and a jacket. She was covered in mud and twigs. I looked at her hard, trying to take in what I was really seeing. Kirra had a long rifle in her hand. *What the hell is going on?* I thought feeling an odd pull in my gut. She was almost acting as if she was drunk, swaying a little and holding the doorframe. Miles and I exchanged a worried glance as we watched our Painting Professor stumble in, shut the door behind her and collapse into my armchair.

Chapter Five

Professor Kirra leaned her head back letting out a groan. Her face caught the light from the paused movie and that's when I saw what was wrong with her. A wide gash cut across her lovely face, from her hairline all the way across her left eye to her right cheek, thick red blood dripped down onto her chest mixed with mud. I jumped to action. There was no reaction, just action. I flipped on all the lights and lamps I had. Miles bolted to Kirra and began getting her long hair off her face and out of the wound.

"Zach! Cam! Out here now!" I yelled at the bathroom door. "Bring me a wet wash rag and a dry towel. Zach, grab my mom's kit, it's under the sink… left side and you and Cam go get the Nurse, Mom and Mom two right now!" I yelled grabbing another towel from my closet.

They both sprang out of the bathroom, with everything I asked for. Cam handed me a wet rag and caught sight of Kirra. His eyes went wide in shock and he raced to the door yelling to Zach that he would get the Nurse. Both boys took off out of my room leaving the door open behind them. I grabbed my kit from Miles and wrenched open the lid of the old vintage metal box.

I have a homemade med kit I had gotten as a gift for my 17th birthday from my mother. It's stocked with alcohol wipes, band-aids, superglue, a suture kit, medical grade tweezers and scalpels, iodine, lots of gauze, Quick Clot for deep wounds and different kinds of homemade pain salves and wound healers made from the cacti around our home in Arizona. I also kept a bottle of *very* strong whiskey as a 'just in case' for calming the nerves for whoever might be injured. People might think this is a strange birthday gift, but when you're poor, you're careful and learn how to care for minor wounds and injuries saving the expensive trips to a doctor or hospital for very serious injuries or illness.

I used the wet washcloth to wipe away the blood covering her face, trying to find where the wound began and where it ended. The gash on her face was deep by her left temple, which worried me. We have an artery that runs up our temples and if that gets cut, it could cut blood supply to the brain. The wound was long, from the top of her left temple, over the eye, nose and right cheek ending at the end of her jaw. Her eye concerned me even more; the lid was shut but sliced open enough to where I could see the eyeball. I swallowed back the bile creeping up my throat and set to work on the top of the wound where the most blood was coming from. My best guess was whatever cut her did in fact nick the artery in her temple. Miles was handing me whatever I asked for and wiping blood away so I could see the cut. Kirra was trying to talk now.

"Please…the Dean. They have come… Small group… I had to tell you. You're the most…important. You four… You're the ones. Others will…they come. They will follow you. Lead them… *You* Skye. *You*." Kirra said. She was starting to sink deeper into shock. None of what she said made any sense to me.

"Kirra, you need to be still, I have to stop the bleeding so we can get you to the Infirmary. I have some friends going to get The Nurse and Professors Warren and Miller. They both have some skill with emergencies. You'll be in good hands soon. Just be still and don't try to talk yet. Miles, please hand me the iodine, butterfly band-aids, gauze and the roll of white tape." I said. Miles handed me what I asked for and I dabbed at the wound with the iodine. I taped some gauze over her wounded eye first, being careful not to tape where it might pull on the wound when removed. I then pulled the flesh together and used the butterfly bandages to hold the top of the wound closed. I put more gauze over the wound and tightly wrapped all the way around her head. Miles had tied back Kirra's hair, tight enough to hold but not so tight it would pull the wound open wider. Once I had the left side of her head wrapped and taped, I started on her right cheek, cleaning and covering the wound. Kirra was between passing out and being fully aware, trying to keep herself still.

I had just finished when I heard footsteps in the hall and the Nurse, my mom and Mom two came in with Zach, Cam and the Dean close behind them. Miles and I stepped into the hallway and let the others get Kirra on the stretcher the boys had brought. My mom stepped out and pulled Miles and I to the side by Miles's room.

"What happened? Did she say anything? The boys told us about how she arrived. Did she say anything to you Skyelaa?" mom asked. She looked very scared and *angry* for some reason. She was still in her black jeans and purple sweater from teaching today, but had her hair pulled back in a messy ponytail like she did it while running over here. The anger in her voice pissed me off a little bit. *Like I did anything wrong*. I thought bitterly.

"Why are you mad at me? I'm the one whose room she decided to come to and I patched her up. I didn't slice and dice her mom!" I said hotly. My mother grabbed my shoulders and squeezed, looking right into my eyes, as if my soul was on fire.

"Drop the attitude. What did she *say?* I know she told you something and I need to know right this instant Skyelaa! *What* did she tell you?" my mom said nearly yelling in my face. There it was again, the fear and the anger. I didn't like this situation at all. *What the hell did that to Kirra's face?* I thought getting worried at the way my mom was acting.

"*Alright* mom, I'm sorry. She said something about, '*They have come. Small group*' and then she said '*the four of you are the ones*' and something about wanting to see the Dean. Then she said…" I said racking my brain. Miles interrupted me as the boys walked over to us.

"She said '*Please…the Dean. They have come. Small group. I had to tell you. You're the most…important. You four. You're the ones. Others will…they come. They will follow you. Lead them. You Skye. You.*' those were her exact words ma'am." Miles said red in the face with smears of Kirra's blood on her cheek. I nodded looking at my mother as Zach's mom walked over.

Zach's mom's looks were like the darker versions of my moms, their faces are the same heart shape, they both are the same height, same curvy size but Melinda has amber eyes where my mothers are cobalt blue. Melinda has short dark brown hair, where my mother's is long and blonde. Melinda is my Mom two. She hugged Zach and turned to my mother.

"Lila, Dean Jacobs told me Miles has an Audio graphic memory, what she said is exactly word for word what Kirra said to them. I think we need to help Nurse Lane get Kirra to the Infirmary. We can discuss this with the kids tomorrow. Zach, once we are gone you may go back to what you were doing before Kirra arrived." she said walking back into my room. My mom looked at my friends and me with an odd look on her face I couldn't read. She pulled me into a hug and patted my head.

"I'm sorry Skyelaa; you know how I get in stressful situations. I demand too many facts all at once. You did well in there. I see you have not forgotten how to quick bind a wound for transport. I will talk to you tomorrow. For now try to get some sleep… And kids?" she pulled out of the hug and looked at all of us. "Please keep this to yourselves. We do not know if it was an animal and don't want students to panic. Boys, thank you for coming to get us, I'm going to pretend Skyelaa called you Zach." she said under her breath, Zach gave her a nod and a thumbs up. "Okay, once we're out of here, you may discuss what needs to be discussed and clean up the mess together." my mom said as she hugged each of us again. It was her way of giving us permission to have a slumber party without actually saying it. This for me sounded great. We now had a lot to talk about and I did not want to be alone with all the thoughts flying around in my head.

Once all the adults were gone, I walked into my room alone. Miles had gone to take another quick shower and change, while the boys helped get Kirra to the Castle. I looked around and took a deep breath. There was blood and bloody footprints on the hardwood floors, bloody towels and Kirra's ripped jacket lying by my chair. My chair had only a small amount of blood on it but was covered in dirt. Thank God, it was leather and I could just wipe it clean.

I looked down at myself. My grey sweat pants had blood and mud all down my legs. My black tank top felt a little stiff in a couple spots from dried blood, and my hands had blood all over them, soaked into my skin. I rushed into my bathroom and jumped in the shower fully dressed. It took a lot of scrubbing to get my hands to look less bloodstained. I hung my sopping wet clothes over the shower rod to dry and then be washed again later. I pulled on a pair of pj shorts and another tank top and washed my hands again in the sink.

When I emerged from the bathroom, I found Miles, Zach and Cam cleaning my room in silence. Zach had raided the cleaning supply closet on the second floor of my dorm, he was on his knees with a spray bottle and a wad of paper towels. I started helping too. After about a half hour and a big trash bag full of bloody paper towels and Kirra's jacket, we all crammed together on my bed. Nobody wanted to sit in the chair. It was as clean as it's ever been, but we just shoved it back it its spot in the corner and huddled together on my bed instead. Somehow, we all fit.

"So, what the hell was that?" I asked, not wanting to sit in silence anymore. Miles sat up a little straighter.

"Well, it looked like an animal got her. Maybe a cougar or a bear?" she said. Zach shrugged, but Cam shook his head.

"No way, they would have done a lot more than just the one hit to the face. We have them out where I live and when they actually attack a human, its *way* worse than what Kirra got. Not saying she wasn't bad, but I just don't see her taking on a large animal like that and not being even more messed up or dead. I think it was something else." he said looking very serious.

"Like what Cam? Sasquatch? Maybe she was attacked by a bear and scared it off with the rifle." said Zach. Cam shook his head again and reached under my bed. He pulled out the rifle Kirra had come in with. I looked at it questioningly.

"I hid it before we ran out of here to get help. You were so focused on fixing her up, you didn't even realize you took it out of her hand and handed it to me. I hid it because I wanted to look at something without anyone thinking I'm weird for checking." Cam said as he started to take the rounds out. It was a 12-gauge pump action shot gun, which held five rounds. He set all five rounds on my bed, checked the barrel again and then did something weird, he brought the end of the barrel up to his nose and sniffed it.

"This hasn't been shot recently. All five buckshot rounds are here and I don't smell gunpowder. It's like I thought... She was snuck up on by something or someone and didn't even get a shot off. I noticed all her holsters were empty too and I didn't see any of her knives on her belt. Maybe she did get a shot off with her hand guns...but I doubt it. Guys I don't mean to sound crazy but I think *someone* sliced her with a knife as she turned around." he mimicked the motion of someone slicing as if they were right handed and holding the knife like we do in training, point towards your elbow, closed fist around the handle. I stared at him in shock. I thought hard about the way the wound looked, it had been pretty smooth. I had bound her wound and there was nothing jagged about the gash. Animals didn't usually make smooth lines when they attacked, even house cats left jagged wounds. I didn't want him to be right but I couldn't disagree with him.

"Cam… you might be right. The wound wasn't jagged. You guys have been clawed by a cat or dog before right?" I asked looking around at all of them, they all nodded. "Okay, have you *ever* been clawed by an animal that left a *straight* line with a clean cut? I sure haven't. It had to be a knife wound…but who would do that to her? And why?" I said.

"I think the better question is, what the hell was she doing roaming around outside at eleven at night in her training gear with a shot gun?" said Zach. That *was* the better question. We all looked at each other. My mind started reeling. *What was she doing?* I thought for the hundredth time. Miles piped up.

"Well, let's look at the facts. Skye, do you have a pen and paper I can use?" she asked and I grabbed an empty notebook and pen from my desk drawer and handed it to her.

"Thanks, okay… so let's break down what she said to us. She might have been in shock so her sentences were broken and didn't seem to make a lot of sense but she was alert enough to be trying to tell us something she felt was important." Miles said as she wrote down; *please…the Dean. They have come. Small group. I had to tell you. You're the most…important. You four. You're the ones. Others will…they come. They will follow you. Lead them. You Skye. You.*

"So we break this down." Miles started saying, I interrupted her.

"You really do remember word for word what she said?" I asked, impressed. Miles blushed.

"I have an *audio graphic* memory, it means I hear something once and I can recall it. It's better if I hear it twice but, when a situation is crazy important I can remember better. It's how I got out of jail when I was caught near that group in Seattle. I…kind of ratted them out and told the police what they were really planning. I'm not proud of that part of though." she said looking ashamed, I nodded and she continued. "Okay, so she mentioned my uncle, that seems obvious, she needed to tell him about the attack. Then she said *'They have come'* in a *'small group.'* So my guess is it was a small group of…maybe people?" She asked looking at all of us.

"I would assume so, if the wound wasn't jagged like an animal wound, and she said *they* and the word *group*. I think if it was really an animal or more than one animal, she may have used the word *pack*. You girls said she was, for the most part, in her right mind, so I think that she would have been clear about an animal attacking her. I agree with Cam, it was definitely a knife or even a thin blade sword." said Zach sitting up closer to Miles. Miles wrote that down in the notebook. Cam started pacing my room deep in thought.

"Miles what did she say about us?" Cam asked mid pace.

"She said *'you're the most important, you four, you're the ones.'*" Miles recited.

"Okay so I'm assuming she meant the four of us. She was sane enough to know we have been hanging out, which is weird because we have only known each other a week. It's not like it's a big secret that we're all friends, but our movie night tonight *was* a secret. So how she knew we would all be in Skye's room at this time of night strikes me as odd. And, why are the four of us so important or *the ones*?" said Cam as he paced and paced talking with his hands. Miles wrote down notes on what he was saying. Zach climbed up into my window and looked outside to the grounds deep in thought.

"So this is what we know. One; Kirra was attacked by a group of humans with a knife or sword but they let her live. Two; we are the *four chosen ones* of something that Kirra seems to know about. Three; we will somehow *lead* and whoever the other *they* people are, will follow us and especially Skye. And Four; Kirra was dressed and ready for a combat situation at 11 at night wandering around in the woods alone and wanted to pass the message on to us, even though she was seriously wounded and should have gone to the Nurse." Zach said looking down at all of us.

Cam stopped pacing and looked up at a Zach stunned. I felt my face get really hot. I was *not* a leader, I just wanted to be invisible to people, not lead them. Miles wrote all that down in the notebook and looked over at me. I wanted to hide.

"Well, it looks like we will have to go talk to both your moms tomorrow and see what we can get out of them. Then, if she's up for it, we talk to Kirra. After that, we write a coded letter to my dad and ask what he knows. I think we need to let Joe know what's happening too Skye. She trusts you and would want to know. And she might be able to shed some light on what the hell is going on too." said Miles, looking down at the notebook. She then started writing a list of whom we needed to talk to tomorrow. I felt like our whole world just turned into a disaster in less than a day.

Chapter Six

We ended up talking long into the night. By the time we woke up, it was well into the morning. Cam and I had fallen asleep curled up together in my chair. Once we had started to get tired, we gave in and finally sat in it. Zach and Miles were curled around each other in my bed. Good thing he was in the bed, at over 6 feet tall his feet hung off the end. Cam was a bit shorter so the chair was a better option for him to sleep in than Zach.

I looked around my room. I had slept through the night without having the nightmare. I blinked a couple times to be sure I was really awake. *Maybe I didn't have it because everyone's here. On the other hand, it could be because I was so tired I crashed out. Maybe it's because I'm cuddling with Cam.* I thought. I wasn't sure but I was glad that I made it through the night. I kissed Cam's cheek as I got up and wandered into my bathroom to take another shower to try getting the bloodstains off my hands again.

I was standing under the hot water staring blankly at the wall, when I heard the door to my bathroom open. I peeked out of the curtain to see Cam using my sink to splash water on his face. I'm not exactly what you call *modest* or conservative, but this seemed a little strange. Zach's the only one who really did stuff like that and it never bothered me. With Cam, it didn't seem to bother me either, which was weird to me, because I didn't know him that well. He finished washing his face and caught me staring at him.

"Hey, what's up?" I said a little awkwardly. He smiled at me. I felt my face get hot again. Blushing seemed to be happening to me a lot lately.

"Hi, nothing… sorry I barged in here, I like to splash cold water on my face when I first wake up, it helps me function. Is it okay if I talk to you? I'll stay out here, nothing weird but I wanted to ask you something." He said sitting on the closed toilet lid.

"Uh, sure…that's fine. What did you want to know?" I asked getting back under the water.

"Well, for starters, we're just friends right?" he asked. *Uh oh, maybe I had been leading him on by sitting in his lap and being overly touchy. Damn me to hell.* I thought but tried to play off the worry.

"Yeah… and we're *The Chosen Ones* too, which makes us stuck with each other…so of course we're friends." I said. Cam chuckled.

"Yeah, I guess we are. Anyway, I was wondering what you thought of Kayla Crew?" he asked. I almost choked on my shower water. *Kayla Crew, Lindsay Cambell's bitch clique member? Where the hell was this coming from?* I thought feeling confused.

"Uh Cam, what exactly are you asking me? Because I'm probably not a good person to be asking when it come to Kayla, or anyone she hangs with for that matter. I have a very *not* nice opinion of all of them." I said peaking out of the curtain again. Cam met my eyes, the silver of his eyes flashing in the light of the bathroom.

"I…well, I think she's pretty. I was thinking about asking her to the Halloween Ball on Monday." he said looking very serious. I sighed feeling relieved that he wasn't crushing on me and annoyed that it was Kayla.

"Well, here's my advice. Don't count on a yes, only because you hang with Zach and me, not because *you're* not cool or cute, but because of us. Her clique would probably disown her for going to the dance with a guy that runs around with *The Poverty Club*…but give it a try it anyways, she *might* not let them run her life like everyone else does. She isn't very nice to me, but maybe I just don't know her that well. And please, promise me that if she says yes and you two start dating or whatever, that you will never change who you are as a person to please her. Promise me? If you do change in the slightest, I will call you out on it in front of everyone and then kick your ass." I said hotly as thoughts of him abandoning us sent me into a tizzy of annoyance. Cam held up his hands in mock defense.

"Alright! Alright! Geeze! I promise that if we do end up dating I won't change my sparkling personality in any way. But I haven't even asked her yet! So relax, I just wanted you're opinion. Now get your butt back in the shower, the curtain is open you know!" Cam said looking right at me…all of me. I threw the curtain shut with a very un-me-like squeal. Cam burst out laughing.

"You keep that up and I might change my mind on us just being friends!" he said between bursts of laughter. I lobbed the shampoo bottle over the curtain rod. It hit the floor with a thud, which caused more laughter from Cam as he left the bathroom shutting the door. Damn him to hell too.

After mulling over the naked incident with Cam, I came out into my room to find it deserted, with my bed made and a note on my pillow. I pulled on a pair of jeans and a black sweater and plopped onto my bed grabbing the note. I pulled on my extra combat boots that I had gotten from Joe and sheathed my custom-made boot knife into the custom holster. The knife has a thin black handle that blends in with the top of the black boot. Joe had made the knife and boot holster herself. The holster was carefully hidden in between the two layers of leather that made up the inside and outside of the boot. I didn't know what we were in for today and I felt like I needed to start being armed at all times. I read the note.

Skye,

We all ran to change. Zach is running to the dining hall

to grab us all something to eat and then we'll go visit Mom 1 and Mom 2.

Then I think we need to go see Kirra.

We will meet you back here in 30.

-Miles

And the rest of the Poverty Club.

I tossed the note onto my desk and climbed up onto my window ledge looking out at the grey morning light. I was still feeling really sleepy; we had stayed up well past two talking about Kirra. I was anxious to find out how she was doing. *Is she going to be blind in her left eye? For an artist that would be terrible. I guess, on the silver lining side of things, it was only one eye and not both of them.* I thought as I sat there thinking about Kirra and what she said and then about Kayla and Cam. My 30 minutes must have been up when Miles came in wearing a heavy jacket, black cargo pants, with a deep green colored beanie and scarf on. I raised my eyebrows at her outdoor attire.

"Hey, I figured we could also go look for the spot Kirra was attacked at." she said sitting down on my bed. I scooted to the edge of the ledge letting my legs dangle over my desk.

"That's actually a really good idea. Might help us figure out what got her. Maybe there are still tracks from whatever it was. We should do that before it starts to rain and washes anything away." I said as I started to climb down. I grabbed my waterproof warm coat from my closet and a black beanie.

"Where do we start then?" asked Miles.

"That's easy silly girl, follow the blood. Isn't your dad in the FBI? Think like he would." I said. Miles grinned at me. I opened up the notebook Miles had been taking notes in last night and skimmed through it. She's *very* organized in her notes.

"Wow, I take it back. You already belong in the FBI, these are really organized notes. Bring it with us so we can use it later when we talk to Mom and Mom two… and Kirra. Might come in handy if Kirra says she can't remember anything." I said and handed her the notebook and pen. She stuck it in her messenger bag and put the pen in her hat.

"I hope to join the FBI someday. I might get to avoid the draft if I get into law enforcement. Maybe you should try that too. I bet you and Zach could both get in if I called in a favor from my dad." She said brightly as her eyes filled with hope, proving that she did have a thing for my best friend. My heart swelled with sadness for both of them. I never wanted so much for two people to be together. Once the letter came, it was near impossible to escape the draft. I put on what I hoped was a reassuring smile.

"Once we figure this mess out, I would be happy to check out the FBI as a career. Thanks Miles, it means a lot that you would do that for us." I said and held my voice steady. Miles grinned ear to ear.

"You guys are the closest thing to best friends I have *ever* had. Nobody has ever treated me like you guys do. Usually people treat me like an Elite rich girl or like the Seattle Director of the FBI's daughter. There are a lot of fake people out there and real ones are almost impossible to find. So thanks, for keeping it real with me." she said. Then she got up and hugged me. I'm a *closet* ball of mush when it comes to emotional stuff but totally not a hugger. It was pretty nice though, like hugging a sister. When we broke apart, the door opened again and the boys walked in. Cam winked at me.

"I see you found some clothes." he said. I rolled my eyes and kicked him in the shin. He hopped around on one foot laughing. I couldn't help but smile. Zach rolled his eyes and passed out toasted croissant sandwiches with ham and cheese from a paper bag. I stuffed my face as Miles filled them in on our plan and we set out for the grounds. We had a lot of grounds to search.

I had us start at the side door, as we found no blood in the hall to follow. I figured the staff would clean that first, keep things secret from students and all. We found a couple drops of blood on the stone steps at the side door, as I thought. I had Miles make a note that only the four of us really knew about and used this door. Kirra might have known it was there but it was supposed to be locked at all times from the outside. The blood trail led us into the woods behind my dorm.

The blood droplets lead to a footpath that leads into the woods. Memories of my nightmare made me hesitate as Cam lead the way first, with Miles behind him. Zach reached back to me and grabbed my hand, knowing why I was hesitant. I took it gratefully and followed them into the dark woods. It was barley noon but in the deep forest, it felt like twilight. We hiked over the rough terrain, branches hitting our faces and legs, for what felt like forever. Finally, Cam stopped at what looked like an opening to a clearing. We gathered around what had been a larger blood pool that had soaked into the ground.

"If I had to guess, I would say she fell down here and lay down for a minute." Zach said. Miles was looking around at the surrounding leaves. As it was fall, they were blooming with colors; reds, gold, yellow, orange, green and brown surrounded us. If I had been out here for just a simple walk, I might have enjoyed it more. Miles pulled off a couple leaves from a nearby tree.

"I don't see any spray, I don't think she was attacked here, but she defiantly laid or fell down here like you said." She said holding the leaf close to her face.

"Spray?" I asked feeling stupid.

"Well, the proper term is *'Blood Spatter'* but spray sounded nicer. When you're cut or shot, the motion is usually very fast and because we bleed as soon as we're cut, it kind of gets everywhere. You can re-created an attack at a crime scene just based on the blood spatter pattern and determine what happened. It's really interesting." said Miles.

"Wow, you really are an FBI agent's daughter, so we look for *blood spatter* on the leaves and ground to find the place she was attacked. My guess is in the open space out there. If she was by the tree line at any point they could have snuck up on her easily." I said looking around at everyone.

"Alright let's split up and check it out. The meadow is a near perfect circle, so we will be able to see each other at all times. Nobody go in the woods alone okay." said Cam. My blood froze. *A perfect circle… a meadow that's nearly a perfect circle?* I thought thinking again of my nightmare freaking myself out. Miles had stopped in her tracks next to me looking shocked. I forgot about her painting. Now I was sure, by the look on her face, that we were having the same nightmare. Though I didn't want to, I knew I would have to talk to her about it later. Zach was looking at the meadow and me, understanding crossing his features. *Later, we will all discuss this later.* I thought as I pressed on, out into the meadow first. The others followed, all looking around for the attack site. I was positive it was the same meadow as the dream but I couldn't hear the river, which was weird. We were looking around the outer edge of the circle when Zach called us over to where he stood, about forty feet from the mouth of the trail.

"I found it. And her guns are here, look." Zach said, pointing to bloodstained leaves and grass. Based on what I was seeing Kirra had been facing her attacker. Most of the blood spatter was in the grass and not on the leaves. Her guns were laying a few feet away but we didn't find her knives. Cam checked the clips in her guns. They were loaded with real bullets and based on his smelling skills, had not been fired. Cam put the clips in the pocket of his cargo pants and the guns in Miles's messenger bag. I looked around for tracks as the rain started falling down. Thunder clapped in the distance. I pulled up the hood of my black jacket and wandered into the woods behind the attack scene, my eyes glued to the ground. I stopped next to a large Cedar tree, a big footprint marked up the mud next to the base of the tree. It looked to me like a boot print of a really big guy.

"Guys! Over here!" I shouted. In moments, it would be gone from the heavy rain now falling down. I looked around, they had been just behind me and I wasn't far in at all, I could still see the meadow through the brush. I turned back to the tree; the print was still there right at the base. Lightening lit up the woods for a split second, thunder rumbling the ground. I looked around again wishing the rain wasn't so loud.

Then the smell hit me. Sulfur and rot. I would know that smell anywhere. I reeled around in a circle trying to see through the thick brambles and pouring rain. I reached for my boot knife. Drawing it slowly I crouched down by the tree and waited. The smell got stronger, assaulting my nose and making me want to vomit. I swallowed hard and looked behind me, back at the meadow. I could hardly see the others moving around out there, maybe looking for me. I steadied myself getting onto the balls of my feet. As I prepared to spring up into a run, I heard it…ragged growling breathing. Like an animal growl, but all too human to be any kind of animal. *It's behind my tree.* I thought as I froze and gently sniffed the air. It took all of my self-control not to hurl up my ham and cheese. It growled low in its throat again. I heard a twig snap and I knew it was going to launch around the tree right at me. With all of my courage, I slowly rotated my body, turning my back to the tree and the *thing*. The hairs on my neck stood on end as I exposed my back to danger.

One…two…three… I counted as I sprang into a run slashing out with my small knife behind my back. I caught flesh and heard a high-pitched growling scream. Unlike the dream, I forced myself *not* to look back. I burst through the thick bushes, out into the meadow and ran smack dab into Zach, taking both of us to the ground hard. I was freaking out. I officially lost my self control; I scrambled off him, knife still in hand and tried to take off again, to where I knew the river would be. I screamed for them to come with me and babbled incoherently. I just couldn't calm down. Zach grabbed for me and missed. I screamed as I was tackled from behind. I hit the ground again, mud spattering my face.

I was flipped onto my back and Cam sat on top of me pinning my arms over my head. He leaned down to my face.

"SKYE, YOUR SAFE!" he bellowed. I froze. The power behind his voice stopped me. I gulped down air and tried to calm myself. Cam watched me, those silver eyes of his boring into me, waiting. Zach and Miles were standing over us. In Zach's hand, I recognized one of Kirra's guns. He was looking around holding the gun ready; Miles held the other one… *Good* I thought. The guns helped, I felt my body calming down. Nothing had chased me, we were alone, but *it* was still out there. I needed out of these woods and to tell my friends about *everything*. *Why didn't it chase me?* I wondered as my heart slowed down and I felt the tingle of calm settling over me.

"Can I let you up now?" Cam asked gently as he wiped mud off my cheek. I nodded as rain pelted my face. He stood up and offered me a hand. I looked up at him and my friends' concerned faces as I took Cam's hand. Zach and Miles came closer to us. Fear was all over Miles's face making her look small and innocent.

"You are going to tell us *exactly* what happened right now. We heard you scream Skye and couldn't see you. Please don't ever do that again. And *both* of you girls need to explain what this meadow means to you. Besides Skye's crazy little freak out moment I could tell from the second we found this meadow, *both* of you are freaked out about it. Zach and I need to know what the hell is going on." Cam said sternly as he gently took the gun from Miles, who looked grateful. Zach looked guilty; he knew about my nightmare but hadn't told Cam. I felt like crap, with everything that has happened in the past 24 hours, I wanted nothing more than to sleep for days.

"Not here, we have to leave this place *now*." I said and headed bravely for the trail back to campus.

We marched out of the woods together. It took a long time. We were probably a mile in; I couldn't believe Kirra made it so far with her face like that. We finally made it to the side steps of the girl's dorm. In my room, boots and coats ended up tossed on the floor just inside the door. I was covered in mud and soaking wet, but I stayed dressed and tried not to think about a hot shower. We all sat in a circle on my floor facing each other. The others were wet and mud spattered too. Zach was holding hands with Miles, which made me feel better… just a little bit. I took a deep breath.

"Okay, I will tell you everything that happened out there, but first I have to tell you about what freaked me out so bad when I saw your painting Miles and then when we saw the meadow." I said looking at each of them. Zach knew the dream, but nothing else. So, I started talking. It was hard to explain everything but they all listened and didn't interrupt me once. When I finished telling them about the nightmare, then what happened in the woods, I realized Miles had tears running down her face.

"Miles? What's wrong?" I asked. She sniffled and wiped her eyes, smearing more mud across her cheek.

"Me too." she whispered. "As soon as I spent my first night here, I started having that same nightmare. But last night I didn't have it. I thought it was gone, which was a nice change. Every night it's been the same dream as yours, but in mine, everything is more blurry. Like everything hasn't completely come into focus yet. But I know the smell you're talking about. It's terrifying that the *thing* is real." she said thickly. I had been sure we shared the same nightmare when I saw the painting and then again when I saw her face in the woods. *We both didn't have the nightmare last night, what does that mean?* I thought racking my brain for anything that didn't seem crazy.

"Skye, you said you may have sliced it with your knife? Do you still have your knife?" asked Cam. I nodded and handed it over. I hadn't put it down until we sat on my floor, then I'd set it beside my leg. It had black sludge looking goo on the blade. Cam carefully took it not touching the blade and sniffed it. He wrinkled up his nose in disgust.

"It smells like what you said. Sulfur and something rotten, like a dead animal. *That* is gross." he said, going to hand the knife back but Zach held out his hand. Cam passed him the blade. Zach sniffed it too. I raised my eyebrows questioningly at this weird action.

"I want to know what it smells like too. Smell is the best way to remember anything important. If this thing is real then I want to know when it's around. Okay, everyone up. We have to take this to Mom and Mom two. They can work together on the…blood, left on this knife and maybe figure out what kind of…thing…it is. Well… see if it's animal or human at the very least. Let's go… It's already three o'clock and we have a lot to do still." Zach stood up and we all reluctantly followed suit. No showers yet I guess. I felt gross now, and the smell of that thing was still in my nose. Ick.

Chapter Seven

When we left my room I couldn't help but notice we actually resembled Lindsay's favorite nickname for us. When we passed through the school's courtyard, her nickname of *dirty homeless riff raff* came to mind. It stopped raining, the autumn sun breaking feebly through the clouds. The students had come out to play football and sit on the benches, hanging out in the weak sunshine. *Fantastic.* I thought. There was no avoiding Lindsay's group this time. They hang out in front of the Gym on the stone steps on weekends when it wasn't raining. All the staff living quarters were above the Gym. I didn't know of any way to avoid it, so I squared up my shoulders and prepared myself as we neared the front of the Gym. I wasn't disappointed.

That Josh guy from my Geometry class was leading a game of catch in front of the Gym. We tried to go around the game but Josh threw the ball at Cam. Cam caught it and hurled it right back at Josh… hard. It hit him in the gut, even though he caught it, he let out a grunt. I held back a laugh. Then the whole group of six guys came over to us, blocking our way to the steps of the Gym. I sighed and just waited for the crap to hit the fan.

"Hey, nice arm man." said Josh, grinning at Cam. I finally got a close look at Josh.

Josh, is as tall as Zach, but built more bulky. His wide shoulders and muscular arms pulled his red sweatshirt tight when he moved his arms. I stared at his face and nearly gasped aloud. His eyes were stunning. They are gold, pure molten gold with flecks of silver and copper, like looking at the setting sun on a hot summer day. I noticed he had a strong jaw and high cheekbones which made his eyes crinkle just a little in the corners, as if he smiled a lot. He had clean cut military style dark brown hair. My eyes surveyed his face; his lips were full and looked delicious. *Oh dear…this is not a good thing to be thinking about.* I thought as I realized I was staring at him. I tuned back into the conversation Cam was apparently having with Josh's friend, Luke.

Luke is dating Lindsay's friend, Carla La'vue, the hot French girl that dated everyone. Luke is pretty too, bleach blonde hair, pretty neon green eyes and a crooked nose that makes him look a little less baby faced. He's built like a linebacker, but shorter than Zach and Josh. If he wasn't such a jerk, I would have been more attracted to him.

"You sure you don't want to play? I know you're busy with the *Poverty Club* kids, but I'm sure you could dump them for a second and get your ass handed to you in a little game of football." Luke sneered. Zach shook his head and went to walk away to the Gym, grabbing for my hand. Miles was standing next to Cam staring at Luke with a look of disgust on her face.

"Luke, back off them." said Josh, rounding on Luke. That shocked me. *Did he just stick up for all of us?* I thought staring at Josh again. Luke took a step back from Josh. Looking satisfied, Josh stepped back and winked at me. I turned red and looked away, looking at Luke instead, as he smiled cruelly at Miles and Zach.

"I think this school has gone downhill, letting trashy low class people in here taking up space and wasting our time. You people are a disgrace to society, no class, no power, your all *nothing…* you're just loser charity cases. My father is trying to stop that from happening here anymore. He's going to make sure this school is cleaned up…

just wait and see. No more scholarships, no more free rides for homeless Science teacher's brats and no more dirty *whores* being allowed in, just because the Dean is their Uncle." Luke said and then spit at Miles.

He actually spit in her face! I flew at Luke, ready to knock his lights out, but Zach was there first. Cam and Josh grabbed my arms as I watched Zach. His fist connected with Luke's nose. The loud crack of bone snapping echoed around the now silent courtyard. Luke flew back into the air, as if he had been thrown and the wind caught him. He landed ten feet away and skidded back another five feet on his back. Nobody moved. We all stood frozen in place, shocked at what had just happened. I realized Josh was still holding my arm, staring at Zach with a hard look on his face. The group of guys around us all gaped at Zach. I had never seen anyone fly that far from one punch. Zach was panting slightly and looking down at his hand in shock. His hand should have been broken from that hit; he was flexing his fingers, still looking angry. Zach's eyes were so icily blue, one look could freeze water.

Carla came running over screaming and cursing in French at Zach. She was the only person who was speaking at all. Carla ran over and flung herself on Luke who was stirring feebly. *How, he is not out cold, is beyond reason.* I thought to myself.

I came to my senses and shook Josh's grip off my arm. I couldn't believe that he even came over to touch me in the first place, after all, I am far below his class. I brushed the thought away figuring he didn't want me to kick the crap out of his friend. I grabbed Zach shoving him towards the Gym. Miles, who was staring at Zach with her mouth hanging open, followed us quietly. Cam grabbed my hand and we walked all together to the steps. I was on my guard as we passed Lindsay, Kayla and Maddie. They just gaped at us as we passed. We weren't bothered by anyone. Nobody said anything mean or rude as we passed by, climbing the steps and through the massive doors.

Once safely inside I let out a breath I must have been holding. We climbed the side steps that rose up on either side of the enormous lobby in silence. The actual Gym sat on the other side of two giant doors at the center of the lobby. The side steps lead to the second, third and fourth floors. Mom and Mom two were on the second floor in a two bedroom, two bathroom apartment unit. Both our moms could have had their own places, but decided to share, since Zach and I were set up in the dorms.

I knocked on the heavy wooden door to their unit. I kept glancing at Zach, who was shaking and looking at his hand still. My mom opened it, dressed in simple blue jeans and a black t-shirt. I couldn't help it; just the sight of my mom did me in. I burst into tears and flung myself into her arms. I didn't even care that I was crying in front of Miles and Cam. We all made it inside, my mom half carrying me to the leather couch in the sitting room. Mom two came out of her room, with tissues for me like she knew I would come in crying. She handed me the whole box and I tried to hold on to some dignity as I wiped my eyes and nose looking everywhere but at the people in the room.

They have a modest sized living room with French doors leading to a balcony. Under each window on each side of the French doors sat their desks. They even have their own fireplace in the living room. The small but cozy kitchen sat next to the front door, separated from the living room by a breakfast bar. My mom's room sat behind the right door and Mom two's room was the left door, leading off the living room. Simple design, very cozy warm dark oak floors and a nice tan color on the walls, made the place feel homey. My art and photos of all of us hung on all the walls. Other than the fireplace, there was no grey rock in the space. I felt safe here. It smelled like chocolate chip cookies, and pumpkin spice candles. Mom always burned pumpkin spice candles in the fall.

Mom patted my back gently and I took a few deep breaths. Cam and Miles were crammed awkwardly together on the loveseat. I pulled myself together, we needed answers. I was here for answers not to be coddled like a baby.

"Mom, Melinda, we need to talk." I said. Melinda sat down next to Zach on the arm of the big leather chair looking grim. My mom sighed and ran a hand over her face. So I started talking. I told them about our thoughts on Kirra's weird statements. I told her about the nightmare Miles and I shared, what we had found in the woods and what I saw and smelled from the *thing*. I gave the knife to Melinda who looked at it wide eyed. Then I reluctantly told them about what Zach did in the courtyard to Luke. Zach hung his head in shame. I figured better to tell them now than to have them find out later. Melinda patted his back soothingly, looking concerned.

"I'm sorry, but you need to tell us what the *hell* is happening here. We're involved now, even though we didn't want to be." I finished looking at my mom, who looked frustrated. My mom looked to Melinda, who nodded, confirming my suspicion that *something* was going on.

"Yes, Skyelaa, I think it's time. I just want you all to know, we didn't tell you before now, for your own protection and because we were sworn to keep it a secret. Miles, Cam, both your parents know the same things we are about to tell you. We have been in contact with them since June when we first were sent here." My mom said to Miles and Cam, who looked at each other looking confused. Melinda piped in and took over for my mom.

"First, we have to talk about Kirra. Be patient with us. This is not easy to explain and you all have to keep an open mind and not interrupt. Do you understand?" Melinda asked looking at all of us. We all nodded. I was ready for answers so I kept my mouth shut for once. My mom gestured to Melinda to start the conversation and got up heading to the kitchen. Melinda sighed looking sad. I had a feeling whatever she was going to say, was not going to be good.

"Alright then, Kirra was on *protection* detail last night. She wasn't alone, but was alone in her patrol zone, behind the two dorms in a one-mile radius. We haven't needed to even have a protection detail until recently." Melinda started as Zach's eyebrows shot up and Cam frowned in confusion. I bit my tongue, holding back questions.

"About two weeks ago, a report came in from Charlie, your dad Miles, saying that the enemy was possibly headed our way. A protection detail was formed for day and night watches but had to be kept secret from students for the time being, until The Council had more details on the situation. The *Council* decides when the student body will be told all the details and that time has come. The school is now on high alert, an assembly will be held on Monday to tell the students about everything. Some students already know because their parents have told them, but have been sworn to secrecy. But, most of the students don't know what they really are and why they are really here." Melinda said looking uncomfortable.

My mom had reentered the living room with a plate of her chocolate chip cookies, fresh out of the oven. Mom set the plate on the coffee table and a tray of six cups of hot coffee. I grabbed a cup, letting it warm my hands. They hadn't explained *what* attacked Kirra yet. I looked over at Miles who was taking notes in the notebook.

"So, as to what attacked Kirra and who the enemy is…It's Demons." my mom said. Miles stopped taking notes and Cam nearly spit hot coffee on the floor. Zach's mouth dropped open. My mom continued as if she hadn't noticed.

"But these are not Demons in the Biblical term. These are the children of the Titian Lord, Typhon. Typhon, asked his mother Gaia, to give him children. Gaia is Mother Earth. Neither good nor evil, she is the earth itself. She gave birth to all the Titans and later the Titans birthed the Gods. Yes…*The Greek Gods, from Greek*

Mythology...anyways, Gaia created the Demons, at her son Typhon's request. She formed their bodies from the flesh and bone of deceased human beings, buried in the ground and formed their souls from the fires of all the volcanoes of the world. Typhon, was waging war alongside Cronus and other Titans against the Gods. The Gods were trying to overthrow their parents reign. Typhon wanted to use Demons to help him and his siblings defeat their own children." She paused looking around at all of our shocked faces. My hands holding my coffee suddenly were shaking.

"Before Typhon could call them to his aid, Typhon and the Titans were defeated by Zeus, Poseidon and Hades and locked away in the depths of Tartarus. Typhon was given his own prison, as punishment for creating the Demons. Zeus, King of the Gods, dropped a mountain on Typhon, Mount *Etna* became his prison. He has been trapped there ever since. However, his children are now trying to free him and the other Titans. The situation has reached the point of affecting humans and the Gods directly.

The Demons are trying to let Typhon out. They have already released Oceanus from Tartarus; much to the displeasure of Hades...The Demons are the cause of all the unrest in the world. The Gods are trying to aid the humans to end the unrest, fend off Oceanus and keep the humans from seeing the Demons and Monsters through the Veil. The Demons work in small groups disguised, searching for the location of their father. They are proving to be more intelligent than we could ever have imagined. They use war tactics, stealth attacks, other monsters and even humans to aid them in their cause." my mother said to a dead silent room. *What? I can't believe these words are coming from my mother. Greek Gods? Titans? Maybe she fell and hit her head? What the hell is going on!* I thought to myself. I started to ask but my mom held up her hand and I fell back into disbelieving silence.

"So, what attacked Kirra and what is threatening the entire

human race is Demons. They will keep attacking and hunting for Typhon until he is released. If he is released, the world will begin to fall into more chaos than you can imagine." my mom said seriously.

"So…those things, or *Demons,* are trying to destroy western civilization and free a real *Titan.* And the *Gods* are *real?* The Gods from *mythology?*" Zach asked slowly. Miles seemed more determined to be open minded than the rest of us. She began spouting out questions, looking excited.

"What's the Veil? And, what does this have to do with telling the students on Monday? Why would the Council want to cause more panic by involving the student body? And…who is the *Council?*" she asked her eyes boring into my mothers. Melinda took over for my mom.

"The Veil is what conceals Monsters, Demons, Titians, Gods and anything unusual from humans. Think of it as a magic mist that only certain beings with magical blood can see through. The *Council* is the *Gods.* They have decided it's time to involve all the Demigods." said Melinda meeting Miles's eyes. Miles emerald eyes grew huge in surprise. Cam finally spoke. He had been sitting in silence looking shell-shocked.

"That's why everyone here has unusual eye color… Isn't it? The eye color indicates what we are. *We*…are *Demigods* aren't we? That also means my parents aren't really my parent's right?" Cam said quietly. I wanted to scream and laugh and cry all at once. Miles actually did start laughing like she thought it was a big joke. Zach started yelling and got up pacing the room. Melinda grabbed him and made him sit back down, while Miles and I sat there staring at my mom. Cam put his head in his hands like he was about to lose it. None of us believed what was happening. My mom got up and walked over to Cam, sitting next to him putting a hand on his shoulder.

"Calm down you guys, I know this is a big shock and a lot to swallow, but you have to trust that this is the truth and was kept from you all for your own protection. Yes Cam, your mother is your birth mother and your father, though not your biological father, knows and loves you no matter what. He was there when you were born. So, he *is* your father and do not think less of him just because you do not share his blood." my mom said gently. Cam nodded mutely, looking off into the distance. Zach took a deep breath and looked to his mother after he finally sat down.

"Who is my dad?" he asked with a hard look in his eyes. Melinda looked upset and gripped her hands hard in her lap. She looked to my mother who nodded.

"Your father is Poseidon, God of the Sea." Melinda said quietly. Zach sat back thinking hard, sinking deep into the chair. I couldn't believe it.

"What about me and Cam?" asked Miles. My mother ran her hand through Cam's hair gently. He leaned into her a little, visibly relaxing, there was nothing like a mother's touch to calm the nerves.

"Cam, your father is Apollo. God of the Sun. Miles, your mother is Athena, Goddess of Wisdom and Battle Strategies." said my mother quietly.

"Why do you and the rest of the staff have eyes like we do? Are you children of Gods too?" asked Zach still looking like he didn't believe them.

"We are Demigods as well. Some of the staff members are born that way, like you. Others, like the two of us, were blessed by a God and given the Blessed Nectar of the Gods to make us Demigods and Immortal…like you all are." said Melinda. *Immortal? Holy cow!* I thought feeling torn between shock and excitement.

"Immortal? Like we can't die?" asked Cam, sitting up straighter.

My mother shook her head and sighed hard, as if she was trying to hold it together.

"Let me clarify that. You have some *version* of immortality, in the sense that your life *span* is longer than any human. You age, but slowly. At 18, the aging process slows down more, so you can pass unnoticed to mortals. They tend to notice when you don't age. So, the Gods chose the age 18 because you can pass as a young adult for a long time. However, you all *can* be killed and wounded easily, you're *still half* human. You heal fast, have more speed, strength, faster reflexes and your senses are sharper and much more refined than a humans are. Zach showed that today when he hit Luke. No human would have lived through a hit like that and no human can produce a hit like that either. It's where your dreams come from too girls. You both have a gift of *foresight*. You can both see what will happen before it does. Although I wouldn't ever set too much store in your dreams, because anything can change based on the choices made. The Fates may set the course, but our choices cause the end result." My mom said meeting Zach's eyes. He looked at his lap in shame again.

"You're all here to learn to harness your skills and powers if you have them. Some Demigods have power over fire or water, similar to a Gods powers. We won't know what your power is until you are in a situation where your instincts would kick the power into gear…so to speak. This school was set up to train Demigods, the *Chambers Family* was really Ares and Athena setting up a place to train you all in the modern world when you would be needed." my mom continued. "The use of Demigods was not needed until very recently, over the past five years. That's why none of the students know what they are and why they are all together now." she said, looking stressed out.

"The Gods decided a long time ago to keep Demigods from knowing what they truly were until they were needed. It was decided that, Heroes would only act as true Heroes when they are truly needed and put in dangerous situations. This was Aphrodite's idea and the other Gods went with it. You are all here, at this particular location, as the front line of defense, to guard Typhon." she said sadly. I looked around at everyone feeling shocked.

"I thought he was entombed in Mount Etna?" asked Miles. My mom nodded and pointed out the window.

"That *is* Mount Etna." I followed her finger, it pointed to Mount Rainier. The quiet snowcapped mountain, which I had just realized, was not as far away as I thought. *Great, the worst Titan is our neighbor. Freaking perfect.* I thought feeling so many different emotions I felt like my head would explode.

"What does the Government have to do with all this? The drafts, the wars, the Silence Act and the Combat Act…how are they involved?" asked Cam.

"They are a mix of high powered Demigods and humans. They know what is really happening and trying to keep it quiet. That's why all the overly irritating laws have been passed. The human government wanted extra protection and to keep everything quiet. So they passed a bunch of laws that require all Demigods to be trained without raising questions to the general population. The Gods want humans trained too, sometimes mortals can be useful. Since the Demons are also using corrupt humans, the Gods using humans seemed like a good idea. Realistically it's a good choice, so our side is ready for any attack. Therefore, they went the legal route. If they pass a law for training teenagers, human and Demigod alike, nobody can raise an eyebrow at it, the same goes for the Silence Act, it was just an easier way to keep everything quiet." said Melinda.

"The Gods are losing control of the situation; they are calling in all the reinforcements they have to fight the Demons, Monsters and Titans that have already escaped. They are becoming overwhelmed." she said. We all looked at each other taking it all in. There was so much to take in; I thought we all would burst from information overload.

I realized something. *My father is a God. Damn it to hell I need air.* I thought as I took a couple deep breaths and looked directly at my mother. She met my eyes as if reading my mind and dreading what she would have to say.

"*Who* is my father mom?" I asked sitting up straighter. My mom sighed again and looked down at her hands.

"You're the daughter of Hades."

Chapter Eight

"What? As in the God that runs *Hell?*" I said feeling all gross inside. *He's the head guy in the pit of fire! And, he hooked up with my Mother! He's supposedly the bad God right?* I thought feeling slightly sick. I couldn't breathe. My hands felt sweaty and my face burned. The others were staring at me as if I had a disease. I wanted to run. I half stood up, eyes glued to the door. Melinda's hand on my shoulder stopped me. I didn't even notice her get up off the arm of Zach's chair.

"I know what you *think* you know about Hades, Skyelaa. However, he is not evil. He is the balance of the Gods. He may be the Ruler of the Underworld, but without him to guide souls to Elysium, or to The Fields of Punishment, the souls of the dead would never rest. He keeps the Titans locked in Tartarus and keeps the darker more frightening things, tucked away in the Underworld. He is not evil." my mom said gently. "You *know* the kind of woman I am Skyelaa, would I be stupid enough to be with *anyone* who had evil in their heart?" she asked looking into my eyes. I found myself nodding to that. My mom *wouldn't* be with someone that was evil or crazy. I didn't know how I felt about this whole thing. I needed to shower and nap or something.

We finished our coffee and my mom packed me some cookies for Joe. I hadn't forgotten about our deal and tonight, training seemed like an excellent idea. It would have a whole hell of a lot more meaning now that all of this *God* stuff had come to light. Melinda said to leave Kirra be and that we had enough answers. We could see her on Monday; apparently, she was a Demigod too and would be healed by then. My mom and Melinda also said to leave what she said about the four of us alone for now. They needed to talk to Kirra to find out what she was talking about, before we got to know. I was fine with that, I had enough to mull over without having to worry about being a *Chosen Demigod*. My mother and Melinda hugged Cam and Miles, telling both of them to come by at anytime, if they needed anything.

We emerged into the courtyard finding it deserted. Which was great, I didn't want to see anyone right now.

"I wonder if anything will be different after everyone finds out?" asked Miles as we wandered towards our dorms.

"I know this at least, we are all equal now. The Elite rich kids are the same as us. Hell some of them are related to us. *That* is my silver lining right there." Cam said as we reached our dorms. Zach was smiling at me.

"What?" I asked him. He looked around at all of us, that silly grin still on his face.

"I'm just starting to feel a little excited about this. I mean we have skills, which we haven't even tapped into yet. I can't wait to tell Joe and see what I got. We have to be there at 6:45 tonight right?" he asked, I nodded half smiling now too. "Okay, I need a shower and I say we all meet at the door and go to dinner and then training together. I want to really look at the others and try to guess who their God parent is." said Zach as we headed to our rooms.

****

At dinner, we sat at our usual spot. None of us really knew how we should feel; we went with temporary acceptance, for now. I think, because it was so huge and so much to take in, we decided as a group to treat it like a game. How else were we supposed to deal with the news? I wasn't very hungry, I settled for a fresh salad and a piece of garlic bread, pushing it around on my plate.

"I think Lindsay is a child of a Titan. That *has* to be why she is such a bitch all the time. I think its Perses; he's the Titan of Destruction. I think that's the one for her." said Miles glaring over at Lindsay's table.

Miles had gotten three books from the library about Greek Gods, Titans, and Mythology. She said the more we knew about them, the better prepared we would be for…well everything. I didn't want to know about Hades yet. I was still trying to wrap my head around *that* one.

I knew Hades was married to Persephone, Goddess of Spring Growth and the kidnapped Queen of the Underworld. Though she had been kidnapped and taken to the Underworld, Persephone fell in love with Hades eventually and married him. Hades, I've heard, is a very jealous, protective man, with power trip issues. He's madly in love with Persephone and would take on anyone to protect her. My mother must have been something special to him. So special that he *cheated* on Persephone with my mother and had me. I was sure my *stepmother* was probably not a fan of that or me for being the result of his cheating. *Damn it to hell…I mean, Hades.* I thought as I tuned back into the conversation.

"I think Carla is Aphrodite's kid. She has a way with guys, like she puts a spell on them." I said trying to distract myself. Cam chuckled; he seemed to be doing better, a lot less surly than he was earlier.

"Dude I'm sure of it. She's so hot and perfect; there's no way that isn't a result of Aphrodite. People have flaws and Carla doesn't seem to have one." Cam said looking over at Carla, who was moodily poking at a salad and talking to Josh, who was sitting beside her. She seemed very cranky and sullen after Zach hit Luke, which I guess is understandable. Luke's nose apparently needed to be reset and he was still in the Infirmary with two black eyes and a mild concussion.

"Oh yes she does, her whole personality is a flaw. She's just a much a snob as Luke, and Lindsay combined." Miles said glaring over at Carla. Zach still hadn't said much. I watched him as he tried to smile at Miles, it was half hearted. I decided we needed to go for a walk.

"Hey, Zach, will you come walk with me for a minute?" I asked him. He nodded and stood up right away. I stood too and looked to Miles and Cam.

"Be back in fifteen guys. I promise we'll keep a sharp eye and be just out front. Keep an eye out for us from here? We'll be on the front steps." I said and both of them nodded. We had all decided on the walk to dinner, that none of us were to go anywhere alone. We had to stay together as much as possible in case Demons come gunning for us. Especially since, we didn't know what Kirra had meant by the *chosen four* thing.

Once outside I looked around to be sure we wouldn't be overheard. The coast was clear so I reeled on Zach.

"Talk...*now*. Something is eating at you and I can tell. You were all gung-ho and excited earlier. What's going on?" I said crossing my arms over my chest. He sighed and sat down on the step. A bright half moon was shining through the thin clouds, casting a creepy light over the grounds. I sat next to him and we looked out over the grounds.

"I am excited. I'm excited that we're Demigods and to learn

about my abilities. I just don't understand what we're supposed to do now. Do we train to fight here and stay here? Are we going to stay and guard Typhon? Are we still in the draft and going to be sent away pretending to be just humans, or as Demigods? What do we do next Skye?" he asked putting his head in his hands.

"We find a way to talk to our dads. They probably have all the answers. I don't really want to talk to mine…*Lord of the Underworld* and all…but I think we should try to talk to Poseidon. I think your dad will be more…uh… personable than mine." I said patting his leg. "Maybe we could even talk to Athena or Apollo. Maybe they will have the answers for what will happen once we're done with school." I said.

"Yeah, maybe…I just thought everything was set in motion. I had accepted the whole draft thing and even knew I could die from it. I *thought* I had it all figured out. I feel like now our promise we made is worth nothing because we have to be all serious now. I was looking forward to being *just* a normal guy going to a rich kid high school, even though I knew it was on a time limit." he said getting agitated, running his hand through his hair. I put my hand on his knee and scooted closer to him so we leaned into each other.

"The promise still stands. We can still do all those things. *Now* we have immortality, sweet reflexes and have to protect humanity from Demons. We don't know if they will attack again. We don't know if they know that Mount Rainier is where Typhon really is. All we can do is train harder, play harder and meet our Godly parents and hope they want to talk. I think it will end up working out…to prove my point, you should ask Miles to the Halloween Ball, its next Friday night you know." I nudged Zach in the shoulder and he nudged back. I caught him grinning in the moonlight. He pulled me closer to him with his arm around my shoulders.

"What would I do without you?" he said kissing the top of my head.

"Be miserable and super lame. I keep you on your toes." I said proudly.

"How are *you* doing, daughter of the Lord of the Underworld? I think your taking this pretty well. I would be freaking out." He said gently. I was freaking out. But, I knew I had to trust my mother. If I couldn't trust her or my friends, I would be screwed.

"I have to have faith in my mom. If she says he's not that bad…then I have to trust her. She may have been a married God's mistress, but I still love her and can't be mad at her. I just hope I don't start seeing dead people or something." I said with a snort. Zach chuckled.

"Maybe Hades is just misunderstood. He has a bad reputation. But, a guy that can take care of souls and send them to Elysium, guard Tartarus, keep a three-headed dog as a pet *and* keep all those monsters in his realm on their best behavior… has to be a good dude. *No way* would someone who does all that be a bad guy. Did you know he controls the Titan Thanatos, who is like the guy the Gods send to kill people that piss them off, like a hit man. He even controls the wealth of the world because all the precious metals on earth come from his realm. Did you know Plutonium was named after his Roman name, Pluto? He's even in charge of controlling that and keeping it from getting out of hand. Once this mess is over I want to ask him why he let humans create nuclear bombs though, that was just *stupid*." he said with a frown. I laughed at that. *Maybe Zach is right. Hades is in charge of a lot of stuff. If that stuff didn't have a place in his realm, the world would be thrown into chaos. Hades can't be that bad.* I thought feeling a little better about it.

"I see you've been reading those books with Miles." I said grinning over at him.

"Yes, he has and I think you should check them out too missy." Miles's voice made me jump as if I had been shocked. Cam's laugher came from behind her. Miles sat down next to Zach and Cam plopped down by me.

"And Zach, I would love to go to the dance with you. Cam and I would like to be in on this promise. Let's try to be *normal* for as long as we can." Miles said grabbing Zach's hand. Normally I would be really mad that anyone had eavesdropped on our conversation, but I couldn't bring myself to be angry. Especially when Miles kissed Zach, full on kissed him on the mouth. I blushed and looked over to Cam, who was grinning. Both of us were trying not to laugh and ruin their moment. I felt…happy. These two had only been with us a short time and we had been through so much now, it was like we had been friends forever. It was amazing how things could change. Miles and Zach finally surfaced and after an awkward silence and some giggles, Cam cleared his throat and spoke up.

"Sorry we eavesdropped on you guys. But, Luke came into the Dining Hall and was looking for you Zach. We overheard him; he's out for blood man. He went up the side stairs with two of his big friends and we wanted to make sure you had back up if he realized you were out here and wanted to start something. Or worse sneak up on you." said Cam.

"Was Josh with them?" I blurted out. *Wait, why does that matter?* I thought. For some reason it mattered, I didn't want him to be with those guys. Cam's pale eyebrows shot up and he looked at me funny.

"Actually no… He was the first person Luke asked and he lied to him saying you guys went upstairs, when I know for a fact that he saw you go out the front. When I was checking out Kayla, Josh was watching you leave." Cam said still looking at me weird. Knowing Josh had even *looked* at me made my stomach flutter a little bit. *Weird. That's a new thing.* I thought as Zach and Miles stood up.

"Time to go meet Joe. We have *a lot* to tell her." Zach said, checking his watch. Cam and I stood up too. I looked around checking to see if Luke and his buddies were around. So far, we were in the clear. We headed down the front steps to the courtyard. I couldn't help thinking; *Let the training of the Demigods begin.*

Miles and I walked out into the arena after we finished getting dressed to find the boys already there. Joe was talking to them while they stretched. She was patting Zach on the leg in a reassuring way.

"You fill her in already?" I asked plopping down next to Zach with Miles right behind me. I passed over the box of cookies to Joe, who gave me a sly grin.

"I am a daughter of Hephaestus, God of Fire and Metal working." she said meeting my eyes.

"AH, hell! I had you pegged for Ares! The God of War for sure! It's all right; Hephaestus is awesome and has fantastic metal skills. I thought he would be mine, I'm a metal sculptor." Cam said excited. Joe smiled at him

"You know it *killed* me not being able to tell you guys what you are? I didn't know exactly who your parents were but I knew you were Demigods. You two have excellent skills but you stifle them because the *Veil* still affects you. Once you accept what you are, your *Sight* will show you what you're missing when your true instincts take over. I will do my best to teach you what I can. So who do you belong to, my favorite cousins?" she asked. I felt my neck get hot and a jolt in my stomach. I felt scared to tell her. The others filled her in, each spouting out facts about what they knew about their parents. I stayed silent. *Am I ashamed?* I wondered. I wasn't sure.

"Skye? Who's your father? I can hone in on your abilities if I know who your parent is. I can also build you custom weapons that you will be able to use like an extra arm. Who is it?" Joe insisted. I cleared my throat, still feeling hot; I looked down at my hands. I was stalling and I hated it.

"I… I am a Daughter of Hades." I said quietly looking at the black mat we were sitting on and back up to Joe. Joe's eyebrows shot up and her eyes widened. Miles came to my rescue spouting out all the facts she knew about Hades and how he was a misunderstood God. Joe held up her hand to silence her.

"I know about Hades, thank you Miles. Skye, you look at me right now. You are not just a daughter of Hades; you are his *only* daughter and his only child. He has never strayed from Persephone before. He must have loved your mother very much. You should feel proud. Do not *ever* let me catch you hanging your head in shame. However, when the rest of the school finds out on Monday we keep this to ourselves. Agreed?" she looked hard to all of us. "We don't need Skye being demonized or treated unfairly because of people misunderstanding her Godly parent. I don't know what this *Chosen* stuff is Kirra was rattling off, but we are not to take it lightly. Her Father is also Apollo, like you Cam. Apollo is not only the God of the Sun and healing but also the God of *Prophecy*; Kirra has this ability more than anyone I know. She's a *Seer*. She can see the future with dreams and visions. So, until she can enlighten us all, we keep things quiet. Understand?" Joe said looking stern.

We all nodded and I let out a huge sigh of relief. It's as if a huge weight was lifted. I felt happy that I could keep it to myself for a while. I didn't need people like Lindsay or Luke trying to humiliate me or something because my dad was the leader of the Underworld.

We spent training working with all the weapons. Joe said she wanted to watch how we handled weaponry to see what type of weapon we favored. She had Miles and Cam go first. Joe already knew I favored knives and the bow. She also knew Zach is amazing with any sword.

Joe set all the basic close range weapons on a table; knives, daggers, long sword, short sword, spear, hammer, an axe and a sweet double blade sword. Then she set up long-range weapons on another table, longbow, cross bow, compound bow and spear. She said any fool could use a gun and we could practice shooting during regular training. Joe explained the bows and spears were weapons used in *real* battles and Demons and Monsters usually need more than bullets to take them down. She had Miles and Cam face the table with their eyes closed and backs to her. Joe stood 40 feet behind them with her shield. She said as soon as she let out a battle cry she would charge and they had seconds to chose a weapon for long range and use them.

"You will naturally select the weapon you are more comfortable with. Do not second-guess this. Just do it. You are Demigods; your reaction to an attack is faster than a mortal. I will be attacking you. Breathe and trust your instincts… Ready?" Joe asked loudly from her position. Miles and Cam said "Yes boss" at the same time and Joe let out a loud menacing battle cry and started to charge. Miles and Cam turned around at the same time, Miles with a spear and Cam with a long bow. They both fired at Joe. Miles's spear planted firmly into Joe's shield right in its center. Cam fired a split second after Miles threw her spear, his arrow hitting the very top of Joe's shield. Both of them ran over to check on Joe who had stopped in her tracks. She peeked over her shield grinning. I let out a sigh of relief; I thought she wouldn't get her shield up fast enough to block the arrow.

"Well, that was excellent! You are definitely a daughter of Athena Miles. And Cam, Apollo would be proud! He also favors the bow." Joe said laughing. Miles was trying not to look proud of herself and Cam was looking at the bow as if it was his baby.

"Alright, so I have to make you both, custom weapons, spear and a long bow with bronze tipped arrows and spear head. Great job you two! Take a break; I'm going to test Zach and Skye again. I know what you both favor but now that you know what you are maybe that will change your weapon choices. Same set up and wait for my signal." She said hurrying back to her start point again. I eyed Zach feeling nervous. His face was set as we took out spots in front of the distance weapons. I closed my eyes and breathed in deep.

Joe's cry echoed around me and my eyes flew open. I grabbed the only weapon that called to me in that split second before I shot at Joe. My arrow sank into her shield before Zach's arrow from the crossbow. His arrow hit her shield next to mine. Joe came over grinning at me.

"What?" I asked feeling confused. *Joe has seen me with a bow before, why is she still grinning?* I thought as Joe flipped her shield around and showed me the inside. My arrow had gone halfway through the metal, the sharp tip and part of the shaft stuck out the other side.

"I'm sorry I ruined your shield Joe." I said feeling worried that I messed up. *Maybe I shouldn't have pulled back so hard.* I thought. Zach was patting me on the back chuckling.

"Joe is trying to give you a compliment and your being difficult. The cross bow I used had the ability to go through a shield if used properly. A long bow, like the one you grabbed can't usually pull that off unless you have massive strength and skill. Nice job little mouse." Zach explained. I blushed. *Yay me, I am freakishly strong.* I thought still red in the face.

"Nice work kid. Now we get to play with the fun toys. Same drill, but I will be only 15 feet behind you with a weapon. I favor the axe and hammer, but this time I'll have a sword instead of those. Pick up the weapon that speaks to you and block my attack. Once our metal meets, we stop. Close range weapons are on the table. Miles, Cam, your first. Eyes closed." said Joe stepping back.

Joe had us run these drills two more times each. Once the drills were complete, we each were to have our own special weapons, made custom by Joe. Cam would get a short sword, cross bow and longbow. Miles would get a spear, and short sword. Zach was to get a cross bow and a long sword. I was the only one who had picked up a specialty weapon that none of the others had touched. By instinct I had grabbed the double blade sword. I just grabbed it during the drills and it became a part of my arm. It's crazy how I just knew what to do with it even though I had never touched one before. I was also going to get a long bow of my own and two knives. All of us were going to get shields, daggers and small handguns from Joe too. I'm not going to lie, I was ecstatic, I'll finally get my own weapons and custom holsters for all of them.

Our training ended and we headed back to our dorms together in high spirits. I just wish we had been paying more attention. We would have been better prepared for what was waiting for us as we passed behind the stables.

Chapter Nine

Hot pain laced through the back of my head. Stars ignited behind my eyes making my vision spotty. My face hit the ground, dirt and mud filled my mouth making it hard to breathe. I could hear grunting and scuffling around me. I knew we had been ambushed. I gently turned my head to the side and took a whiff of the night air. No rot or sulfur smell. Relief flooded through me. *No Demons.* I thought as anger took over the relief.

Near my head, two sets of feet shuffled around. I looked up and saw Cam facing off with Luke's giant friend. Everyone called him Big Mike; the name fit him like a glove, thick like an ox and taller than Zach. He's surprisingly fast for a guy his size but even more surprising, Cam was still standing, not only *taking* Big Mike's hits, but landing quite a few of his own. I heard Miles yelling. *I have to get up.* I thought as I forced myself to come up fast, it made me dizzy but I stayed up, looking around me. Adrenaline began to pump through my veins like fire as it became clear as to what had happened; *someone sucker punched me from behind.* I didn't know who, but they were not about to get away with it. Nobody hurts my friends or me.

I surveyed my surroundings looking for a target. We were behind the stables; I could hear the horses getting upset from the shouting and fighting out in the open. I counted five guys that jumped us. Big Mike was fighting Cam, Luke, was scrambling around Zach, trying to land a good hit, but by the look of the blood coming out of Luke's nose, he wasn't doing very well. Two other guys, twins by the look of them, whose names I didn't know, were preparing to help Luke but just hanging back a little, waiting.

Miles held her own against a small measly looking guy, named Kirk. Kirk is small and wiry, with a mean chiseled face, jet-black eyebrows, long greasy black hair and red glowing eyes like tail-lights. If he wasn't so tan, he could almost pass as a Demon. Miles landed a great hit, right into Kirk's stomach, dropping him to his knees. I nodded briefly at her as she met my eyes, rage etched all over her face.

I caught Twin One make a move at Zach's back out of the corner of my eye and lunged into his path knocking his hand aside. I faced off with Twin One, taking in his appearance. Stocky, built very broad in the chest, but skinny looking legs. His round face and shaved head make his features appear slightly squished giving the impression that he frowned a lot. His mouth was hidden by a thick sandy brown moustache and beard, if he didn't have such a round chubby face I would have taken him to be in his late 20s instead of attending a high school. His voice came out as a growl.

"What's the matter? Afraid to take on a *man?*" he growled at me. His twin chuckled watching the two of us circle each other. I didn't let him bait me. I wanted him to attack first so I could look for weak spots. *It looks like the only thing that might be weak on this guy is his legs.* I thought looking him over feeling slightly worried. His jeans were a little baggy, making it more difficult to tell if his legs even could be the weak point I needed.

I smiled mockingly at him, trying to push his buttons and waited. The smile worked, he came at me like a freight train swinging with a right fist at my head. I dodged it feeling the whoosh of air as his fist passed. He over stepped his punch, in that split second, giving me an advantage, I took it and punched him in side, landing another hit to his stomach. He staggered coming back up swinging, he faked a hit to my face with his right fist. He landed a poorly aimed punch with his left, to my side. I blocked with my arm, as he staggered to the side. His twin stepped forward taking his place.

Realizing I now have to fight both of them, I got more pissed off. They seemed to have a system; taking turns while I had to keep going the whole fight. I took a deep breath as Twin Two stepped up to take Twin One's place. Twin Two had no moustache, but everything else was the same including the thick sandy beard. *Maybe he'll make the same mistakes?* I thought hopefully… I let my guard down just long enough to look at him for a weak spot. He caught my jaw with a left hook after faking a right jab causing me to nearly go down and stumble over my own feet. Rage at my own mistake flooded over me.

That's when something overtook me, like I suddenly came out of a daze. Time dropped into slow motion, kicking my instincts into overdrive. Twin Two came at me with blinding speed, with another punch aimed for my face with his right fist, as I was turning from my half crouch to meet him again. Before he could break my face open with his flying superman hit, I dipped down lower in my crouch, seeing my only chance. I tucked my head just enough for him to miss me and used all my rage behind a punch of my own into the side of his knee. His leg snapped, awkwardly jutting out to the side. I more than likely dislocated his knee and probably broke a bone in his leg. He let out a howl hitting the ground *hard*. I kept going. I was a machine, with no off button and no mercy. I leaped on top of him connecting hit after hit to his face. Twin One came at me to help his brother; I ducked, rolling to the side under his swing and used a leg sweep taking him down onto his back. Twin One cowered on the ground, covering his face causing me to stop in my tracks before I could jump on him and beat him into the dirt. Twin Two rolled on the ground clutching his busted up leg. I had won the fight and left both of them there, searching for my next target. Zach and Luke were closest to me. I raced over to them.

I watched them fighting, both of them using skills from combat training to try to take the other to the ground. I noticed Zach was being more defensive instead of offensive. Zach usually never fought defensively, then I noticed the glint of a knife in Luke's hand. Looking harder at the situation I saw Zach holding his left arm funny. Blood flowed down to his fingertips from a deep gash on his bicep. More blood soaked through Zach's grey sweatshirt from what appeared to be a shallow knife slice across his chest. Pure boiling rage filled me. Luke brought a *knife*. This was no longer just a regular schoolyard fistfight between a bunch of silly teenagers with pride issues, this was *wrong*.

I charged at Luke, shoving Zach back behind me and jumping in to take his place. Without hesitation, Luke lunged at me with his knife. I side stepped his lunge; cross punched him in the bicep, deadening the muscle in his knife arm. I dropped down and leg swept him causing him to fall to the side. He caught himself before he hit the ground. As he began to come back up, I landed a punch to the side of his head. As his head snapped to the side, my other fist was there to meet his face. Just like Twin Two tried to do to me. Spinning on my heels, I jabbed from the front and hit his nose, which cracked under my closed fist. The hits fazed him, but not enough to stop him. Luke came at me fast, landing a hit into my shoulder causing me to turn, exposing my right side. He caught my mistake and sliced the knife at my right side. He caught the flesh through my sweatshirt and I felt the hot sting of a deep cut. I stumbled back a step, feeling that the slice to my side wasn't too deep but it was deep enough to bleed a lot. If his arm hadn't been weakened by my first blow, he probably would have done more damage. Feeling hot blood trickle down my side I decided, I was *so* done with this clown. I took my lead step as Luke went to take a swipe at me again with the knife. With all my strength I leapt into the air and roundhouse kicked him in the face. My boot connected with a sickening crack across his cheek and nose. I landed in a crouch watching as he went down, out cold and not moving. I felt eyes on me and whirled around.

Miles watched me while holding wiry creepy Kirk down on his back, with his hands up, yelling that he was sorry. Cam and Big Mike stood side by side staring at me. The Twins were helping each other head over to where Luke lay, a few feet from me. They stopped and held up their hands as if to say they were done. I nodded at them and stepped back a few feet so they could get Luke. My breath came out in heavy gasps as I stood shaking trying to shut off my instincts and adrenaline. Slowly after a few deep breaths my heart began to slow down as my adrenaline slowly left my veins.

I looked at my feet taking more deep breaths trying to calm down, as Zach walked up next to me. Cam headed over to where we stood by the wall of the stables after saying something to Big Mike. I leaned against the wall feeling my wounds for the first time as Zach leaned against the wall with me holding his arm gingerly. My face started to hurt from the punch Twin Two landed. I still couldn't feel the wound on my side yet, but I could feel the blood soaking my shirt and seeping down into the top of my jeans.

I couldn't believe Luke brought a knife. *What a jackass.* I thought. At least he hadn't been trying very hard to use it. I had seen Luke in combat training with daggers; he knew how to kill with small blades. Thank the Gods he didn't try too hard to really cause damage.

"I can't *believe* he brought a knife. It's one thing to want to fix your pride and get one over on you for punching him." I said looking at Zach. "But, to go farther by bringing five guys and a *weapon*? What the hell was he thinking?" I asked feeling suddenly tired.

"I think it was more that he wanted to show off. He didn't pull it out until I was gaining the upper hand. I don't think he wanted to *really* use it, just scare me with it. He waved it around and threatened me without actually making a move. I lunged at him and landed a couple good hits. It's really *my* fault… I made him use it. Seeing it pissed me off too much and I lost my self control." said Zach quietly. Miles and Cam joined us and we watched the Twins and Kirk try to get Luke up. He started moving a little bit, but seemed really out of it still. I almost felt bad…almost. Big Mike made his way over to us. I felt us all tense up, ready for anything. He held out his hand to Cam. Cam looked at his hand confused and then took it slowly, shaking hands with him.

"That was an *excellent* fight. You have skills man. Luke just *had* to get his pride back, probably picked the wrong way to do it, but he's my boy and I have his back. But, I want you to know, you have my respect. You need anything, you let me know." Big Mike said in a deep smooth voice. Smiling, Cam nodded.

"You too, I didn't think I would be able to hold my own against you. Your fast man. You need anything from me, let me know." Cam said. Big Mike smiled; he actually had a sweet smile, making him look like a big cuddly brown teddy bear. His eyes looked like deep grey storm clouds and they crinkled in the corners when he smiled. Big Mike turned to me holding out his hand. *What?* I thought feeling confused.

"You're good too. I was watching when you laid out Luke. That was a *hell* of a kick little girl. You need me, say the word okay?" I took his massive hand and shook it feeling stunned.

"Thanks…Big Mike. All I ask, for now, is to call it even with Luke. If you could pass the word to Luke when he comes to? Tell him to stay away from us from now on too. And, to sweeten the deal, the four of us will help get everyone to the Infirmary. I'll even tell Nurse Lane and even the Dean that we were all playing football and got too rowdy with it." I said making up the story on the fly, thinking of when Zach had punched Luke earlier in the courtyard.

I didn't want any of us to get into trouble, if that meant covering for Luke and his cronies, so be it. Rowdy football seemed like a good enough story to me. Josh popped into my head; I kept picturing him throwing the football and his golden eyes. *Damn me to Hades, I have to stop thinking of that guy.* I thought. Big Mike chuckled deep in his belly, bringing my attention back to the real world.

"Agreed. Let's get these guys taken care of. I like your style little girl." Big Mike said patting the top of my head. I slightly wanted to punch him for all this *little girl* nonsense, but he was smiling and I liked that better than his *angry fight face.*

It took all of us to help get Luke, Twin Two and Kirk who had apparently broken his ankle, courtesy of a *sweet* block from Miles, to the Infirmary. Kirk had tried to kick her in the face and she caught his foot, with a twist of the wrist, she snapped his ankle. It was gross but it worked when you wanted to end a fight without killing anyone. Miles was untrained and had done that on pure instinct. I was proud and a little grossed out. It took Zach and Big Mike to carry Luke. Miles and I had Kirk, who whined and squealed about his ankle. Twin One had Twin Two's arm over his shoulders, helping him walk. The twins were not as nice as Big Mike. They were both pretty upset a tiny little girl took them in a fight. *I guess this whole Demigod thing works wonders when you know about it.* I thought as they grumbled about the fight being unfair. I was shocked at how my instincts had taken over and even allowed me to take on three big guys in a fight. I would have to talk to Joe about it at some point.

When we finally hobbled into the Castle and to the Infirmary, Nurse Lane, was beside herself. She bustled around muttering about the dangers of football and that we should know better than to play so rough. I was just happy she bought the lie, but I could tell she may have just settled for hearing it instead of wanting to know the truth. It took *forever* for her to patch us all up. Zach's arm needed ten stitches, his chest, she sealed up with medical glue. Miles had a black eye and a broken pinky finger that was put in a tiny cast. I laughed at it, her finger stuck out off to the side making it look like she permanently had a teacup in her hand, it looked ridiculous. Laughing hurt my face and my side. I ended up with a bruised jaw and eight stitches in my side. Cam fractured his right wrist and was forced into a cast by the angry nurse. He also had a great deal of bruises on his face and arms. Big Mike had a concussion and a busted lip.

Luke was a mess, two black eyes, a re-broken nose, three cracked ribs, a broken arm, another concussion and a fractured cheek. The face wounds were mostly my fault. I felt guilty and even worse when I found out that Twin Two had a broken leg in three places and a dislocated knee. *Whoops, I guess I need to save all that rage and crazy for fighting Demons.* I thought as I heard the report of injuries. We were sent away and didn't get back to our rooms until two in the morning. I stripped out of my bloody filthy clothes and fell into bed in my underwear falling asleep instantly.

I sat in Natural Science Class next to Miles. My mom's lecture on Earth's precious metals, made me think of Hades. I zoned out and stared out the window at the mountain.

Miles nudged me trying to get my attention, but before I could blink or speak, a loud screeching sound cut through the air. My hands flung to my ears. Everyone else did the same, all looking around with fear in their eyes. I didn't know what this alarm was for; everyone grabbed up their things as quickly as they could and rushed into each other trying to get out the door to the stairs. My mom yelled for them to calm down but her yelling went unnoticed. I grabbed my bag and Miles's hand running towards my mother, dodging chairs, other students and desks.

"MOM! What is that?" I yelled over the alarm. My mom grabbed my shoulders.

"Skye, it's the emergency evacuation alarm! Take Miles, meet up with Cam and Zach and get to the bunker under the Castle! Do not get separated! Go down the servant's staircase to the door on the left at the bottom, follow the steps down. Go to the door at the end of the tunnel and stay there! Go now! I have to make sure the floor is clear with the rest of the professors and we will be there shortly. Go right now! Don't look out the windows and do not stop no matter what you

see or hear! Do you understand!?" she yelled. I knew this was bad, she never called me Skye. I could see the fear in her eyes. I wanted to tell her no and make her come too, but I knew she wouldn't go until everyone else was out.

I glanced out the window and saw them. Grey skinned, black clothed…hundreds of Demons ran towards the Castle. I turned to Miles, whose eyes were wide with terror . They were here. Then, the world exploded around me. Hot fire whipped past me as I threw Miles to the floor. Glass exploded, slicing my face and arms. I felt hot blood trickle down my flesh as I tried to get up. The earth shook. Heat seared my skin again as the world went black.

I woke up covered in sweat. I felt all panicky and jittery looking around my room. It was morning; a dark morning, raining like crazy and windy outside. I looked over to my clock by the bed, 9am on the dot. I pulled up a pen and paper and jotted down the dream and the time. My mom said I was some kind of *Seer*, so I figured I should probably keep track of my dreams. I heard soft breathing in the corner and looked over at my chair. Zach slept awkwardly curled up with his long legs tucked under him. I sighed getting up and shook him awake. He moaned and groggily looked around like he didn't know he had come in. I helped him stagger to my bed making him lay down. He fell asleep right away softly snoring. I snuggled back in next to him and tried to sleep too, I was still really tired. I didn't sleep, but just laid there going over the dream in my head. It was scary but not as scary as the first one, probably because I knew what the Demons were now. I knew I had to tell Miles about it and my mother too. I really wanted to talk to my father about all of this. I knew he had most of the answers to this whole confusing mess. I just wished I knew how to contact him, but I was pretty sure The Underworld didn't have a phone number.

About an hour later, my door opened, Miles and Cam came in. They had both showered but were in sweats and sweatshirts. *It's going to be a lazy Sunday.* I thought feeling relieved. Both had brought food from the Dining Hall and their homework. I crawled out of bed feeling really sore and went to get into the shower. When I came out, also dressed in sweats, I felt a little better but my stitches were itchy. Zach was awake and sitting with Miles on my bed eating breakfast burritos. I snatched one of the yummy burritos off my desk and plopped down on top of Cam in my chair. He was ready this time and only grunted. I leaned back into him munching on my food with my eyes closed. Miles spoke up making me open my eyes.

"Did you dream last night?" she asked seriously. My mouth was still full so I nodded. She sighed and shook her head. I pointed to my notepad by the bed and Miles began to read it, eyes wide.

"It's the same but from your point of view. I had the same dream and wrote it down too. So, there will be a Demon attack at some point. Only, this time they are going to openly attack us. This *foresight dream* crap sucks. I hope it's not true. We need to talk to our parents soon and find out what they know. My dad will know the Demons movements. My mom…she just needs to tell me more about myself and what being her daughter means." Miles said as she settled into Zach, being careful of his chest wound.

"I think our mothers will know how to reach them. We'll have to ask them. But today, we need to finish our homework and rest. I don't know about you guys but I feel like I was hit by a bus." Zach said barely stifling a yawn. We all nodded, my body hurt and I was ready to tear out my stitches, they itched so bad. Cam was trying to stick a finger under his cast to itch his arm. I reached past him to my desk and handed him a pencil, he took it gratefully and shoved it in the cast scratching his arm. I looked around at my friends, who were itching their injuries from our epic adventures from last night and it dawned on me. *We are freaking Demigods.* I thought as I leapt up off Cam's lap startling him.

"What the hell Skye! Is your ass on fire or something?" Cam groaned rubbing his legs. I bolted over to Zach and Miles.

"Take off your shirt Zach." I ordered. Miles raised an eyebrow at me.

"Why? What's your deal little mouse?"Zach asked, eyeing me knowingly as a smile crept up his face. He took off his shirt and stood up facing me. I looked at the cut across his chest. It had nearly healed already. It may have been a shallow wound, but shouldn't heal this quickly. It will probably just be a thin scar in another two days or less. I ran my finger along the cut feeling that it was fairly smooth and most of the medic-glue the nurse had put on it was already gone.

"We are *Demigods* guys. We heal faster than humans do. Miles look in the mirror. Your eye isn't black and blue, its already yellowish green and healing. Cam I bet you're going to be out of that cast by Tuesday. You and I can probably take out our stitches tomorrow!" I said excitedly pointing at Zach's arm wound. I ripped up my shirt and looked down at my side. No wonder it was itchy, the skin had pretty much sealed up and it wasn't swollen. Instead of being less than a day old, it looked like it was a week old. We all assessed our injuries, all of us trying not to smile.

"Well, that's really cool. No wonder we all feel so tired. We're healing so fast that our bodies are using much more energy than a normal human does. This is pretty awesome. I can't believe I never noticed before, I've been hurt so many times and never noticed I heal faster. This is crazy." said Cam from my bathroom, as he looked in the mirror.

We spent the rest of our Sunday, finishing our homework and looking through Miles's books on Greek Gods and Demigod Heroes. By the time the sun set, we were all exhausted again and went to bed right after eating a hurried dinner we brought back to my room. Monday was going to be crazy; the whole school was going to be told the truth.

Chapter Ten

I sat in my chair looking blearily around the Dining Hall. Zach, Miles and Cam looked around sleepy eyed too. We had gotten plenty of sleep but all still felt tired. I was able to pull out all of my stitches when I woke up. Cam cut his cast off too before we walked to the Castle together for breakfast. Zach had Miles pull out his stitches too. We all still itched and were exhausted but were at least nearly healed. The only part that sucked about it was how sleepy we all felt. After our overly eventful weekend, I wasn't surprised.

"When do you think they are going to call for the assembly? To tell everyone what's going on?" asked Miles. I looked around at all the students eating breakfast, laughing and joking with each other. They were about to have their tiny little worlds rocked. I would feel bad for them if Lindsay wasn't pointing at me, talking to Carla and Josh about me and my friends. I hoped she freaked out about it, had a nervous breakdown and they sent her away. *Alright* so, sometimes I can be cruel, but she is such a mean selfish person I worried that she would take this Demigod thing too far and become an even worse bully.

Cam watched Kayla chat with Big Mike, his face determined. Suddenly, Cam got up, walked over to their table and sat down in an empty chair right across from Kayla. Lindsay's eyes got wide at whatever Cam was saying to Kayla. Miles, Zach and I watched anxiously over the backs of our chairs. We couldn't hear what any of them were saying, it was too loud in the Dining Hall. I looked around at the people at the table. Big Mike was smiling and nodding, Josh kept looking from Cam to me.

Why is he looking at me? I thought feeling my face turned red. *Great… I love blushing in front of everyone…so irritating.* I thought.

I focused on Lindsay. She looked *really* mad. She waved her hands around, talking really fast to Kayla. Kayla seemed to be ignoring her and looked stunned. She smiled a big glittering smile at Cam. I took that as a good sign. Cam had said he was going to ask Kayla to the dance. By the look on her face, he might actually get a *yes* out of her. Kayla stunned me again, getting up and walking around the table over to Cam, holding out her hand to him. He took it and they walked off together hand in hand, out to the patio. Lindsay looked furious; her face was red and splotchy as she hurried over towards the three of us with Maggie, Josh, Big Mike and Carla behind her. *Great… I am not in the mood for another fight.* I thought as I quickly turned back around in my chair. Lindsay marched around to the front of my chair blocking my view of the fireplace with her really short hot pink dress.

"Your boyfriend needs to back off Kayla!" Lindsay shouted at me.

Whoa, still too early for loud shrill noises. I thought, feeling my anger rise in my veins. Josh and Big Mike hung back and watched Lindsay yell at me, while Carla and Maddie flanked her.

"He's not good enough to even *look* at her, or ask her to the dance! Her father *runs* Wall Street. *He* is a big deal, *she* is a big deal! Your dirty low class friend needs to stay away from her! I will *not* have *my* best friend hooked up with a low class pile of trash! I will make all your lives hell if you don't *back off!*" she shouted, practically spitting on me.

Now I was really mad. *How dare she talk about Cam like that.* I thought as anger bubbled in my chest. I held it together and stayed seated, it took all my willpower not to jump up and crack her in the mouth. Zach got up to talk to Big Mike and Josh while watching Lindsay yell at me. Miles scooted closer to me, flanking my left side, tension rolling off her in waves.

"Easy Lindsay…*First* of all; Cam is one of *my* best friends, so watch your *dirty mouth.* Second; he's his own person and can make his own decisions *and so can Kayla.* I don't care who she is in the social world. We live in the *real* world." I slowly rose from my chair barley reaching eye level with Lindsay. "Back off okay. I think *you're* the one with the problem, Kayla didn't seem to have an issue with Cam talking to *her.*" I said as I moved closer to her, causing her to take a step back. "*And…* if you *ever* threaten me or my friends again, I'll make sure to rearrange your pretty little face… *Am I clear?*" I asked my voice low. Maddie glared at me, her round pudgy face getting red. Carla put her hand on Lindsay's shoulder.

"I am theenking we should go. We do not need to talk of this now Lind see." Carla said in her thick French accent. Lindsay dropped her eyes. Taking a step back, it's like she couldn't help herself, she swung out to punch me. I could sense it coming before she did it. I caught her fist mid-swing, twisted it up and spinning her around I pulled her arm behind her back, pushing her elbow up. I pushed it up a little more, causing her to let out a pained cry. If I pushed a *little* more I would dislocate her shoulder and tear the ligaments. Maddie let out an outraged scream and lunged at me. Big Mike, Josh and Zach rushed over to break us apart. Big Mike grabbed up Maddie in a bear hug, holding her back while she shouted profanities at me. I still held Lindsay's arm. Miles squared up to Carla, who was backing up with her hands raised jabbering in rapid French.

"Are you done now? Or would you like to keep going?" I whispered close to Lindsay's ear.

"Yes! I'm done. Let go! You're going to break my arm!" she squealed. I let out a creepy laugh, which is *very* unlike me.

"That's the idea, you spoiled little *bitch*." I growled. Once I said it, I realized how sick that sounded. Reluctantly, I let her go, but held my stance in case she whirled around to hit me. She didn't. Instead, she let out a strangled cry and stormed off grabbing Josh's hand. He made eye contact with me and pulled his hand out of her grasp. She looked at him, burst into loud sobbing tears and took off running out the front doors. Maddie and Carla ran after her, leaving Big Mike, Josh, Miles and Zach staring at me. Actually, the whole Dining Hall was staring at me. Heat crept up my face and I plopped back down into my chair, looking into the flames of the fire as the anger left me, replaced by exhaustion.

Soon the normal buzz of people chattering and cell phone sounds filled the Dining Hall. Someone sat down in the chair Miles had been sitting in. I looked over, it wasn't Miles. *Josh* was sitting there, his golden eyes boring into my soul. My face flushed again. I glanced back behind my chair; Miles and Zach were holding hands leaning into each other talking with Big Mike. I looked back over to Josh, he was grinning at me.

"Sorry I tried to break your girlfriends arm. Are you here to tell me off for that? My only defense is… she swung first and I just don't like her. She's a mean person." I said feeling lame.

Mean person? Really, that came out of my mouth? I thought, feeling like such a moron. Damn it to Hades. Josh chuckled.

"Uh, she isn't my girlfriend. She thinks she is though… but no, not my girlfriend. And yeah she *is* a mean person, especially lately." he said, his voice sounded rich, smooth and deep. I could listen to him talk all day. However, I didn't trust him. He's guilty by association; he hangs with all the mean kids, even though Big Mike is okay. I felt my temper spike again. *What does he want then?* I thought feeling cranky. All I ever wanted was to fly under the radar and be left the *hell* alone.

"What do you want then?" I demanded, not caring if I sounded rude. His eyebrows shot up and he snorted.

"Wow, you don't seem to be cooled off yet. I just wanted to introduce myself. My name is Josh Stafford… Son of Zeus." he whispered. I sucked in a breath and turned to face him again.

"You know? How long have you known?" I asked hastily, glancing around to be sure, we weren't in hearing distance of anyone. Big Mike, Miles and Zach were gone. I felt a little panicky. Joe said not to tell anyone who my parent is yet. I didn't know how to get out of this one. *Maybe I'll lie and tell him Poseidon is my father too, people already think Zach and I are like brother and sister.* My mind whirled.

"I have known for the past five years…since I was thirteen. My mother told me and then my father came to see me. He said I needed to start training right away because in a few years there would be a great war and all…people like us would have to fight. I know you're one of the top 12; your instincts are too fast to be a lesser God's child. Who do you belong to?" he asked quietly. There it was. The question I was dreading. I swallowed hard, preparing myself to lie to this child of freaking *Zeus*.

"I'm Skye Miller and I am a child of…Poseidon." I said and held my breath. He nodded. I let out my breath. *He bought it… thank The Gods.* I thought.

I hate lying. I only lied to keep people out of trouble. I tried to convince myself that I was keeping myself out of trouble this time, in a way, that's true. He smiled at me, his eyes getting brighter.

"Nice to officially meet you Skye. I was wondering… would you like to go for a walk with me after the *big assembly?* It's going to be a mad house here and classes are going to be canceled the rest of the day. I'll meet you in the lobby of the Gym after it's over?" he asked. I blushed again, my stomach fluttered. I couldn't believe it; he wanted to hang out with me. However, my realistic side kicked in.

"Sure… I guess. But… why do you want to hang out with me? All your friends hate me, Luke hates me, like a lot. Kirk and the Twins *defiantly* hate me. Lindsay wants to pretty much destroy me. And, I *know* Carla and Maddie hate me, probably Kayla too. What's the thinking here… running around with me? They're just going to be mad at you." I said trying to look him in the eye. Those beautiful eyes were going to be the death of my self-control. I found myself wanting to touch him.

I went rigid… *don't touch him weirdo*. I thought to myself. Josh laughed a little; he had a pleasant laugh, low and rumbling.

"Maybe, I don't care what they think. Maybe my only real friends in that whole group are Big Mike, Kayla and Luke *before* he went nuts. *Maybe*, I'm fascinated by you and want to know more." he said. Now I was beet red in the face and felt hot all over. *Great, how much can I blush during breakfast, it's exhausting.* I thought as I looked down at my hands and took a deep breath.

"Alright. But, I still don't trust you. I feel like this is one of Lindsay's set ups. Maybe it is, maybe it's not and you're being real. I'll give it a shot. But I'm warning you. I'm hard to love and even harder to get to know." I said. *Ah hell, I said love… bad, bad, bad!* I thought feeling panicked and flustered. His eyebrows quirked up, telling me he caught the L word too.

"Alright then. It's about time to head to the gym. I'll see you after. Then maybe, you will someday, trust me enough to tell me the truth about who your dad really is." he said as he got up and headed out the front door. *Uh oh. So busted.* I thought realizing I really needed to learn how to lie better. Zach and Miles took up the empty seats around me again, both looking smug.

"So... how did that go?" asked Miles. Zach was trying really hard not to laugh at me. I was still flushed and felt all jittery.

"He *knows*. He's a son of Zeus. And I'm a *terrible* liar; I tried to tell him Poseidon was my father." I said and put my head in my hands. Zach laughed at me; I reached out and slapped his arm.

"Yeah you're a really bad liar. But, don't worry; he probably won't push you too hard to find out. Big Mike was saying Josh was the most honest, loyal guy he's ever met. Oh and Big Mike knows too. It's not shocking, but he's a child of Ares. I guess Luke, Maddie, Carla, Kirk and Lindsay don't know yet. But they will in about fifteen minutes." said Zach checking his watch. Not a second later, a bell buzzed and the Dean's voice came over the speakers.

"*All students to the Gymnasium for an emergency assembly. This is a mandatory assembly. You have ten minutes to get to the Gymnasium. Again, this is an emergency assembly. Classes with be canceled the rest of the day to assure all student questions are answered. Please file into the Gymnasium in an orderly fashion.*" The bell buzzed again and the speaker cut off. The students were silent and then everyone started talking all at once. The three of us got up grabbing our things and headed out the front doors into the windy cold courtyard.

****

The Gym was full of noise and phone sounds. It looked like everyone had listened to the Dean and not skipped out. The four of us sat in the very front, closest to the exit. I'm not a huge fan of crowds, so the closer to the exit we were, the better for my anxiety. I scanned the crowd. It was easy to tell which students knew they were Demigods. They were in small groups whispering to each other, looking serious. More knew than I had originally thought. What impressed me more, it had remained a secret. The kids at Chambers Academy are notorious for epic rumor spreading abilities. Secrets normally, never stayed secret for long.

"I wonder how this was able to stay a secret for so long." I asked Cam, who sat closest to me. He shrugged and glanced around behind us. Kayla was sitting a few rows above us, she saw Cam and waved. He grinned and waved back. I held back an eye roll with *extreme* difficulty.

"I think they were threatened with something big. Or, only the ones who are *loyal* and *true* were chosen to be told." he said. I caught a double meaning behind that last part. I quirked an eyebrow at him.

"What do you mean by that?" I asked.

"I heard, from two really good friends of mine, that you had a little chat with Josh Stafford. You know… Zeus's kid. All I'm saying is I think he might be one of the good guys. Look at Big Mike. Big Mike runs with a crap crowd sure, but he turned out to be a great guy, who's also in on the *big secret*. Maybe… Josh isn't like the others? I've figured out that Kayla isn't like them as much as we both thought." Cam said knowingly. *Damn him and my big mouth friends to Hades.* I thought as I glared over at Zach and Miles. They both looked away like they weren't listening. *Right… like they're deaf.* I thought feeling flustered.

"Maybe I will. I *am* meeting up with him after this *big reveal* for your information. How did it go with Kayla, really? She looks pretty happy. What's the deal?" I asked changing the subject. Cam grinned.

"I asked her to the ball and she said yes. Then, we went for a walk around and literally just talked. I guess she noticed me too, when I first got here and was curious about me. She was shocked that I was even interested in her. Apparently, I put off a super confidant vibe and she didn't think she was good enough to get my attention. Can you believe that? I thought that was crazy! Like I wouldn't notice *her*!" he said excitedly. I didn't want to be miss rain cloud, but I'm a realist.

"You do give off that vibe. It's not a bad thing though. But… don't you worry that she's lying?" I said seriously. Cam shrugged.

"Yes and no. I like to believe that all people have good in them. I think she's telling the truth. Besides, life is too short to worry about something that could hurt you. You have to get out there and take chances or you're not really living. All I'm saying is, I'm keeping my promise. I'm living; I'm being a normal teenager. You made the promise too. Don't break it just because you're scared your heart will hurt. I can think of plenty of things a hundred times more painful that could happen to us at any time, especially with what's happening right now." Cam said his voice low and serious.

I took in what Cam said for a moment. I was still scared but felt a little better about it. I leaned over and kissed him on the cheek. I realized I kissed him in front of Kayla and turned around realizing I might have crossed a line with her. I was surprised when she winked and smiled at me. I didn't know what to do, so I waved and turned back around. *Damn it to Hades, now I really have to nice to her.* I thought to myself, feeling glad that she wasn't the jealous person I thought she would be.

The Dean took the podium and the Gym fell into silence. All the professors were sitting in chairs behind him, all looking worried. I met the green wolf-like eyes of my Geometry professor. He winked at me. *Weird…* I thought, as I focused back to Dean Jacobs. I never noticed before now, Miles and Dean Jacobs looked a lot alike. His eyes are the same color as hers. His face is heart shaped and his hair is blonde, but cut so short it was hard to tell. He wasn't very tall either, but the proud chin and pronounced facial features make him seem 10 feet tall. Unlike Miles, his very presence demanded respect. He's pretty intimidating just by the way he carries himself.

"I want to start by requesting that all students hold their questions until the end of the assembly. Your professors are available for the rest of the day and private meetings the rest of the week as well, to answer all the questions you may have." He said as a general murmur sounded in the Gym. Dean Jacobs held up his hands and the room fell silent again.

"So, I brought you in here today because The Council has decided it is time to inform you of the happenings at this school…I am just going to come out and say it. You have all been brought here, over the past five years, for the possibility of needing a front line of defense against an enemy. This enemy is of higher intelligence than we originally thought. The time has come to get you all informed and *battle* ready.

You are all attending this school, not because of money, power, or your scholastic achievements, but because of the blood in your veins. Each and every one of you… are Children of the Greek Gods… also known as *Demigods*." He said surveying all of us. I held my breath waiting for crap to hit the fan. Silence… Absolute silence. Nobody seemed to even breathe. Most of the students' faces drained of color; others looked to be stuck between laughing and crying. Dean Jacobs looked a little surprised; he must have been expecting shouting. He didn't have to wait too long for the crap to hit the fan, all at once, everyone started talking.

Then, everyone *did* start shouting. Maddie and Luke were the loudest. Carla was crying, she wasn't the only one, many were. Lindsay was screaming at Josh, her face full of rage. The students, who knew, stayed silent. The noise was starting to hurt my ears. Dean Jacobs just stood there, waiting. The staff just sat there looking around. This struck me as odd; some students were squabbling with each other, accusing people of knowing and lying. Tempers were rising as students accused each other of lying and keeping secrets; a fight would break out soon. I wanted to run out the doors.

The Gym lit up. Blinding white-hot light lit up the entire space, blinding me. I snapped my eyes shut. Heat seared my face. The ground shook, as if it was going to rip open. People screamed. I grabbed Cam's arm in a death grip. For a crazy moment, I thought of my latest nightmare and thought about running. As soon as it started, it all stopped. People stopped screaming, the light was gone and the earth was still. I opened my eyes. My jaw hit the floor.

Standing next to the podium, was a man unlike any I had ever seen. The man stood at ten feet tall. He wore a brilliant white tunic and white pants. Golden-strapped sandals covered his bare feet. The man's hair was long brilliant white, braided down his back. A long white beard fanned out past his chin. His skin was smooth and thickly corded with toned muscles, without a single wrinkle. Up his bare arms were ever changing golden tattoos of ancient symbols, that *glowed* with light, from under his bronzed skin. I nearly jumped out of my seat when I looked at his eyes. His eyes were frightening and intriguing. White with no pupils, instead light golden flames flickered like real fire, which made it impossible to tell where he was looking.

The room had gone silent again. The tall man's thick white eyebrows came together as if he was surveying us.

I glanced over to where Josh was sitting across the bleachers. He stood, bowing his head, crossed his right arm over his chest and placed his fist on his heart. People were either staring at Josh or at the man, whom I figured was *Zeus*, King of the Gods. I don't know what made me do it, but I stood and mimicked Josh's show of respect. Immediately, Miles, Zach, Cam, Big Mike, Kayla, the entire staff and about 100 others did as well. I peeked up at Zeus. His eyes had turned to normal molten gold like Josh's, but they flickered gently like flame still. Zeus caught me peeking and winked at me, a smile quirked up his beard and moustache. I couldn't help it, I smiled back at him. We all sat down again, staying silent. Dean Jacobs sat in a chair next to the podium and gave Zeus his undivided attention.

Zeus surveyed the room and began to speak. His voice was deep and rough, like...well... *thunder.*

"Hello children... I am Zeus. Head of The Council, King of the Gods and Ruler of Olympus. I am here as *proof,* to what the Dean has spoken... I am real... You are real. The time has come to defend Mount Etna. Mount Etna *must* be protected. The Titan Typhon remains entombed within the mountains depths. He must *not* be freed. This is of the up most importance for the protection of the world and the human race.

Your professors will give you the true details; I am here to show you what you do not believe. *You...* are the Heroes of this new age, as Hercules and Perseus were before you. The Council has decided that there will be need for more than one Hero. The threat is large enough and treacherous enough to require your help. The Gods do *not* ask for help...So consider this request an honor. Take the time to let this news sink in. You have until sunrise to accept and request information. Many of you do not know to which God you belong. You will know soon. Each God will send their children written word and a gift. You will know which blood runs in your veins before the night falls.

You will attend classes tomorrow, but they will be new to you. You will be focused on learning new skills to assist with your full training as a Hero. Those of you with metal working skills will make weapons and armor. Those with strategic skills will work to develop battle strategies, defense of the school and Mount Etna. Those with Healing skills and abilities will learn to heal and care for the wounded. Those with skills with animals will train them to aid in battle. Those with leadership skills will be trained to lead properly... There are many skill sets I have not mentioned, you all have them, you only need to accept them. *All* of you will learn to fight. You all have the skills already. We do not have much time, but enough to make you true Heroes. Before I take my leave, I thank you. You are our best hope for keeping Typhon, forever entombed in his prison and saving the world as you know it." Zeus finished, giving all of us the same bow we gave him. With that, a brilliant flash of lightening and an earth-shaking clap of thunder…he was gone.

Chapter Eleven

We were released from the assembly after Dean Jacobs issued directions to go to the professors if we had any questions. Many students were following behind the professors in small groups to go to the classrooms for the information they needed. Many were crying hysterically, others were very *angry*. Cam, Miles and Zach left me in the lobby, so I could meet up with Josh. I didn't really want to after what just happened, but I keep my word. I really wanted to go with my friends to my room and talk. The other part of me *really* wanted to just sit and stare at Josh all day. Damn it to Hades.

Josh weaved through the thick crowd, heading in my direction. My tummy fluttered and I looked down at my feet. For a weird reason, I had been really careful about what to wear. Normally I just threw on jeans, cowboy boots and a sweater. For some reason, I had picked deep blue skinny jeans, my new knee high brown boots, a tight V-neck white t-shirt, and my brown leather jacket with my red scarf. I even brushed and braided my hair off to the side. Apparently, I wanted to look good while I got dressed in my sleepy haze. It all worked out like I was dressed to impress him, I wasn't sure how I should feel about that. I wanted to try to take Cam's advice, but I'm afraid of boys though I would never admit that to anyone. The only boy I have been around is Zach. I have dated boys before at our old school, but they usually got bored with me because I didn't sleep with them, or because I like nerdy things, like books. I hoped that Josh would find me interesting enough to hang out more than just once.

Josh finally made it to me, he grabbed my hand and we headed out the doors onto the grounds. The wind had died down to a light breeze and the rain was gone. The sky was still grey and looked like a storm would be rolling in. He led me behind the Gym to a cluster of trees that stood in the open meadow near the pastures for the horses. One beautiful very old maple caught my attention. Its branches were thick and low hanging. The maple stood taller than the other trees around it. I'm terrified of heights but love to test myself all the time and because I'm a closet adrenaline junkie, I tugged my hand out of Josh's and began to climb it. He chuckled once he figured out what I planned.

"Impressive, I didn't even have to tell you what we were doing here. Most girls would ask and then get all offended at the suggestion of climbing up a tree." Josh said laughing as he watched me climb up through the branches. I wanted to reach the top.

"I like to climb trees. It's one of my many weird passions in life. I would have done it even if you said we were going somewhere else. *Tree climbing…* That's actually really cool for a first…whatever this is." I said laughing. He chuckled again, climbing up behind me.

When I finally reached the top, I looked out. It was beautiful sight. I could see everything. A huge valley spanned out in front of me that the school property sloped gracefully down to. Not far off the valley's end, were three rolling hills covered in greens and fall colors. Mt. Rainier…or Mt. Etna, lay just beyond the peaks of the rolling hills. Its white capped top hidden in the thick dark clouds. I could see the glittering river as it raged cutting a thick path through the valley.

Josh perched up next to me on the thick branch. We sat straddling the branch, facing each other. Josh leaned into the thick tree trunk; I leaned back into the up curve of the branch. I kept glancing at him, soaking him in, realizing how ruggedly handsome he is. He wore simple blue jeans, a black sweatshirt and black work boots. He caught me staring at him, which of course made me blush up to my hair.

"What are you looking at?" I asked, feeling slightly shy all of a sudden.

"I'm looking at you. I can't figure you out. I don't know... There's just something about you. I just want to know more. All I know about you, is you can hold your own in a fight and your fiercely loyal to your friends." he said smiling a little.

"Well, I told you before. I'm hard to get to know. I like it that way. It keeps me from getting hurt. It also protects the ones I love. I don't want them getting hurt either. Besides, you already have me figured out. Loyal and fighting is all there is to me, well and sarcasm...I've got that in spades." I said meeting his gaze.

"I can tell. I saw the incident with Lindsay. You want to know why I brought you here?" he asked. I nodded, praying to the Gods that it wasn't something bad.

"Two reasons. The first, I want to apologize for what happened with Luke. He shouldn't have done that. I'm pretty old fashioned and I don't believe in attacking a girl, *ever*. It's one thing during training, because the girl is aware of what she's doing there, and she is there to learn to defend herself. What he did to you and your friends, was wrong. I wish I had been there to stop him. He should have never laid a hand on you and for that I apologize." he said as he reached out and touched the fading bruise on my jaw line. Goosebumps lit up my skin, and my blood surged. It felt like fire and ice racing across my skin. His fingers left a trail of flames and icicles across my jaw. I shuddered, trying to hide the whirlwind of emotions storming through my body. His hand moved from my face to holding my hand.

"It's okay, I pretty much put myself in the middle of it by jumping in between Luke and Zach. Really its my own fault, I just got mad and let that take over. Luke shouldn't have brought a freaking knife though. That's what sent me into a tizzy of crazy." I said feeling like I needed to explain it better. Not like I wanted to defend Luke for trying to take me or Zach out with a knife, but because I couldn't let Josh think it was only Luke's fault. Josh shook his head a little as if he caught what I was trying to do but still thought it didn't excuse Luke's actions.

"That might be, but he still should be man enough to have at least dropped the knife and fought you one on one fairly. I'm impressed how you still managed to kick the snot out of him and walk away fairly unscathed. I know how Luke fights and how good he is, so for a little thing like you to do the damage you did is kind of awesome." Josh said making my cheeks light on fire with embarrassment. I giggled a little trying to figure out how to feel about that statement.

"Thanks…I think. So…uh anyways…what's the second reason you asked me here then?" I asked trying to change the subject. Josh's golden eyes constantly looking at me were making me feel all tripped out, like he was seeing into my soul. It made me giddy and a little uncomfortable. Josh chuckled, no doubt noticing the lame attempt at a subject change. He took the change without question.

"The second, Skyelaa Miller, daughter of a *secret* God, would you like to accompany me to the Halloween Ball this Friday night?" he asked, meeting my eyes again. My stomach fluttered with millions of butterflies as heat rose to my cheeks. I grabbed his other hand.

"Yes. I would love to…. But on three conditions." I said, trying to keep myself together. He was leaning towards me, close enough I could see the copper and silver flecks in his eyes. *If I leaned in to him…those delicious lips could be mine.* I thought getting distracted. I blinked hard trying to clear my muddled brain.

"Name it." he said, his voice low.

"We leave my God parent out of it; I'm not ready to talk about that yet. Second, if you're planning a stunt at the dance and dump pigs blood on me when I get named prom queen or whatever, you promise to *let* me beat the hell out of you without a fight. Third, we pretend that we are just *normal* teenagers and not Demigods during the Ball?" I said trying not to smile. I meant all those things, but I was really excited that this was even happening. His dark eyebrows shot up looking surprised and shocked.

"I promise this is not a stunt. But if it were, I would let you do that. I promise to wait until you're ready to talk about your dad. And, I promise it will be a normal teenage date to a dance. Seriously, I'll step on your toes, make you wait for a while when I run off and talk to my friends, we'll get in a tiny little fight. I *might* even kiss you and then won't call you for three days. Good... Deal?" he asked smirking at me. I whacked him in the shoulder.

"Ass... Urgh, yeah all right... deal." I said and held out my hand, he quirked up an eyebrow and reluctantly shook my hand.

"You're a strange little girl...I think that's my favorite thing about you." he said meeting my eyes again. I laughed. He was surprisingly charming, which I knew could be trouble for me. We sat in silence for a few minutes, looking out into the valley.

"So, your dad is...fascinating. He reminds me of Father Time or something. He looked like a nice guy. Except those eyes, I could see his *wrath*...or whatever they call it, before he changed them to look kind of normal." I said trying to create conversation. He looked at me with shock on his face. *Ah man, I probably should have talked about the weather.* I thought to myself.

"You... could see his true form?" he asked still looking at me as if I slapped his mother. *Great, now I'm some kind of freak.* I thought feeling nervous.

"What? Well yeah, he was in front of all of us. He's your *dad*. Your telling me, you have never looked at his eyes? They're white and full of golden flames with no pupils. It's kinda scary. Then, it's like he changed them to have pupils or something, but the flames still flickered there. You never noticed? I thought everyone saw it and because they were all freaking out I thought maybe Zeus changed his eyes to make everyone calm down a little." I said hastily trying to explain. Josh let out a breath, running a hand through his hair.

"I know I promised not to bring it up... but you're *sure*, your father is *not* Zeus?" he said meeting my eyes, looking serious. I suddenly understood the concern, but not the eye thing. *He thinks I might be his sister, gross. Apparently, he really might like me if he's worried about it.* I thought trying not to laugh.

"No, I'm not your sister. Gross, that would just be gross. I know Demigods are all technically cousins and what not, which doesn't matter for dating purposes in our world. But, dating someone from the same parent...to me, that would be a little bit of a line crossing." I said still smiling. He sighed in relief.

"Okay, I feel the same way about that. Well, you can only see their true form if you're a child of the top three Gods. Hades has never had a child. I thought you were lying about being a daughter of Poseidon. I guess I was wrong." he said looking relieved. Guilt ripped through my heart, I wanted to tell him the truth but I didn't know how. He continued.

"When Zeus showed himself today, only children of his and Poseidon's could see his eyes and the tattoos. To everyone else, his eyes were gold like mine and he had no tattoos. He really isn't as tall as he was today when he visits me...that was for effect so the students would believe him. His face is a little more intense too, but today he kept it light. I can't wait to see what he sends me. What do you think Poseidon will send you?" he asked. *Oh my Gods. This is going to turn into a tangled web of horrible lies. I hate lying.* I thought feeling slightly sick about it. I thought of Zach, what he would want as gifts and went with that.

"A sword…or maybe a good set of knives, I collect knives and wouldn't mind one that was made by a God. That would be pretty cool." I said trying to be convincing. I racked my brains trying to think of what Poseidon favored. *Dolphins and…horses…the Trident. Ugh; I really need to read more of those books Miles has.* I thought.

"Maybe you will get a knife set and a horse. I know Poseidon probably can't send you a dolphin here." he said laughing. I tried to laugh too. It sounded a little fake and high-pitched.

"I still don't want to talk about him please. How about we go back to the Dining Hall and grab lunch together?" I asked trying to save myself from having to lie more. Pretending to have *daddy issues* with a dad that wasn't even really my dad is a huge pain in the ass. Josh smiled at me sheepishly.

"Sorry, I won't break the rest of my promises. I just panicked a little when you said you could see Zeus's true form. It would be weird to have a *thing* for my half sister." he said and started to climb down before I could even respond. *A thing…trouble… this is going to really be trouble.* I thought as my stomach did a flip with excitement.

"Oh… a *thing* huh? You can't just say that and scamper down a tree!" I hollered down to him. *Ugh, I'm flirting, and I like it…this is bad.* I thought, as I watched him climb. He was laughing as he reached the bottom; I began to make my way down.

"Did you just use the word *scamper?* That has to be the cutest thing I've heard out of your mouth yet!" he said laughing at me. I reached the bottom and jumped down. He grabbed my hand and we walked together to the Castle talking about random things. We arrived about two hours early to lunch so we sat by the fire and talked about everything and nothing at the same time. It was the most I had ever spoken to anyone outside of my little circle of friends. It was nice, but I still kept my guard up just in case.

By the time people were coming to lunch I could tell things had changed. For one our lunch group had expanded again, Kayla, Josh and of all people, Big Mike now sat with us. Most of the other students were gone still talking with the professors while the others that had come to lunch seemed either overly excited or extremely freaked out. I tried to focus on the new people that now sat with us all of a sudden, like we were their friends before Zeus dropped by and changed life as we knew it.

We had moved the chairs closer to the fireplace making a half circle to all see each other better and talk. It's the strangest thing, all of us from different backgrounds hanging out together. We were all talking about Greek Gods, Heroes, Monsters and discussing the Demons. The original members of the Poverty Club, left out Kirra's attack, but we told the others about the Demons and what we knew about them. Miles and I left out our weird dream-sharing stuff too. We didn't know these people that well and didn't need them passing around our secrets like candy. I never thought in a million years, I would be sitting with Lindsay and Luke's friends. I was sure they all hated us.

I glanced over to Lindsay's usual table, she and Maddie were deep in conversation with Luke, while Carla, Kirk and The Twins were listening intently. All of them looked furious and kept looking over at us. *Maybe not right this moment, but later, I know this is going to become a huge issue.* I thought. Lindsay didn't like to share friends and *really* didn't like to share guys she's in love with. I just prayed this wasn't a set up, for all of our sakes.

As a daughter of Hades, I was starting to notice things about myself that I could only figure were *Hades* traits. I realized I had quite a temper; my fuse seemed to be shorter. I also was starting to like fighting, I liked it before because it was something I was good at, now though, it felt like I liked having it as an option to solve my problems. I didn't like that very much, in fact it made me a little sick. I was also starting to notice my hearing was increasing. If I looked at Lindsay long enough I could hear her whispering to the others. I couldn't make out the words, but I knew it was her voice. I figured this was what Zeus and Joe meant when they said *acceptance* will improve my skills. I tried it on the fire. I looked hard at it, tuning out the other talking and noises. After a few minutes of concentrating suddenly I heard the crackling of the wood and the gentle hum of the flame. I felt a twinge of excitement and focused harder. Someone shook my shoulder. I blinked a few times as I lost the sound and looked up, meeting a concerned look from Zach. The whole group was staring at me, my face got hot.

"Earth to Skye, what were you doing? Your eyes got…well they were glowing, like a cats. I thought it was the light reflection, but I think they actually glowed! What were you doing?" asked Miles, excitedly. Now I was *really* hot in the face. Josh was staring at me, a half smile teasing his lips. He *knew* what I was doing. I had forgotten he already had five years to train and learn his skills.

"I was listening. Mom said we had better senses than a regular human's right? I could hear…fire. Over the sound in here and you guys all talking, I could hear it. I just focused on it and tuned out everything else." I said pointing at the fireplace. Miles wiggled in her chair excitedly.

"I want to try! Watch my eyes, see if they glow too!" she said as she focused on the flames. We all watched her with bated breath. Nothing happened at first and then after a minute her eyes got brighter, then the emerald color of her eyes seemed to radiate light, but gently. It was both insane and awesome. We spent another hour watching each other's eyes glow. We learned if we focused on the sound, we were also *seeing* more clearly, like looking through a magnifying glass. Josh walked everyone through the new sight and sound skills explaining, if we practiced, they would improve. *Maybe we need him to come to our Saturday training sessions with Joe.* I thought watching him explain everything with ease. On the other hand, maybe I just wanted to be around him so I could stare at him.

The four of us said goodbye to the others and headed back to my room to discuss things. Sitting in our usual spots, we talked about Zeus and what tomorrow would bring for our new classes. Things were changing drastically. We also decided talking to Kirra needed to happen soon. She hadn't been at the assembly, which worried all of us. We still needed to figure out what she meant by all the *Chosen Ones* stuff.

"I still think she had a vision about the coming war with the Demons. Based on your dreams I would say that was the start of the war, or at least an attack that would lead to one. We already figured the first dream was Kirra's attack. The night she came to us both you girls stopped having the dream about the meadow. We just didn't know you were seeing Kirra's point of view. Based on the facts, I think we can take your dreams pretty serious." said Zach, tucked with Miles on my bed.

I leaned into Cams chest more; I found that, like Zach, Cam calmed me just by touch. I felt anxious and jittery again. Between Josh, Hades, Kirra, Lindsay and all the changes in our little world, my nerves felt...thrashed.

"I agree, the whole school knows now, but they don't know what we know. I think *something* is going to be our responsibility somehow. I just don't know what without talking to Kirra." said Cam as he unknowingly played with the end of my braid. We all sat deep in thought for a while. A hard knock sounded on my door. I looked around to the others. Nobody moved. The last time there was a knock, a wounded, lost Kirra was behind it. I shrugged and opened the door. I found myself face to face with my grey haired, wolf-like Geometry professor. I stood in shock as he eyed me down with his crazy green eyes.

"Are you going to let me in, or make me stand out here?" he asked. I gulped; we were more than likely going to be in trouble. *Great more trouble.* I thought as I stepped back into the room and he followed shutting the door behind him. Zach, Cam and Miles looked shocked and guilty. The professor gave a snort, his wolf-like eyes resting on me again.

"Well, I see the rules are *not* being followed. *Shame* on you girls. I was hoping as child of Athena, Miles, you would know better than to fall for a son of Poseidon. As a daughter of Hades, I was hoping to recruit you Skye. Shame, it's a real shame." he said shaking his head. We looked around at each other confused. Nobody but my little family and Joe knew who I belonged to.

"What? What are you talking about professor? Recruit me for what?" I asked. He chuckled and took a few steps back from us.

"Sorry, I forgot I was in this form. Please shut your eyes, this will be bright." he said. A flash of white light filled the room, like when Zeus appeared, but cool instead of hot. I slammed my eyes shut. Cool air, smelling of pine trees and crisp morning dew, swept over me and then was gone. I cracked my eyes open. The light and my professor were gone.

Standing in his place, stood a beautifully fierce woman. Her thick silvery blonde hair was braided down her back, held with a thick leather cord. Her face was perfect, not a single flaw, with high cheekbones and luscious red lips. Her skin glowed with silvery light and shimmering silver tattoos. The Tattoos were shimmering silvery symbols and pictures of animals, flowed up and down her bare arms. She met my eyes. Her eyes were almond shape and exceptionally beautiful. Like Zeus, her eyes showed no pupils, instead crystalline silver and white shimmered like moonlight dancing on a stream, reflecting light from the lamps in my room. She wore black and silver army fatigues and a black t-shirt, which were *very* tight fitting against her perfect curves. I noticed a beautiful silver longbow and quiver strung over her back. I had no idea what to say or do, so I stood there like a fool and stared at her.

"Hello, little cousins. We have *much* to discuss. I am Artemis, Goddess of the Hunt." she said in a gentle soothing voice. *What!? The freaking huntress, Goddess of the Moon is my math professor? Damn it to Hades.* I thought feeling amazed.

Cam stood right away and bowed the way we had in the Gym to Zeus. Miles, Zach and I did too. Artemis bowed as well and sat in my leather chair. Cam and I crammed onto my bed with Zach and Miles.

"Well, this is a lovely chair." Artemis said setting her bow and quiver on my floor, snuggling into the chair, tucking her legs underneath her. I somehow found my voice.

"Thank you...Goddess." I said unsure of how to respectfully address her. She smiled at me, her face was youthful, like she was the same age as me, it made me feel a little more relaxed.

"You my dear, have fantastic manners. I saw how quickly you followed Josh when he bowed to Zeus today. I'm a little surprised. Hades can be...well, an *ass*. I wasn't sure how you would really be personally. This is a lovely surprise." she said smiling at me. I gulped, realizing that a Greek Goddess was sitting in my room talking to me and wanted to meet *me*.

Chapter Twelve

Cam seemed to come out of our silent stupor first. He was grinning from ear to ear. I figured it wasn't often he was around a smoking hot Goddess.

"So, Goddess, are you here to tell us about what Kirra meant by us being the chosen four?" he asked excitedly. She smiled gently at him, her eyes twinkling like silver glitter.

"Cam, I'm afraid the answer to that, is not a happy one. The answer is both yes and no. I don't know all the details but I will tell you what I do know. You are going to be the leaders of the Heroes of this new age, which will be a *very* difficult journey. You will suffer losses and achieve great triumphs. I don't know who will save the human race and this world, but I know the answer lies with the four of you. There has been a Prophecy, Kirra has come to be the possessor of this Prophecy and all the true details of what the future holds for you lies with her. That's all I can tell you, because that's all I know. The rest of the answers you seek, lie with Kirra. She is, unfortunately, in a coma. Nothing I can do will wake her. Because she's a Seer, she has the ability to send her soul to the Underworld to wait until her body heals and it's safe for her to come back." Artemis explained.

"Her *soul* is in the Underworld… but she's still alive?" asked Zach glancing at me.

"Yes, Seer's have the ability to do that to avoid being taken hostage and tortured by the enemy. Think of it as a *Soul Vacation* only for Seer's." she said looking serious.

"Does that mean Skye and I can do that too?" asked Miles a little hope shone in her eyes. *I guess I'm not the only one who wants to escape the dreams or the general stress of life.* I thought. Artemis shook her head sadly.

"I'm sorry Miles, no you cannot. You both are not Seers, you have *Foresight*. It means your dreams can give you a *glimpse* of past, present and future events, but not the paths that lead to the event. You can only see the event and the event alone. Kirra can see the paths that lead to the event, the whole event and the end result. It can be exhausting. Once people find out what she is, especially with what's coming, she would run the risk of being taken hostage. So leave it be for now, you will have to find out soon enough what the Prophecy says anyways, stressing about it won't do you any good. Trust me, you need to be focused on training right now. So, you're probably wondering what I'm doing here? I am here to see how you all are doing and to keep an eye on you. I'm like a guard to the four of you. Zeus wants you protected until we figure out what is going on. I watch the school too, but I'm here for you guys, think of me as another mentor, like Joe." she said smiling at all of us kindly. "So, what other questions do you have? I know your parents are going to send your letters in the next couple hours, so that will explain some more things."

"How can the Gods not know what's going on?" asked Zach.

"It's simple, we are not all knowing. Humans, Demigods, Titans, Monsters and even Demons are blessed with Free Will, which as you all know is the ability to choose or change your minds at any given time by your own decision. We have powers of persuasion, foresight and can even control others, but we can never be absolutely sure as to what will happen in the future or even who will be responsible. All we as Gods can do, is use our powers to keep the balance of the world intact." Artemis said as if it were just that simple.

I looked around at the others; they all looked stunned, confused and excited. I leaned into Zach thinking about where to start and clam my nerves. He put his arm around me as Miles absentmindedly grabbed my long braid running her fingers through my hair, while she leaned into Cam's chest. Artemis bit her lip and looked hard at all of us.

"You four, *have* to keep this bond. I have never seen one form so quickly, that is so real. No matter what you face, remember to love each other every day and never lose each other." she said beaming with pride. I smiled at her, she reminded me of my mother.

"Yes Goddess, I would like to ask another question." I said meeting her eyes. She nodded for me to continue, so I took a deep breath.

"Can I, as a daughter of Hades, travel to the Underworld and find Kirra's soul without having to die? I don't want to disturb her, but we do need to know *what* is going on here. Who are the others? How am I going to lead people and for what? There are a lot of things about that statement that need some clarification and she's the only one I can ask." I said. Zach squeezed me gently.

"Yes, you are one of the only ones who can travel to the Underworld, without having to pay passage, die, or become a God. A Child of Zeus may also travel to the Underworld, but they would have to be brave enough." she said meeting my gaze. My stomach fluttered when I thought of the only son of Zeus I knew. Artemis's eyes bore into me like she was reading my thoughts.

"I know who you're thinking of, Daughter of Hades. He is brave enough. I do not approve of relationships with any man. Men destroy strong, brave women and usually treat them as though they are beneath them… No offense boys. I have seen it for thousands of years. I travel the earth and offer the strongest women a chance to be forever free of the overbearing wrath of men. I let my Hunters have the power themselves to make their own decisions, be forever on the Hunt to protect the world and other women from harm. This is what I wanted to offer you Skye. You are welcome to join me at anytime. You will become fully immortal, but will never be at the mercy of a man, who might break your heart or your spirit." she said looking serious and deadly. I felt the boys tense up a little bit.

I felt honored that she would offer that to me, but it freaked me out a little. *That seems…lonely, but free, free from heartbreak and fear at the very least.* I thought. I didn't want to answer right away.

"Thank you Goddess, it would be an honor above all others. I would like to think on this choice for a while. I will not be able to provide an answer until this war is over. I don't want to be a chosen one, or a leader. But, if it's my destiny, I will have to see it through to the end." I said surprised at my own words. Artemis beamed at me.

"Spoken like a true Huntress. You are full of courage Skye; I can see it in you. I can also see that it scares you. Do not be afraid, embrace it." she said still beaming. Her gaze rested on Miles, who had been very quiet. Usually, she was Miss question-all.

"Miles…sweet Miles… you look troubled, what's on your mind little one?" Artemis asked gently. Miles sniffled, trying to hold herself back from crying. I felt bad for her. She's so sweet and gentle, like she could break at anytime. However, I had seen her defend others, question everything and go looking for answers on her own. It's why I loved her, the hidden courage that everyone can see but her.

"I…just don't know if I can do this, Goddess. I don't know how to be a Hero." Miles sniffed. Zach reached out and grabbed her hand, while Cam gave her a squeeze.

"Of course you don't little one. No Hero does. That is *why* they become great Heroes. You have so much to offer, you are stronger than you think. You are also the most intelligent of Athena's children. All you need is to have the strength to believe in yourself. That is more difficult than battling a Titan. A true Hero; is pure of heart, courageous, honest, loyal and above all, has the ability to love. As much as I can't stand Aphrodite's *Love conquers all* crap... she has a point. If you don't have the courage to love, you will never have the courage to defend, protect and fight for what you believe in. You love the ones around you right? *That* is all you need to focus on and when the time comes, your courage will aid you to do the right thing." Artemis said kindly.

"The Goddess is right Miles. But, for all of us, I love you all and I will fight until my last breath to protect you. We are all each other has. Where one of us is weak, another has the strength. If we stick together and stay true, we can do this. We can lead the other Demigods into battle and save the world. We just have to trust ourselves that when it's needed, we will find the courage to act." said Zach firmly. I wanted to cry or scream, I was terrified like Miles that I would let everyone down.

"Zach, you are correct. I have to leave, but before I go. I have added homework for all of you. Miles, you are to begin research of battle plans and strategies through each and every history both Greek and Human. You will draw up defensive and offensive plans of this school and Mount Etna. Also, study up on weapons and train with them as often as possible.

Zach, you are to begin working with Miles on those battle plans. You are also, to begin your training with the horses. You are a son of Poseidon, which means you can speak to them, train them and understand them better than anyone here. We will need them in battle soon.

Cam, you are to team up with Joe. Work with her, learn to make and mend weaponry. You will need to learn to use your healing abilities as well. I recommend working with Nurse Lane on those. You will need to train with the one you call, Big Mike, on hand-to-hand combat as well. Big Mike will be your asset in many battles.

Skye, my dear, you will have to tell Josh who your father is. You will need him with you to travel to the Underworld and find Kirra. You must do this soon; you will have to travel there in a very short time. You will need to study with Miles as well, she will teach you battle strategies, listen to her and learn from her. My last task for you will be difficult. You will need to learn from Hades, how to travel to and from his realm and to call to the precious metals of the earth to bend to your will. You are the *only* one who will be able to do this, other than Hades himself. It will be needed later.

You *all* will add Big Mike, Josh and even Kayla Crew, to your secret training sessions with Joe. They *will* end up being very important. I am requiring all of you to work with Joe and only Joe, each afternoon from noon until five. The seven of you will not have afternoon classes anymore. Please achieve these tasks as soon as possible. I will check in with you when I can. As of now, I must join Zeus to strike against Oceanus, he is getting stronger. I will be aiding the Gods against the Titan as well as trying to be here as much as possible. For now I say goodbye." said Artemis giving us a stern look.

Before we could speak, light flashed around my room, washing over us, smelling of the forest and the Goddess of the Moon was gone from my chair.

I blinked looking around at the others. *This is just getting more and more difficult. Not only do I have to save the world, I have to team up with a guy I just lied my butt off too, somehow meet my father and learn to teleport to the land of the dead, while moving treasure around. Ugh, why couldn't I get to train horses!* I thought feeling irritated. Damn courage to Hades.

"Well…I never want to get on her bad side. At least she gave us a direction to follow. That's all I ever wanted, just to know where to go from here." said Zach calmly like our past couple days had been normal, like Gods and Goddesses hadn't been flitting around, blinding us.

"Me either, it's weird but she's…actually really nice. I wouldn't want to cross her though. In my books, she's not as nice and is *epic* in battle." said Miles proudly.

Miles hearing that she is good enough for this from a Goddess, appeared to be really good for her. I could have probably told her those things for days and it wouldn't have made nearly as much of an impact. Cam put his arms behind his head.

"I bet she's *epic* at everything.…Well, tomorrow we have new tasks, new goals and from the sound of that, a real chance to get things going. I'll take all the help we can get." Cam said slowly, deep in thought. I giggled as I leaned back into Zach again.

"Right and the fact that Artemis is the hottest woman to grace us with her presence has nothing to do with this?" I asked winking at him. He flushed a little.

"Okay fine, she's beautiful. But, she hates men and she's my…what, aunt?…sort of? Anyway, like Zach didn't have drool running down *his* chin." said Cam laughing.

"Easy man, I can contain my drool…I *may* have gotten just a little in your hair though." he said wiping the top of my head. I tickled under his thigh causing him to squirm and bump into Miles. She tickled him in the side, making him let out a less than manly squealing sound. Ten points to Miles and me.

Light flashed in my room again causing all of us to stop wrestling with each other and shield our eyes. Wind blew over us in a rush, smelling of the ocean. In a sound like a wave crashing to shore, the light, wind and smell of the sea left the room. On my chair was an old green glass bottle with a rolled up yellowing parchment paper sticking out the top. Engraved in the glass of the bottle was one word ZACH. I felt him tense underneath me, somehow in our wrestling match; I ended up on top of him. I crawled off him and he got up slowly, grabbing the bottle off the chair, carefully pulling out the paper. He looked afraid of it, like it might bite him.

"We all read them to each other. That way none of us have any secrets. Deal?" he asked looking hard at all of us. In unison, we all said "Agreed" and he sat in the chair carefully setting the bottle on the floor. He read aloud;

Zach,

I would have rather met you in person, but because of Oceanus, it would not be smart for me to abandon my realm. I know this has come as a shock to you. I apologize for not being able to be a part of your life. I know words cannot change the years I have missed. I have been able to keep in contact with your Mother about how you have been. I want you to know, I love her very much, as I love you. One day, you will better understand.

The point of this letter is to tell you about your abilities. You are my Son, which means you have many of my abilities, but they are restricted, because you are part human. Do not be discouraged by this. Your courage and strength out match many others. I heard about what you did to a boy called Luke. Hera was very upset that you bested her son, I am proud. Don't ever let anyone make you feel like you are less than they are and always honor your friends.

As to your abilities, you will be able to survive in my realm if you so wish without the need to breathe, all you have to do is ask the water to not enter your lungs and it will follow your wishes. You have the ability, as I do, to use water to your advantage as a weapon. Try it, you will see, the trick is, wanting it to do as you wish, but, you must respect it. Water is an element and demands our respect. You also have a kinship with sea creatures; they will come to your aid if you send word using the water to carry your message. It works the same way as when you call to it for help. You will find that you are very skilled with swords and the cross bow in battle. Trust your instincts to fight, trust yourself to know what to do. You will find that you will know how to draw battle plans, based on where water runs under and above ground. You will always know where water is, at all times and call it out of anything. Everything on Earth is made of water.

I am proud to call you my son. Be true and loyal, respect life and the lives of others. I hope that I will meet you soon. Your gifts are outside the door. One of the gifts is probably hungry, I would take him to eat, he has had a long journey and may be moody. His name is Earth Shaker. He likes to be called Shake. Tell him hello from me.

-POSEIDON

Zach finished reading the letter with a slight smile on his face. It was actually a nice letter, all things considered. There was a loud snort from the hallway; we all rushed to the door. Zach opened it and stood face to face with a huge, deep chestnut colored stallion, with a long black mane and tail. Zach's jaw dropped. The giant horse leaned his head down and nudged Zach in the chest, nearly knocking him back into my room. The horse had battle armor made of bronze covering his chest. His black saddle had a bag attached to it with more armor peeking out the top. A pair of swords were also sticking out of the bag. Zach unsheathed both of them, expertly looking them over. They were polished brilliant silver and shone like diamonds. Each hilt was encrusted with black pearls and emeralds. They were beautiful. Zach sheathed the swords again and looked at the horse again looking startled.

"I can hear him!" Zach said in shock. "He... I can hear him, in my head! I can understand what he is saying! A horse! I'm talking to a Horse!" Zach said excitedly. The horse snorted in an agitated way and nudged him again.

"Oh... sorry... this is new to me. Uh, guys, this is Earth Shaker... Er... I mean Shake, the gift from my dad. I have to take him to the stables. He says it's nice to meet you all. Skye, you make him nervous, but he will try to get over it and tell the other horses you're cool." Zach translated. I eyed the horse wearily, he made me nervous too. I figured we had to get the crap out of the way now. So I addressed him directly, it's a weird thing, talking to a horse.

"Hi...Shake. It's nice to meet you. I'm sorry I make you nervous, you make me nervous too. I know you could trample me to death, which freaks me out a little. May I ask why I make you nervous?" I asked. Shake snorted and tossed his head a little. Zach spoke for the horse.

"He says... you remind him of the Fire God and that he and the Fire God's dog, Cerberus, don't get along and you smell like fire and smoke. He says...you don't seem mean, so he will give you a chance. You may pet him and give him green apples anytime...unless you are mean… I would pet him now Skye." said Zach trying really hard not to laugh.

I found myself smiling; I liked the smell of wood smoke and fire so that didn't offend me. I reached out and pet Shake's long neck, he tensed for a minute and then visibly relaxed, shifting his weight. Once I finished petting him the others did too. Zach was glowing with pride. He had never had a pet before, though he had always wanted a dog. His mom couldn't afford to feed a dog so he had never gotten one. Zach was beaming from ear to ear, as he lead Shake down the hall to the wider steps that lead down to the main lobby.

Chapter Thirteen

Cam and I stayed in my room while Zach and Miles took Shake to the stables. I snuggled against Cam on my bed while we waited. He leaned over and sniffed my hair.

"What the hell are you doing weirdo?" I asked half laughing.

"You kind of do smell like fire. And…Cinnamon, I like it… wood smoke and spice. That horse is full of it, you don't smell scary at all. You're too small to be that scary. I'm not going to lie; I can't wait until Hades sends you your present. I bet it's a dragon or something." Cam said excitedly. *That would be my luck; I get a freaking dragon that will eat everyone.* I thought feeling nervous and slightly amused.

"Oh Gods, I hope not. I was thinking, after what Artemis said, I need to come out with who my dad is right away. I shouldn't be ashamed. If I'm supposed to lead other Demigods, I don't think it would be good to start by leading into it with a lie. I don't want to be a leader but I don't think I have much choice if it's the right thing to do. Joe said people will come gunning for me, but if we have Josh, Kayla and Big Mike on our side too, others will probably follow their lead. What do you think?" I asked. Cam thought for a minute.

"I think your right. We have to try to do this right. Honesty is a good start. Like you telling *me* the truth about what you and Josh talked about." Cam said with a wink. Damn him to Hades. *Ugh, he knows everything*. I thought, feeling my face heat up.

"Really, we're back to this? Ah hell. He asked me to the Ball…I said *yes*, okay. I think he's *very* attractive and I'm going to try to take your advice. But…I'm an idiot and started it with a lie. He thinks my father is Poseidon. I'm going to have to set it right. Hopefully he will forgive me." I said looking out my window. The dark clouds had rolled in again and rain pelted the window while the wind roared through the trees.

"He will. I don't think he can hold that against you. Any of us would lie; Hades has a bad reputation, at this school anyone would lie about that. Everyone here is so concerned with social status in the outside world, lying is a way to protect yourself from being bullied. The people here are professionals when it comes to bullying. Stop worrying so much, you must *really* like him then, if you're freaking out about it this much." he said chuckling.

We were in the middle of a very intense pillow fight when Miles and Zach walked in. Miles had a potted plant with her and a teeny tiny little grey spotted owl on her shoulder. She was beaming as she plopped into my chair, upsetting her little owl. I took advantage of the minor distraction to whack Cam in the side of the head with my pillow.

"Guys! My mom came through and sent me my letter and my gifts! *This* is an Olive Tree. And… this little guy is Warfare or War for short. He can talk to me, just like Shake can talk to Zach! Isn't that amazing!" she said, her voice getting higher pitched the more excited she got. The little owl's big grey eyes surveyed me. He's very cute, white and grey with little black spots and fluffy feathers. Those eyes were a little unnerving, there's high intelligence there, which freaked me out a little. Cam got up and gently pet War's head.

"So what does your letter say Miles?" I asked sitting back farther on my bed. War took flight and landed on my knee startling me. He pecked at my kneecap tentatively; I pet his tiny head with one finger. He closed his eyes and settled onto my knee.

"He likes you; he says you remind him of his mother…his mother is with Hades, in the Underworld. Hades loves owls too so War's mother is working as a messenger for him. War says, once you get your ability to go to the Underworld, he will go with you. To see his mother and be able to carry messages to us and back… Isn't he sweet?" Miles cooed at him. I laughed loving the fact the she's a ball of mush sometimes. I pet his fuzzy head again.

"War, I will gladly take you to see your mama. You and I are going to get along just fine. You take good care of Miles for me okay?" I said to the little owl.

"He says he will protect me at all costs…so I got my letter, he actually brought it to me. It's kind of short, but War told me my mother gets to the point and doesn't mess around." Miles said pulling a very formal looking thick white paper from her coat pocket. We settled in and listened as she read her letter.

Dearest Miles,

It is time for you to begin your work. You must develop a plan to defend the castle, the grounds and above all, the defense of Mt. Etna. My child, you are the most skilled and intelligent when it comes to battle strategies and warfare. You are my daughter; you have the skills to become a great leader. You only need to believe in yourself and study hard.

Your abilities are as follows;

-Healing when you are needed most.

- Excelled hand-to-hand Combat skills.

- Complete accuracy with a spear.

- Heightened senses, above all other Demigods, when you focus.

- The skills to turn any object in your immediate surroundings into useable tool.

I am sorry I did not get to tell you this in person. You understand that during times of war, one must focus on the battle at hand before enjoying other activities. The Olive Tree I have provided is from my own garden. Please remember to put it in a bigger pot soon, it will grow fast. The tree will provide olives shortly. I have personally blessed this tree. If you are suffering from an injury, eat one Olive and all your ailments will be healed. More than one will kill you. Study hard and stay focused at all times.

Sincerely,

Athena

Miles finished reading the letter, blushing a little. I felt bad for her. *Athena seems a little cold to me. I suppose it has to do with the fact that she's so smart, her mannerisms come across as cold, when really she is trying to help.* I thought hoping with all my heart that was all it was.

"That's great Miles! She sent you a tree that can fix you if you get hurt, you got *two amazing* gifts! Plus your abilities are better than any of ours! That's awesome!" I said trying to point out the more upbeat side of the letter. Miles smiled a little as if to prove my point, War landed on her shoulder again and nibbled her ear. Miles giggled looking much more herself. I just hoped she understood the list of skills better than I did. Athena didn't explain how to *use* any of the skills, which worried me. I didn't dwell on it too long.

A weird scratching sound made us all freeze. It was coming from my door. I got up and opened it looking out, not seeing anyone. I looked down the hall again and still didn't see anything. Feeling confused I shut the door. When I turned around, an orange and white fluffy thing was standing on Cam's chest as he leaned back on my bed. The orange thing was making growling sounds. Zach was about to grab it from behind when Cam held up a hand, his face going from shocked to focused. We all froze again.

"This is Orion… he's my gift…and a long bow in the hall…" said Cam slowly. Orion, who happened to be a fox, turned and sat on Cam's chest facing the rest of us growling a little in his chest. I grabbed Cam's bow and quiver from the hall. I almost didn't want to hand them to him. The bow, made of gold and bronze with symbols probably in Greek were etched into the metal, it was stunning. His black leather quiver was full of beautiful arrows, also gold, with red hawk tail feathers and bronze tips. A letter was wrapped around the handle of the bow. Cam unrolled the letter looking excited and worried. He read aloud,

Dear Cameron,

It is wonderful to be able to write you a letter! I am most pleased with the way you have accepted your true talents and taken to the arts! I have seen your sculptures and am proud that you have indeed been blessed with true talent! If only I could get you to sing and write poetry as well. Alas, one can dream!

As to the requirements of this letter, I must tell you about your other talents! Because you are my son, you will be able to shoot any bow, at any time and never miss a target. You also have the ability, (like yours truly!) to call upon the light and heal anyone

or anything. The sun provides life, the light of the sun may be used to heal, or as a weapon if you so wish. All you must do is call to it. Focus and show need of the light and it will come to your aid. I do hope you enjoy the gifts! I hand designed the bow myself and the quiver will never empty as long as you are living.

Orion is a wonderful companion. He can be a little mischievous at times, but it's all in good fun. He will be your eyes and ears when you need him most. I hope all is well with you and I hope to see you soon!

Yours Truly,

Apollo

Cam set the letter on my bed looking a little disgusted. Orion nudged him and curled up next to Cam's side, resting his head on his hip. Cam scratched behind the foxes black tipped ears. I didn't want to say it aloud, but Apollo…is a little *pompous*.

'So…my dad is…interesting." said Cam looking a little confused. Zach spoke up and came to the rescue.

"Dude, Apollo might be a little…self centered…but he's a really hardcore fighter. He has won many battles and *really* never misses when he uses a bow. Him and Artemis killed a giant, called Tityos, who tried to take advantage of their mother. He literally beat Tityos down to dust. So seriously, Apollo is not such a bad choice to have as a father." Zach said as he examined Cam's bow. Cam chuckled.

"Yeah he isn't that bad. Just a little…over the top…Orion says my dad is a nice guy and that I should be glad I'm not Aphrodite's child. Apparently she sends her kids perfume and makeup as gifts." said Cam as he picked up his quiver. We all laughed. I was really jealous. *A quiver that never emptied, that would be the best present ever.* I thought.

I felt pretty nervous all of a sudden. I hadn't gotten my letter yet. *What if he forgot?* I thought, feeling more nervous. I had to get one soon, I needed to know what skills I actually have. Tomorrow we started new training and completing our homework for Artemis. My palms were getting sweaty. The others were looking at Cam's bow and Miles's plant, making small talk with each other. They were doing it for me, all of them not wanting to point out that I hadn't gotten my gift yet. The sun was nearly set now from what I could tell through the dark clouds. We would have to head to dinner soon. *Oh Gods, what if Hades sent my gift during dinner! What if it's a giant dragon and everyone freaks out!* I thought. I felt all panicky as the minutes ticked by and I stared out the window.

Miles screamed, pulling me out of my panicky thoughts. Still trying to string together a sentence, she pointed to my closet. Thick black smoke billowed out from under the door. Zach ripped my closet door open as bright orange and blue flames licked the doorframe. He jumped back bumping into me. Cam bolted over the bed running into my bathroom, coming out with a glass of water as the flames licked the floor and walls outside my closet. Miles ran into the bathroom coming out with wet towels, throwing them over the boys. Black smoke billowed out of the closet filling the room and choking us.

"Zach! Put it out! Use the water! Do it!" Cam yelled over the roar of fire coming from my closet. I felt a pang for all my new clothes I had just gotten from Miles. Zach closed his eyes and focused with his face scrunched up in concentration. The glass in Cam's hand exploded, drenching him in a wave of water, too big to have been in the glass. He yelped and jumped back, blood running down his hand from a cut on his palm.

"I'm sorry! I didn't mean to! I was trying to get the water to get bigger and attack the fire!" Zach said reaching for Cam's wounded hand. *All right, now I'm pissed. My room is smoky, my clothes are gone, Cam is hurt and the animals are terrified. Enough is enough!* I thought feeling pissed. I held my hand as close to the hot fire as I could stand feeling my veins burn with anger. I didn't know what else to do, so I screamed.

"*STOP!*" I yelled…the flames froze, no longer rampaging around, like hitting pause on the TV. I looked hard at the fire, getting close enough to smell the heat. I gently touched a frozen flame; it was still alive, burning hot. I figured if the word *stop* works… why not try another word.

"Be Gone!" I yelled at it…and to my shock, it went. The fire disappeared with a whooshing roar and a blast of hot air. I looked in the closet; everything was there, not a scorch mark on anything. I stood there with my mouth open like a fool for a few moments staring into my unusually tidy closet. Zach and Cam dropped the wet towels to the floor with wet thumping sounds, staring at me, eyes wide. *I can't believe that just happened.* I thought in confusion. Deep booming laughter came from behind us causing me to whirl around.

A very tall man stood in my room. I looked him over before deciding what to do about him. He had short copper hair and a black and copper beard trimmed neatly across his jaw line and neck. A strong jaw, thick dark eyebrows and high cheekbones made him look intimidating. He wore simple blue jeans and a plain red t-shirt. The t-shirt showed off his dark bronze muscled arms covered in tattoos, which danced like red fire across his skin. I met his eyes, orange and blue flames flickered in his white eyes. *This man is a God.* I thought feeling awed and pissed off.

"Well… you make that look easy kid… I feel pretty damn proud right now." said the God. I crossed my fist over my heart and bowed. The others did as well. The God bowed back. *Good… now that we got that out of the way.* I thought as I let my temper take over.

"What the *Hell* was that for? It's not funny to set a girls closet on fire! You could have burned the dorm down! Who are you?" I yelled at him. Zach was staring at me wide eyed. Miles was trying to hang onto War, who seemed to be trying to fly away from her. The God smiled.

"Hi to you too…*Daughter.* My, my…we *are* being a brat today. I am Hades, God of the Underworld and your Father. I wanted to meet you, in person." Hades said, a slight edge to his voice. Black smoke swirled around him as he spoke. I gulped. He cast a dark look at me then faced Miles, addressing her directly and the smoke disappeared.

"May I pet him Miles? He's getting mad at me for not saying hello to him, and I don't want to be *rude.*" Hades said casting a dark look at me when he said the word *rude.* He smiled at Miles as he held out his large calloused hand to War. Miles smiled tentatively and gently placed War in the palm of his hand. Hades brought War close to his face. For a wild moment, I thought he was going to eat the little owl; instead, he nuzzled War lovingly. I wanted to burst out laughing. *Hades, Lord of the Dead, being mushy towards a teeny little owl.* I thought trying to keep my mouth shut. It was like watching a lion kiss a mouse on the cheek. I cleared my throat and tried to adjust my tone.

"Uh, I'm sorry…Father. I sometimes have a hard time controlling my temper when my clothes catch fire…it's a pleasure to finally meet you." I said, wondering if I hug him or shake hands…awkward moments suck. Hades apparently was a forgiving man when he was nuzzling tiny owls. He chuckled deep in his chest. He handed War back to Miles, who sat down on the bed next to a bemused looking Zach and Cam. Hades patted Orion on the head and faced me again.

"Ah, it's alright. You wouldn't be a child of mine if you were all sunshine and daisies. I wanted to see your reaction. You just discovered one of your abilities. You can control fire...*shocking* right...I figured telling you in person would be better than writing a long winded letter." He said as he sat in my chair. I sat on the edge of my bed next to Miles and took a deep breath as I looked at my father. I was ready for answers. I couldn't help smiling a little bit too; he and I are a lot alike.

"I guess I'm more like you than I thought. Sarcasm is my favorite past time. It would appear it's yours as well...So I can control fire? How does that work?" I asked meeting his gaze. He was smiling, his eyes crinkling in the corners.

"Cheeky little thing aren't you. Don't ever talk to me like this in front of the other Gods. They have this whole air about how Demigods are supposed to talk to us, this is not it. If you spoke to me like this with them around I would have to kill you for disrespecting a God." he said sternly, making me gulp again, as Miles tensed up beside me. He cracked a smile.

"But, when it's just us, please feel free to be yourself. I like this side of you better, it's more...real. Anyways...yes kiddo, you can control fire. You *can't* call it up from the depths of Tartarus or anything, but if you have something that can create flame, you can bend the fire to your will. You can also visit me, by using fire as your transportation. Start a fire and take it into your hand and tell it to take you to the Underworld. The fire will engulf you and bring you to me if you ask it to. It won't burn you either. It will feel hot, but won't burn you unless you tell it too...but don't ask it to do that, my arm still stings from the last time I let it burn me." he said itching up near his shoulder, lost in thought. *Control fire...that seems cool and now I have a way to get to the Underworld and find Kirra. One task from Artemis down. I* thought feeling a little excited.

"Uh...dad, what else can I do? I had a visit from Artemis earlier;

she said I need to ask you about the precious metals?" I asked cautiously. He nodded turning serious again. He pulled a baseball sized rock from his pocket and held it in his hand. The rock seemed like a boring plain grey simple stone. I looked closer noticing a black thick line running through its center.

"I like her, she's my favorite niece, she's cheeky too. Anyway, yes… you can call the metals of the earth to you. Like with fire, you can control them. If you need to pull the iron from someone's blood, you could because it's an element of the earth. It would kill them of course, so unless you want someone dead, save that little trick for enemies. Try with this stone. Think about the object you're pulling from, hold out your hand while concentrating on getting the metal to end up in your hand. You have to focus and want it. Go ahead, try it out. I'm here in case you need help." he said as he held the rock closer to me.

I shut my eyes, thinking of the rock in his hand. I figured the metal was in the dark line. I thought about how I wanted the rock to push out the black stuff for me. Then I thought about how I wanted the black part in my hand. I kept thinking of it like that, for a few minutes nothing happened. Then my friends gasped and I felt something cool touch my palm. I opened my eyes and saw the black line sitting in a ball in my hand, but it was no longer black. It was a ball of pure gold the size of a marble.

"That's it kiddo! You got it! How did you know there was gold?" Hades asked me, pride written all over his face. I blushed a little, feeling shy all of a sudden.

"I didn't… I saw the black part in the rock and figured that's where a metal or gem would be. I literally just guessed." I said meeting his fiery eyes.

"That was a hell of a guess kiddo. Black sand hides gold. You did great. Be careful doing this though. If the wrong people see it, they will get greedy and try to use you. Don't use this ability for greed *ever*. I will know how much you are pulling. If there is a lot leaving my realm I will have to discipline you and then you'll wish you were *dead*." he said sternly, I believed him, as I watched the fire rampage through his eyes.

"Yes dad. I won't let you down." I said and I meant it. He grunted his approval.

"Alright kid, your last skill that we need to discuss, is *shadowing*. You can hide in the shadows, as if you were really a shadow. The dark is your friend. Tell your body to become a shadow and the shadows will become part of you. Like fire and metal, you have to ask for it and accept it. The number one rule to all of your abilities is, do *not* disrespect them. If you abuse them and don't respect them, they will drain your life force. As it is, using your abilities will make you tired anyways. It takes a lot of energy to harness these powers. So use them wisely. I have to leave, but before I do I have to give you your gifts." he said, then he let out a loud ear-piercing whistle. I tried to hand him the ball of gold, but he winked and shook his head. I figured this was my one freebee, so I stuck it in my desk drawer. Mom was going to love it.

There was a loud thumping sound from the hallway and loud panting. *Oh dear, please don't be a dragon.* I thought as I rushed to the door. With Hades and my friend's right behind me, I slowly opened the door. On the other side I found myself face to face with the bright orange eyes, like my own, of a pure black wolf. Only this wolf stood just a *little* smaller than Zach's horse. I froze. The wolf let out a yip and licked my face. From my neck to the top of my head, I got covered in dog drool. *Gross.* I thought as I felt a very large hand on my shoulder and heard the deep rumbling chuckle from Hades. He wiped my face with a red handkerchief.

"This is *Chaos*; he's a Hellhound from my realm and your first gift...Chaos, *small*..." He said to my new pet. Before my eyes, my new *Hellhound* shrunk down to the size of a small Husky. I smiled at him. *This is a much more tolerable size.* I thought as I reached down and scratched behind his ear. His fur was surprisingly soft and fluffy.

Hi, when do we get to eat? I'm pretty hungry. I eat red meat, just so you know… no dog food please. That stuff is gross. I heard Chaos talking in my head. *Wild…this is totally wild.* I thought.

"Okay, red meat it is. No dog food for this pup." I said to my new dog. He yipped again and licked my hand.

Thanks boss, you're the best! Chaos said excitedly. Hades chuckled again. He could probably hear Chaos talking too. Zach, Cam and Miles started petting him and scratching behind his ears. Chaos was babbling to me about how nice my friends were as Hades drew my attention back to him.

"Alright kiddo, *this* is the next present. Use it well." he said as he pulled a black corded handle from his pocket. I looked at it confused.

"Take it in your hand and step back into open space. Then, press your thumb on the cord that feels like it's bigger than the others." he said. I did as he asked, stepping farther out into the wide hallway. I found the thicker cord and pressed it. Twin black blades shot out from either end of the handle. It was a double bladed sword, but smaller than the one I picked up in training. At the base of each of the blades were two rubies and a key engraved into the metal. Hades smiled proudly at me as I whipped the sword around.

"This is amazing. Thank you. How did you know I would be good with this sword?" I asked, closing the blades again.

"Joe of course. She passed the word to Hephaestus, who passed the word to me. I had her and Hephaestus forge the blades for me, I did the carving and the rubies. I also blessed the blades. They will never dull; they will never break, or get dirty. They can also never be turned against you, or ones you love. You could try to run through

Poseidon's kid over there and it wouldn't even scratch him. You may also turn it into two swords. Run your finger up the thicker cord and they will separate. Put them near each other and they will go back together if you will them to…this is you third gift." he said handing me a necklace on a leather cord. It was a black skeleton key like the ones on my blades, old fashioned and a little heavy. The keys handle had an odd-looking stone in the middle, bright red and fiery orange. I turned it over watching it glimmer in the light. I put it around my neck; it fit perfect, not too long and not strangling me. I looked up at Hades…my dad. He was smiling again.

"Wear this at *all* times. It shows that you belong to me. You are *my* child. Anywhere you go in the Underworld, you cannot be harmed with this on. *Never* take it off Skyelaa. It's very important. Always wear it." he said seriously. It was beautiful. I met his gaze, looking up at him.

"What kind of stone is this?" I asked.

"My own. *Flame* encased in a Ruby. I named it for your mother. I call it *Lila.*" he said resting a hand on my shoulder again. I wasn't sure what to do, so I gave him a brief hug. Hugging wasn't his thing; he patted me awkwardly on the back. Pulling away, he met my eyes.

"I have to go. Stay out of trouble, stay cheeky and stay strong. See you soon kiddo." Hades said and with a flash of fire and the sound of a chuckle, he was gone.

Chapter Fourteen

Apparently everyone in the Dining Hall had gotten their gifts. It sounded like a zoo had a massive breakout. Different kinds of birds, dogs, *mini* livestock and snakes were making all kinds of noises. The students had changed drastically. There was excitement in the air, and a mass display of many different kinds of weapons being shown off. I sat at our usual place in front of the fire, Chaos sat by my feet, watching birds fly around the high tower.

Can I eat one Boss? He asked, his orange eyes meeting mine. I laughed as he tried to make the cute puppy face and apparently, Hellhounds can't make that face. His lip was curled up in a half snarl. I reached out and pet his head.

"No, those belong to other Demigods. How about I go get you a nice steak?" I asked. He stretched and got up.

I'll go with you; I don't want to let you go alone. Some of the Demigods here smell like trouble. I don't like it. Can I call you by your name, or do I have to keep calling you Boss? He asked as we wandered to the back wall with the food tables. I laughed again; I really was starting to like this dog.

"Yeah, call me Skye. Just remember though, you can't eat other Demigods pets. I know you won't eat War or Orion, but try not to eat Shake okay. That's Zach's horse and he would probably cry if my dog ate his horse." I said sternly to Chaos as I loaded a plate with a lot of meat. He sneezed, curling back his lip and let out a growl.

Horse! Gross! Horses taste terrible. No thank you. I promise I will never even take a bite out of that horse…can I hunt deer? There are tons of them up here, I can smell them.

"Yeah, deer is okay. I know you probably eat a lot more than what I can feed you. So, I'll do my best to make sure you can hunt as often as possible. Sound good?" I asked him. He yipped his approval.

"First sign of insanity…talking to a mutt." came Lindsay's voice from behind me. Chaos, promptly raised his hackles, started growling and bared his teeth. If she got nasty enough with me, I would be tempted to tell him to get *Big*.

"Easy Lindsay, he bites rude *ugly* people." I said coolly, turning to face her. She had a white Cockatoo sitting on her shoulder; it squawked at me and then crossed its beady eyes. She patted the bird's foot and looked down her nose at Chaos.

"He better stay away from me, nasty dog… Anyways, I'm here to simply request that you leave Josh alone from now on. I am a Daughter of Hera; he is a Son of Zeus. We belong together. He loves me and he is mine. *You* are just a filthy child of the Sea God; he could never be with you. He just feels sorry for you. Don't take it *too* personally, he's nice to everyone because he has to be. Him and I will be attending the Halloween Ball together, *not* the two of you. Sorry to burst your sick little bubble but, I *told* him to leave you alone and not lead you on. As it turns out, he thinks you're so pathetic, he felt like he *had* to ask you to the ball. Unfortunately, you won't be going with him. It's like I told you before, I will make your life hell if you don't back off and I mean it… Stay away from Josh." she sneered at me. I was about to unleash the wrath of Chaos on her stupid bird and light her on fire, but thought better of it.

The fact that she thought I was a child of Poseidon and *knew* he asked me to the ball meant that Josh talked to her about our discussion in the tree. My heart sunk. Him and I were totally alone and the only way she could know anything we talked about is if Josh talked to her about it. I found it hard not to believe her when she said it was a set up.

Josh was setting up some kind of prank or something then. He was really going to ditch me and go with Lindsay… Why even ask me then? I thought and my heart ached. I couldn't understand why it hurt. *I should feel angry… I don't know him and this shouldn't hurt this bad.* I thought feeling…betrayed. This is worse than *me* being the liar about who my Godly parent is. Now I have to be around him constantly, because Artemis said so. *Looks like I will have to play it off, like everything is okay. Great… more lies.* I thought as I played it cool and smiled at Lindsay.

"Don't worry Lindsay… he isn't my type. We were just talking. But, I am *not* a child of Poseidon. He got that wrong. Sorry to let you down. Oh and my dog… he really *does* bite, so I suggest you leave *me* alone. Always nice chatting with you….*Chaos,* come." I said taking my plate and his plate back to our spots by the fire. He let out a deep booming bark, making Lindsay jump and tottered beside me. I felt pretty proud of myself for not hitting her…or pulling out my new sword and slicing her head off.

Next time, I get to eat her stupid bird. That girl is just as rude as Hera is. Don't like her at all. Chaos said as we sat down with my friends. I set his plate on the floor at my feet and he began to eat. The others were talking excitedly about their God-parents gifts and letters. I listened as I ate my salad and mashed potatoes.

"I couldn't believe it! I always knew I was adopted, but a Daughter of Hephaestus! I did *not* see that one coming! But it makes sense because I love crafts and welding. I know… welding is a weird thing for a girl to like to do but, it is what it is. My dad totally hooked me up. I got a bunch of wicked tools to use in the armory with Joe, my new sister…and he made me a pure bronze short sword that turns into a dual headed axe if I press on the right stone in the hilt. Joe is going to freak, this is so cool… and I have a *sister*." Kayla was saying to Cam and Miles, excitement lighting up her yellow cat eyes. *Well at least she's still here, being nice to us.* I thought crankily. I looked around noticing Josh hadn't shown up yet. Good thing, because I didn't want to look at him yet.

"That's great Kayla, wait until tomorrow. We're going to start training personally with Joe, every afternoon. You're going to love it. She can teach you everything about weapons and fighting." said Cam, absently stroking Orion's white belly as he lay across his lap. War was picking scraps of meat off Miles's plate as she listened to Kayla talk and *boy*, did she talk. I was starting to get the feeling that she wasn't allowed to talk much when she hung out with Lindsay and Luke. Big Mike and Zach were in a very deep conversation about Ares and Poseidon and how they fought during battles. I tuned everyone out as a golden Eagle caught my attention circling above us and settling on the fireplace mantle. I couldn't think of the God that had a thing for the Eagle.

"Cool dog. I thought Poseidon was a horse and dolphin guy? Since when did he get into wolf dog breeds?" Came a deep delicious voice from behind my chair. *Ah, Zeus likes eagles.* I thought as Chaos yipped baring his teeth.

"Poseidon *doesn't* like dogs." I said glancing up at Josh as he hovered over the back of my chair. I *was* going to tell him the truth, but I couldn't bring myself to do it yet. After what Lindsay had said, I didn't feel like he needed to know. The Eagle flew off the mantle and landed on his shoulder. If he didn't have broad shoulders, the massive bird would have fallen off.

"Huh, that's weird. Anyways, this is *Alke* my gift from Zeus. His name means *courage*. What's your dog's name?" he asked sitting on the arm of my chair. I tried not to lean into him…or push him off the chair.

"*Chaos*...no definition needed." I said coolly as I patted my dog on the head. Zach had stopped talking to Big Mike and was watching me closely. I met his eyes and he nodded, getting to his feet. He said a quick word to Miles who passed the word to Cam under her breath. Cam met my eyes and nodded briefly, returning to the conversation with Kayla as if nothing had happened, like him noticing my surliness.

"Sorry Josh, I need to borrow little miss sunshine for a few minutes. We'll be right back." Zach said reaching for my hand. I reluctantly took it and we headed out the front doors with Chaos following behind us. We made it down the stone steps and hurried over to the side of the Castle by the trees. The wind was blowing like crazy, stinging my eyes.

"What's going on? What happened back there? You were all goo-goo eyes over him a few hours ago. If we're going to be bringing Josh, Kayla and Big Mike into our lives, we will have to all get along and know each other. I could see the look you had, you look like that when you're ready to rip someone's face off." said Zach as he sat on a stone bench facing the Castle. I sat down next to him, feeling ashamed that I liked a boy who only pitied me. I sighed and told him everything Lindsay had said to me. He scooted closer and put his arm around me, Chaos rested his chin on my knee. *I'm surrounded by so much love, and my heart still hurts, Damn it to Hades.* I thought feeling annoyed.

"What pisses me off the most, is that he *told* me he wasn't with Lindsay and never has been. Then she comes to rub it in my face that she knows *everything* we talked about in the tree. How could she know that unless he told her? Nobody was around. It was just me and him." I said practically whining.

"That... just plain sucks. I don't think Josh is the type to pull something like that. Unless my judge of character is way off. You *do* have to keep in mind; Lindsay is a liar, and a gossip queen. She could have over heard you two, or over heard him talking to someone else about it. Don't write him off yet. Artemis said we need him... mostly *you* need him. I was talking to Big Mike earlier; Josh is Zeus's *only* son. I am Poseidon's *only* son. This time the top three Gods only had one child each. When you go to the Underworld, you will only have Josh as an option, or go it alone. I know Hades is your father and that will offer you a lot of protection, but his protection doesn't cover the Demons, or the Humans that are aiding them. I *hate* the fact that I can't go with you to protect you. I'd rather have Josh there than you running around by yourself in the damn Underworld." Zach said. Chaos yipped at him and growled.

Tell the Sea Kid his brain is full of Kelp. I'll be with you. I can protect you. Chaos said as he grew a couple sizes, reaching the size of a donkey. I laughed a little, as Zach's eyes widened.

"He says, he can protect me...and your brain is full of Kelp." I said giggling. Zach looked uncomfortable. He spoke directly to my dog.

"I know you can. You understand that I just worry about her, don't you? I know you will be there for her always, *but*... the more of us that can protect her, the better. *Right?*" Zach said sternly. Chaos cocked his head and shrank back down to husky size; he yipped at Zach, showing he understood. Zach reached out and cautiously pet his head. Chaos lay down at our feet and huffed out a breath.

I guess I like the Sea Kid. He's not so bad. I don't like that Kid of Hera's. She's mean and smells all wrong. We should kill her. Chaos said to me. *Indeed... sometimes, I wish it were that easy, it would make my social life more tolerable, but that's not a good enough reason to end someone's life, no matter how mean they are.* I thought with a sigh.

"No, she might be mean, but she's just a stupid girl, not evil or anything. We don't kill innocent people just because they're mean." I said to him. Zach quirked up an eyebrow at me looking a little confused about my comment to Chaos.

All right Skye, I won't hurt anybody unless they try to hurt you first. You take the fun out of everything. I might pee on her leg though if she keeps trying to bully you.

'Deal… that'll be funny." I said to him and patted him again. We sat in silence again, looking out to the Castle and the grounds.

"I guess I'm just not used to having this many people involved in our personal lives. One minute it's just you and me. Then it's me, you, Miles and Cam. Now it's *seven* of us, all different people who are tossed into the pot together, expected to become the leaders of a Demigod army to beat down Demons and a Titan. It's bad that I'm starting to miss the days when it was just us and our biggest concern was the stupid draft letters. Sometimes, I just wish that we could run away and hide." I said exasperated. Zach sighed, and pulled me closer to him.

"I know. I miss that too sometimes. But it was *lonely* sometimes when it was just the two of us. This is really a good thing when you look at the big picture. We have more people who care about us, that we care about too. Besides… I *am* falling for Miles. I can't help it. Without all of this, I would have never met her. The more time I spend with her, the more I want to know her. I like Cam a lot too. He's cool and he keeps *you* calm when you're all worked up. You have to give the others a chance. I know you love Cam and Miles but, you have to try to love Kayla, Big Mike…and even Josh too. Artemis said that *Love* will help us win. We have to win this war…or die trying. I couldn't live with myself if I ran away from this. We've spent so much time hiding from the world, maybe I'm ready to finally do something that means something." said Zach, his features turning hard.

In that moment, I realized I *had* to do this for him. Not for the world alone, but for him. Zach is the kind of guy who always wants to help and do the right thing. If I ran away I would be running because I'm selfish, Zach is always trying to make me a better person and I knew I had better step it up and protect everyone I could. Growing up, it was us usually protecting each other and blocking everyone else out. This time, it was bigger than we were.

I sighed, knowing all I needed to do is shut off the emotions and uncertainty, then we had a chance at becoming a team and saving the world.

"You're right…as usual. I promise to try. Easier said than done, but I will try. I'll give the others a chance; tomorrow I'll tell them the truth when we all train with Joe. Okay?" I said.

"That's all I'm asking Skye. We will find out if Josh is playing games. I don't think he is, but for now, play it off as if you know nothing, go to the Ball with him and enjoy rubbing it in Lindsay's face. I really think…no, I really *hope*…this is all just coming from her, I don't think I could handle Josh being the guy to break your heart." he said. I stood up and felt anxious about what Zach would do if it were true, I decided to change the subject.

"Well, tomorrow everything officially changes. I think I'm going to call it a night and head to bed now. See you in the morning?" I said to Zach. He nodded and hugged me. I watched him head back into the Castle.

I didn't want to go to bed quite yet, it wasn't raining for once, so I sat back down on the bench and mulled things over in my head. I sat there in the dark and wind for a while, when suddenly Chaos started growling. My hair stood up on my neck making me want to run. My senses screamed at me, *something* was coming. I slowly stood, listening hard over the wind as it rustled the trees. I heard the sounds of twigs breaking under heavy footfalls.

"What is it?" I whispered to Chaos. He grew to his full size,

hackles raised and growling deep in his chest.

Turn to shadows Skye. Do it now, I smell Demons. He said. I started to panic. *I've never shadowed before, hell I only found out about it a couple hours ago!* I thought to myself as I stepped back into the tree line out of the moonlight. It took all my focus to shut my eyes and calm myself down. I focused on the dark around me, taking deep breaths. I begged the shadows to help, to make me disappear. I begged in my head and in a small whisper hoping the Demons couldn't hear me. Cool air crept over my skin, as if I dipped my arms in cold water. The cooling sensation edged its way up my legs and over my body. I kept my eyes shut trying to stay focused. The sensation stopped and I cracked open my eyes looking down at myself. I knew my body was there but I couldn't see it. I looked like nothing more than a dark space between the trees. Shocked I tentatively stuck my hand out into the moonlight. My hand flickered from nothing more than a shadow of a hand to my pale hand, gleaming in the moonlight.

Okay, this is crazy. I thought as I pulled my hand back out of the light and it turned to shadow again. I tucked myself back farther into the trees and waited. Chaos had shrunk down to mini pony size, shadowing next to me. I realized I could still see him even though I knew nobody else could. My eyesight is keen in the dark when I shadowed, I could see everything, as if it were bathed in sunlight. Grateful, I sent a huge thank you to the shadows. They responded with another cool caress over my skin. I crouched down and waited. Two figures came through the woods about twenty feet from where I was crouched. The wind carried over the scent of the Demon. I fought back a gag. Chaos moved silently closer to me and let out a little snuff.

Ugh, those things smell worse than the dead. I can see they've been blessed by Spirits. See the tattoos on the Demon's skin? The tattoos give them life and intelligence. This is even worse than Hades thought. Who is that with the Demon? It's not another Demon... It's a Demigod. I can smell their blood from here. Smells like…grapes… Child of Dionysus. Chaos said. I shivered and gave Chaos a nod, too scared to say anything to him even in a whisper just in case they could hear me.

What! One of our own was helping the Demons! Frickin fantastic, no wonder they were able to get on the grounds so easy and attack Kirra. I thought as I looked through the trees using my keen sight to see the persons face. They kept their back to me and had a hood on. I could tell they were probably male but nothing else. I listened hard focusing on them with all my might, hoping that my eyes wouldn't glow and give me away. Their words carried over to me. I have never heard the Demons speak in my nightmares. Frankly, I didn't even think the Demons could talk. This Demon, spoke perfect English in a gravelly rasping voice.

"…you are sure, beyond all doubt? My Father lies under the mountain they call Mount Rainier?" The Demon asked. I didn't recognize the Demigods voice, which sounded high pitched with fear.

"*Yes,* Why would I lie about that? You would just kill me if I were lying." said the Demigod. I wished they would turn around so I could see their face. The Demon pulled out a long sword with a jagged blade and put it under the Demigods chin.

"Indeed I would. *You* are the reason we came out here. You told us our Father was here and the one that created the Prophecy was here as well. We will never get to hear the Prophecy because that wretched *Seer* is gone. Her soul has left her and will not return unless it is forced. Only Hades or his child can return the soul. Hades and his child are the only ones that can even find the entrance to our father's prison and open the door… if you're telling the truth of course and he truly does lie under *that* mountain. Is there a child of Hades at this school?" asked the Demon, lowering the sword. The Demigod visibly shuddered.

"No, I haven't heard of one yet. But, people only just found out about their parents today. I'll need more time to find the child of Hades. Then you can force them to bring back the Seer. Then you will know the Prophecy and the child of Hades can get you into the mountain." said the Demigod in a shaky voice.

"Good, you have two weeks. That is how long it will take the others to get here. My brothers are under orders to not harm the Seer. We will need her alive to hear the Prophecy, then we will know how to win the war. If we know the Prophecy, we can kill the ones who will stop us before they even get a chance. My brothers will be watching you. Two weeks, little Demigod, if you fail... You die." said the Demon. Then he disappeared in a cloud of ash. I shuddered at the thought of Demons being able to puff in and out of anywhere like the Gods.

The Demigod sighed heavily and went back into the woods. I tried to see their face, but even with my excellent eyes, I couldn't see them. Their hood covered all of their features.

This is really, really bad. I thought knowing I had to tell the others right away. Worse, I had to keep lying to everyone about my dad, or we would all die before we had a chance to do anything.

Chapter Fifteen

"This is a *disaster!*" Miles said as she plopped heavily into my chair. War hooted softly from the back of the chair, where he perched. Once the coast was clear, I had run to the Dining Hall and grabbed Miles, Cam and Zach. Thank the Gods for the moonlight, or I would have given myself away by coming in as a pure shadow. I had forgotten to release the shadows in my panic when I raced out of my hiding spot.

Chaos sat curled on my bed next to Zach, watching us intently. I was pacing my room, while Cam sat perched in my window with Orion. I had just told them everything I heard and saw in the woods. Zach filled them in on what had happened with Lindsay in the Dining Hall. It was now past midnight.

"So we really *can't* tell anyone who your father is now Skye. I want to trust Big Mike, Kayla and Josh, but for now until we know who the traitor Demigod is, we'll have to keep it quiet." said Miles sadly.

"Maybe not… we know the Demigod was a child of Dionysus. That rules out Joe, Kayla, Josh, Big Mike, Lindsay, Luke and even Carla. Carla is a child of Aphrodite, like I had thought before. It could be anyone else though. If Chaos can smell the blood of a Demigod and know who they belong to, we have a way to weed out all the children of Dionysus and keep tabs on them. I still say we tell the others soon, Artemis wouldn't set us up to be killed by making us tell the wrong people." said Cam looking down at all of us.

"You have a point. We have two weeks to train and get a defense plan going. That's not much time at all. Skye, you will have to find Kirra's soul as soon as possible. We need to know the Prophecy; now I feel sure she was trying to tell us before she sent her soul to the Underworld. She just didn't have the time or strength to do it. We need to know what it's about so we have a direction to take, or at least before the enemy gets a hold of it. We have to tell Mom and Mom two first thing in the morning. Miles, you have to send word to you father. He might need to send us back up and spruce up the defense of the entrance to Typhon's prison. I would actually set up a couple traps and false entry points to throw the Demon's off. We're going to have to tell Joe and the Dean as soon as possible. We are the leaders of this new army, according to the Prophecy. Now is when we start taking charge. " said Zach sternly.

"Right. We're going to have to take this on faster than I thought. We have to start on the plans tomorrow. I'll get on the research as soon as I can. I will also need the plans and layout of the entire school and mountain range. If we're going to set up a defense grid, I need the full layout. I guess Artemis wasn't kidding about me doing this as soon as possible… I'm going to send War with a letter to my dad. He would be a better option than trying to use the actual post office. We're going to have to skip out on all our classes and just train and plan with Joe, Mom one and Mom two. We had better get to bed. We have an early start tomorrow and not a lot of time to get things done." said Miles, as she stood up. Cam held up a hand to stop her.

"Before we do that, I need to know something. What are the words tattooed on the Demons?" he asked me. I looked to Chaos who hopped off the bed and came over to me. I pulled out a pen and paper and sat at my desk.

They have been blessed by <u>The</u> <u>Algea</u>; The three spirits of pain and suffering. <u>Achos</u>; spirit of trouble and distress... <u>Ania</u>; spirit of ache and anguish... <u>Lupe</u>; spirit of pain, grief and sadness... I also saw the markings for <u>The</u> <u>Androktasiai</u>; spirits of battlefield slaughter... <u>Bia</u>; the spirit of, force, power, bodily strength, and compulsion... and <u>Deimos</u>; the spirit of fear, dread and terror.

I wrote them all down. This didn't seem to be a good mix of spirits to be blessing one creature all at the same time. *Great...the Demons are the very definition of evil.* I thought with a sigh and handed the paper to Cam who read it with eyebrows raised, letting Orion read it too. Orion let out a growl.

Orion says this is really bad. Those spirits usually never bless anyone. Usually they are just around to influence human's decisions. Somehow, they were able to transfer their powers to the Demons to give them strength...this isn't good Skye. Chaos said. I patted him on the head as Cam passed the paper silently back to me. Miles was at my shoulder, looking over the words.

"Hang on a second, let me see that." she said as I handed her the paper. She started writing and crossing things out. She handed it back to me after a few minutes, all of us looking at it together.

The Algea- Αλγεα

Achos- Αχηοσ

Ania- Ανια

Lupe- Λυπε

The Androktasiai- Ανδροκτασιαι

Bia- Βια

Deimos- Δειμοσ

"How did you remember what the symbols look like from your dream?" I asked looking at the weird writing.

"I didn't, this is the Ancient Greek translation of those words. The symbols are written in Ancient Greek. That's why only Chaos, War and Orion can read them and know what they mean. The Gods would be able to read it too of course. I've been studying ancient Greek; I wanted to know more about it. It was sort of just a hobby to help with reading old books, but I think it's really good to know what the tattoos say. Bia is the spirit of compulsion, force, power and strength. I think the key word with this particular spirit for us to watch for is *Compulsion*. If the Demigod that's helping the Demons has *Bia's* symbol tattooed on them, it's possible they are being controlled by the Demons, or worse they are not being controlled and they are tattooing it on others. Which would mean it's possible innocent people could be controlled by the Demons. I just figured it's something we should look out for." said Miles looking at the paper and underlining the Bia symbol.

"You're a genius Miles." I said giving her a quick hug. She smiled at me and patted Chaos on the head.

It was nearly two am when I finally laid down to sleep. We had been talking so long about everything I thought my head would soon explode from too much information again. I drifted off to sleep with my Hellhound curled at my feet, thinking not of the possibility of war or Demons and Prophecies, but of Josh. I tossed and turned as my mind reeled.

I have to face facts. I like him a lot. I thought as I rolled over to look up at my window. I don't know why, but I couldn't get him out of my head most of the time and got pleasantly flustered whenever he's around. It didn't make sense to me. *I really don't know him that well...maybe that's a lie. I know he likes being outdoors, because of our tree climbing adventure. I know he isn't a follower, but a leader, based on the way he defended us that day when Zach punched Luke. I know he's brave because of that too. It takes real bravery to stand up to your friends. I also know he's the best fighter in our training classes, because Sergeant Scott said so during training.* I thought as I felt a pull in my gut at the thought of Josh.

When I told Lindsay he wasn't my type, it had been an outright *lie.* There's just something about him that I couldn't put my finger on, something that drew me to him. Besides the fact that he is very attractive, just his gaze lit me on fire, realizing that made me feel even more confused. I had never really *looked* at him in school before…probably because I figured he would never be an option for me.

I rolled over again upsetting Chaos, making him grunt and growl at me. Sighing, I thought of the Ball again. With everything going on, I wasn't sure if it would even happen. I'm not really a ball gown and diamonds kind of girl, but I really wanted to just be a girl and go out with a cute boy who made my tummy flutter. Liking a guy is so *complicated.*

****

The morning rolled in with a massive thunderstorm. It woke me up before my *Demon attack* nightmare even had a chance to finish. Rain pelted my window as the sky rolled with grey and black clouds. The wind ripped through the trees and lightening cast sinister blue flashes across the raging sky. *Great, this is going to be a long miserable day.* I thought crankily as I rolled out of bed and wandered into the bathroom, excited for a hot shower. When I emerged with my hair in a long damp braid, Zach was sitting on my bed watching Chaos eat a large bowl of raw meat.

"I went to talk to Shake and feed him early this morning and figured I would stop by the slaughter house for scraps." Zach said seeing my look of disgust at the bloody carcass in the giant bowl.

I really like the Sea Kid. This cow meat, is really good stuff. Chaos told me. Gross, cow meat looked *way* less appetizing when it was still bleeding. I decided I needed to dress for the weather as I scanned my closet. We would probably have to do some hiking today for Miles and Zach to get a lay of the land. Zach dressed in his combat gear, fully armed with his swords from Poseidon strapped across his back, crossbow on his hip and a black beanie on and our uniform jacket. After looking him over I looked back at my closet.

"I should probably steal some uniforms." I said looking for anything that might work. Zach snorted pulling a big brown paper bag from under my bed, stuffed full of something.

"Oooh presents! Is it my birthday?" I said faking girly excitement in a high pitched squeaky voice. Zach laughed at me and rolled his eyes.

"Yup, I got you a brown bag and a cow, but Chaos got to it first." he said chuckling throwing the bag at me. It was surprisingly heavy, I ripped it open. It had all my combat training gear in it, an all weather jacket and black beanie. I grinned at him and pulled off my sweats, slipping into my gear. I strapped on my belt, which I noticed had a custom sheath for my new sword and additional holsters for more knives.

"I stopped by Joe's cage too. She modified all our gear. We'll have to get our custom weapons from her in a couple days... but for now, she set us up. We won't get guns for a few days too. Wear your boots she gave you over the summer." he said as he watched me sheath my knives. I finished filling all the holsters and we headed out the door. Miles met us in the hall dressed in her gear. Cam was waiting at the side steps with his quiver and bow across his back, geared up as well.

We looked pretty intimidating, armed and uniformed. We went straight into the Castle to grab a bite to eat and catch our moms before classes started. People stared at us. The students were all armed again today, showing off their gifts, but without gear on. Something about being geared up made me feel more confident. I walked with my head held high through the Dining Hall. Chaos sniffed people as we passed.

There's so much mixed blood in this room, its making it hard to find out whose smell is whose. I think it would be easier if I were able to sniff them one at a time. Chaos told me. I quietly told the others the dilemma. Orion lay across Cam's neck, like a scarf with teeth. He dropped down to the floor walking next to Cam with his nose in the air, sniffing. Apparently, though his nose wasn't as strong as a Hellhound, he could smell the Demigods scents too.

"We'll have to be careful about that… but, because people think you're only a dog, it won't seem too out of the ordinary. When we're passing people in smaller groups, you can sniff them out. Don't worry about it too much for now though buddy, we've got bigger things to work out today." I said under my breath to Chaos. He snuffed at me and seemed to relax more.

We grabbed hot egg and bacon burritos and headed up the back steps to the second floor to the staff offices.

"We should talk to them and the Dean at the same time, it would save a lot of time. And I think we need to have Joe there. She should be included. I consider her my Sergeant and my Uncle will have to go with us on that. I won't let her get left out from the important stuff ever again." said Miles, as we reached my mom's office. I nodded and opened the door to the small office. My mom looked up from a stack of paperwork and smiled at us.

"I was wondering when you would come and see me. How was your chat with Artemis and Hades…Why are you all armed and in your gear?" she asked. *Okay good, so she knows Artemis and Hades spoke to us.* I thought. I was about to tell her about the uniforms when

Chaos bounded into the office, knocking me aside and licked my mother's face. She laughed and scratched behind his ears.

"Good to see you too old friend. I've missed you." she said to him. I should have known they knew each other and could mind talk too. I cleared my throat; it was time to get down to business.

"Mom, we need Melinda, Dean Jacobs and Joe here… *now*. We have a *lot* to fill you in on." I said meeting my mother's eyes. Concern passed over her features as she picked up her phone and paged them.

"What about Charlie? Miles have you contacted your dad?" My mom asked.

"I sent War, my owl from Athena, with a coded message to him this morning. I hope that the weather won't be an issue for him. I didn't want to risk calling him or sending a letter by mail. Those can be intercepted. An owl is less noticeable." Miles said meeting my mother's stern gaze.

"Smart girl. Your right of course, I'm really glad your mother had the good sense to send you that little owl." Mom said nodding. A few minutes later, Dean Jacobs, Melinda, and Joe came into the small office. We all crammed in and shut the door. Chaos sat nearest the door to listen in case someone was outside. Melinda patted him on the head absently as she looked around, concern flooding her features.

"What's this about Miles?" asked Dean Jacobs.

"We have to fill you in on what's happening. Something happened last night, Uncle, it's an emergency." she said meeting his powerful gaze.

"By all means, let's hear it." he said and sat on the edge of my mother's desk.

It took all of us to tell them about Artemis's visit, Kirra being the holder of the Prophecy, Hades visit and the Demon/evil Demigod combo in the woods. Miles showed them the tattooed symbols Chaos had explained to us. I explained that we needed to be excused from classes, as well as Kayla, Big Mike and Josh. I explained how Artemis told us the seven of us were going to be the fate of this coming war; I made it *very* clear that the first battle might be on our doorstep.

I left out my concerns with Josh's loyalty. Lindsay might be a rotten person, but she wasn't smart enough to be working with the Demons or at least I *hoped* she wasn't. Besides, I truly believed, thanks to my talk with Zach, that our little drama triangle had nothing to do with the issues at hand. Miles explained about the Demigod being a child of Dionysus and that we only knew it was a boy. After an hour of explanations, the Dean jumped to action.

"Alright, I knew this day would come. It came sooner than I would have liked, but I will send word to Charlie for back up and some other trustworthy contacts I have in the Government. I will also send word to Dionysus personally about what one of his children are up to. He might be able to help. However, like Hermes, Dionysus has quite a few children. Probably because Hermes and Dionysus are thick as thieves and breed like rabbits." he said, more to himself than the rest of us. Gross, thinking of the chunky drunken God of Wine making babies... not a pretty picture to me.

"I will lead the training daily with you all. We need you ready sooner than later. You will all have to be excused from classes of course, that gives us a lot more time. Sgt. Scott and the other trainers will have to get all the other students trained and ready as well. I say we focus on students 16 and over. The youngsters will need to know defense, but I will not be responsible for the deaths of children by allowing them to fight in the front lines." said Joe sternly.

I had forgotten that the school age ranged from 14 to 18. I didn't want them fighting either, that would be blood on my hands as well as hers. The thought made me suddenly feel uncomfortable.

"Agreed. Skye, you will continue to keep who your father is a secret. Clearly, we have a mole at this school, probably have more than one… it's not a surprise. The people in this room, Charlie and your group of seven are the *only* ones to know. I have eyes and ears all over this place and if anyone spills the beans on the Prophecy, or details of this conversation I will know and detain the offender indefinitely." he said gruffly, eyeing us all down. He cleared his throat and continued issuing out orders. Fine by me, I did not want to take the lead on this; I wouldn't even know where to start.

"Well, your orders are as follows; Joe; finish the weapons for these four immediately and prep for training. Skye; your group of seven is excused from classes until further notice, you will report to Joe everyday at 8am sharp and will not leave until she sees fit. I will call Josh, Mike and Kayla into my office within the hour and fill them in on everything, including your father Skye, so be prepared for possible backlash from that. I know you haven't been open about Hades with anyone. Good thinking on Joe's part for that." he said to Joe, who nodded. My heart leapt into my throat, I wasn't ready to let them in yet. Zach gave my hand a squeeze. At least I knew I had him, Miles and Cam on my side. The Dean kept going.

"Lila, you need to get a message to Hades about the Demons plans in case he wants to pop by. He will need to come disguised. I would like to pretend, for the time being, his child is not here and he has no interest in this mountain range *at all*. I also would like to request that he finds Kirra's soul and places it under protection in his own realm. I will contact Artemis and let her know we need her back as soon as she can be spared. Zach and Miles get going on the battle plans. The school's blueprints, ground layouts and maps are in my office, I will get them to you right away. Cam, you will lead a perimeter walk with the seven of you together today, you have the best sense of direction because you are Apollo's child, you will know where the sun is at all times. Use that skill to navigate and draw up maps. We need to know all our weak points and area's we can set traps or send troops for open field battle. You will report to Joe by 7pm tonight. Melinda, keep your eyes peeled for anyone with any of the symbols of any of the spirits. You and Lila will begin your classes on time with the new curriculum as requested by Zeus." The Dean paused and checked his watch. "Its 8am now, Miles, Cam, Zach and Skye, you will report to my office by 9:30 sharp. I will have told the others what's happening and you will leave together. I will have the maps and blueprints for you as well. Joe, you will need to bring Josh, Mike, and Kayla's gear so they may change…Let's get to it. I want reports *daily* of progress and *any* news." said the Dean in a stern voice.

He reminded me of a general in military movies. I saluted him as I do when there is a God around, the others followed my lead. The uniformed salute was like putting an official stamp on the fact that we were now the leaders of a Demigod army…scary.

Chapter Sixteen

My nerves were making me jittery while we waited outside the Dean's office at 9:25, as he asked. I felt like when Josh, Kayla and Big Mike came out of the office, I would be punched, ignored or possibly hugged. I was really hoping for hugging. Because I was nervous I kept shifting my weight, unable to sit still, making the others and our animals feel my nervous energy too. Cam was pacing the hallway, with Orion pacing beside him. They were talking to each other; Cam kept saying random things under his breath in the fox's direction. Miles kept wringing her hands and trying to make small talk with Zach, who was cutting pieces off an apple with his knife, only half listening to her as he leaned against the wall. Chaos kept whining a little.

"What's wrong?" I asked my dog. He had been really quiet since we left my mom's office. We ended up in the library after leaving the office. We occupied our time by looking up historic battles, Greek mythology and Greek spirits. We didn't have much time to look really hard into anything, but we were all feeling anxious and needed to feel busy.

I'm really hungry, and your nerves are getting to me. I can sort of feel your emotions when they are really strong. You need to calm down. When we go on our walk, can I hunt a little? He asked.

"Of course you can. I'm sorry, I can't help it. I really like Josh and I think he's going to be mad at me…or he really doesn't like me anyways and is in love with Lindsay. It's such a mess." I said. Chaos snorted at me.

You humans and your weird love crushes. Just tell him you like him and see if he likes you back. It's easy. If he could hear me, I would ask him for you and settle this. Your emotions are really confusing when your thinking about him, it makes me want to gnaw his leg off for making you feel like that. He said as he leaned into my leg. I laughed picturing my dog attached to Josh's leg. I'm a sick person. I felt a little better though.

"You're the best dog of all time. Thanks for having my back on everything. I'll try to keep the girly love crushes to a minimum." I said scratching behind his ears. He yipped at me and licked my hand. The door opened and Big Mike, Kayla and Josh emerged, fully geared up and armed with all eyes on me. *Crap…damn hugs to Hades.* I thought as I blushed up to my hair.

"Okay… Are we ready to do this? We have a lot of ground to cover. I'm thinking we should travel on horseback. It would make sure we'll be back in time to meet Joe." said Kayla, trying not to stare at me. She caught me looking at her and winked. Yup I liked her. Cam picked a good one, she was trying to be nice to me and I appreciated it. Zach smiled at them.

"Sounds good to me, Shake was begging to go out for a ride this morning. He's going to love this." Zach said sheathing his knife. Miles smiled up at Big Mike, who was looking a little nervous. He kept shooting glances at Chaos and me.

"I'll probably have to take out one of the Belgians. I'll be too much weight to ride one of the quarter horses." said Big Mike still looking uncomfortable. Josh was looking surly and not meeting my eyes. That hurt a little. I couldn't keep my mouth shut anymore. I looked around to make sure we were alone.

"I'm sorry I didn't tell you guys... I should have. You understand why I didn't though? We don't know each other that well and I was afraid you would judge me... I was wrong. I'm not used to making friends or trusting anyone. From now on, it's all or nothing. We're in this together and I will do my best to be as open as possible, with all of you." I said forcing myself to look at Josh. He avoided my eyes still. Later, when I could get him alone, I was going to call him out about Lindsay. He promised me he would tell me, I really didn't want to be mad at him.

Kayla, of all people, patted my shoulder in a reassuring way. Miles smiled encouragingly at me.

"I understand why you didn't want to say anything. *Besides* the fact that you would be probably dead right now, I know for a fact that Lindsay would have taken that information and ran with it. She's my friend, but her ways of doing a lot of things, are just not right. I got your back, as long as you swear to have mine." Kayla said looking me in the eye. I was floored. I didn't expect that from her.

"I swear, to all of you. I have your backs in everything." I said. Josh nodded once, his face like a mask, unreadable. Big Mike still looked nervous. Cam called him out.

"Big Mike, you good man? You don't look so sure. If we're on the same team, we need to know you're really with us. You heard from the Dean how big of deal this is. You're in or out, regardless of how you feel about Hades and his kid." Cam said right to Big Mike, his silver eyes boring into Big Mikes deep grey eyes. Big Mike took a step back eyes wide.

"No man...I mean I'm good. I told Skye after the brawl I had her back and all of yours. I keep my word, regardless of who people's parents are. I...I just don't like...dogs." he said eyeing Chaos cautiously. Miles was trying really hard not to laugh.

"What? Ares loves dogs. They're one of his favorite animals. You're genetically made to like dogs. What happened to make you not like them?" Miles asked, gently touching Big Mike's arm. He visibly shuddered.

"When I was five, a Doberman chased me home from school. He got out of his yard and went on a rampage. He ran me down for seven blocks and finally caught me. When he did, he bit my calf and threw me into some old lady's yard. She whacked the dog with a broom and it took off. I ended up in the hospital and needed forty stitches. I haven't liked them since. Your dog scares me Skye." he said. Chaos cocked his head to the side, looking slightly offended. I felt bad for Big Mike; it's a sad thing seeing someone of his size cower at a dog. I sighed; we were running out of time and needed to go.

"I promise he won't touch you...and he's not a dog. When we get to the woods I'll show you everything, for now... ignore him. Please?" I said. Big Mike nodded and we all headed down the stairs. Classes were going to let out soon and we needed to go. I needed to show everyone what Chaos really was to start with. *In training tonight, I'll show them what I really am.* I thought, feeling slightly nervous.

We reached the stables and Cam sent Orion to check for people who might be around. We didn't want to be followed. Thunder and lightning tore across the sky, as the wind fiercely bent the trees nearly in half. We picked a bad day to ride. We saddled up the horses setting out past the maple tree Josh and I had climbed. I rode double with Zach, since I made the other horses nervous. Chaos downright freaked them out. Josh let out a whistle and his eagle Alke, flew ahead of us, swooping down gracefully towards the valley.

We reached a cluster of thick forest past the grazing pastures near the beginning of the valley, below the school property and stopped. Orion scampered off to check for Demons and anyone else. We dismounted and I called Chaos over to me. Zach told the horses to stay over by the thick trees and under no circumstances, run away. Once Orion returned, Cam gave me thumbs up. Everyone gathered around.

"Okay, Chaos is not at dog. He's a Hellhound from my father's realm. He will not harm any of you unless I command him too, which I never would. This is not his normal size, don't freak out, I assure you, he's safe...*Chaos*...*Big*." I said sternly as the Kayla, Josh and Big Mike watched him, their eyes wide. Chaos grew to the size of a horse, causing the horses to rear and whinny loudly and my friends to gasp. Big Mike stumbled, backing away from Chaos. Zach ran over to calm the horses, while I walked over to Big Mike. The others were petting Chaos, Josh stood off to the side, his face still a mask.

"Mike, it's okay. Do you trust me?" I asked, slowly he nodded. I took his hand and walked him over to Chaos. Big Mike's eyes were wide, but he made himself walk right up to my Hellhound. Chaos sat and lowered his head waiting. Slowly, Big Mike forced himself to pet him. Chaos responded with a yip and tail wagging.

Tell him, I would never hurt him. I am here to protect you, but I will protect all of them if I can. Chaos said. I smiled, progress was great.

"He says he will protect us always." I told them, but mostly I was talking to Big Mike. Big Mike was actually smiling.

"It's so cool that he can talk to you, I never thought I would be standing near a dog again, especially one the size of a horse... thanks Skye...and thanks Chaos. We should probably get going then. Let's get a map made of the area. Are you going to ride him?" Big Mike asked.

I hadn't thought of that. I looked at Chaos, who gave me a booming bark and lowered himself down so I could climb in his back. I climbed up and held onto the thick mane of fur on his neck. Everyone saddled up and we headed out again. Riding a dog, through the forest was an odd experience. It took a lot of getting used to, he moved very different from a horse. The plus side, I realized was that Chaos can travel faster and more stealthily. Eventually I was able to kind of predict his movements.

We rode for a little over an hour through the valley following the river. We could have probably reached the mountain in twenty minutes but we had to stop often and check patches of woods for weak points or vantage points during a battle. We followed the river upstream, with Zach's help, to a pass through the smaller hills near the mountain. Once we reached the hills, we had the cover of the trees from the screaming wind and sideways freezing rain. The storm had become downright raging. I was starting to think we would have to think about finding shelter and stay for the night. Once in the forest of the hills, the trees offered a lot of protection.

After another hour of mapping trails and the valley, the seven of us finally reached the base of Mt. Rainier, which is *massive. This is going to be a pain in the ass to protect. We're going to need more soldiers, more weapons and just... more of everything to keep this place surrounded.* I thought craning my neck to look up at the massive snowcapped rock. The thought was frustrating, considering we only had two weeks to get it handled.

I shivered looking up at the mountain. I was freezing and because we were up to a higher elevation, light snow blew sideways in the wind. I looked around at the others watching them. Miles stopped often taking photos, writing notes and muttering to herself. Zach stood a few feet away talking to Shake and making a map of underground water sources. Kayla, Big Mike and Josh were discussing surveillance options and possibly trying to get some of Hephaestus's Automatons to stand guard. *Whatever an Automaton is.* I thought moodily. Josh sent Alke to fly around the mountain and look around.

I hopped down off Chaos's back next to Cam's grey horse. Cam dismounted too; looking up at the mountain with his mouth open. I sent Chaos to go hunt for food. I watched as he tore off into the woods, past large white and blue glacier formations. I surveyed our surroundings. We stopped at the end of dense thick forest, which stopped abruptly by massive glaciers. The mountain rose up into the black and purple rolling clouds, so only the base was visible. The top rose up so high, it hurt to bend my head back that far too even look up there. The base itself seemed to go on for miles. It would be treacherous to even reach the actual mountain's base with the massive glaciers surrounding the bottom. The glaciers themselves were the size of mini mountains, formed from slick ice, with cracks, and probably thin spots that lead to death. My teeth chattered from the cold and the snow stung my eyes.

I looked over at Cam, who had a light in his hands near his face, with Orion cuddled around his neck. I walked closer to him. A light wasn't *in* his hands; it was coming *from* his hands. It looked like he held a mini sun in the palm of each hand just under his skin.

"*What* is that Cam?" I asked watching his hands. He smiled over at me and opened his hands a little more causing the light to shine brighter.

"I called the light. Apollo said I could use it and it's really cold up here and I haven't tried it yet. This is pretty cool." he said, looking proudly at his hands. After I got over the amazement of Cam holding sunlight in his hands, I had a thought.

"Try throwing it at that little glacier. Maybe you really can use it during battles if you need it. This is the best place to test it; nobody else is around in case you can't control it." I said, pointing at a smaller glacier near the two of us. Cam nodded and whispered to his hands. He closed one fist as if he held a baseball and pulled back his arm. He threw it, like he was a pro pitcher, launching a ball of pure white-hot light, across the air. It blasted into the ice with a bright flash, making it steam and sizzle. Cam and I ran over. Sure enough, the light left a deep, wet looking hole in the ice of the bluish white glacier. Cam looked down at his hand and said thank you to the light.

"That was frickin awesome! I can't believe that you can do that! We are going to have to practice our skills as soon as possible." I said, thinking about all the training we still had to do. *Gods, two weeks is not enough time to learn all of this stuff…two weeks if the Demons can keep their attack to that timeline and not sooner.* I thought. I had no idea how we were going to pull this off. The others came over, Kayla, kissing Cam on the cheek as she passed by to check the melted spot in the ice. They had all seen Cam throw the ball of light and were very excited. Josh finally smiled.

"I'll help train you guys with your fighting skills. I can help with abilities, like eyesight, hearing, reflexes and combat skills to get you all ready. I've been working on those things for quite a while and if you're all okay with it, I'd like to help teach you." said Josh looking around at everyone. They all nodded talking excitedly about training tonight. I noticed he didn't look directly at me once. This *ignoring* act he was pulling was not only hurting me a little, it was annoying me. If he was mad or hurt, I felt like he should at least be mean to me, or something. We were now stuck together, supposed to be teammates and have each other's backs on a battlefield. I shot him a glare. *We are defiantly going to need to talk later.* I thought, dreading just the thought of it.

"Cam, I'm freezing, where's the sun so we can get home? I think we'll have to come back here in the next couple of days. The valley will be the schools weakest point; we are going to have to do some serious thinking to find a way to protect this mountain and the woods. There is a lot more area to cover then we have resources for. We should get back, grab dinner and head to training." said Miles, looking over her notes and a map.

I felt a little guilty. I had no notes and not been paying attention to the area as much as I should have. I let out a whistle for Chaos to come back so we could leave. Cam lifted his head towards the sky with his eyes closed. After a minute, he opened his eyes and pointed towards the trees again. Chaos bounded up to us from somewhere off in the woods behind us and I climbed back onto his back. We headed off back into the trees away from Mt. Rainier. If the weather was nicer, I might be sad to be leaving the beautiful place, but at the moment, I was tempted to have Chaos *sprint* back.

By the time we reached the valley, the storm was so intense it was like night had fallen and the rain had turned to sleet. We had taken too long to get to the mountain. The sleet blasted through the trees stinging our faces. Josh and Cam were in the lead and both stopped at the tree line. Thunder and lightning ripped across the sky, briefly illuminating the valley. Even I knew we had a two more hour ride based on the storm. We had to cross the valley, travel up the sloping hillside and through the woods. In this storm, we would have to stick to the tree line for cover instead of going straight across the valley, and that would take two hours alone and possibly turn to much more. Chaos has a thick coat of fur, but the horses appeared cold and tired. Chaos and I moved closer to the group.

"We're probably going to have to camp out for a few hours to see if the storm calms down. The horses are tired, cold and starving. I don't want to push them too hard through this weather." Zach shouted over the wind.

"I agree we're going to have to find some cover. It wouldn't be smart to keep going through this mess." said Kayla looking out into the valley squinting against the wind.

"So we find somewhere to stay. I say we travel as a group. Nobody goes off on their own...Skye, I'm talking to you. We don't need a repeat of last time, so stay with the group." said Cam eyeing me down. I rolled my eyes at him. *Yeah, like I wanted to do that again.* I thought as I wiped more ice off my hair.

"Okay *dad*... I say we head back into the trees a little ways, where the trees are thicker. Once we find a place, I'll shadow with Chaos around the perimeter and make sure we are really alone." I said.

"What do you mean *Shadow?*" asked Big Mike, moving his giant horse closer to me, reaching out and petting Chaos's neck.

"Let's find a place to camp and I'll show you. My eyesight is like night vision when I do it, so it's the best way to hide *and* be able to see everything." I said smiling at him.

We all headed back into the safety of the trees. It didn't take long to find a good tight circle of pine trees with thick branches to provide cover for us and another spot for the horses. I just prayed that Joe wouldn't send out a search party in this weather. They would end up with way too much ground to cover.

"Skye, can you do your shadow thing after we get a fire going? I brought a lighter with me and some matches. I figured you could make it burn faster with your powers." asked Miles, as she looked under our tree canopy for dry branches. I hadn't tried to use my fire skills yet, the thought made me nervous.

"Okay, but can we try it farther away? I don't feel like lighting our shelter on fire if things get out of hand." I said.

We moved out into a more open area. Miles brought a stick with dried moss wadded up and stuck to its end. The others, curious to what we were up to, came to watch. Miles lit a match and laid it gently on the forest floor. I focused on the tiny flame, willing the fire to jump to the stick. The match began to spark and pop like a firecracker. I focused, asking the flame to jump to the stick again and again. The match turned into a ping-pong sized ball of flame. The ball of fire, with me gently coaxing it on, bounced once then leapt up growing to the size of a basketball and engulfed the end of the stick. However, it exploded once it touched the stick, Miles squealed and dropped it. I ran over to her, past the basketball sized flame lying in the dirt. The others moved closer to her. Zach reached her first and helped her up.

"I'm sorry! Did I burn you?" I asked feeling frantic. Miles faced me, not a scratch on her, thank the Gods. She smiled at me.

"I'm great, it just startled me. When it grew the heat off it was pretty intense, but it's okay, I over-reacted a little bit. See... no burns." she said showing Zach and me her hands. I let out a sigh of relief. It would be my worst nightmare if I lit one of my friends on fire.

"Can I see this shadow thing you can do?" asked Big Mike. Kayla nodded looking excited, while she held Cam's hand.

"Wait for me! Just let me put this in the shelter, where I set up a fire pit. I'll be right back okay." said Miles as her and Zach hurried back into the tree shelter. Josh was eyeing me suspiciously, still not speaking to me. Miles and Zach rushed back over as I let out a low whistle to call Chaos over so he could show them too.

"Alright, I have to step back into the trees a little bit, so I don't catch any light off the fire. Watch me and Chaos closely and you might be able to see what happens." I said stepping back towards a couple trees. They all gathered around, none of them wanted to blink. I shut my eyes and asked the shadows to cover me. The cool sensation of the shadows danced over my skin from my feet and up the rest of my body. The others gasped; I must have looked pretty crazy. I opened my eyes and looked around. The night vision worked great, I could see everything around me that had been in the pitch black.

"I'm going to do a walk of the perimeter with Chaos." I said closest to Zach who had been looking right at me and not realizing it. Zach jumped back a step. Cam called to the light and lit up both his hands. Warm light hit me, causing the shadows to flicker on my skin.

"That's insane. The light makes you flicker into existence, like you're in a strobe light at a dance party!" Kayla said excitedly. I giggled. *Me at a dance party, that's hilarious.* I thought to myself.

"Okay, she needs to check the area. I'll send Alke to fly over us. You and I will be on the ground with Chaos...I'm going with you whether you like it or not. I don't need to *shadow* to see in the dark." said Josh in a surly voice, like he wished he didn't have to check the area with me, like I was an inconvenience to him or something. I was annoyed but also a little happy about it because now would be a great time to talk.

"Okay, be back in 20 you two. I don't think any of us should split up for too long. I've seen horror movies and that's how people die." said Big Mike. Josh gave him a sharp nod and followed me into the woods. I sent Chaos in the other direction, so we could meet in the middle. Josh whistled and Alke swooped down landing on Josh's arm. After Josh asked him to check from the air the eagle took off again. I stomped into the woods without waiting for Josh. He still followed me, surprisingly quiet as we wandered about fifty feet from our camp.

"So...can the *oh-so wonderful perfect son of Zeus* see me or do I need to send away the shadows?" I asked, sarcasm dripping off my words.

"You should probably send them away so you don't get too tired. Using a power can drain a Demigod. But, I can see you. I already have night vision." he said quietly from behind me. I let the shadows go, thanking them for protecting me. I was already tired and didn't need to prove anything to Josh by wearing myself out, just out of spite. I'm not going to lie, I enjoy pushing people's buttons sometimes, but not so much when I liked someone a lot. We wandered in silence for a while, stopping to listen over the wind and thunder for any sounds. I sniffed the air, terrified I would catch the

Demon's scent, so far nothing but fresh cold air.

"Why didn't you tell me?" Josh said quietly from behind me. I slowly turned around to face him. *So he is mad.* I thought feeling my stomach fill with anxiety.

"Why would I? You seem to just run and tell everything to Lindsay. Just like I thought you would. I *told* you… I'm hard to get to know. Lindsay told me about the real plans." I said meeting his eyes. His eyes lit up in the dark, telling me he was using his Demigod vision to look at me even more closely. I returned the favor and focused on really *seeing* in the dark. He shimmered into focus, like he was standing in the sunlight, it made me feel elated that I figured out night vision without shadowing or his help. Josh huffed out a breath and shook his head.

"What *exactly* did I tell her? Please enlighten me, because I haven't spoken to her since before the assembly." said Josh hotly.

"*Really?* You expect me to believe that! Especially when she cornered me at dinner to make sure I was aware of what you told her? She *knew* I said yes to you about the Ball. She *knew* I told you my dad was Poseidon. How could she know that when we were alone in the tree? You're the only person I've had to tell that lie to, nobody else has even asked who my father is. Oh and just so you know, the guilt for that lie, haunted me and kept me up last night. As for the Ball, apparently you and *her* are going together. You asked her and had it planned this whole time. I'm just the last to find out. I *knew* it was too good to be true. The worst part about this whole thing…I take people's promises too seriously and that's *my* fault for trusting you. But, come to find out, the only reason you asked me is because you feel *sorry* for me for being lower class and *poor*. You're just like everyone else, a rich stuck up *jerk!*" I yelled at him as I stepped closer to him.

My temper was at the surface, boiling over. I took a step back from him so I wouldn't punch him. He just shook his head, not saying a word. I originally wasn't even going to say anything either, I guess I couldn't help it. Damn my big mouth to Hades. I looked down at my feet, feeling torn between screaming and throwing myself at him. His hands grabbing mine startled me. He stepped closer...too close, my body burned with fire and ice. I met his scorching golden eyes, trying to keep my brain clear.

"I didn't say anything to her. I would've never even thought about asking Lindsay to the Ball. I don't like her like that and never will...I was really waiting for the right time to ask you. I've been watching you, hoping for my chance to just talk to you. I noticed you, the first day I got here this summer. You were walking with Zach through the courtyard, laughing about something and you glanced in my direction. That's when I saw you're smile. You're so full of life... so free and *happy*. You're smile is like sunlight and fire, it drew me in. I knew at that moment, *I* wanted to be the reason for that smile." he said moving closer to me still.

I wanted to believe him with all of my soul. I was scared. The way I felt for Josh absolutely terrified me. I stood perfectly still waiting for him to do something. My body was screaming for him to kiss me. My breathing became more difficult as he leaned in towards me. He rested his forehead against mine and let out a sigh.

"I'm sorry you felt like you couldn't trust me. I understand why you didn't tell me about your father. It's even more important now that *nobody* knows you're a child of Hades. I'll prove to you that I can be trusted. I'll never hurt you or lie to you. That's a promise. I still want to have the chance to go with you to the Ball. I think we all need one night of normal in this nightmare. I want to spend that night with you, if you still want to spend it with me...we can also find out *together* how Lindsay found out about everything." he said in a whisper. My heart melted somewhere between my gut and my toes. I gave in to easily. I just didn't want him to be one of Lindsay's minions. Zach told me to trust people more and I knew he was right so I forced myself to push aside my fears.

"As long as we promise to tell each other the truth, no matter what happens." I whispered back. He smiled his charming beautiful smile and kissed my forehead gently.

"I promise." he said, walking ahead of me as we finished up our perimeter walk.

Chapter Seventeen

It was dawn by the time we reached the Castle grounds. We had spent the night trying to sleep in turns and listening to the raging wind. None of us really slept well in the cold and thunder. It had rained and snowed and even hailed on us through the shelter. I was exhausted now.

I had gotten back on Shake with Zach once we entered the valley so Chaos could pretend to be a dog again. The storm settled down enough for us to haul butt straight across the valley. Without having to stop and draw maps we got to the edge of the grounds within an hour this time. The only part that had been an issue was trying to cross the swollen river as it raged in its banks. Zach had used his powers to stall the waters just long enough to let our horses cross. It was crazy how he just asked the river to calm down and it did, like it was frozen in time. The only downfall was it made Zach so tired I thought he was going to pass out on Shake's back.

The storm started gearing up again right as we rode into the stables. At a couple points I had fallen asleep leaned awkwardly against Zach's back. Zach shook me awake right as we rounded the corner of the stables to put the horses away. Joe, the Dean and both our mothers were waiting for us. Their faces were full of relief and sleep deprivation. Like us, none of them slept last night. I hopped down off Shake and hugged my mom.

"You scared me to death. The only reason I'm didn't come barging out looking for you is because Josh sent Alke with a note telling us you were all safe and had to take cover in the storm." My mother said. She walked over to Josh and shook his hand thanking him, leaving me feeling grateful for Josh and his beautiful eagle. Even Miles and her brilliant mind hadn't thought of that. Dean Jacobs ordered us to go to bed for a few hours and report to him once we were rested. I didn't argue and headed straight for my room.

A few hours later after we all napped and showered, we met up in the training center. Joe had us meet in the Gun Range. We all sat around a table the Dean brought in for us. While we were out scouting, Dean Jacobs decided to use the Gun Range as a War Room. Maps covered the bullet proof glass, preventing anyone from seeing into the room. Realistically the range was the best room for us to set up shop. The doors locked from the inside, it's soundproof and full of bullet proof glass and it's fairly big. As soon as we all settled into our seats, Miles, Zach and Kayla gave Joe and the Dean the details of the area we were able to map out.

"I really think we'll have to set traps around the mountain. I'll see if my mother can get us surveillance equipment too. We need to be careful though. The Demon that Skye overheard wasn't sure that the traitor Demigod was right about this actually being Mount Etna. It would be a dead giveaway if we set up obvious protection around it. We'll have to be subtle." said Josh to the Dean. Dean Jacobs nodded taking notes.

"What does your mother do?" I whispered, meeting Josh's eyes. He smirked at me.

"She's an investigator for a law firm that handles corporate criminal cases and large scale class action lawsuits. She gets the evidence to take down big-wig companies who are breaking the law. It has to be under the radar so the companies can't destroy incriminating evidence. So, she has really good connections for top of the line surveillance equipment. We could get some great stuff from her and probably Miles's dad too." Josh explained to me. Miles overheard us and nodded taking more notes.

"Perfect, I'll ask my dad as soon as he sends War back with his response letter. You should send Alke to your mom and see what we can get from her. We have very little time to get things set up." said Miles looking around the table. My mother and Melinda spoiled us and left cookies, *lots* of coffee and even brought sandwiches during lunch. Kayla sipped her third cup of coffee, looking over notes and maps.

"Joe, I think you should contact Hephaestus. See if he would be willing to send us a few Automatons. We need to keep the students safe. I say we post them around the school perimeter and hide them around the edges of the valley. Make it look like they are guarding the school from there but really they are watching the mountain. We have to be sneaky about it but I think he could make some that can be camouflaged easily." said Kayla. Joe smiled at her affectionately. This sister thing seemed to be really good for Joe.

"I think that's a great idea. You know we could probably build a couple of our own too. With Cam and your welding skills, my mechanical skills and Melinda's brain, we could build them... oh speaking of that... I have your weapons! I had to change it up once I found out about your gifts from your parents, but one can never have too many weapons. I'll be right back!" said Joe excitedly, as she ran out of the War Room.

"What the hell is an *Automaton* anyways?" I asked. I'd been hearing the term a lot over the past few hours and it still confused me.

"They're basically robots. The difference is, you bless them with the markings of a God instead of using computer programming. Once they are blessed with the right symbols only the God or a child of the God can control them. They last as long as the God, because the blessed markings tie the Automaton to the Gods lifespan. Basically they become immortal robots that don't have to rely on batteries or anything else as a power source. They're really helpful in battles and to guard anything, because they are very difficult to kill. Hephaestus makes them all the time for Ares and his battles." said Kayla. I nodded, finally understanding what they were.

"Speaking of Ares, I never asked you Big Mike…what did Ares send you as a gift?" I asked as we waited for Joe. Big Mike grinned ear to ear and slowly stood up from the table stepping back a few steps. He held up his left wrist showing off a big gold and bronze watch.

"I got a shield… and short sword." he said. With a flick of his wrist the watch made a clunking sound of metal on metal and turned into a full sized gold and bronze shield. Battle scenes of Ares and monsters were artfully carved into every inch of the shield. Black onyx stone shone as the center piece and ran all around the edge as trim. Big Mike's shield is a real work of art. I got up and looked at the scenes carved into the metal. Big Mike pulled a small straight blade knife from a side holster of his utility belt. He pressed the end of the black handle, a bronze blade shot out from the end replacing the knife blade. The hilt encrusted with more black onyx stone and gold pieces. Big Mike smiled proudly showing off his weapons. They were perfect for him.

"Those are fantastic Mike! Perfect for you, I think Ares nailed it." I said feeling really content in the War Room with my friends. I jumped as light flashed around the room bringing with it the smell of the forest.

"Ares can get some things right." Artemis said, appearing in the corner of the room. Once my heart calmed down a little I looked her over. She looked a little worse for wear. Her braid was messier, her tight black and silver fatigues were a little dirty and she had a silver sword on her hip in addition to her bow and quiver. We all stood at attention and bowed to her. She bowed back and plopped down into a chair at the table. Joe came in with her armor cart behind her. She stopped in her tracks, bowed and took a seat. Our weapons would have to wait.

"I got your message Steve. I'm sorry it took me so long to get here. I have news though." she said directly to Dean Jacobs. I had no idea his first name was *Steve*. The name didn't really fit him.

"No apologies needed. I understand the situation with Oceanus. What news do you have?" he said bowing his head in respect. I'm pretty sure Gods *never* apologize for anything. Artemis earned even more respect, in my opinion, just for that.

"Thank you. Well, as you can probably tell by the thunder storms you've been having lately. Our fight is not going too well against Oceanus. Zeus is outraged at the news of the Demons discovering that Typhon is here because of a traitor. I warned him when he wanted to make that speech to the whole school, but he didn't listen. Anyways, Dionysus is searching for the rouge Demigod, when he's not drunk or helping us fight. I'll be here as often as possible to help find the Demigod. The news I have concerns all of you. I'll just go down the list... One; Oceanus is tearing up the Pacific Ocean. Poseidon thinks he is trying to get *here*. Right now he's still being held off in the middle. Hawaii is a bit of a mess, but it's the best we can do for now. If he does reach here, batten down the hatches, the entire west coast will have some serious storms to deal with. Two; Dionysus is having trouble finding the Demigod. We think they have been branded by a Spirit like the Demons have, making them invisible or even appear to be his child when they really are not. Three; the Demons have begun their assault on the Underworld. They are searching for Kirra's soul and trying to free more Titans. Hades is throwing what he can at them. If they infiltrate the Underworld, they will release the rest of the Titans, take over and get to Kirra." she finished looking deadly serious.

My heart crawled up into my throat. I wanted to scream, cry and possibly throw up.

"How many Demons are there? Have they started using Monsters too? What's Hades doing and how can we help?" Zach asked sounding slightly panicked. I scooted closer in my chair to him and rested my hand on his leg. Miles dropped her head into her hands looking stressed. Cam let out a breath of frustration and leaned back in his chair.

"Easy you guys. This sounds worse than it is. Hades is very capable of protecting his realm. As far as we can tell the Demons are not using Monsters yet. Apparently there are a lot more Demons running around than we thought. There are enough Demons at this time for them to not need to call any Monsters to their aid. The Demons have the Spirits and Titans right now." Artemis said with a head shake like even she was surprised.

"Hades has unleashed Thanatos and the Furies. He also has a whole army of undead, Hellhounds and a mess of other creepy crawlies to defend himself. He will be fine. However, Skye, this makes your journey even more important and more difficult. You will have to be more stealth about going to the Underworld. If a Demon see's you at all using any of your abilities, you will be known for what you are and they will try to capture you. Once they get their hands on you, it's over. They would be able to use you to get Kirra, release the rest of the Titans, open up Mount Etna and raise the punished dead of the Underworld." said Artemis looking a little sad.

"What do you mean...*raise the dead?*" I asked feeling slightly sick.

"You are your father's daughter. Once in the Underworld, your powers are more extreme. You *could* raise the dead, but the use of that power would kill you. It goes against nature. If you were fully immortal it would weaken you greatly, but you would live. You're half human, so using a power that defies your very existence as a human being would drain your life force entirely. It's an ancient law that goes back to the beginning of all existence set into place by the Creators of all things." she said seriously, her silver eyes lighting up with power. I gulped feeling my face heat up. Artemis leaned across the table meeting my eyes again, raw power radiating off her. *So leave the dead...dead at all costs.* Chaos said from under the table where he had been napping.

"You have two days to travel to the Underworld. Josh as discussed with Dean Jacobs, you will be going with Skye, so be ready. The Gods are calling some Titan allies of our own to come help with Oceanus. So I wouldn't worry too much about that. Stick to your tasks. Get it done as soon as possible... I see Joe has finished your weapons. Let's see what she has." said Artemis kindly to Joe as she changed the subject. My stomach squirmed at the last statement about the dead raising thing. Thank the Gods for Joe and her weapons to distract me, or I might have run out of there screaming.

"Thank you Goddess, I have indeed finished all your weapons and armor. By the end of the week, thanks to the new classes the rest of the school is taking, each student will have their own armor and weapon made by my armory students. Your armor is waiting for you in your lockers. So, for our leaders...here are your weapons." said Joe proudly pulling her heavy solid steel covered cart to the middle of the room.

She hit a large button on the side and the steel case sprung open, revealing a weapons display like something you might see in a showroom. The distraction worked, making me push aside the fact that I could raise the dead. My mouth watered at the beautiful display of craftsmanship. Joe had out done herself. The case was full of knives, swords, bows, arrows, spears, axes, hammers, daggers, crossbows and hatchets. All the weapons were made from bronze and stainless steel metals, with leather corded handles, leather sheaths and holsters. Joe began passing out our custom weapons.

Zach got a cross bow made from bronze and steel. He was given over 100 arrows made of bronze. Miles was given two bronze daggers with custom thigh holsters and two steel spears with bronze spear tips. Cam got a cross bow like Zach's, arrows and a gleaming bronze short sword with a leather sheath. Kayla got two steel handled, bronze head hatchets and four bronze throwing knives. Big Mike was given two spears like Miles, and a dual headed axe with a steel handle and bronze head.

For Josh, Joe spoiled him. He got two steel and bronze spears, a cross bow, arrows, two knives and a dagger. Joe carefully presented me with my weapons. She gently handed me a steel and bronze long bow with a quiver full of bronze tipped arrows, plus 100 more arrows. She also gave me two daggers that strapped into thigh holsters like what she gave to Miles.

All the weapons could be packed around comfortably thanks to Joe's custom holsters for each weapon, made especially for us. Each of our weapons had Joe's custom stamp and our names etched into the metal. We all tried the holsters and moved around with them on. Artemis and Joe gave us tips on how to wear the weapons and make them more accessible. I gave Joe a big hug. The words *thank you* just didn't feel like enough.

We decided we needed to train. We had already wasted most of a day in our short time limit having meetings and sleeping. Each of us had a lot to learn and with Artemis there, we figured pointers from a Goddess would help out a lot. We had come in fully armed and in our gear so we were already ready to go. It seemed like none of us would be wearing normal clothes anymore. Dean Jacobs remained in the War Room going over our notes and maps, writing letters to the appropriate people for aid. I decided I wanted to spar with Josh. If Sgt. Scott says he's the best fighter, I wanted to try my skills with him.

"Want to spar? I hear you're the best and if you're going with me to the Underworld I want to see you prove it." I said feeling flirty again. Damn flirting to Hades. Josh smiled at me and started to remove all his weapons and holsters.

As I took all my weapons off, I looked around at the others. Cam and Zach were working with Artemis on using their bows properly and how to use the bow itself as a weapon if you were out of arrows or the target had gotten too close for shooting. Miles, Big Mike and Kayla were working with Joe on hand-to-hand with daggers and axes. I stepped onto the mat and started stretching out my muscles. Josh joined me sitting on the mat.

"You ready for this little girl? I'll go easy on you, since you and I have never fought." he said meeting my eyes. I snorted, playfully giving his shoulder a shove.

"This isn't my first rodeo. No need to be easy on me." I said smugly. He huffed out a breath and shook his head as he stood up.

"Alright…but remember, you asked for it." he said grinning at me. I jumped up and got into my stance, ready to make a move first. Suddenly, I was on my back, my head ringing. He had come at me so fast I hardly saw him and didn't even have a chance to defend myself. I'm not even sure which moves he used to take me down.

"You okay Skye?" he asked kneeling over me. The ringing in my head had started to fade, thank the Gods for Demigod healing powers.

"Yeah…the next time I act like a cocky jerk, do whatever you just did and I'll behave myself… I promise…what exactly did you do? I can't even tell where you hit me…*everything* feels like it got hit." I moaned rolling over slowly and getting up on my hands and knees. My head spun again and I plopped over onto my butt. Josh plopped down on the mat beside me.

"Actually, I didn't hit you at all. I did a takedown. I attacked from the front, but brought my knee from the right into the side of your thigh, stepped to the left, gave your center a good shove and you went down over my left leg like a stone." he said as if it were simple. He moved so fast I hadn't even seen it coming.

"*What*…that's all you did? How did you move so fast? I didn't even have time to know what happened. All I know is one minute we faced off, the next…I'm on my back!" I said feeling a little embarrassed now. He chuckled low in his throat.

"You forget I've had five years to train and harness my skills. You can move just as fast as I did. All you lack is the training. You're a Demigod. You have more strength and speed than a human. All you need, is to learn how to use them. Get up, let's go again but I'll slow it down. Remember to focus and let your instincts take over. Clear your mind." he said, his golden eyes boring into me. I stood up taking in the way he carried himself. He stood at the ready, his arm muscles pulling his black t-shirt tight and his hair looking a little rumpled. *Clear my head…right…like I can think straight when I'm looking at him.* I thought as I tried to look at him without really looking. I got into my stance and prepared myself.

I spent most of the day on my back and not in a good way. Josh moved faster than lightening. I finally was able to focus enough to block him and stay on my feet the last two times. We decided to call it a day. I was sweaty, tired and sore. Josh looked perfect, like he had been sitting around all day doing nothing. I thought about punching him in the face just to make him look like I felt. I put on all my weapons and holsters, planning to shower in my room. Kayla and Miles were headed to the locker rooms, I caught up with them.

Kayla, Miles and I walked into the locker room together talking about what we learned. Training for the rest of the school was going to start in a few minutes, so girls were changing into gear when we got to our lockers. Since I had come in my gear, I planned on just grabbing more sets of t-shirts and pants. I wished I had skipped out on even going to the locker room. Lindsay walked over to me with her nose in the air, dressed in her gear with a short silver sword strapped to her hip.

"*So...* How's the *Poverty Club* enjoying its newest member?" she said directly to Kayla. *Crap...I forgot they were best friends. This is not good.* I thought. I kept my mouth shut this time. I didn't want to make things worse for Kayla. Kayla stepped around me and faced Lindsay. Kayla is one of the only girls at the school who is the same height as Lindsay; they stood eye to eye, staring at each other.

"You got a problem with who I hang out with?" Kayla demanded. I stood back with Miles beside me, waiting. I found Maddie and Carla trying to hide behind the row of lockers next to us. I smiled and waved at them. Reluctantly they both came out of hiding and flanked Lindsay, both of them looking like they didn't want to be there.

"Yeah...I do. You always said Skye was a loser charity case. *You* always talked about how much you wished we could make her and that *freak* she hangs out with leave the school for good. I just find it strange...you said you hated them, tried to get her mother fired, started all those rumors about *poor innocent little Skye* and now you're hanging out with her, now... *your* one of them? *They* don't belong here. This school is for people who are important to the world...people who *matter.* What happened to you?" Lindsay sneered. Kayla held her ground and purposefully stepped into Lindsay's space, causing Lindsay to step back.

"*I* had a change of attitude. Maybe I did think all those things once. *Maybe* I was being a selfish petty jerk. Did you ever think that *maybe* everyone around you acts like that because you make them feel like *nothing* if they don't? I don't want to be a part of it anymore. We were best friends once. You and I shared *everything* and now you care more about social status and money than the people in your life. It's pathetic...You heard the Dean. There's a *War* coming and *we* are the ones who have to stop it, we all have to be a team. As soon as he said that, I realized there are *bigger* things going on and I want to help see them solved. If you have a problem with *that*... your just heartless and *worthless* to humanity. Skye, Miles, Zach and Cam are real friends to me, they are as true and real as it gets. I'm allowed to be myself with them. I *never* could with you and that hurts more than anything. So unless you want to say sorry for the mean things you say and do, stay the *hell* away from me and my friends." said Kayla firmly. My heart swelled with joy, those were the nicest things anyone has ever said about me.

Lindsay's eyes filled up with tears and her face turned beet red. I thought she was going to run out of the locker room but instead, she swung out and punched Kayla in the jaw. I yelled in outrage getting ready to attack, but Miles grabbed my arm. Maddie and Carla were just standing there watching, not trying to fight or help, instead they both took a step back and looked shocked. Kayla recovered fast and punched Lindsay back, catching her in the eye socket. Then Kayla landed another hit to Lindsay's ribs, one to her jaw and took her to the floor like Josh had taken me down. Lindsay hit the floor hard with Kayla standing over her breathing heavily.

"You need to decide what's more important. Social status, or helping save the world. This isn't a game Lindsay. I know the girl I grew up with is still there; when you find her again, let me know. In the mean time...back *off* my friends." Kayla said looking down at Lindsay who lay on the floor on her back with tears running down her face. Kayla grabbed up her gear and weapons, slammed her locker shut and marched out of the locker room. Miles and I scrambled, grabbing our stuff and running after her.

Miles and I found Kayla sitting on the ground in front of the stables. She wasn't crying, but seemed like she was thinking about it. We plopped down next to her, one of us on each side. All three of us sat in silence for a minute, as the wind whipped around us.

"I'm sorry you guys." said Kayla sadly. Miles patted her knee.

"Don't worry about it. Honestly, I've said nasty things about you to Zach. The reality is; we never gave each other a chance, that's both of our faults. But, it's water under the bridge. We were both wrong and whatever happened before doesn't matter anymore. I stand by what I told you, I got your back no matter what. I know you have mine, I trust you with my life." I said meeting Kayla's beautiful bright yellow eyes. She smiled at me a true glittering genuine smile, leaning back into the wall of the stables.

"Thank you. I don't think I could do this without you guys. I really am sorry about the way I was…before. I'm just glad I can be *myself* with you guys. I also…think I'm falling in love with Cam… is that weird for you guys?" she asked sounding a little shy.

"Really…that's great actually! I know he really likes you too… to be totally honest I would rather have him be with you than anyone else. Don't worry about before, like Skye says, its water under the bridge. We're a team now." said Miles still patting Kayla's knee.

"A team…I like this. Let's get going, get cleaned up and go to dinner. I'm starving and want to go pretend to be normal for a little while." Kayla said getting up and grabbing up her gear off the dirt. Miles and I followed her lead and headed to the girls dorm.

Chapter Eighteen

The Dining Hall was all ours with the rest of the students doing combat training. We sat around the fire like usual talking about training. We left out most details about anything that could be over heard just in case. Zach and Cam excitedly told us about what they learned from Artemis. Miles, Kayla and I didn't tell the boys about the incident with Lindsay. That's something we didn't feel the need to worry them with, especially since it really had nothing to do with anything important. The three of us girls decided we all had enough on our plates without having to worry about overly dramatic gossip queens.

"I think the school should still have the Halloween Ball. It would boost morale. The students know they face a battle and know it's going to be soon. Joe said everyone is training hard and they all know how important the situation is. I think everyone deserves to have something semi-normal in their life. *All* of our lives have been turned upside down in the past few days, if we don't push for the Ball...I think our *army* will be less enthusiastic about this whole situation." Miles said, holding Zach's hand.

"Your right... I don't like that it will take time away from training, but it needs to happen. I also don't like that we would all be gathered in one space. That might make us more vulnerable to an attack." said Big Mike as he absently scratched Chaos behind the ears.

Big Mike and Chaos had bonded really well over the past 24 hours. Big Mike's fear of dogs had disappeared, oddly enough, thanks to a Hellhound.

"That's true Mike, but I think we might have to risk it. I say we take it to the Dean and see what he thinks." said Josh winking at me. I blushed and looked away from him.

Once we finished eating and talking about the Ball, we headed off to our rooms for bed. Miles and Zach went to see the Dean about the Ball together, so I walked to my dorm with Chaos for company making small talk about little things.

I lay in bed thinking about everything and talking to Chaos about our adventure into the Underworld. I would have to leave the day after tomorrow. Thursday, the day before the Ball, my date and I would be going into the pit of fire. If that's not a bonding experience I don't know what is.

I think you'll like it in the Underworld. It's warm down there and it smells like flowers and pomegranates. The Palace is made of black onyx and silver, with precious gems all over the place. It sparkles from the fires of Tartarus. You can't even hear the screaming from the Fields of Punishment. Chaos said wagging his tail with excitement. I smiled at him, but couldn't help thinking the Underworld didn't sound as *cheery* to me as it did to him. I may be a daughter of Hades, but I was raised out in the sunlight, not down in a cave.

"Is there really a river of fire?" I asked feeling nervous about this whole thing. I played with my key necklace around my neck, feeling a little comforted by its weight.

Yup, it's called the Phlegethon. It's in the Fields of Punishment. So is the Acheron; the river of pain and the Kokytos; the river of wailing. The Lethe; the river of forgetfulness, flows in front of the gateway to Elysium. That way the dead can decide to forever forget their life on the Earth or pass it by to Judgment. The

River Styx flows in front of the Palace so Hades can oversee Charon while he ferries souls to the Field of Waiting. Chaos said stretching out along my legs.

"I'm scared Chaos… what if the Demons find me while we're down there? I won't go looking for them or anything, but it's going to be hard not to try to help if they happen to be attacking Hades while we're there. Why do I even have to hear the Prophecy anyways? Maybe it's better if I don't know what it says." I said meeting his blazing eyes.

You need to hear it. Through all our history, the Heroes of the greatest battles have had to gather information from the dead. This time, will be easier because the soul you're seeking isn't actually dead, so there is no chance of a wasted trip. Once a soul passes into Tartarus or Elysium you won't be able to speak with them, only a God would be able to do that. Plenty of Heroes have gone through the trouble of sneaking into the Underworld and not been able to find the soul they seek. You won't have to. Plus, you're a child of Hades, which means you will still have all your powers while you're down there. They will actually improve immensely. You have to hear the Prophecy. The Gods need you to hear it because for the first time, none of them even knew about it until now. I bet Apollo has his toga in a bunch about that. He usually knows all the given Prophecies at all times, it's weird that he missed this one, he never has before. Chaos said seriously.

The whole thing made me uncomfortable. I wasn't just on a mission of my own to aid us to win the battles and find out my purpose, I was on a mission for the freaking Gods.

"That's not helping me. I think that makes it feel a little more complicated. The whole fate of the world rests on the fact that I find Kirra's soul, hear the full Prophecy, make it out of the Underworld without getting kidnapped and then, lead an army of untrained Demigods into battle. What if I fail? The world is resting on my shoulders and I feel like I'm not the one that is supposed to be the Hero. I'm not Hero material." I said feeling panic rise in my chest.

Chaos licked my hand and whined at me.

I know you're afraid. You have a lot to deal with and take on. I'll be with you the whole way. I know all the places to hide in the Underworld. I promise I will keep you safe. I'm less worried about the Underworld trip and more worried about the battle with the Demons. It will be harder for me to watch you in the middle of a battle. He said changing the subject. I sighed and scratched behind his ears.

"I was actually thinking you and I could go as a team. I make horses freak out as it is and once the Demons attack the Castle, they'll figure out real quick who I am. I'm not going to *not* use my powers in a battle. Once I throw some fire at them or disappear into the shadows, they would know. I would rather ride on *your* back than a skittish horse. You're more useful than a horse anyways because you can fight with your teeth while I'm using my sword and bow from your back. What do you think?" I asked him. He yipped and jumped up licking my face excitedly.

That would be great! Then I would never be away from you and could be with you the whole time! Maybe we can get Joe to make you a custom saddle? I don't want you to fall off when I'm running and twisting around during a fight. He said wiggling around like a hyper active puppy. I started laughing at him, trying to get him to lie down. Eventually I drifted off to sleep with Chaos sprawled out across my legs.

The Demon attack nightmare woke me out of a dead sleep again. This time I woke up screaming and thrashing around. Chaos stood over me at the size of a donkey with Zach standing next to him. I had apparently been crying based on the wetness across my cheeks. Zach sat down next to me and pulled me close to him. I cuddled up nestling under his arm sniffling, trying to slow my breathing. Chaos shrunk down to his Husky size and lay down at my feet again.

"You scared me this time… I couldn't wake you up. You were

screaming and crying…this is worse than the last nightmare isn't it?" he asked gently rubbing my back.

"Yeah, but not because it's more scary…it's that now I *know* there could be truth behind it… that's what makes it downright horrifying. It could actually happen in real life and not just in my dreams. I just hope it's like Artemis says and it's not really going to happen that way… Zach…I'm scared. I feel like I'm going to fall apart at any moment. There's so much at stake…what if I can't do this?" I said sniffling as I leaned against him. He sighed and gave me a squeeze.

"You can do this. You're the strongest person I know. I can count on you for everything. It's okay that you're scared. You would be crazy if you weren't. I'm scared for you… but you have to remember you're *not* alone. The *four* of us are together on this. Then we have Joe, the Dean, our moms' and Kayla, Big Mike and Josh…plus, the help of Greek Gods and hundreds of Demigods. You're far from being alone little mouse." He said holding me tightly against his chest.

"I know…but, I can't help feeling like it rests on me. Like I hold the fate of *everything* based on my choices and the paths I take. It's just so much to handle in a week. We haven't even known about this very long and all of a sudden it's like bam! *You're a Demigod, a child of the one and only Lord of the Underworld and the fate of the world is up to you…* How on earth am I going to do this! What if I can't do it and I fail?" I said crying hard now. Chaos whined at me and scooted closer.

"You ask for *help*… you've always tried to do everything on your own. You're strong, smart and loyal. You would die to protect people. You try so hard to fix everything for everyone else without ever asking for help. It's what makes everyone love you but, sometimes that's your biggest flaw. Skye, you don't have to do any of this alone. We're *all* in this together, which means you have to let others take on what you can't. You have to be strong enough to ask for help too. It's the only way to keep yourself from breaking. If you try to take it all on your shoulders and don't share the weight with the rest of us… you'll break down. I don't want to see that happen to you when the answer is so simple." Zach said gently, running his fingers through my messy hair. He let out a gentle sigh and kissed the top of my head.

"It's killing me that I can't go with you to the Underworld. This is going to be the hardest thing I've ever had to do, just letting you go without being able to follow. I'm terrified that something will happen and I won't be able to protect you down there. I know Josh is more than capable of keeping you safe. I know he really cares about you too but, I would rather be there because I know you better than anyone else. I told you before that I really want to be with the others and make new friends, but I can't do that without you too. You better come back to me. If I lose you…then I will break." he said tipping my chin up to meet my eyes. I sniffled and met his sea green eyes, seeing everything that made me love him. His love, kind heart, intelligence, loyalty and fierce courage made him *My* Zach. Only *I* got to see all of him.

"I promise to try. I won't do anything stupid when I'm down there. I'll hide in the shadows as much as possible and stick close to Chaos and Josh at all times. I promise I'll always come back to you…no matter what." I said thickly through my tears. Zach kissed my forehead gently and I snuggled up closer to him.

"Look at the bright side. Miles and I convinced the Dean to still have the Halloween Ball, which means you have to make it back so you can laugh at how bad I am at dancing. We got our one night of normal and I need you there for that." he said smiling.

We sat in silence for a little while, just holding on to each other. I cried some more but then the tears dried up and I started to feel better. I guess I needed to let myself be emotional and get it all out so I could focus. I usually feel like I'm being weak when I cry or get upset, but Zach never lets me feel like its weakness. I reluctantly drug myself out of bed and tried to get ready for the day, knowing I needed to train up and prep myself for the next day's trip to the land of the dead.

Zach and I stuck together all morning, grabbing a quick breakfast and walking to training through yet another storm with intense wind. We were late, but still stopped by to see Shake at the stables. I figured being a little late to training this one time would be fine. We walked into the training arena to find Cam and Big Mike sparring hand-to-hand while Joe coached them. Miles, Kayla and Josh were working with Artemis on bow training and throwing knives. They were all pretty occupied so nobody really noticed we were there. The Dean came out of the War Room with Nurse Lane scurrying behind him. He spotted me and headed in my direction. *Here comes the 'don't be late' speech.* I thought to myself.

"*There* you two are… we were getting a little worried about you. I was going to send Miles to your room and get you, well, I'm just glad you're here now. Nurse Lane was just telling me that we have a full team of 10 students who are children of Apollo, skilled in healing abilities. We also have another 15 students who are children of Aphrodite who are also skilled in healing abilities. So at total of 25 students, whom are gifted healers, will be training with Nurse Lane to assist as battle field medics and to treat the wounded in the Infirmary." he said.

I didn't quite understand why I needed to be told this, until I remembered that I am the leader of the whole army. The thought made my stomach turn. I nodded at the Dean and remembered Cam has healing abilities from Apollo as well. This gave me an idea. I called Cam over to us. Cam walked over to us with his eyebrows raised in confusion.

"Okay that sounds great Sir. Cam, Nurse Lane has gathered up 25 students with healing abilities and I'm thinking you could lead the team of medics? I know it's a lot to ask so, only if you're willing to take that on and lead them in battle?" I asked him seriously. Cam's eyebrows furrowed as he thought about it.

"You know that's not a bad idea. Apollo said I am able to heal anyone by using the Light. I'm willing to train with a unit of my own, just as long as I'm fighting along with the rest of you. I won't be that guy on the sidelines. It's not my style to just watch." Cam said meeting my eyes. I nodded in agreement, looking to the Dean.

"I think that's an excellent idea Skye. Then Nurse Lane would be able to stay in the Infirmary to treat the wounded instead of having to be in the field. So it's decided, Cam will be in charge of directing the Medics in the field. I'll speak with the other professors over the next couple of days to establish groups of fighters based on their abilities. Each of you will be leading a team of fighters based on your own skills and abilities. So, for now get to training… and Skye, work with Josh, prepping for tomorrow." said the Dean firmly. I saluted the Dean and walked with Zach over to where Josh and the girls were working. I decided to tell everyone to be ready for getting their own teams so I called a halt to training to have a quick discussion with them. They all gathered around including Artemis, who looked stunning as usual. Zach and I bowed to her.

"I just had a quick chat with the Dean about groups of fighters needing leaders. Cam will be leading all the field medics during any battles. They will be fighting as well as getting any wounded taken care of. The Dean will be gathering teams of special units like that together for each of us to be in charge of. I'll leave those decisions up to him and you guys to figure out, so be ready to suddenly have a group of students under your command. Remember the *Mole* is still here so be careful about what you talk about in front of your fighters. I know what I am is going to come out, but the longer we can hold off on that, the better off we'll be. I just wanted to make sure you were all in the loop." I said feeling a little stupid trying to sound like I had my crap together. Miles looked at me with a half smile, like she could tell how uncomfortable it is for me to make speeches.

"That's sounds great. It's actually a really good idea to have specialized units. All major branches of the armed forces do, I don't see why we can't. Thanks for letting us know Skye." said Miles giving me a wink and a bow. I bowed back to her not knowing what else to do with myself.

"You all won't be alone. I contacted Charlie this morning and we will be getting Demigod soldiers sent to us from the US Army. Even your human Government knows how important this is, so they are helping us out. The Army can't spare a lot but are willing to send 300 men to help us fight and defend the school and Mount Etna. They will be here by Sunday." said Artemis grinning at all of us. I breathed out a sigh of relief. *Thank the Gods we will have some highly trained men to help. A bunch of students pretending to be an army scares the crap out of me; at least with the Army here we might stand a chance.* I thought feeling a little better. Josh tensed up next to me when Artemis said *Army,* I couldn't figure out why that would be upsetting to him. I looked over at him seeing his face was a mask again. I shrugged it off and felt excited for the Army to get here.

We split up again to work on different training. Josh and I went to the mats to spar with swords this time. We decided to use the less dangerous wooden replicas from the weapons wall. Joe thought ahead and had a double blade wooden sword like my own for me to practice with. I grabbed it and got into my stance with the double blade at the ready and waited for Josh to make the first move. He used two swords and came at me full steam ahead. I moved fast spinning the dual headed wooden blades blocking each blow. After a few minutes I began to lose focus and he disarmed me, knocking my sword to the ground and taking me down too. I landed on my back with a thud as he held both sword tips to my throat.

"You're dead…what happened? One minute you're blocking

everything I have and then it's like you gave up." he said standing over me. I huffed out a flustered breath and knocked his blades away sitting up.

"I don't know. It's like I lost my head and all of a sudden got clumsy. What's that all about?" I asked. He gave me a hard look. When we train, Josh is all business and no games. He helped me stand and faced me, eyes blazing with golden light.

"This isn't a game Skye. You have to be focused. If this were a real fight you would be dead in a second. You're a Demigod, not a clumsy weak human. You lost confidence in yourself, I watched it happen. You have to remember to let your instincts guide you in a fight. If you try to control them or push them back, you get caught up in the Veil. The Veil is around us at all times, as Demigods we can push past it and use our full powers and skills as long as we accept them. If you don't accept them, our human side lets the Veil take over, which weakens us. It's both a gift and a curse… Get your sword and focus on nothing but my attacks. Get *into* the fight and push down the human instinct to think things through. I know you well enough to know you usually act before you think. You need to do that while fighting not just when you run your mouth off." he said sternly. *Okay that stung a little bit. I might not think before I speak most of the time, but I don't run my mouth off.* I thought as I grabbed my sword and faced off with him again, still feeling stung about what he said.

He attacked again full force, gracefully swinging each blade like they were extensions of his arms. I blocked him, spinning my blade through my hands, side stepping his strikes and lunging with my sword. I let my body do the thinking, like he told me. It worked for a while. I blocked, lunged and spun using my blade and my body as a unit. We kept at it and I did really well until I saw Zach go down from something Artemis did to him, causing me to lose my head entirely. In that second Josh stabbed me in the stomach knocking the wind out of my body and I went down. I lay there panting still looking over at Zach, who was slowly getting up, but appeared perfectly fine. Josh looked over at Zach and Artemis and back at me again, his face twisted up in frustration. He helped me up again.

"What the *hell* was that?" Josh demanded. I looked down at my feet, feeling stupid.

"I panicked when Zach fell…I'm sorry. I caught it out of the corner of my eye and lost focus again." I said to my feet, afraid to meet his eyes. Josh huffed out a sigh.

"You can't be distracted by that. If we were on the battlefield you wouldn't be able to help *anybody* if you're dead. People are going to be falling and fighting all around you. You will see your friends get hurt and possibly die. The only way to protect *them*, is to stay alive, win your own fight and then go help them." he said, his voice hard as a rock. I met his eyes seeing anger and pain there. *Where is that coming from?* I thought to myself.

"I said I was sorry. This Demigod thing is all really new to me. I know you have known for years but remember, I only found out a few days ago. So back off a little bit." I said hotly feeling defensive. He shook his head and picked up my blade shoving it into my hands again.

"We go again. Stop acting like a human. Get in your stance." he demanded. My temper spiked up and I attacked first. I used the anger as fuel and purposely forced him to defend himself. Again and again our blades met, each strike harder than the one before, causing my teeth to rattle. His face twisted into a mask of focus and anger. He switched it up on me and suddenly I was on the defensive again, not able to even attempt attacking him.

On and on it went, I realized the others had stopped what they were doing and were watching us. I tried a spin move and came around to his side hoping to catch him off guard. He blocked my blow easily, forcing me to step back and be on the defensive again. I blocked a blow to my side, spinning my body out of the way, while blocking a second blow to my neck. I tried again to force him back, but got distracted by the Dean rushing in the door. He struck my unguarded right side and caught me in the ribs. I gasped and hit the mat again. *Damn wooden swords to Hades.* I thought annoyed with my mistake. My ribcage felt like it was on fire. Josh stood over me breathing hard, looking angry again.

"You lost focus *again* Skye. You almost had me when you switched to offensive that last time… but, you lost it when the Dean came in. This is getting *ridiculous*. You'd be dead three times just because you can't seem to pay attention. This isn't a joke *little girl*. You think this is some kind of game?" he said in a low menacing voice. Anger burned fire through my veins. *Who the hell does he think he is?* I thought feeling my blood pump faster. I stood up ignoring my burning ribs and faced him, my head just reaching his chin.

"What the *hell* is your problem? I told you this is new to me. I'm trying my hardest to do everything everyone is asking me to do. I don't need some arrogant jerk screaming at me about my focus every two seconds! If I almost had you at any point that just tells me that you have never had to *really* fight for *anything* in real life! I've never been in a battle, *none* of us have! Just because you're a freaking high and mighty *Son of Zeus* who *thinks* he knows what it's like fight for real, doesn't mean you can treat me like I'm stupid!" I shouted at him. I looked into his eyes, which were full of fury and pain. His face hardened into a mask and I couldn't tell what he was thinking anymore, the pain now gone, replaced by nothing at all.

"If that's what you think Skye." he said. Without another word he marched out of the training arena. I stood there fuming for a moment and then realized, the others were still watching, their faces shocked. Artemis watched me, showing no emotion in her face, I cringed as her silver-white eyes bored into my soul. My face turned red as I tried to ignore them all and pick up our discarded wooden weapons. The Dean cleared his throat, drawing everyone's attention to him.

"I…uh…there's been another attack. I need you all in the Infirmary. Miles, it's your dad." he said, that's when I noticed the tears in his eyes.

Chapter Nineteen

My heart felt like it stopped as I watched Miles's beautiful face drain of all color. She took off at a dead sprint towards the exit, Zach racing to catch up with her. Artemis blitzed out with a flash of light and wind. I looked around wide eyed at the others feeling confused. The Dean left right away hurrying out the door behind Miles and Zach. Chaos came hurling out of the War Room, where he naps when we train, probably sensing my fear.

"Let's go... Skye, go get Josh, I think you owe him an apology and we need him with us. Miles will need *both* of you. Go now and don't argue." Cam said sternly. I nodded and stood in shock watching as Kayla, Big Mike and Cam left.

"You *do* owe him an apology you know. Josh has been through a lot of things that would curl your hair if you knew. When you can, ask him about it...I'm going to the Infirmary too. I'll meet you in there in a few minutes." Joe said firmly. I sighed and nodded to her as Chaos and I rushed out the doors.

We sprinted past the stables as I thought hard about where Josh would be. He was nowhere to be seen so I figured he must have taken off running. I decided Josh might go to the big maple tree he took me to when he asked me to the Ball, so I headed that way to check first. I sprinted around the pastures, behind the dorms and Gym to the tree, leaving the others behind me. Another storm was brewing, black clouds rolled over the sky and the cold rain stung my cheeks. I finally reached our tree and sure enough, Josh sat against the trunk up on our branch. I climbed up as quickly as I could, knowing he wouldn't be able to hear me over the wind even with his Demigod hearing. *I have to get back to Miles as soon as possible.* I thought as I climbed. Chaos paced around the base of the tree, whining slightly.

"Hey…how'd you find me?" he asked in a sullen voice as I reached the branch. I crawled up across from him, out of breath from my race to find him.

"I know at least one thing about you. Your father is the God of the sky, which means you're more comfortable in high places than with your feet on the ground. Other than that, I don't really know that much else about you. I would like to know the real you and also apologize for what happened earlier. But right now that doesn't matter, we'll have to come back to this conversation later. It's okay if you're mad at me and whatever but we have to go *now*. The reason the Dean came rushing in, is because there's been another Demon attack. Josh… I don't know how but, they got Miles's dad. We have to go to the Infirmary right now." I said feeling panicked. I knew the longer we took the worse things could get for Miles. I needed to be there for her and so did Josh, she needed all of us. Josh's eyes widened in shock as his hardened mask melted off his face allowing me to see his fear.

"Let's go, right now. We can talk about everything else later." he said firmly and began to climb down. Once we reached the bottom we began to run towards the main Castle. By the time we burst through the front doors of the Castle, we were both breathing hard and soaked to the bone from the pouring rain. The Dining Hall and Library were empty of students as we ran through the Library towards the Infirmary, which rests behind the big center staircase at the back of the Castle. I wrenched open the big dark wooden double doors into the Infirmary.

Set up like a hospital ER, we passed the door to Nurse Lane's office, rows of beds separated by curtains and medical equipment on carts and trays of smaller medical tools. We came to the end of the main room, where the private intensive care rooms were located. Only one door stood cracked open and we could hear muffled talking from inside. Chaos sat down next to Orion beside the door to wait for me.

I slowly opened the door to the large room. Everyone was there standing around Miles's dad's bed. Heart monitors made quiet slow beeping sounds. My mom, the Dean, Mom two and Joe stood in the far corner of the room by the rows of white cabinets, having a serious discussion in whispers. Artemis was nowhere to be seen, which struck me as odd. I felt like she should be there.

Nurse Lane stood by a machine in her white lab coat, golden blonde hair pulled in a tight bun, taking notes on her clipboard. Kayla, Big Mike and Zach were seated on a bench which sat below the window. Miles had a chair pulled up by the head of the bed, her back to us, with her head down on the edge of the bed. War perched on the bed near her head making soft hooting sounds.

I looked at her father in the bed. He resembled the Dean a lot. I could see some of his sandy blonde hair from under a *very* bloodied bandage, which covered the whole right side of his face and head. Even though his face had scratches and small cuts all over it, I could tell he was handsome. His skin was pale, like Miles, with chiseled cheekbones and a light brown beard across his strong chin. I looked the rest of him over, his left arm rested in a heavy bandage across his broad chest. His left leg was also heavily bandaged and rested out of the sterile white blanket that covered him. He looked much taller than the Dean. Blood seeped through the bandages on his head, arm and leg. He was able to breathe on his own, but it sounded weak as air rattled in and out of his lungs.

Josh walked over to Zach and sat down next to him, talking quietly. I reached out and rested my hand on Miles's shoulder. She looked up meeting my eyes. Tears pooled in her beautiful emerald eyes, her face as pale as the blanket over her father. I pulled up a chair and sat next to her holding her hand. She heaved a huge shaky breath and lay her head back down on the bed by her father's unwounded arm.

I'm not sure how long we all stayed that way; the only sounds in the room were the beeps of the medical equipment and low whispers of the others. My mom pulled up a chair on the other side of Miles. Miles started crying, my mother pulling her close, holding her while she cried hard. I felt terrible for Miles and guilty. I know it wasn't my fault, but part of the reason the Demons were here was because they were looking for me, not just Typhon. I made eye contact with Cam motioning for him to follow me out of the room. He whispered something to Kayla, kissed her cheek and followed me out. I shut the door behind us. Chaos stood and started pacing with Orion pacing behind him like an orange and white shadow. If I wasn't so stressed, the sight of the two of them pacing like that would have me cracking up.

"Can you heal him?" I asked Cam, my hopes up just a little. Cam's face fell and he shook his head.

"He's been marked, like the Demons. I can't read Greek and neither could Nurse Lane, the mark is burned across his chest, like he was branded. I had Orion look at it. It's the mark of *The Arae*, the Spirit of curses... Orion said he's been cursed as well as wounded. Until we can lift the curse, Nurse Lane and I can't heal the wounds. The curse keeps the wounds from healing and we don't know what else it does. It's what we worried about with the rouge Demigod, the Demons do have the ability to mark people with Spirit markings." he said sadly, running his hands through his hair in frustration. My heart hurt when he said that. The Demons were using Spirit markings to hurt people. The situation just went from bad to *awful* real fast. Light flashed around the Infirmary and wind blew over us, signaling the entrance of a God. Artemis stood next to us looking grave.

"I'm sorry; I had to go tell Zeus and Athena what happened. Athena couldn't be here, but is *very* angry about Charlie being attacked. She said to tell Miles to remember the Olives? Whatever that means." said Artemis with a sigh. *The olives! Of course!* I thought feeling hopeful again.

"He's cursed so Cam and Nurse Lane can't heal him with their powers. Would olives from a blessed healing tree work for his wounds?" I asked Artemis seriously. Her brow furrowed deep in thought.

"It might. It won't hurt him even if it doesn't work. If you could heal his body you would have a better chance of getting rid of the curse…or at least more time." she said. I about jumped into the air with joy. A little tiny ray of sunshine was better than nothing.

"Can you find out how we can break the curse? Or at least what we need to do to find a way to break it?" I asked her. She smiled gently at me, I've been learning to fear that look from her, it usually means *I* have to do something *unpleasant*.

"You can ask tomorrow how to break the curse…when you travel into the Underworld. You will have to seek out Thanatos. He is the spirit of death, dealer of death and Hades right hand. He will have the answer for you." Artemis said meeting my eyes. *Great, I totally want to hang out with the Grim Reaper and chat about curses.* I thought to myself. I sighed hard and nodded, pushing back my fear.

"Alright then. I'll go get the olive off the tree. Then, Josh and I leave *tonight*, not tomorrow. Based on what happened, we have officially run out of time. The Demons seem to be attacking people randomly now, as well as having the ability to mark whoever they want with the Spirit tattoos. What was Miles's dad even doing anyways?" I asked Artemis.

"He was coming up here early to help get things ready for the incoming soldiers. He wants to set them up in the dorms, which means a lot of moving around for the students. He would have to be here anyways to lead the soldiers, but he decided to come before they did. He was attacked on the main road up here. He got out of his truck because a tree had fallen across the road and was attacked by four Demons. Apparently they are watching the roads to the area, which means the soldiers will have to come in quietly now. If War hadn't been with him, he would probably be dead. War went for help right away finding Sergeant Scott and Melinda. Once Sergeant Scott got there, the Demons had gone, leaving Charlie alive and branded with the Spirit's markings. It's a terrible situation, but now at least we know the Demons are in fact watching the roads. Charlie wanted to come early enough to surprise Miles and see her off to the Ball." she said sadly. My heart wrenched in my chest painfully.

"That makes this even more urgent. We leave tonight. I'm not going to be able to sleep tonight anyways and Charlie needs to be with his daughter. Miles *needs* him. Without him, she will be alone. I can't have that happen to her, it's my job to protect her and keep her safe. I'll get it done. Oh and Artemis, would you please do me a favor and tell Athena thank you for the tree." I said with a respectful bow. Her lip twitched like she wanted to smile but she kept a straight face and bowed back.

"I'll let her know right away… Do not leave for the Underworld until I return. Understood?" she said sternly. I nodded and she was gone in a flash of light.

"Okay, Cam go let the others know what the plan is. I'll go to Miles's room and grab an olive as fast as I can." I said taking off towards the doors as Cam nodded heading back into the room. Chaos followed me out of the Infirmary. Apparently we had been in there a while because lunch had come and gone, the Dining Hall was now being set up for dinner by kitchen staff. I rushed out the front doors into the raging storm, racing to the girls' dorm thinking about Miles. Chaos and I tore into Miles's room leaving water drops and mud all over the place. I found the little olive tree sitting up in her window sill, which is identical to mine. I climbed up onto her desk and carefully plucked the one and only small green olive.

Whatever you do, don't smush it okay. That's the only one. Chaos said watching me like a hawk. *Like I want to wreck her dad's only chance by smushing an olive.* I thought giving Chaos an eye roll.

"Just make sure nobody gets in my way. Classes should be letting out by the time we get back to the Castle...bark, growl, be an irritated dog and keep my path clear." I said.

Oh, this is going to be fun. Stay right behind me and don't clench your fist. Let's go. He said heading out the door. I followed behind him back out the front doors into the miserable storm. With all the running I seemed to be doing, I wouldn't need to work out for a month. Once we made it through the front doors of the Castle again, classes had in fact let out. Students flooded the front stairs, front entry, Dining Hall and part of the Library, all of them headed in different directions. I grabbed Chaos's tail, trailing behind him. He did what I asked and boy could he clear a crowd. His deep booming bark echoed around the Castle, he snarled and even nipped at a few people as we hurried through the sea of students. Everyone moved out of the way for him, jumping back or letting out screams of fear. I tried not to smile at the effect a *mini* version of a Hellhound has, they would be crying if he came at them like that in his full size.

I burst into the room, trying to keep quiet so I didn't startle anyone. Miles turned and gave me a weak smile. I held out the olive to her.

"I didn't even think of my olive tree. You're smarter than I am

Skye. Thank you…for everything." she said standing up and hugging me.

"When you get a chance to meet her, you can thank Athena, it was her idea." I said as I looked around, noticing my mom, mom two, Cam and Joe were all gone now. Kayla leaned on Zach, looking like she had just woken up from a nap. Big Mike sat in a chair in the corner reading over some of our notes, while Josh stood staring out the window. The Dean sat in the chair my mom had previously been sitting in, closest to Miles.

"Is it possible for him to eat the olive?" I asked feeling worried. Miles's dad was unconscious and I wasn't sure if he was even able to wake up.

"Yes, Nurse Lane will be in soon to give him a shot of adrenaline. It will wake him up long enough to eat the olive. We don't know how he will act once he wakes up because of the curse, so she's going to strap him to the bed. Cam went with her to help and see how to properly fill the syringe." said Miles. I nodded and leaned against the wall waiting. A few minutes later, Cam and Nurse Lane came in with straps and a big scary looking shot.

"This could be a very dangerous situation. I need all of you to back away from the bed and stand against the walls. Do not try to help, that could overwhelm him when he comes to. He also may be dangerous depending on the type of Curse, especially with a dose of adrenaline in his system. He was made a Demigod, by Athena herself. He may have powers from her which could be intensified from the curse. The Curse may also have given him abilities that could be dangerous. Miles, I ask that you do not touch him. We don't know what Curse he has and he could pass it to you or try to harm you. Do you understand?" Nurse Lane asked gently. Miles sniffled and nodded backing away, moving to Zach. Zach wrapped an arm around her and held her close. We all backed up to the walls as requested, while Cam and Nurse Lane strapped Charlie's arms, ankles, legs and shoulders to the metal frame of the hospital bed.

"I'm going to inject the shot directly into his heart. It will look scary, but it's the only way to apply the dose." said Nurse Lane. She stabbed the needle hard into his chest and pushed down the plunger. As soon as she pulled the needle out of his chest, his eyes flew open wide and he sucked in a giant breath of air. Nurse Lane stood back near Cam, gently taking the olive from a shocked looking Miles.

"Charlie, can you hear me? It's Nurse Lane, you're in the Infirmary in the Castle at Chambers Academy." she said gently still keeping her distance. Charlie pulled against the restraints, his shockingly bright apple green eyes bulging, making him look slightly crazy. The Dean stepped forward like he wanted to help; Big Mike put a firm hand on his shoulder stopping him.

"Demons! I'm burning! The fire…the fire! Get it off me! I'll burn alive! I have to find Miles! Where is Miles! I'm on Fire! Help Me!" he screamed pulling against the restraints hard, rattling the metal bed frame. He pulled and thrashed around screaming, making the hair on my neck stand up. Miles tried to go to him, tears flowing down her cheeks as she screamed and pulled against Zach, who firmly held her back. Nurse Lane waited until Charlie's mouth opened up and shoved the olive into it. He abruptly stopped screaming and tried to spit it out. Cam leapt forward, right hand glowing with his brilliant healing light and held it over Charlie's mouth as he thrashed. After a tense moment Charlie swallowed the olive and stopped thrashing around, collapsing back into his pillows. Cam lifted his glowing hand from Charlie's mouth slowly and released the light, whispering gently to it as it left his hand. Charlie's breathing slowed, growing more even with each passing second. I let out a breath, not realizing I had been holding it in. Miles cried hard against Zach in fear and relief. After a moment Charlie's eyes opened again and he looked around the room, confusion crossing his features.

"Who are you? Where am I?" he asked looking around at all of us. Miles stepped forward, hope shining in her eyes.

"It's me dad…Miles. You were attacked. You're at Chambers Academy…my school." she said looking like she was trying really hard not to reach out and touch him.

"I don't have a daughter. You must have me confused with someone else my dear. I don't feel like I was attacked by anything. What would attack me?" he said seriously as Nurse Lane began removing his bandages. Sure enough the olive had done its work and all his wounds were gone. The only proof of them having ever been on his body was the bloodied bandages Nurse Lane removed and very pale pink scars from a lot of different size cuts. Miles's eyes filled up with tears.

"Daddy…you really don't know me?" she sobbed, looking at him. Her dad had a silly grin on his face as he watched her cry. It was slightly sickening to watch. Kayla, Big Mike and Josh were watching the exchange with looks of pity on their faces. Kayla had tears in her eyes, as she gripped onto Cam's arm tightly. The Dean was probably at the end of his rope and bolted out the door trying to hold back tears.

"Nope…this must be one of those silly game shows like on T.V…ha ha very funny…where are the hidden cameras? I think…Urrgggaahhhh! I'm on Fire!!! Put it out! Put the Fire out! Help me!" Charlie screamed thrashing around again. Blood curdling screams filled the room as Miles's dad thrashed around thinking he was on fire. Miles started screaming too and pulling against Zach's grip on her waist. I threw my hands over my ears and forced myself to stay in my spot against the wall. Nurse Lane rushed to him and held her hand just above his head not touching him. Soft calming white light poured from her hand, like Cam's light, to Charlie's head. His eyes fluttered closed and he lay still, fully asleep. Nurse Lane let the light go from her hand gently, walking over to Cam whispering to him about something.

"Miles…don't listen to what he said. It all has to do with the Curse. He knows you or he wouldn't have asked for you. I think you should go…you're dad will be safe now. He's going to be sleeping until Skye can find a way to lift the Curse. You need to go get some food in you and rest." Cam said gently laying a hand on her shoulder. She shook her head hard, pulling out of Zach's arms. Zach met my eyes; I could see his eyes fading to grayish blue, telling me he was hurting.

"I can't! What if he needs me! I can't do it Cam!" she wailed, crying again. I walked over and grabbed her shoulders, making her look at me.

"He will be sleeping until I get back from the Underworld. Once I get back with the answer, he will be better. You won't be any use if you're falling asleep where you stand. Zach is going to take you back to your room. You need to take a hot shower, eat something and then if you really want to you can come back here and sleep here. I'll make Nurse Lane put you out right now if you don't listen to us. Josh and I will be leaving for the Underworld as soon as Artemis gets back. I want you there when we leave. I have to get ready to go and I don't know how much time I have until Artemis returns. Please Miles? Let Zach take care of you." I said looking into her tired eyes. She sniffed and nodded in agreement, but reluctantly. Zach wrapped an arm around her shoulders and walked her out of the room, kissing my cheek as he passed by. I let out a huge sigh of relief.

I turned facing Josh, Kayla, Cam and Big Mike, I noticed their fear from earlier had gone, replaced by hard courage. Just the sight of them gave me strength of my own.

"Josh, get ready. We leave for the Underworld in a matter of hours. Kayla…You, Joe and Melinda get started on those Automatons *now*. We're going to need them to get the Demons away from the roads so this doesn't happen again. Contact Hephaestus for as many of his Automatons as you can get. Tell Joe to get the armory stocked up and the metal working students working full time on weapons and armor. Cam, work with Nurse Lane and your unit on fighting skills and treating wounded while in the middle of a battle. Big Mike, you are to take over for Miles as of right now. Next to her, you're the best at preparing battle plans. Get going on that as soon as possible. Get my mother to help you with that. Cam, tell Zach to start training up the horses as soon as he can, also let the Dean know I've issued these orders as soon as possible. I have to go get geared up and grab some food. Once Artemis gets back, Josh and I leave." I said sternly. They all bowed to me and we left Charlie's room going our different ways to our tasks.

Once back in my dorm room alone with Chaos, I looked around seeing everything differently. It had been hard knowing the fate of the world could rest on my shoulders, now that it was up to me to save Miles's dad, I no longer felt afraid. I felt courage swell up inside my chest and shove the fear down. *I have to save him for Miles. I will find the answer from Thanatos or die trying.* I thought.

I dressed in clean combat gear deciding to leave without the jacket. Chaos said it would be warm down there; the jacket would be unnecessary weight. I strapped on my knives to my belt, daggers on each thigh and sword in my side holster, feeling comforted by their weight. I tucked my key necklace from Hades into my shirt. Once I was done I gave my room one last look. Not that long ago, we had been giggling and watching a movie, without a care in the world. I wanted to get that time back for all of us.

Someone softly knocked on my door. I opened it to find Josh standing there fully geared up and armed with both his elegant bronze swords strapped across his back, his crossbow and quiver strapped to his hip and daggers in each boot and one more on his other hip. In his hands were my bow, a full quiver of arrows and two small bottles of amber liquid. I took my weapons from him eyeing the amber liquid questioningly.

"This is The Nectar of the Gods. Alke brought it to me a few minutes ago with a note from Zeus. The note said if we are injured; take one small sip to treat any wounds. If one of us is captured by the Demons, he said to drink the entire bottle and we will die, preventing them from using either of us. Tuck this somewhere safe." he said handing it to me. The thought of being captured sent a shiver up my spine. I tucked the dangerous little bottle into a clever hidden pocket inside my boot. I strapped my bow and quiver over my back and met his shimmering golden eyes, full of strength and courage. Feeling full to the brim with bravery myself, I stepped forward, gently pulling his face down to mine and rested my forehead against his. Josh didn't resist, instead he closed his eyes and let out a soft breath, making my heart flutter.

"I'm sorry about earlier. You were trying to teach me and I was being stubborn and rude. One day, I want to hear about everything you've been through. I'm glad it's you going with me… I trust you." I whispered still resting my forehead against his. He sighed again, running his hand gently down the side of my face, making my stomach flutter as he left a trail of fire and ice down my skin.

"I trust you too and I won't let anything happen to you. We're in this together, you and me against the world, always." he said, his voice low. My lips were begging for him to kiss me, before I could kiss him first, he kissed my forehead gently and pulled away. I let out a sigh as Josh, Chaos and I walked out of my dorm together headed for the Castle, ready to go into the depths of the Underworld.

Chapter Twenty

I found myself feeling separate from the rest of the student body as I grabbed some food to take back to the Infirmary. Josh and I loaded up plates with food for us and Chaos and made our way through the crowd to the Infirmary doors. Lindsay caught my eye glaring at us with a look of disgust on her face. She tried to engage Josh in conversation as we passed by her table, reaching out trying to grab his hand; he shrugged her off not saying a word. She shouted something at me as we passed the grand staircase. I ignored her, it didn't matter what she said. Her rude comments didn't matter right now. *I've got much bigger things to deal with.* I thought as we walked into the Infirmary.

We sat with Kayla, Big Mike, Zach, Cam and a much better looking Miles, around a small table, eating dinner in the middle of the Infirmary. Nurse Lane was in with Charlie giving him nutrients through a tube in his arm. Nobody really talked as we all tried to eat. My nerves were besting me, making it hard to eat while my stomach rolled around uncomfortably. Bright light flashed around the Infirmary making all of us squint and cover our eyes. Artemis stood before us looking battle worn, her long silvery blonde hair let loose from her braid, billowing around her in some unknown breeze. Soot and dirt smeared her lovely face and tight fatigues, making her look like a wild huntress. We all stood and bowed respectfully to her. She returned the bow, her face serious.

"It's time Skye... I just came from the Underworld. It's currently under attack by the Demons. Thanatos and Hades are at the front lines trying to keep the Demons out. The Demons are trying to use the River Styx as an entrance. The river runs into the mortal world at only one point, deep down in a cavern. In ancient times this was used for humans to make sacrifices to the Gods by throwing offerings into the river. The Demons have found the entrance. So far Hades and Thanatos are holding them back with their army. I provided some aid while I was there and alerted Hades wife, Persephone, of your arrival. She is currently in charge of Kirra's soul and guarding the Palace with her own army of Hellhounds and soldiers." Artemis said looking grave. I tried to swallow but my mouth was dry and my stomach felt like it was full of bats.

"You will be entering the Underworld on the outskirts of the realm inside the Fields of Punishment. The Fields are quite large so if you enter in the middle, it would be the farthest point that is safe for you to enter unnoticed. The main fight is, as of right now, closest to the outer edge of Hades realm near Elysium. Tartarus rests behind the Fields of Punishment, beyond the Rivers, so you won't be too close to it either. Make your way out of the fields, cross the River Styx and go into the Palace from the back through the Garden. Chaos will know the way. You have never traveled by flame before, so let Chaos take the lead once you're incased in the flame. We do not have time to teach you how to properly travel by fire. Do not fear the fire and keep your minds empty of all thoughts of places and people you know. Josh, to survive the trip, you *must* be touching Skye or Chaos. If you let go during your travel, you will burn up and be killed. Is that clear?" Artemis asked. If Josh felt any fear, he didn't show it. He gave her a tight nod, his face a hard mask of determination. I took a deep breath and we stood up moving to the middle of the room. The others got up and hugged each of us, nobody really knowing what to say. Miles hugged me and whispered in my ear.

"You are the best friend I could ever have. Thank you for saving my dad. Be safe and come back to us. War is already there, he will travel back and forth sending word and keep us in the loop as much as he can…I love you Skye." she whispered. I wanted to choke up and cry, but I kept it together and kissed her cheek. Cam hugged me without saying anything, his face serious. Zach pulled me into his arms holding me tightly. My heart jumped into my throat, nearly cutting off my air.

"You come back to me. I love you little mouse." he whispered gently kissing my forehead. I tried to speak, but I couldn't even choke out a sound, so I just nodded. Everyone stepped back giving us room. I grasped Josh's hand tightly as Chaos grew to the size of a donkey. Josh grabbed the thick fur on Chaos's neck and gave a tight nod to Artemis.

Kayla pulled out a match striking across her belt and held the flame out to me. I opened my palm, forcing myself to trust the fire. She set the match gently in the palm of my hand, the flame feeling hot, but not burning my hand. I smiled at the flame as it danced gracefully around my palm, warmly tickling my skin. I took a deep breath and speaking to it inside my head I coaxed the fire to cover my body. Slowly it crept over my arm, warm and gentle, like being wrapped in warm sunlight. I asked it to cover all of me and it danced over my skin and clothes happily, making me feel at home.

My body fully incased in fire now, I gently pushed it to Josh with my mind. Once it touched him, a slight smile crept to his lips as he watched it cover his body. Chaos caught fire and wiggled with excitement. We probably looked *insane,* all three of us incased in orange and white flames, I hoped nobody walked in and saw us. Artemis stepped forward speaking directly to Chaos.

"Take them now and keep both of them safe. Lead them to the Palace as fast as possible…I hope to see you all soon. Good luck." she said bowing to the three of us. I gave her a nod and closed my eyes clearing my mind.

Once we are in the Underworld I'll be able to speak to both of you. Right now we are all connected by the fire. Chaos said, Josh huffed out a breath of surprise next to me, letting me know he could hear him too. *Clear your mind, relax and hold on tight to each other. This will feel weird, it might be best if you both close your eyes. Skye, grab my fur with your free hand and hold on tight.* Chaos said gently. I reached out and grabbed his thick fur on his back.

Chaos let out a mournful howl and I felt pressure building around my body as the fire heated up. I squeezed my eyes shut and told myself over and over that it would be okay. The fire began to roar in my ears, I kept my eyes tightly closed, forcing my mind to be empty. Josh's grip tightened like a vice on my hand. Suddenly, my feet weren't touching ground at all, making me want to panic. The sensation of falling brought my stomach up to my throat. I clenched my teeth, hoping I wouldn't throw up. The fire roared louder like a train thundering through a tunnel. The fire started to crackle and pop like fireworks, across my skin heating up again. The dropping sensation halted and the flames roared again.

With a screeching sound, like it had never been there, the fire left, only the original tiny flame dancing on the back of my hand gracefully. I opened my eyes feeling that my feet were on solid ground, the solid ground of the Underworld. I whispered a thank you to the little dancing flame and let it leave me. The little flame puffed out with a little curl of white smoke. I looked around feeling strangely at home and freaked out. I glanced over at Josh who was shaking his head like he was trying to clear it.

We stood in a huge field of waist high black grass, swaying gently in an unknown warm breeze. Looking around more closely, I could tell we were in the *punishment* part of the Underworld. Fires burned behind me in the distance, casting a sinister red-orange glow over the grass. The fire made me sure that Tartarus was below those flames burning behind us. I shuddered, thinking of all the horrible things that were kept in that pit being eternally punished. I could hear crying, screaming and wailing of the dead that burned in the fires and drowned in the rivers that Chaos told me about.

The dead wandered aimlessly around the grassy field, looking like they were still alive but really creepy versions of what they used to be. They wandered looking for something they would never find, with vacant expressions and white eyes. None of the dead had eye color or pupils, just void, empty, white space behind tired looking eyes. It freaked me out. I looked out beyond the vast field using my Demigod vision, which worked effortlessly down here, catching sight of a wide river surrounded by the dead and giant rocks that glittered from the light of the fires. Just past the river I caught the glint of the Palace towering over everything. I looked up, we were underground, but the ceiling appeared as high as the night sky on Earth, glittering with stars. *Stars... underground... what in holy Hades...* I thought feeling confused.

Those are glow worms, crystals and precious gems. Chaos said in my head answering my silent question. I looked at him closely seeing his full, true form. He stood as tall as a horse, but more broad in the chest. His fur looked shorter and sleeker than it did before. His eyes were full of dancing orange flames, instead of their still orange color.

You can hear me... inside my head? I asked feeling shocked.

Yup, our connection is stronger in our home realm than it is on Earth. I can hear you and you can hear me. We are a unit; I can feel your emotions better and hear all your thoughts. Your eyes are like mine too, by the way. Look at Josh's eyes, his are different too. He said with a yip. I turned and looked at Josh, who was looking around too with his mouth open. His eyes looked like bright molten gold with silver and copper flecks dancing across the gold. Light seemed to come *from* his eyes, instead of catching the light around us. He caught me staring at him and his jaw dropped when he caught sight of my eyes.

"Wow…your eyes…are on *fire*." he said stepping closer to me brushing a strand of hair off my face.

"You should see your own. It's like golden light is coming *from* them… like looking at the sun, but with the stars out too." I said looking at them, wanting to kiss him again.

Ahem…this is where our connection gets awkward. Could you please stop that? Chaos said whining.

You're right…sorry…we need to go right now anyways. We're wasting time. Lead the way Chaos…how do we get out of here? The dead are coming this way and freaking me out now. I said, watching as a dead woman in a short red dress and two men in orange prison uniforms started wandering over towards us. The screaming grew louder from the fires behind us, making the hairs on my neck stand up. Josh unsheathed his crossbow looking around, appearing nervous for the first time. I pulled my bow off my back and notched an arrow.

We need to leave here. A wall of fire will engulf this field soon and you don't want to get caught in it. Let's move, keep your eyes peeled for Demons. They should be far away from here, but that could change at any second. Chaos said heading in the direction of the Palace. Josh nodded at Chaos telling me that Chaos had spoken to both of us that time.

"Okay Chaos, I'll take your word on that. Let's get out of here." Josh said. We stuck close behind Chaos, weapons at the ready. I was perfectly okay with putting the sounds of the punished dead behind us. We walked as quickly as we could through the vast field passing the dead as we made our way towards the river. I couldn't help but stare at the dead as we passed them. Some were sobbing quietly, lying in the grass; others were talking to themselves aggressively and pacing around. There were a few who were just standing in one spot screaming, never pausing or drawing breath, just forever screaming. Some of them were aware of their surroundings and watched us as we passed by. Their white eyes staring at me were setting my nerves on edge.

As we got closer to the River Styx, the tall grass had thinned out, replaced by black gravel and giant obsidian rocks, shining in the light of the orange glow of the Underworld. Rubies, diamonds, emeralds and chunks of gold littered the gravel of all shapes and sizes, just lying all over the place.

All this money just lying around on the ground…crazy. I thought. Chaos let out a huff, but stayed quiet in my head. His ears were perked up and he kept looking around. We reached the bank of the River Styx, which was at least a mile wide. The waters of the fast paced river shimmered black and deep green. The waters were so clear you could see the bottom, which looked like it was covered in black sand and sparkling precious gems. I looked across the river seeing the looming black Palace in the distance, set up on a hill top covered in trees of every color known to man, plants, shrubs and sloping orange and black grass. I figured that was the *Garden* Artemis was talking about. Suddenly, the ground under our feet began to rumble, rattling my teeth. A loud roaring sound, like a stampede of horses, drowned out the sound of the rushing river waters. Chaos barked in a panic.

The fire is coming! Get behind me and that big rock! Get down on the ground and DO NOT touch a drop of the river water! Don't move until I tell you! Chaos's panicked voice rang through my mind.

My heart rate hitched up and I felt my adrenaline spike. Josh and I threw ourselves behind a giant obsidian rock, right at the edge of the river. The dead wandering near the bank of the water grouped together and stood, staring at the water in silence. Before I ducked down behind the rock and under Chaos's belly, I watched a wall of raging blue and orange fire tearing across the Field of Punishment at alarming speeds. The wall of flame reach near a mile high, burning everything it touched. The screams of the dead rang out over the roar of the fire. The dead gathered on the bank began to scream like a demonic church choir, sending chills over my skin.

I flung my head down behind the rock, Josh wrapped himself over top of me and Chaos crouched over top both of us. The wall of flames reached us and the bank with an earsplitting roar. The hellfire consumed our rock making the ground shake violently. The heat was unbearable, like my flesh was melting off my bones. The sound of the raging fire overtook the sounds of my own screaming. I could barely hear Josh roaring in pain from the heat as he pressed his body hard against mine. Chaos's chest heaved against us as he howled out in pain, taking most of the fire upon himself. I felt like I couldn't breathe, the heat seared my lungs like inhaling hot ash. I was sure I would die right here, burned alive. The fire kept coming, but stopped at the bank of the river unable to pass the waters as if blocked by an unseen wall of glass. Suddenly with an ear piercing screech and a whoosh of burning air the fire pulled back and was gone leaving nothing but steaming scorched earth in its wake.

I lay with my face and body smashed into the gems and gravel underneath Josh, both of us panting. Chaos let out a pitiful whine and fell over on the other side of our rock. I lifted my head and looked around through my dry scratchy eyes. Steam rolled off everything including Josh and my clothes. The group of dead that had been screaming, stood in their same spots. They no longer looked like humans, they were now charred statues, their flesh blackened and peeling off. I looked away feeling grossed out and burnt. Slowly Josh and I got untangled from each other, both of us stiffly moving. I felt sunburned, but after looking myself over, I didn't see any actual burns. My flesh was red and did look sun burned everywhere, even under my clothes, but nothing I couldn't handle. Josh was leaning near the river water. I reached out and grabbed his hand stopping him from touching it.

"Don't touch it. It will kill you unless you're swearing an oath upon its waters." I said, my voice coming out hoarse from my scorched throat. I crawled around the rock over to Chaos. He lay whimpering on his side. Most of his sleek fur had been burned off; his light pink flesh charred and blistered in patches all over his rib cage, back, legs and neck. Bright neon red blood, seeped out of a deep burn on his neck. My heart broke a little in my chest at the sight of him. He saved us.

"Chaos…please…what do I need to do to help you." I whispered to him as I crawled up to his big head and pulled it into my lap. Josh crouched down and looked over the wounds down Chaos's side. Chaos whined more, panting hard.

I…will heal, but it will take time. It's okay…I'm okay. His voice in my head sounded strained, like it hurt him to mind talk. His whining got louder and his breathing more ragged. I gently ran my hand over his head, fur and charred flesh stuck to my hand and came off the side of his face. I held back a gag and held up my hand to Josh who looked at me with wide eyes. I wiped my hand on my pants feeling sick and worried.

"Can we give you some Nectar big guy? Will you be able to use it?" Josh asked gently. Chaos's tongue lolled around in his black mouth as he let out another whine. Tears leaked out of my eyes, feeling cold against my burnt cheeks.

Yes, but I wouldn't be…able to drink it again. Ever…just a drop will do, we don't have the time for me to heal how… I normally do. Chaos said sounding weak. I hoped with all my might that we would never have to use it ever again. I decided we needed to risk it, we didn't have time to let him heal, even though Hellhounds healed fast, it wouldn't be fast enough. I pulled my bottle from my boot, pouring a drop into the twist cap so I didn't dump too much into his mouth by accident. I tipped the cap onto his lolling tongue. He swallowed hard and licked his lips. I capped the little bottle, put it away and waited, gently petting the one spot on Chaos's head that wasn't burnt.

We sat for a few minutes watching as the Nectar went through his system. His neck wound began to close before our eyes, the blood flow stopping entirely as the flesh knit together, as if being stitched by an invisible needle and thread, turning into a thick pink scar. The burns shrunk down, vanishing like they were literally being erased. New pink flesh replaced the charred flesh and black sleek hair grew fast, looking a little fluffier than the rest of his fur. It only took a few minutes; Chaos stopped panting and began to breathe normal deep breaths. I laid my head on his, petting him and kissing his big nose. He licked my face from neck to hairline covering me in dog drool, I didn't care. Chaos slowly stood and stretched out, Josh and I standing next to him. For good measure, Chaos turned and licked Josh's face.

"Gross…thanks for the bath. I'm glad your okay big guy." Josh said with a smile wiping the drool off his face and patting Chaos on the head.

Okay…wow that stuff is great! I feel like a pup again…thank you guys. We better hurry up, the wall of fire will come back again. So now we just need you to call for Charon, Skye. He will take us across the river. Grab a stone from the bank and throw it in the water, but, don't touch the water, not even a drop. Chaos warned. I did as he asked and threw a good sized stone into the rapid black waters of the wide river, the stone didn't even splash as it hit the water, it just sunk down as if it had always been there.

We didn't have to wait long for the Ferry Master to make his appearance. Where I had thrown the stone the water stilled. The current moved around the stilled spot in the like water around an iceberg. A moment later ripples formed on the glass-like surface, moving slowly. A long sharp black mast broke the surface of the river, followed by an eerie black carving of a screaming woman with empty eyes and her hands tied over her head, mounted to the front of the boat. The boat broke through the water silently, not making a sound as it came to rest on the surface, unmoving by the current of the river. Made entirely of ancient black wood and the size of a school bus, the ferry glided silently sideways to our shore leaving the water undisturbed at the bank. The ferry had no sails, no motor and no ores to make it move like that. Once it got close I realized how tall the sides were. I couldn't see over the sides onto the deck. I shuddered as a wrought iron black ladder dropped down on the bank in front of us. Chaos bounded over the ladder and right onto the boat in one jump. Josh and I looked at each other, he gave me a tight nod and reluctantly I began to climb the ladder. I climbed over the side and finally noticed the silent Ferry Master, Charon standing at the back of the boat. I nearly fell back over the railing at the shock of his appearance.

Charon must be where humans came up with the idea of the Grim Reaper. He towered over us, as tall as Chaos. A ragged black cloak covered his head, most of his face and billowed down to his feet. Black skeleton hands gripped a thick wooden stick, which I assumed was the rudder for steering the boat. A black chest stood at his covered feet, the lid open showing it was full of thick heavy looking golden coins. What I could see of his face had me wanting to get off the boat as soon as possible. His skin seemed to fade away when he moved his head, like looking at a ghost of a man one minute and a skeleton the next. His skull shone in the lights of the fires, shiny black like the onyx rocks on the shores of the river. His eyes were nothing more than empty sockets with a creepy green glow like the river waters. Josh made it over the edge of the ferry and stopped in his tracks, staring at Charon.

"*Payment.*" said a deep voice from where Charon stood. His mouth didn't move, but I know he must have spoken. *Chaos…we forgot to bring him money for passage to the other side…what do I do?* I thought feeling panicked. I did *not* want to experience Charon angry. I shuddered, thinking of the endless possibilities of what he could do to us.

Show him the necklace Skye. Josh, stand close by her side. Chaos said. Josh gave a nod and moved right beside me. I fumbled with my shirt collar and pulled out my key necklace from Hades, making sure Charon could see it.

"Ferry Master, I am Skye...Daughter of Hades. If...if it's not too much trouble, I...I mean we, the three of us, need to get to the other side of the river right away...Please it's an emergency." I said lamely. Charon stared me down. Well, I *think* he was looking at me, with no eyes he could have been looking anywhere. Charon let out a rumbling chuckle, like the ones in bad horror movies right before the villain takes over the world. The little hairs on my neck stood up at the sound. Josh moved in tighter to my side, our arms touching.

"*Ah...I see. The key to the realm... Very well little daughter.*" Charon said with another chuckle, sending more chills up my spine. He pulled the heavy wooden stick and the boat turned gracefully, facing the direction of the Palace. Charon moved with a slow moving grace unlike any being I had ever seen. He did nothing that was not necessary, he kept his body still, only moving his arms to keep the boat on a steady path across the vast river. I gripped the side of the boat expecting to be thrown off, but the boat glided so smoothly, I couldn't even tell we were on water or going against the flow of the rapids.

Josh pulled a small canteen of water from one of his pants pockets and handed it to me. I took two long gulps of the cool water handing it back to him, watching the colorful hill side and Palace loom closer. Chaos hung over the side of the boat, with his tongue lolling out like a golden retriever hanging out a car window. Chaos was right; the sounds of the screaming dead were nearly gone, as we got closer to the Palace. It was nice not to constantly hear the depressing sounds of the miserable dead.

The ride to the other side went by in only a few minutes. I watched as the sloping hillside of colorful trees drew closer. Charon eased the boat to the shore at the base of the colorful hillside and dropped the ladder down for us. Chaos bounded over the edge with an excited yip.

"Thank you Charon." I said in a small voice, still feeling unnerved by him. I approached the edge of the boat ready to get off the ferry and away from Charon's eerie glowing eyes.

"Thank you Ferry Master." Josh said with a bow. Charon dipped his hooded head to Josh and then with sudden alarming speed, Charon whipped around, facing up river. A terrifying black and silver sickle appeared in Charon's hand in a puff of black dust, making him really look like the Grim Reaper.

"Go...go now Children. Finish your task little daughter, as quickly as possible then leave this realm. Run and do not look back." Charon said in his deep voice. I didn't need to be told twice, I readied myself to climb down the ladder, when an explosion rattled the entire Underworld. The ferry launched back from the shore with a bone wrenching jolt, knocking me off balance. The ferry jolted again from another deafening explosion that sent me cascading face first over the side of the boat towards the thrashing black waters of The River Styx.

Chapter Twenty-one

Frantic screams tore out of my body. My fall seemed to last forever, as I watched the raging waters come closer to my face. I slammed my eyes shut, right before my face hit the water. Pain shot through my torso as I felt my ribs bend under some unknown pressure. I felt my body wrench violently to the side, as I was pulled by nothing but my ribcage. Pain laced through my head as my face hit something hard. *I must be dead. This much pain running through my body, must mean I'm dead.* I thought as hot pain tore through my core.

Slowly, I realized I wasn't drowning or under any kind of water, but on land. I rolled over to my back with a groan. My midsection felt like it was going to fall off me. I wrenched my eyes open to see Chaos standing over me, panting with part of my shirt stuck on one of his teeth. I was lying safely on the black gravel shore of the deadly river. Josh ended up by my side, his eyes wide and full of fear. I didn't need to ask to know what happened. Chaos had jumped up and caught me in his mouth mid fall. I couldn't believe how many times in a couple hours my dog had saved my life. I could feel the hot gooey trickle of blood running down my left cheek. I went to wipe it away finding gravel imbedded in my face. Fire tore up my side as I moved my arm, making me gasp out loud.

"Apparently...I need... to be babysat down here...you saved me again Chaos. Thank you...I feel terrible, but at least I'm not dead." I said, slow to form the words. I groaned out loud as another wave, of what felt like acid tore though my body. I felt myself trembling hard, unable to control it. Josh crouched down over me and moved my hair off my face. I tried to say thank you but only a wail of pain came out again.

Sorry, I couldn't let you fall in the river. It's going to be okay, I know it hurts. You have a pretty bad gash on your side from my teeth. You will have to drink some Nectar before my saliva gets too far into your system. Hellhound bites can kill. Our saliva is like poison to humans. It will shut down all your organs and then your heart if you don't drink Nectar right away. Chaos said with a whimper. He must have been talking to Josh too, because Josh pulled out his Nectar and dumped a drop into the twist cap forcing me to drink it. It tasted like honey and green apple. I wanted to drink more because it tasted so good; instead I swallowed and tried not to move. My insides burned like fire, but now a cooling sensation crept slowly through my body, putting out the burning pain. I could feel my sides healing as the skin pulled back together with odd tugging sensations. The fire ebbed away from inside my body and the pebbles that had been stuck in my face fell out next to my ear with little clunking sounds, which is gross considering they were falling out of my face.

Josh leaned in close watching my wounds heal up. His face looked hard and slightly angry again, like when we got in our spat during training. I tried to reach out and touch his hand but my hand just trembled in mid air.

"Don't you *ever* scare me like that again…I thought you were going to die in the river. I was *right there* and should have caught you. From now on I go first, *not* you. If Chaos hadn't been there…" Josh said in a hard voice, making me feel guilty and a little irritated. I huffed out a sigh and nodded, not wanting to argue with him again.

The ground rumbled again making my heart rate pick up. Josh looked over his shoulder behind him. I noticed the ferry was gone and the once calm river now raged, barley contained in its banks.

Slowly I sat up, feeling pretty darn good considering what had just happened. My shirt was torn up a little but all my weapons were still in place, including my bow and full quiver. I silently thanked Joe and her amazing skills with the holsters. The ground rumbled again making my teeth rattle.

"Josh, what is that?" I asked feeling really great now. That Nectar worked wonders, I felt like I could run for a thousand miles and never get tired. I hopped up and walked next to Josh. He pointed off past the curve of The River Styx. I followed what he was looking at feeling nervous. In the distance I could see what could only be described as *paradise.*   Elysium lay beyond the Palace, on the other side of two rivers and another field of black grass. I remembered Chaos had told me The Field of Waiting lay between the River Styx, The Lethe; the river of forgetting and the Palace. The beautiful paradise on the other side *had* to be Elysium. I stared in wonder, as the River Styx glittered next to the River Lethe, flowing side by side in front of the tropical paradise. The black glittering ceiling of the Underworld melted into vibrant blue skies over the rolling green hills and white beaches of Elysium. Palm trees, white sand, a massive variety of colorful fruit trees and teal waters from a mini ocean lay beyond the black grasses and darkness of the Underworld.

Black smoke billowed up from beyond a lush hillside in Elysium. I felt my heart speed up with anger as I noticed one side of Elysium appeared to be burning. *This is not right.* I thought. The Demons were there, attacking Elysium, working their way closer to the Palace and Tartarus. I wanted to go help my father. I felt outraged that the Demons would disturb the resting dead and destroy a place so beautiful.

"We need to go. They will make their way here if we don't get what we came for. Skye, we have to find Kirra and then find a way to help Miles's dad. We'll have plenty of time to kill Demons. Let's go…Chaos lead the way." said Josh seeing the look on my face as he firmly grabbed my hand turning me away. Reluctantly, I followed tearing my eyes away from the fires that didn't belong there.

I followed behind Chaos as we worked our way up the gravelly river bank and onto the grasses of the colorful hillside. We passed fruit trees, grape vines, pear trees, banana trees and every tree and plant that grew anything good to eat. My mouth watered at the sight of all the delicious looking fruits and vegetables. Josh followed close behind me with his crossbow at the ready, eyes peeled for anything. Besides the sounds of the battle raging in Elysium, it was silent, which sent my instincts buzzing. The trees moved lazily as if they were in a breeze, making their fruit look more tantalizing than ever. The soft breeze carried the delectable scent of each fruit and vegetable making me want to eat one bite of everything.

Tinkling laughter filled the vast Garden making me stop mid-reach for a crisp looking green apple. I hadn't even realized I was reaching out for the fruit. I shook my head feeling a little foggy. *With the Nectar in my system I shouldn't feel loopy at all.* I thought as my instincts screamed at me to stop and not touch a thing. The bell-like soft laughter sounded again. I looked around catching sight of Josh as he reached out to pluck a big red strawberry off a nearby bush. I ran over and slapped his hand before he could touch it. Chaos was rolling around in the grass on his back, appearing perfectly relaxed. Something wasn't right with this Garden; I pulled out my bow and notched an arrow. Josh seemed to be in a trance of some kind, looking at the hand I had slapped like it was something new to him. *Okay, something is defiantly wrong if he's acting like that.* I thought looking around cautiously. The laughter sounded again, sending chills up my spine. I whipped around sensing someone behind me.

"You cannot shoot me, I am the night." came a soft silky woman's voice from all around me. I spun in a circle feeling scared and slightly stupid.

"Show yourself! I am a Daughter of Hades and will not be toyed

244

with in my own realm!" I shouted over the pressing silence as I pulled back my bow string, ready to launch an arrow. The tinkling laughter sounded again, sending me spinning in a circle again.

"I am the night, I am the dark. This realm is mine as much as yours, little daughter. Do not eat the fruit or you will never leave." said the woman's voice again from every direction. A shadow flickered in front of me, slowly taking form of a person. She flickered into existence out of the shadow, like I can when I'm shadowing. I stared down the shaft of my arrow and waited, ready to let it fly if I had to. As she came into focus through the rolling shadows, I felt the cool caress of the shadows as they crawled up my own body. I welcomed them to me like an old friend. I looked over to Josh and Chaos, both of them lay frozen on the colorful grass as if time had stopped entirely. Josh was still staring at his own hand crouched by the strawberry bush and Chaos was mid roll with his tongue lolling out a few feet away. The shadow woman appeared clearly now through the dark shadows, her features all dark as night. She had long raven hair that blew behind her, melting in and out of the darkness that billowed like black mist around her. Her eyes were black like the night, but still appeared soft and gentle. She was short like me with a long strapless silk black dress that covered her feet. Pale skin, like moonlight, flickered through the shadows as they caressed her skin. She smiled gently at me, the shadows moving gracefully over her features.

"Who are you? And what happened to my companions?" I asked not feeling threatened by her now with the shadows dancing over my skin. I lowered my bow and put my arrow back in my quiver. She smiled again, making her look lovelier than ever.

"I am Nyx, Goddess of night, shadow and darkness. You call for me when you call to the shadows. I will not harm you, little daughter. Your companions are halted; they will be fine once we are done. We have much to discuss before you reach the Palace. We do not have much time." Nyx said in her lovely silky voice.

"I am Skye, Daughter of Hades. It's a pleasure to meet you, Goddess." I said with a respectable bow. Nyx dipped her head gracefully in return.

"You must not eat any of the food in this Garden. It will curse you for all time and you will not be able to leave this realm. This Garden is how Persephone became Queen of the Underworld. She consumed one pomegranate and could no longer leave the realm except during springtime. As a Goddess the curse does not affect her the same as a Demigod. The Garden will try to entice you, ignore it and pass through quickly. The food however, will not affect Chaos, so do not worry about him. As soon as you enter the Palace and hear the Prophecy, I will send Thanatos. I understand you have need of him?" Nyx asked, her face turning serious.

"Yes Goddess, I need his help as well. If I do not speak with him, my best friend…will lose her father." I said meeting her black eyes. The shadows swirled around us gently, while Josh and Chaos sat in the grass, still frozen in time. I wondered how she knew I needed Thanatos but felt so happy that she wanted to help I didn't ask. She was a Goddess and I've learned that Gods and Goddess's just know stuff.

"Understood. You are pure of heart and full of light. But you are also full of darkness. It is not always bad to give into the darkness as long as you do not get lost within it. You must press on; the battle will reach the Palace shortly. Persephone will not be there to greet you, she has been called out to fight with Hades. Kirra is expecting you, protected by Hellhounds, in the back of the Palace. You must leave as soon as you have what you need. Do not help, do not try to fight. You will be faced with the Demons soon enough little daughter. Once you hear the Prophecy, you must try to alter certain things; you will know them when you hear them and they come to pass. Remember, Prophecies can be changed based on the path you choose to take. Follow your heart, it will guide you when you think all is lost and save you when you need it most. I must go, do not try to help your father. If you are seen by the enemy, certain events of the Prophecy will be set into motion and you will die. Good luck little daughter. Call the shadows

when you need them and they will always answer." Nyx said as the shadows covered her entirely and she disappeared with the same bell-like laughter as before.

I wasn't sure if I liked the sound of what she said. I noticed the shadows covering me had gone, while Josh and Chaos were un-frozen again. Josh appeared to have come out of the weird daze of the Garden and was looking around confused. He caught the look on my face and jumped up from his crouch knowing something had happened.

"What's going on? I missed something big didn't I...you're okay right, nothing hurt you?" he asked looking me over with a little panic in his eyes. Chaos bounded over to us, seeming to be in a very cheerful mood.

She must have talked to Nyx, the Goddess of the darkness. She's pretty nice. Nyx has been around since before the Titans, if she told you anything I would listen to it Skye. The shadows know all the secrets of the world and she knows all the shadows, do exactly what she told you to do. Chaos said seriously to Josh and me.

"She told me to find Kirra on our own as soon as possible. I guess the battle happening right now is going to reach us in a little bit. Persephone is gone to help my dad fight. There are more Hellhounds inside watching Kirra and protecting the Palace. Nyx said she would send Thanatos here as soon as possible, so we don't have to try to find him on our own. We need to go now. We're out of time. And don't eat anything from this garden." I said. Josh nodded and as if to prove my point, the ground shook again and more fire licked the hillside in Elysium. Josh sighed and set a fast pace towards the Palace. I could smell the luscious scent from the berries and tress, but focused on the task at hand. We weaved in and out of trees and bushes making our way up the hillside as quickly as possible.

When we finally reached the top of the hill, the Palace shone in the dark, reflecting the fires from the entire Underworld. The Palace made the Castle at Chambers Academy look small and insignificant. The Palace was massive, probably more than 10 stories tall, with towers all over the place. Dragon sculptures of all sizes rested around the whole perimeter of the Palace and on top of the roof and towers. Smaller sculptures of owls, hellhounds and keys covered everything from window ledges, doors, balconies and down massive stone staircases. A dark jade marble courtyard surrounded the entire Palace with black stone fountains, stone benches and statues all over. We passed odd looking plants that appeared to have teeth, all over the courtyard in pots made of black stone.

I had Chaos lead us to the back entrance, it was too hard for me to tell which door was the back and which was the front. Chaos led us around a particularly large statue of a dragon, to a hidden door resting behind the dragon's tail. He placed his paw in the middle of the door and the stone melted away in a puff of black smoke. With the door gone, I could see a tall narrow tunnel with torches set in ancient iron brackets that led deep into the Palace. The torches cast an eerie red glow from the red flames guttering low in the dim. I didn't want to go in there at all, but I took a deep breath and followed behind Chaos with Josh right behind me. We both had our swords out and ready.

Be ready, the other Hellhounds will be on high alert and ask questions second if you know what I mean. I'll announce our presence once we reach near the end of the tunnel. This tunnel leads to a room with only one door as a way in besides this tunnel, where Kirra will most likely be. Skye, have your necklace out of your shirt in plain sight. We are coming near the end of the tunnel. Chaos said. I steadied myself as I watched Chaos raise his hackles and let out a deep howl that echoed around us through the tunnel. Josh stepped right next to me, tensed up like he was made of steel. We waited in silence as a higher pitched howl came from the other side of a solid stone wall at the end of the tunnel. Slowly the wall melted away and brighter orange light poured into the dark tunnel. I raised my sword just a little higher waiting.

Chaos stepped half way into the room first, blocking my view of the inside. Then all hell broke loose. Chaos snarled as a big grey ball of fur growled and came at him like a speeding car with fur. The grey Hellhound collided with Chaos in a frenzy of snarling and barking. A full on dog fight started, the sounds of it echoing loudly through the tight tunnel. Josh and I were pushed back deeper into the tunnel as another smaller Hellhound with reddish brown fur came through the doorway yipping and snarling. The three Hellhounds rolled and bit each other crammed into the tight space. Chaos seemed to be the biggest of the three and was able to push the grey and brown Hellhounds out of the tunnel and into the room.

Josh and I followed behind the snarling dogs, with our blades ready. I stepped into the room behind Josh. Good thing the room was enormous. The three Hellhounds fought and rolled around knocking over heavy looking dark wood tables and armchairs, scattering furniture all over the place. My adrenaline was begging for me to jump into the dog fight and help, but I held myself back knowing one bite from any of the Hellhounds could kill me. Josh stood protectively in front of me with his deadly looking swords raised at the ready, watching the fight like a hawk. We moved around past the tunnel door, to the other side of the room near the massive black stone fireplace. I couldn't take it anymore. Chaos was holding his own well enough, but had some pretty bad bites from the other Hellhounds on his shoulder. I shoved Josh to the side and stepped as close to the fight as I dared. I pulled flame from the fire behind us and coaxed it into my hand. I could only hope I knew what I was doing and didn't hurt Chaos.

"Stop! I command you to stop!" I yelled over the sounds of the fight as I threw my hand out letting the fire fly out and roar over the Hellhounds. As soon as I let the flame go, I pulled it back to me as quickly as possible. I wanted to scared them, not fry them. It worked. All three Hellhounds stopped mid-fight, whimpering with their heads down on the floor. The three of them whined a little bit and kept their heads down in submission. I felt like I was safe enough now, as I walked up to them. Josh moved close to my side again with his swords still held at the ready. I lowered my sword and pulled the blades back, only keeping one out. Chaos was by far the biggest of the three. I was able to look closer at the two new Hellhounds. The grey one, had a thick silvery grey coat, with white feet. He glanced up at me showing his crystal blue eyes. He was large, nearly the size of a donkey, but was smaller than Chaos. The brown one had to still be a puppy. The brown Hellhound was only the size of a mini pony with a coppery tone to it's fluffy coat and whimpered more than the grey one.

"Chaos, you may get up. You two...what are your names?" I asked still holding a firm edge to my voice. The other two slowly sat down, keep their heads bowed, not making eye contact. The grey one spoke in my head first.

I am Blade. I guard the Palace and Hades. You are his daughter aren't you? I can smell it. The grey Hellhound said. His voice was deep like Chaos's but raspier.

"I am. My name is Skye, Daughter of Hades; this is Josh, Son of Zeus. What's your name?" I said addressing the small brown one. The copper one whimpered and kept looking up and down again, appearing to be shy.

They call me Blaze. I just got old enough to be a guard. Blade is my big brother; please don't burn me Miss Skye. I'll be good okay. The little brown one said in a soft sweet voice. I shouldn't have been surprised that there would be female Hellhounds, but I was anyways. I reached out and pet little Blaze on the head and behind the ears. She responded by leaning into my hand, looking up at me with lovely soft hazel eyes. Josh pet Blade on his muzzle, while Chaos stood by and watched.

"I won't hurt either of you. I'm here to speak with Kirra, the soul you're guarding. Is she here? It's very important that I speak to her. You two also need to be ready for a fight, we spoke with Nyx, she told us the Demons will be here shortly looking for Kirra. It is very important that they do not get to her." I said seriously. Both Hellhounds nodded.

"Sometimes, I worry that you need your eyes checked." Kirra's voice came from behind me. I whirled around to find her standing right behind me, smiling. She looked the same as she did before she was attacked by the Demons, her scar wasn't across her lovely skin anymore. She wore plain black combat gear and her long raven hair flowed freely down her back. I met her sparkling teal eyes and warm lovely smile. I ran forward and hugged her, excited to find that she was solid and not like a ghost. She returned the hug tightly. We broke apart and Kirra held my shoulders looking into my eyes.

"Skye, we don't have much time. We are literally down to less than an hour. I will tell you everything. The Prophecy has already begun. Please listen closely and do not react when I start. When I finish the Demons will be at the Palace, you need to leave as soon as possible, just run and get out of here. Do you understand?" she asked me as her eyes bored into mine. I nodded and she let go of my shoulders and addressed Blade and Blaze.

"Go watch the tunnel and the door with Chaos. Do not put yourselves in harm's way; simply warn us if they are coming. Go now and stay sharp." She said as all three Hellhounds went to the only two doors in the large room. Josh up righted three chairs and we all sat down, Josh keeping his crossbow trained on the door where Blade stood, while Chaos paced between the two entry ways. I faced Kirra sheathing my sword and pulled my bow, notching an arrow, in case of anything.

Kirra put her head back and rolled her shoulders. She took a deep breath as a shudder ran though her body. When she brought her head down to look at me again, her eyes were no longer teal, but entirely blacked out. I nearly jumped out of my chair. She opened her mouth but didn't move her lips, just left her mouth gaping open. Her voice started speaking while her lips stayed still on her open mouth. I wanted to slap her or run. The sight of her turned my blood to ice. Her raspy voice speaking caught my attention.

"From the Mother, for the Son
Rose up the might of The Dark Ones
From under The Mountain through blackened skies
The Dark Ones shall aid He to rise
Titans will come from the depth of flame
Aided by Dark Ones, Titans shall rein
Darkness and chaos will consume all life
Forever shall the World be turned to night
The mighty Gods shall fight and fall
The Titans now shall rule them all
Only the Children, bore by Gods
Can unite together to beat the odds
The suffering shall end at the hand of Four
The Chosen Ones will halt the war
Child of The King of the Dead
Will bring all the chaos to end
Child will fall without the other Three
Given to Dark Ones, the power to free
Child of the God of the Sea
Has the power to fall the enemy
Child of the God of the Sun
Shall harness the light, to fall the One
Child of the Goddess of Wisdom
Has the power to hold the Prison
Trials and perils the Four shall see
Leaders of all the Children, the Four will be
One will pass through darkness whole
To emerge with scars upon their soul

One will fall to enemy hands
Returning broken, with their plans
One will watch the others fall
Finding power to save them all
One will face the enemy alone
To save the world, both sky and below
The suffering will end, at the hand of Four
The Chosen Ones will halt the war."

Kirra's raspy voice said, while chills climbed up my spine. Kirra rested her chin on her chest and took a few deep breaths, when she lifted her head she looked normal again. Chaos had stopped pacing and sat in the middle of the room looking at us, whimpering a little bit. I thought over what I had just heard.

The Prophecy clearly said, without the *four chosen* ones fighting together or even alive, the enemy will win. *That's the key.* I thought. The Demons would need to know that to win the war. If they killed any one of the chosen four, they would win and be able to capture me. I looked over at Josh who had a pen and paper in his hand writing fast while War perched on his shoulder. I had been so absorbed in Kirra, I hadn't even noticed the little owl. Josh tied a note to the little owl's leg and War flew to my knee, let me pet him and took off again down the tunnel. I looked over at Josh feeling confused.

"I sent word that we are okay, just waiting on our *Hit man* friend then we'll be home." Josh said. I understood the coded message. Thanatos was the Gods hit man, that way if War was caught with the note, nobody would know we had already heard the Prophecy and now waited for Thanatos. Kirra stood up facing the door leading to main part of the Palace, her eyes wide. Her form began to fade and flicker, like she was becoming a ghost. She turned to me, right before she faded out to nothing.

"Run." She said as she faded out, right as the whole Palace shook, throwing me out of my chair.

Chapter Twenty-two

Blade barked and flew back from the big stone door barking madly as cracks spider webbed across the door and walls. I jumped up from the floor, right as Josh moved to my side with Chaos and Blaze. Blade bolted over to us as the ground shook again. I called the fire from the fireplace over to me and put up a wall of flames in front of the cracking black stone door. I let more fire engulf me. It was time to go. Our time was up. My heart ached for Miles as I thought of not being able to speak with Thanatos.

Not in here Skye! We have to be outside the Palace before we can travel by fire. Quick, out the tunnel! Blaze and Josh go in front of her and make sure the way is clear, Blade and I will follow. Skye, keep the flames hidden in your hand and stay behind all of us. Do not be seen! Go Now! Chaos bellowed in my head. I let the fire travel to just my fist and closed it tight, drawing my sword again. I threw my dropped bow over my shoulder and followed Blaze and Josh out of the room into the dark tunnel. The light from the torches blazed hotter, lighting the way, casting flickering sinister shadows over the tunnel walls. We ran to the end, Blaze letting out a high pitched bark, causing the other door to seal off the room and open the door at the end to the Garden. I could see the dragon tail as we ran. Another explosion shook the tunnel dropping pebbles and dust from the ceiling. We picked up speed all of us bursting out the other side.

Once outside, fires burned all around the lovely Garden and the complete chaos of battle surrounded us. Demons were battling Hellhounds, flying serpents, dragons and the dead dressed in black armor. Dead soldiers rode on black winged horses cutting down Demons. Large burley men so tall they had to be Giants dressed in bronze armor, picked up Demons with their bare hands and ripped the Demons bodies in half. I caught a glimpse of my father near the river bed. Hades was by far more frightening than the Demons. He stood more than ten feet tall dressed in black armor encrusted with rubies, his tattoos fully ignited in flame. He cut Demons down with a long black sword engulfed in blue flame. White hot flames shot from his other hand turning a Demon to dust. His eyes were full of the brightest orange fire it made the fire around us look dim. Pure rage made his face blur with flames from the light of his eyes.

I itched to go help, my adrenaline screaming through my veins as I felt the fire heat up in my hand. Josh reached out and grabbed my elbow, leading me to behind the massive dragon statue and pulling me into a crouch.

"We have to go right now. We're still hidden right here, so stay down. Remember the Prophecy, if you're seen using any powers, the whole thing is over now because they will come for you. We *will* fight. Let's go *now*." Josh said firmly gripping my arm. I met his swirling golden eyes and gave a tight nod. I didn't want to go, but he was right. Chaos came over and I grabbed his sleek coat engulfing all of us in flames. Blade bounded over, towing a struggling Blaze in his teeth by her tail.

Take her. Please! She is too young and I will not stand by and let her get herself killed. Take her now! Please daughter of Hades! She must survive! Blade said whining while little Blaze struggled against his hold on her tail. I nodded and reached out grabbing Blaze's thick coppery brown coat engulfing her in fire. She whined and pulled against me, but Chaos grabbed the nape of her neck in his mouth and held her in place.

Goodbye brother. I will see you again. I promise to keep her safe with us on Earth, Skye and I will protect her. Fight hard and stay alive. Chaos said to Blade. Blade huffed and took off towards the fight in a flash of grey fur. I felt the fire burn hotter as Chaos took the lead; I slammed my eyes shut and focused, as I felt myself falling again. The sensation of falling caught me off guard a little, I thought we would travel up this time around. The fire roared in my ears as I began to sweat, gripping Josh's hand hard, when my feet finally landed on solid ground. I opened my eyes as the fire dwindled down to nothing and I let it go with whispered thanks.

We were back in the Infirmary, but it was daylight. I looked around confused. The room was empty. Nobody seemed to even be here. Josh looked around confused too. Chaos was back in husky size with a little brownish copper colored husky puppy still in his mouth. Blaze whined sadly and Chaos gently set her down licking the side of her cute little face. She whimpered and looked up at me, making my heart melt. I walked over and scooped her up holding her against my chest.

"It's okay little Blaze. My father will keep your brother safe." I said to her. She didn't respond in my head and I shot a worried look to Chaos.

She hasn't bonded to you. So when you're here in the Earth realm she can't talk to you. You can only talk to me… She says she knows and it's okay. She just misses him and is scared. Chaos said with a little whine. I guess that suited me okay, too many voices in my head would probably send me to the loony bin.

"So…what do we do? We have to tell the others about the Prophecy and what happened. Where is everyone?" said Josh still looking around as if they would pop out of the cabinets. I walked over to Miles's dad's room and found it also empty. *What the hell is*

257

going on? I thought to myself. Slowly we checked all the rooms and Nurse Lane's office finding everything deserted. *Something doesn't feel right. People should be in here.* I thought feeling unnerved.

We slowly walked out of the Infirmary doors, under the grand staircase, still seeing no one and hearing nothing. It's like the whole school picked up and left. I set Blaze down and had her get up to large husky size with Chaos. I pulled my bow and notched an arrow. Josh pulled his sword and let out a low whistle calling for Alke. I looked around, the Castle was deserted but the Dining Hall had been transformed into an elegant ballroom. Fall decorations hung from the rafters, lined the windows and covered the tables, which had been pushed to the sides around the dance floor area in the middle. We slowly crept to the front doors, eyes peeled for any sign of life.

"Once we get outside we won't have much cover. Let me go first, you watch my back. Chaos and Blaze, you two watch our sides. Remember to stay quiet." Josh whispered sheathing his sword and pulled out his crossbow, loading an arrow. He slowly opened the door, grey stormy daylight creeping into the entryway. Cool air breezed past us smelling of sulfur and rot. My adrenaline spiked up, kicking my senses into overdrive. *Demons.* Chaos growled in my head. Josh crept out first, headed to the woods for cover. I followed with my bow at the ready. Blaze and Chaos came out with their hackles raised, sniffing the air. Blaze snuffed and sneezed once she caught scent of the Demons. Chaos growled moving closer to my side.

Something is wrong. I smell Demon flesh, but don't hear anything. I can't even hear birds. Chaos said with another low growl. We hurried to the tree line and hid in the low hanging branches. I called the shadows right away, this time covering Josh as well. I didn't think it would work but it did. I thanked Nyx with a whisper, feeling a cool caress over my face, letting me know she heard. Josh looked down at himself with a slight look of shock then nodded at me. We pressed on towards the dorms, sticking to the tree line moving slowly and quietly. I was getting worried about everyone. The Demon smell still billowed in the wind, but the school seemed frozen in time and vacant. *Did they kill everyone?* I thought as fear tore through my gut.

We finally reached the secret steps to my dorm and snuck inside. I couldn't hear anything as we climbed up the steps and reached my floor. I went to my room and opened the door finding it empty. I let the shadows go that still covered us, feeling tired for the first time since I drank the Nectar in the Underworld. I headed out of my cold room and we checked Miles's room. Her bed hadn't been slept in and everything was still neatly in place. I looked around feeling worried now. A tap on her window made me jump and nearly let loose an arrow. Alke, Josh's eagle, sat perched on the outer window sill. Josh hurried over and climbed up the desk and let his beautiful bird inside. Alke fluttered down to Miles's desk chair and perched there. Josh seemed to be listening to whatever the eagle had to tell him. I waited patiently for news, trying my best to not interrupt. After a few minutes my impatience took over. Damn patience to Hades, I needed answers.

"What's going on Josh?" I said with a slight edge to my voice. Alke fluttered up to Josh's shoulder and Josh finally faced me. He had a grave expression on his face, which I did not like at all.

"Everyone is in the training center. The soldiers that were supposed to come in on Sunday have been showing up in smaller groups to avoid the Demons. Hephaestus sent in some Automatons last night. The Demons attacked a group of soldiers on the road early this morning. Thanks to the Automatons and our team, we only lost three soldiers. The Demons that had been watching the road that didn't escape are dead. The whole school is in combat training right now and the kids under 16 years old have been sent away already secretly. Skye, we were in the Underworld for nearly two days. It's Friday afternoon." Josh said looking shocked. My mind reeled. *Two freaking days! I thought it was only a few hours!* I thought feeling shocked and relieved. Apparently time worked very different in the Underworld. We needed to get to the training center and find out what happened.

"Josh we need to get over there. I have to break it to Miles that we couldn't save her father. Then we have to tell the others what the Prophecy said. Miles is going to hate me Josh…so you will have to convince her to help us figure out what the Prophecy means." I said sadly as I met Josh's molten golden eyes. He brushed a strand of my hair to the side sending the feeling of fire and ice across my cheek.

"She won't be mad. You did everything you could do Skye…it will be okay." he whispered still touching my face gently. I shuddered as he pulled away. We left the room and headed out to the training center, weapons ready.

We began to see more signs of life once we reached the stables, which made me let out a breath of relief and put away my bow. Students were training with the horses, both human and horse in full battle armor taking down straw dummies in the outdoor riding arenas. I spotted Zach on Shake's back shouting orders to the riders. It took all my self control not to run across the arena to him and jump on him and his silly giant horse. I settled for a wave and Chaos barked. Zach's face lit up and he waved back. Zach rode over to another rider said something to them and headed our way at a full gallop. Zach dismounted gracefully and leapt over the fence. He pulled me into his arms and flung me around in a circle laughing.

"I'm so glad you're back little mouse! I was so worried about you. Come on we have to talk to the others right away. Their all in the War Room, you two missed a lot and we need to hear everything about…the east side of the mountain." Zach said looking around realizing other students were listening. I shot Zach a questioning look as we headed towards the training center. Zach explained in whispers that they had to come up with a plan once we left. Apparently the Dean had realized we wouldn't be back very quickly so he came up with a cover story saying that we were scouting the east side of Mt. Etna, just in case the rouge Demigod caught wind of the plans.

We got into the large indoor training arena to find students full on training for battle. Every mat was full with students sparring and every practice weapon was out and being used. Soldiers in green Army fatigues were leading groups of students barking orders and showing them different techniques. I spotted Big Mike right away as he showed off his axe and shield skills. Big Mike had his own small group of fighters and was showing them to move as a unit with their shields, like the Spartans. He saw us and nodded calling a halt to his group. He followed us into the War Room. Everyone was in the War Room; Mom, Melinda, Miles, Kayla, Cam, Nurse Lane, the Dean and Artemis. I hugged everyone, feeling relieved that they were all here. I pulled Miles to the side feeling a lump in my throat. I felt like I was going to break her heart…it was killing me to have to tell my sweet Miles that I failed her.

"Miles…I couldn't get to Thanatos. The Demons attacked the Palace and we had to leave right away. I know it was two days up here, but down there it was only a few hours…I…I'm so sorry I couldn't save your dad. I'll go back on my own and find Thanatos again. I'm sorry I broke my promise." I said looking into her glittering emerald eyes. She was smiling though. *Why is she smiling? Did she not hear me?* I thought to myself. Miles pulled me into a hug again making my heart break again. She should be mad at me or disappointed at the very least. She pulled out of the hug still grinning from ear to ear.

"Skye…you did exactly what you said you would do. Nyx said she would send him to you right? Well she didn't say *when* she would send him or *where*. She sent him yesterday. He saved my dad in literally a split second. He removed the curse…but it came with a price. My dad is bound to Thanatos now. My dad was turned fully immortal and as long as he stays as Thanatos right hand man, no curse will ever hurt him and he cannot die. He's in the Underworld right now fighting the Demons alongside your father. You probably *just* missed him." Miles said. I breathed a sigh of relief and sent a silent thanks to Nyx.

"How did you know I spoke to Nyx?" I asked. She smiled again right as War landed on her shoulder.

"Josh sent word to us with War, remember? Thanatos himself showed up right after War did. I'm so glad you weren't hurt. We were all really worried you know. Zach was about to come down there last night, but I *knew* you would be back. Come on we need to get to work. Let's sit down and hear the Prophecy and come up with a plan." She said walking to the table. The others were already seated waiting for me. Coffee and my mom's cookies sat in the center of the table. I nearly jumped at them, as I sat down and poured myself a hot cup of coffee and shoved a cookie in my mouth. Kayla had left when I was talking to Miles and brought in some steaks from the nearby slaughter house for Chaos and Blaze. Blaze had taken to Kayla and sat curled in her lap down to the size of a little husky puppy again. Kayla caught me staring at her and smiled at me.

"We bonded Skye. It's crazy that I would bond with a Hellhound from your father's realm, but I could hear her as soon as she walked in this room. Can I keep her?" Kayla asked with hope in her pretty yellow eyes.

"Of course you can Kayla. I wouldn't have it any other way. I'm glad she found you, I honestly didn't know what I could do to help her up here without her brother." I said sincerely. Blaze whined and yipped at me wagging her tail.

"Thanks Skye…from both of us." Kayla said as she cuddled Blaze, petting her head gently. Joe walked in causing the chatter around the table to halt. Joe pulled me into a quick hug and then shook hands with Josh, as she sat down at the head of the table. Apparently I missed a lot; if I wasn't mistaken, it seemed Joe was now the commander of the army.

"Alright people. Let's get started, questions at the end. I need to hear everything Skye. What happened from when you got there to when you left? I need the whole Prophecy as well. Then we can tell you what happened here while you were gone. Sound good?" Joe said meeting my eyes. I nodded and saluted her.

Josh and I told them everything. From the Fields of Punishment to The River Styx, Nyx, Charon, the garden and the Demon attack. Josh had written down the Prophecy, but in his own code so only he could read it. I was glad for that because I couldn't recite it word for word. The lines about four of us facing trials and death set my heart rate up, making me feel panicked and freaked out. Josh pulled out his paper from a pocket in his cargo pants and began to read it out loud.

"From the Mother, for the Son
Rose up the might of The Dark Ones
From under The Mountain through blackened skies
The Dark Ones shall aid He to rise
Titans will come from the depth of flame
Aided by Dark Ones, Titans shall rein
Darkness and chaos will consume all life
Forever shall the World be turned to night
The mighty Gods shall fight and fall
The Titans now shall rule them all
Only the Children, bore by Gods
Can unite together to beat the odds
The suffering shall end at the hand of Four
The Chosen Ones will halt the war
Child of The King of the Dead

Will bring all the chaos to end
Child will fall without the other Three
Given to Dark Ones, the power to free
Child of the God of the Sea
Has the power to fall the enemy
Child of the God of the Sun
Shall harness the light, to fall the One
Child of the Goddess of Wisdom
Has the power to hold the Prison
Trials and perils the Four shall see
Leaders of all the Children, the Four will be
One will pass through darkness whole
To emerge with scars upon their soul
One will fall to enemy hands
Returning broken, with their plans
One will watch the others fall
Finding power to save them all
One will face the enemy alone
To save the world, both sky and below
The suffering will end, at the hand of Four
The Chosen Ones will halt the war."

He finished reading as chills ran up my spine. The fate of the world sat heavy on my shoulders, making my insides squirm uncomfortably. The others looked around in silence.

"Well...that seems easy enough. I thought it was going to be all death and destruction." Cam said with a chuckle. I couldn't help but laugh too. There was nothing else to be done except face it and move forward. The others laughed as well.

"I'll pass the word on to the Gods. I'll be back tonight for the Ball. I'm glad you two are alright. See you soon." Artemis said with a bow as she flashed out with a blinding light and the scent of the woods.

"The Ball is still on?" Josh asked once Artemis had gone.

"Yup, we all decided after the attack the students needed something to fight for, like a reminder that life is still normal most of the time and this war will pass. It was Miles's idea and we couldn't say no, because as usual, she's right. The students are really excited and with the soldiers arriving early, we have guards during the Ball." The Dean said proudly, making Miles blush a little.

"Perfect." Josh said with a wink at me, which of course caused me to blush right away. Damn him to Hades.

"Okay so what did we miss? I hear we were gone for *two whole days*. In the Underworld it was literally only a few hours…this is nuts how much time we missed. We heard there was an attack on the road?" Josh asked looking to Zach. Zach nodded his expression turning grave.

"There was, we lost three good men but wiped out the Demon guard on the road. Obviously, we knew they were watching the road because of Charlie's attack, but with all the students still untrained we didn't want to risk open attack on them without help. Joe sent word for the Automatons and her dad came through. Hephaestus sent us four Automatons right before the attack of the soldiers. They are pretty cool. They are disguised as statues that now guard both roads leading up here to the grounds. They wiped out the Demons and sent the rest scrambling. We don't expect them back until they re-group. That gives us more time to train up. It also gave Artemis time to get all students under the age of 16 home. For now only students who are of combat age can be here. The General of the US Army gave us those orders right after you guys left anyways and after the attack on the road we jumped into action." Big Mike said as he pet Chaos on the head.

"Yesterday we each got our own group to train with. Mike is training Children of Ares and Athena for front line defense. He has them trained up a lot like the Spartans, moving as a single unit. Zach is in charge of Children of Hermes, Athena and Demeter. They will be the second line on horseback. Kayla is training up Children of Hephaestus, Hera and Ares to mend and make weapons as well as provide the third line of hand-to-hand defense. I have the medics and archers, all Children of Apollo, Aphrodite and Hermes. Miles is working with a group on stealth attacks and traps, all Children of Athena, Ares and Hermes. The Children of Hera and Dionysus are working with Joe on a little bit of everything. Josh would you mind stepping in and helping everyone with their groups? You're the expert on use of our super senses and I think it would help everyone if you could teach people to use them." said Cam meeting Josh's eyes. Josh nodded and gave Cam a salute.

"What about me? What can I do?" I asked feeling a little left out.

"You will be working with everyone as well. I want you to stick with Josh and train up on everything you possibly can. We want to keep you a secret still and by sticking you with Josh it makes you look like a Child of Zeus." Zach said in a tone that told me not to argue, which made sense all things considered. Working with Josh gave me authority like a child of Zeus but didn't put me directly into a group where it might come out that I belong to Hades, like around the horses who clearly hate me. *Perfect, because I don't know where to even start.* I thought feeling slightly relieved.

"Okay, you're up to speed and so are we. Go rest and shower. We will see you at dinner and the Ball. I think you deserve to rest up for now. Tomorrow starts a whole new round of intense training and you will need to be well rested for that. Now, get out of here and enjoy tonight. I put a dress for tonight in your closet Skyelaa." My mom said from the corner of the room where she and Melinda had been working on maps and plans while we were all talking. I didn't need to be told twice. I got up, hugged my mom and mom two, said my goodbyes to everyone and headed out of the War Room with Chaos and Josh.

"So…would it be weird if I stopped by your room after I change and shower?" Josh asked. My heart rate picked up and of course I blushed. I made sure we were outside the training arena before I answered him. Lindsay and her weird friend Maddie were watching us like hawks. Maddie made me feel nervous whenever I was around her, it was probably her neon purple eyes, or the fact that she never seemed to smile. Once we were out of their sight I turned to face Josh noticing soot and dirt smudged his handsome face making him look rugged and rough. *Like I can tell him no when he looks like that.* I thought to myself.

"Sure, that's fine with me…so I guess I'll see you in like an hour?" I said looking up at him. He winked at me and pushed my extremely messy hair off my forehead.

"Sounds good. I'll be there in an hour." He said and kissed the back of my hand.

Chapter Twenty-three

My stomach swarmed with butterflies as I pulled on a pair of black sweat pants and a tank top. I was really thinking like a girl, feeling torn between being comfortable and wearing something cute. After staring into my closet for a while I settled for the sweats and flopped down on my bed next to Chaos feeling exhausted.

If you're planning on doing anything shockingly human with Josh please let me know so I can leave the room. Chaos said in a sarcastic tone. He had been hanging out with me too much, his sarcasm had vastly improved. I laughed at him trying to keep my fluttery tummy calm.

"Good Gods Chaos...I'm not that kind of girl. You know I really like him and all, but I still worry that he might not really like me back once he really gets to know me. All he knows about me is I'm clumsy, stubborn and not as good of a fighter as I thought." I said feeling a little embarrassed. Chaos snuffed at me and licked my hand.

Well that's true...but he will love the other things about you. You're brave, loyal and funny too. I know that about you. It's the best thing about you, you're different than most humans because you're more than just one thing. Chaos said and he licked my face. I wiped my slimy cheek off on the back of my hand.

"Thanks pup that's gross. I guess we'll have to wait and see what happens. Just don't let me do anything overly stupid." I said right as someone knocked on my door.

"Come in." I said as my tummy fluttered again. Josh opened the door dressed also in sweat pants and a sweatshirt. He had a paper bag with food in it and set it on my bed.

"Hey, I thought you might be hungry so I brought lunch…or pre-dinner I guess." He said sitting on the edge of my bed. He pulled out two turkey sandwiches, two green apples, two waters and a bunch of my mom's cookies. My mouth watered as I set up our picnic lunch on my bed. Chaos snuffed at Josh, who laughed at him.

"You think I forgot you? No faith in me dog." Josh said as he pulled out a paper plate and two steaks wrapped in white paper. Chaos yipped happily and licked Josh's face as he jumped off my bed nearly knocking me over. Josh set Chaos's food down on the floor and we all ate in silence. I had no idea I was starving until all my food was gone and I was thinking about checking my junk food stash for more. Josh finished his food and put the trash back in the paper bag and lay back on my bed.

Okay…I'm going for a run and to see if Blaze can come too. I don't want to be the one to witness weird human mating rituals. Can you open the door? Chaos said making me blush ten shades of red. *Oh my Gods this damn dog and his dirty mind.* I thought as I opened the door for him.

"You have a filthy mind pup. There are not going to be any *human mating rituals* happening here…Go on… I'll leave the door cracked so you can get back in here. Be careful okay." I whispered to him out in the hall. He snuffed at me and took off down the steps. I came back in the room to find Josh sitting up watching me.

"I heard that…*Demigod* remember." Josh said with a crooked smile. I felt my face turn redder, which should have been impossible and I put my face in my hands. Josh started laughing, deep and low in his chest. I walked over and punched his shoulder, which made him laugh harder. I sat on the edge of the bed debating whether or not to hit him again.

"I love it when I make you blush. It's the cutest thing, cuz all your freckles stand out. It's a huge compliment that I can make you do that." He said once he stopped laughing at me. I half heartedly slapped his arm again, but couldn't help smiling. He shocked me by pulling me into his side and laying us down together. My heart rate kicked up and heat rolled over my skin. He snuggled up behind me with his face buried in my hair and an arm thrown casually over my waist. We fit together like puzzle pieces.

"You smell like cinnamon. It reminds me of Christmas time." He said causally through my hair.

"That's what Zach's horse said. But he said I smell like smoke too and he didn't like it." I said and instantly felt stupid. I couldn't believe I started talking about what a freaking horse said about me. Damn it to Hades. Josh chuckled.

"Quit being nervous…You have no reason to be. I like you and I love the way you smell. That horse is an idiot anyways. After all we've gone through I just wanted to be with you before the Ball, just the two of us. You and me against the world right?" he said softly.

"You meant that? Even though you were mad at me before we left?" I asked rolling over to face him. His eyes were closed and he cracked them open at my sudden movement.

"Yeah, one thing you will learn about me is I never say anything I don't mean. Yes I was mad at you, but it was wrong for me to be mad. You don't know the whole story or why I train and fight the way I do. I get really hard core when I'm training others. I'll be nineteen in January. I've already served six months in the Army. When I turned eighteen last January I opted out of high school and served my six months instead of waiting until after graduation. After what happened during my deployment, the Army decided to place me at this school, not just for finishing my education, but to become a Combat Trainer next year. I'm interning with Sgt. Scott. He was my squad leader in the Army. He saved my life in Ukraine…I was the only one he could save." Josh said his voice low and gruff. I could tell he didn't want to talk about it. I felt shocked that he wasn't a high school student, but an intern and almost 19. I didn't see that coming, but I guess I never asked. I kept quiet and let him keep talking.

"We were on a scouting mission in a small village in Ukraine. There were 15 of us fresh out of boot camp and thrown under Sgt. Scott's command. It was supposed to be an in and out mission, no combat. We were there to gather intelligence, or so I was told. Late on our fourth night in the village, Russian rebels on their way to a larger town decided to pass through the village instead of going around. My squad was sleeping in an abandoned house near the village courthouse. Two of our night guards had fallen asleep on watch, they had simply gotten too comfortable with the villagers. The rebels came in peaceful and quiet at first, but the villagers decided they wanted to fight back.

We woke up to gunfire and hand-to-hand fighting between the rebels and villagers. My squad tried to get out…just leave unnoticed, we had strict orders *not* to interfere. The villagers knew we were there and expected us to help them. The rebels saw us trying to leave the house. Gunfire came at us, killing two of my friends instantly in front of my eyes. We took cover behind the house and shot back. There was too many of them and not enough of us. I killed more of them than I want to know. I went into survival mode. Sgt. Scott and I were the only Demigods in the squad, so we were faster and better fighters than the others. The rebels tried to take us hostage then. We fought with hard… cutting them down. I watched my friends fall all around me, so to death…others just injured. I let it get to me and faltered, that's when I took a knife to the chest and a bullet through the arm. Sgt. Scott pulled me back and hurled a grenade at the rebels. It killed most of them and we were able to escape…but it also killed the injured guys still alive in our own squad. Some of them were *only* wounded and we didn't save them." Josh said with a hard look on his beautiful face. I reached out and rest my hand on his cheek, feeling the heat of his skin and rough stubble from not shaving. He had no tears in his eyes, but I could see how much it still hurt him.

"That's not your fault, or Sgt. Scotts. I'm so sorry… I don't know what to even say… you guys shouldn't have even been there. Maybe look at it this way… maybe you had to survive so you could help me. I don't know how fate or destiny works, but I know that I need you…I need you to help me, because I can't do this on my own…I don't know how to lead an army or save the world and I'm scared. I'm sorry I pushed you that day in training. I didn't know, but now that I do, I'm glad it's you teaching me, I don't feel so afraid when you're around. Will you help me?" I asked looking into his molten golden eyes.

"Yes… as long as you promise to listen." He said with a half smile. I moved closer to him, watching his lips, wanting more than anything to kiss him and take away the entire memory of that day. He sucked in a deep breath, slowly letting it out as he reached over and ran his rough calloused hand down my face. My skin ignited with heat and chills…fire and ice raced up and down my whole body.

"I want to kiss you now." He whispered making my stomach flutter. I wanted to say something clever but all that came out was a gasp.

His lips met mine. My body responded with the feeling of fire and shadows covering every inch of me together. The kiss started slow and soft, slowly becoming deeper and more desperate. His hands firmly grasped my waist as he pulled me against him. I ran my hands down his back, thoughts ripping off his sweatshirt racing through my mind. He rolled over top of me, kissing down my neck and back up to my lips. I gave up my reservations and tore his sweatshirt over his head in one fluid motion, tossing it to the floor and finding his lips again. I ran my hands under his t-shirt feeling the tight corded muscles of his back. I decided to remove that darn t-shirt as well. He kissed me harder, breathing heavy, his hands going under my tank top across the skin on my stomach and sides. I started pulling up the t-shirt when he suddenly pulled away, his breathing heavy and cheeks flushed. I was out of breath and my lips tingled, while the fire and ice still raged over my body.

"What's the matter?" I asked feeling pleasantly flushed and warm all over. He sat back against my wall with his eyes closed. I waited wondering what I might have done wrong, feeling a little worried.

"Nothing...I had to stop. As much as I want to keep going right now, I won't be that guy." He said meeting my eyes.

"What do you mean by *that guy?*" I asked sitting up and running my hand through my tangled hair.

"The guy that makes you feel sorry for him and takes advantage. I won't do that to you. I respect you too much for that. I'm old fashioned and like to date a woman before... going in the direction we were headed." He said running a hand over his face.

"Oh...I'm sorry Josh. I normally don't...don't do this...ever. I mean I never have...you know...with anyone." I said feeling embarrassed. His expression looked a little shocked.

"You mean never? Now I feel *really* bad." He said putting his head in his hands with a groan. I laughed, I couldn't help it, I never thought I would ever be in this situation where the guy is the one who felt bad, normally they got mad at *me* for it.

"Don't feel bad...I'm the one who decided to rip off your clothes...I...okay how about this. We have a date tonight, we both need sleep, so let's go to sleep and plan on kissing again later. We can save the other stuff for another time. Good?" I asked and that got a laugh out of him. He shook his head at me, smiling.

"You're a silly girl. Okay sounds good. I'll try to keep my composure but I'm warning you it will be difficult for me… so don't egg it on. There is something about you that I can't seem to wrap my head around. I make no promises if you come at me first." He said lying down again. I lay down next to him and cuddled up with him behind me like before.

"Deal…I'll try…but *I* make no promises either." I said and forced my eyes closed trying to calm down the butterflies. He snorted into my hair.

"Fine…I'll take it." He said in a muffled voice from being snuggled up in my hair again. We both fell asleep right away laying in each other's arms.

A few hours later, Miles woke both of us up shaking my arm. I didn't have any nightmares this time which was nice. I rolled out of Josh's arms and sat up.

"I was going to knock but this is *way* better." Miles said with a giggle. Josh chuckled sleepily and stretched with a big yawn.

"How long do we have until the feast before the Ball?" Josh asked looking up at Miles.

"About an hour, but the feast lasts for two hours before the Ball officially starts. You get outta here, I have to try and get our *fearless leader* dressed as well as myself. Zach and Cam are going to meet us girls by the fire place in the Dining Hall. You can wait with them. Kayla should be here in a few minutes too." Miles said as she heaved a suspicious looking black case onto my desk.

"Alright, I'll meet you there. Miles, I suggest you don't put her in heels, she might fall and break an ankle." Josh said with a cocky grin,

I wacked him in the arm pretending to be offended even though he was right. I could wear boots with heels, but those thin strappy girl heels caused me injury in the past. I just hoped my mom picked a long dress so I could wear my boots underneath. Josh got up and kissed me on the lips gently, making me feel warm all over as I thought of earlier.

"I'll see you soon." He said as he pulled away. He threw on his sweatshirt that I had thrown on the floor and headed out my door right as Kayla opened it. Kayla came in with a dress in a long black garment bag and a look of shock on her face. She said bye to Josh and shut my door, turning to face me. I blushed and shrugged.

"You're supposed to sleep with the guy *after* the date." Kayla said as she hung the bag on my open closet door and Miles laughed. I huffed and flung myself back onto my bed looking up at the ceiling.

"Nothing happened like that. *Gods* get your mind out of the gutter." I said making Kayla laugh now. Miles opened her black case on my desk revealing its contents, which was tons of makeup and hair stuff. I wanted to crawl in bed and hide from all the crazy looking products. I pretty much stuck with the minimum amount of makeup and hair stuff. Miles set up all her stuff and plugged in a bunch of hot hair tools. Kayla went around and turned on every light I owned before helping Miles.

I sat on my bed and watched them get ready together. Miles curled her pretty blonde hair and pinned all of it up in a cute messy bunch of curls. Each pin had an emerald jewel at the end and glittered in the lights of my room. Kayla used a waver hot tool, giving her long raven hair shiny waves down her back. She pinned it half way back with a couple golden pins and pinned a big beautiful white lily on one side, making her look exotic. I watched them apply their makeup. Each of them drew masks around their eyes in intricate designs. I could tell Miles was going with peacock colors, while Kayla was sticking with whites, gold's and yellows, like her flower. Miles pinned a few real peacock feathers in her hair then turned and looked at me. She looked stunning. Her mask was swirls of jewel tones of emerald, purple and blue, outlined in black and white. It made her eyes sparkle. Kayla's mask curved up like flower petals with golden yellow tones and sparkling white glitter, bringing out the lovely yellow hues of her eyes.

"Why did you two do masks?" I asked marveling in how beautiful they both looked. Miles smiled and spun slowly making me laugh. She was still in her sweats and zip-up hoodie; her dress lay carefully in the bag on my armchair.

"It's the *Halloween Ball* dork. I'm going as a peacock and Kayla is going as a lily. Come over here…it's your turn." Miles said grinning at me. I didn't know what my dress was so I didn't know what they were going to do to my face. I plopped down in my desk chair and waited.

"I don't know what my dress even looks like." I said feeling bad that I hadn't even looked. My mother has excellent taste and knows me better than anyone so I wasn't that worried. Miles and Kayla exchanged a look and both smiled at me.

"We talked to your mom and know what you'll be wearing. No peeking." Miles said as she came at me with eyeliner. Kayla attacked my messy hair and pulled and pinned it up all over my head. I was able to hold still and not complain. They were having a really good time giggling like girls and gossiping about everything. I even joined them, making small talk about silly things like boys and scantily dressed girls at our school. It was really nice, after all this was our one night of *normal* for Gods know how long.

It didn't take very long for them to finish my hair and makeup. Miles held up a mirror and I gasped out loud. My mask was red and golden fire, which sparkled in the light with red and golden glitter. My eyes were lined heavily in black and gold making my orange eye color stand out beautifully. The mask arched over my eyebrows and ended from the corners of my eyes to my hairline on the sides of my face in delicate flame designs. My hair was pinned up like Miles had done hers, but with golden pins with orange and red jewels. Red and orange feathers were artfully pinned into the curls and waves of my hair. I smiled up at the girls, I felt and looked amazing.

"You two are the best friends I could ever have. What am I?" I asked.

"The Phoenix… your mom came up with it. She figured it fit you. She's right you know. You're the definition of what the Phoenix represents. The Phoenix *is* fire and the destruction of the darkness. You are the fire we all fight with, the light we all fight for and the one who carries us to the end." Kayla said meeting my eyes. The weight of her words rested heavy on my shoulders.

"You are the reason we all feel brave every day. Because of you, we all know everything will somehow be okay. We all stand behind you Skye. Don't ever forget that. Now…let's go make those boys of ours drool." Miles said with a smile, though her eyes were set and full of determination. My sweet little Miles had found her strength, like Artemis had said she would. I hugged both girls while I held back tears.

Kayla and I helped Miles into her dress first. It was a true ball gown, with a corset lace up back and no straps. The bodice was made of cobalt blue silk, with a full floor length skirt of emerald, black and cobalt blue fabric. The top layer of the skirts was made of genuine peacock feathers, held underneath a thin silver rope like belt, riding along Miles's hips. She looked amazing.

Kayla's ball gown was also a corset top but with thin straps over her shoulders. The whole dress was made of a lovely pale yellow silk with golden stitching along each seam. Her skirts were the same yellow as the top, fading gracefully to white down to the bottom of the dress. Miles pulled out the bag with my dress from my closet and made me close my eyes as they helped me get into it.

I looked in my full length mirror on the back of my closet door and didn't recognize myself. The dress was strapless with a lace up back, the bodice was made of blood red silk with thin golden stitching of flames running down to the full skirts. The skirts were floor length and full, with reds and oranges blending gracefully together. The golden flames went all the way down the dress, only noticeable when they caught the light. I smiled as I looked in the mirror feeling truly beautiful for the first time.

We all decided to be on the safe side and wear our combat boots under our dresses. The dresses were long enough to hide our feet anyways. Both their boots had been equipped like mine with hidden boot knives. We also each strapped a thigh holster on with a dagger under our layered skirts. None of us felt safe without being armed anymore. It's a sad thing, but it made us feel better about playing normal life for a night. The three of us headed out the door to the side steps together to go meet the boys. We were only going to be ten minutes late, which I felt was pretty darn good considering we all looked like we spent all day getting ready. I silently thanked Zeus when I opened the side door to find clear night skies and a full orange harvest moon. It was still freezing out but at least the night was clear and the wind was calm.

Blaze and Chaos met the three of us with War in front of the girl's dorm. War perched on Miles's shoulder while Chaos and Blaze walked next to Kayla and me. For the first time since I found out I am a Demigod, I felt proud and excited about it. I just hoped the dance would be worthy of the excitement.

Chapter Twenty-four

One thing great about Chambers Academy is they truly go all out when it comes to having a Ball. The front of the Castle was lit with little white lights, lining the front steps and patio. Black lanterns hung all over the place on wrought iron hooks, with white candles lit, casting a warm glow over the courtyard. Pumpkins and Jack-O-Lanterns sat glowing with sinister faces along the walkways and near the front doors. Corn stalks sat in the corners of the front entrance with fall leaves twisted into the stalks. The Castle looked amazing, like something out of a dream.

We walked in the front doors to find the place full of students eating and laughing. Orange, white and red twinkle lights hung from the ceiling trusses with strings of fall leaves wrapped around them making the leaves glow. All the tables were lit with black lanterns and white pillar candles. Fall leaves, pine cones and Jack-O-Lanterns of all shapes and sizes sat on the centers of all the tables. All the tables made a half circle around the dance floor where some students were standing around talking and laughing. A DJ was setting up his equipment on the landing of the grand staircase, while soft string symphony music played on the school's sound system. All the girls wore full ball gowns of all colors, with masks painted on or strapped on. All the guys wore black tuxes with black masks making it hard to tell who they were.

Zach, Cam, Josh and Big Mike stood together over by the fireplace all of them in black tuxes and black masks. We headed over to them while Chaos and Blaze went to the open library to hang out with the other student's pets that could be inside. Even they had a good set up. A blazing warm fire in the fireplace, bird perches, cushions of all shapes and sizes and food dishes full of anything an animal could eat. The boys were all deep in conversation which promptly came to a halt when the three of us walked up to them. For a moment all of them just stared at us.

"My *Gods*...I didn't recognize any of you without your weapons. You look beautiful ladies." Cam said with a wink. He held out an arm to Kayla who seemed to be glowing with joy and kissed her gently on the lips. They walked over towards the food table together having a whispered conversation. Zach's mouth was hanging open a little bit as he stared at Miles. It made her fidget with her dress.

"Do you not like it?" she asked looking uncomfortable now. Zach shook his head as if to clear the cobwebs, walked right up to her and kissed her. I choked back a giggle as he picked her up by the waist kissing her harder, making the rest of us turn politely away from them. I tried not to laugh out loud at their display.

"Well...you look amazing, *Phoenix* huh? I think it fits you pretty good Skye. I like it. Oh, there's my date... do you guys mind if she sits with us?" Big Mike asked as Carla La'vue walked over in a beautiful pale blue strapless gown covered in silver glitter. Her hair was up in curls on top her head with silver and white feathers pinned delicately into the curls. Her mask was painted on with silver and white feather designs, making her sea green eyes shine brilliantly in the candlelight.

"Nice job Mike... how did you land that one?" I said in a whisper elbowing him gently. He smiled sheepishly, his grey eyes sparkling from behind his mask.

"Luke… is an ass. He started to get kind of violent with her and I couldn't stand it anymore so I put him in his place and she just kind of stuck by my side. This happened the night you left on your mission and she's been following me around ever since." Big Mike said as Carla arrived kissing his cheek gently, standing on her tip toes. I felt bad that she had to deal with that from Luke. *She might be a snob, but nobody deserved to be treated that way.* I thought watching her as she stared up lovingly at Big Mike.

"You look lovely Carla. What are you going as?" I asked even though I was sure I already knew. She smiled at me still clinging to Mike's big arm.

"I thank you Skyee. I am going as zee Angel. My mozzier picked out zee dress, tis lovely no? You are zee fire bird no?" Carla said with a sincere smile. I nodded, that was the most I had really heard her talk. Her French accent was lovely but really thick, catching me off guard a little.

"It is… your mother has excellent taste." I said with a smile. Carla nodded politely as her and Big Mike walked to the food tables together. I turned around to find Josh standing right behind me smiling down at me. His black mask made his golden eyes stand out and shine in the light of the candles.

"You are making it very hard for me to keep my outstanding self control little Phoenix. You look beautiful." He said making me blush. He leaned down and kissed me softly on the lips making my heart flutter.

"You don't look so bad yourself. You clean up pretty good, Son of Zeus." I said as I pulled out of the kiss. He smiled down at me as he grabbed my hand, leading me to the food tables. I tapped Zach on the shoulder as we passed by him and Miles, who were still kissing. Thank the Gods that's all they were doing this whole time, people were starting to stare at them. I giggled as they broke apart, both of them looking like they forgot where they were. Zach set Miles back on her feet and they both followed us looking flushed and slightly embarrassed.

The kitchen staff had out done themselves. Fresh fruit, salads of every kind, fresh veggies, grilled chicken, soups, pasta, fresh fish and desserts of every kind lined the food table. I loaded up my plate with a little of everything that would fit, finishing it off with a mug of hot apple cider. We took our plates back to the table where Cam, Kayla, Big Mike and Carla sat eating and chatting. We sat enjoying each other's company for a while when the DJ started playing music to start up the dance.

Hip hop music thumped loudly over the speakers as the chandeliers and twinkle lights dimmed lower, making it darker in the Dining Hall. People moved to the dance floor and started dancing. I watched as Carla and Big Mike started dancing, Carla being provocative in front of Big Mike, who is a surprisingly great dancer, keeping up with Carla. Kayla and Cam were doing the Robot dance laughing together. Zach and Miles were dancing near Kayla and Cam laughing along with them. Josh stood up standing in front of my chair with his hand out.

"Come on little girl. You *know* you want to." He said with a silly grin on his face. I took his hand and let him take me out on the dance floor with the others. We danced for quite a while like a bunch of idiots, when a slow song finally came on. Josh wrapped both hands around my waist and pulled me tight to him. I lay my head against his shoulder and chest feeling utterly relaxed swaying with the music. When the song ended another fast song came on, Josh leaned down to my ear making me shudder. Damn him to Hades.

"You want to go outside and get some air?" he asked. I nodded and let him lead me to the outdoor patio. Surprisingly, we were the only people out here except for two Army guards watching the woods. I said hello to them as we passed them by and sat on the same bench I had overheard the Demons plans. Josh put his black tux jacket over my bare shoulders as we sat down. I leaned into his side and he threw an arm around me. We sat in silence for a few minutes just looking up at the stars.

"You two look fantastic. Skye I love your dress." Artemis said from the woods behind us causing both of us to jump and spin around. Josh held out a dagger he pulled from who knows where, making Artemis smile.

"Good reflexes. I'm patrolling the edges of the woods and wanted to say hello. Are you two enjoying the Ball?" she asked walking over to us as Josh sheathed his dagger up his sleeve. Both of us bowed to her and sat back down. Her hair was braided down her back and her black and silver army fatigues oddly blended with the moonlight and forest behind her. Every time the moonlight shone on her skin, her silvery tattoos lit up, swirling over her.

"Yeah…it's nice pretending to be normal for a night. I'm really glad the Gods were okay with this still happening." I said wrapping Josh's jacket tighter around me as a breeze chilled my bones.

"The Gods do love a good party, even in the middle of a war. Well, I guess this isn't the middle… it's more the beginning of one. Tonight, all that doesn't matter… enjoy yourselves we shall discuss business tomorrow. Skye…remember my offer though. As long as you keep your virtues, my offer still stands." Artemis said seriously.

"Thank you Goddess. I will keep that in mind." I said eyeing Josh's hard expression out of the corner of my eye. We both stood and bowed again as Artemis walked back into the woods silently and disappeared.

"She asked you to join the Hunters didn't she?" Josh asked seriously, his expression hard.

"Yeah but I'm still thinking about it. I didn't tell her yes, if that's what you're asking." I said wondering why he seemed irritated.

"Do you really want to?" he asked. I thought for a minute. It would be nice to just hunt all the time and work with Artemis, forever protecting the innocent. The trade off of never being able to love a man or lose everyone I love and know, sounded less intriguing. I didn't want to walk away from all of them *ever*.

"I don't think so anymore. When she first offered it I sort of wanted it, but for the wrong reasons. I wanted to run away instead of honorably accept the offer because I wanted to protect the innocent. I don't think I could walk away from everyone. I think it would make me miserable." I said meeting his eyes. He smiled and kissed me on the lips gently.

"I won't stop you but I would probably try to talk you out of it first. I really want to give this; *You and Me against the world* thing a try…if you're interested." He asked holding his hand against my face looking into my eyes.

"Are you saying you want to make this… you and me thing… permanent?" I asked feeling the butterflies in my stomach going crazy.

"Yes…if you're okay with turning down all those other boys for dates. I want you all to myself if that's okay with you?" he said with a wink. I giggled kissing him.

"I would like that. But I don't have to turn down any guys… ever. Remember I'm the leader of the Poverty Club?" I said making Josh chuckle low in his chest.

"Well I like the whole Poverty Club and think I'm a member anyways. Will Zach be okay with us being together?" Josh asked seriously.

"Yeah, he has Miles now. But, you have to be okay with the fact that he is my best friend. He's my rock... well my whole world really. You've seen how we are together and you have to be okay with that or this is a *no deal*." I said meeting his gaze. Zach is the only person I have ever been able to count on and I wouldn't give him up for a jealous boyfriend, no matter how amazing the boyfriend could be.

"I can agree to those terms. I like him, between the two of us you will always be protected from anything. I have huge respect for Zach and the way he takes care of you. He's a good man." Josh said and kissed me again. The kiss was deep and soft, he pulled me into his lap kissing me gently down the bare skin of my neck and shoulder. He found his way to my lips again. I tried to make the kiss more intense but instead he stopped it, picked me up and stood, setting me gently on my feet again. I huffed out a breath causing a little cloud of moisture in the cold night air.

"Come on *Phoenix*...let's go back inside, it's getting pretty cold out here." He said as he took my hand leading me back to the patio side entrance.

We danced until everyone felt tired. All of us sat down at our table snacking on desserts talking about random things. Everyone stopped talking when Lindsay, Luke, Maddie, Kirk and the Twins walked up to the table. I hadn't seen much of the Twins since the fight behind the stables. Lindsay was dressed in a long white gown covered in white feathers. Her mask wasn't painted on but a huge white feathered mask on a stick each feather tipped with yellow glitter. The neon yellow feathers sticking out of her hair made it apparent she was a cockatoo. Maddie had a deep purple dress with long sleeves and an open back, which seemed to clash with her neon purple eyes. Her dress also had sheer wings that hung down her back. Her mask was also on a stick with dragonfly wing designs all over it. Kirk stared at us silently; his red eyes looked creepy as they glowed behind the eye holes of the mask.

"Hey guys. Are you having a good time? It's a nice break from training right?" Josh asked casually. I had nearly forgotten they were his friends. Luke was glaring hard at Big Mike through his black mask. As if to prove a point Big Mike put an arm around a scared looking Carla's shoulders. Carla settled closer into Big Mike and stared determinedly back at Luke. Luke let out a huff and crossed his arms over his chest.

"Hi Josh…I was wondering if I could talk to you?" Lindsay asked in a sweet voice. I didn't trust the sweetness at all. All it did was annoy me.

"You needed a whole group of back up to come *talk* to him? You scared of something Lindsay?" I said looking up at her. She smiled at me sweetly, which made my adrenaline spike.

"Skye… as always it's a pleasure to see you. No, I'm not scared of anything thanks. They just wanted to say hi to *their* friends…that's all. Josh…could we talk now?" Lindsay said turning her back to me and facing Josh. I looked at Miles and Kayla, both of them had hard looks on their faces. Josh glanced around at all of us seeing how irritated we all were.

"Sure Lindsay, what's up?" Josh said looking up at her expectantly.

"In private if you please. What I have to say might offend people of lower intelligence." Lindsay said smoothly. Cam laughed out loud at that.

"Your cute sweetheart, but I think we can handle it. As much as you don't like us you might want to speak to us with a little more respect. We *are* your commanding officers remember. Don't forget, we're on the same side. So unless you're rollin with the Demons now, I suggest you check your tone because I have *no* problem throwing your sweet little ass in a holding cell for a few days. Is that clear enough for you?" Cam said standing up now. I about jumped for joy. I forgot we were in charge of the specialized units of our little Demigod army. Luke stepped forward like he wanted to hit Cam, but Zach stood stepping in front of Luke. Luke faltered and stopped glaring up at Zach, but not making any moves.

"Calm down all of you. Pull up some chairs and sit the hell down now. *That's an order.*" Kayla said standing up too. After a tense moment everyone pulled a chair from the surrounding tables and sat down at the table with us. Once everyone was seated an awkward silence settled over the table. I couldn't take it so I spoke first trying to sound like a leader instead of an irritated teenager.

"Alright, so now that we are all here feel free to talk about whatever it is that's on your mind. Does this have to do with the Demons or is this a personal issue?" I asked looking around at everyone. Maddie shifted uncomfortably in her seat looking hard at me and her eyes kept darting from Luke to Kirk which struck me as odd.

"Okay, so we know that we all don't like each other, which is fine. This is about the Demons. I heard a rumor that they are looking for a child of Hades. I also heard that if we hand over the child of Hades they won't attack the Castle. I think we should do that to avoid a real war." Luke said surprising me and making me feel nervous. None of my friends even glanced my way, thank the Gods. *We still don't know which Demigod is working with the Demons and this conversation feels suspicious.* I thought not liking the way the conversation was heading.

"Even if we knew *who* that was, handing them over wouldn't change the fact that the Demons are trying to free Typhon. They would still go after Mount Rainier anyways. Remember Zeus said it was our duty to defend the mountain. If Typhon is released this school would be the first place he destroys. So really it wouldn't do us any good to hand over the child of Hades. We don't even know if a child of Hades is here. The Dean is checking other schools and military bases looking for this kid and so far they haven't been able to find them. For all we know the kid is in the Underworld with Hades himself." Josh said smoothly. I had to give him props; he was doing an excellent job of lying.

"Still, maybe we could negotiate with them or something. I just don't think going to war over one kid is worth it. Think of how many people could die because of this." Lindsay said looking around at all of us. My heart sank a little at the thought and guilt tore through my stomach.

"It's not just about that *one* Demigod. This is about all of us and the rest of the world. If they get the child of Hades, they will still release Typhon and the other Titans and take over the world anyways. They would still attack us even without the kid of Hades, we are the first line of defense for Typhon's prison, so they would come for us regardless. Why is this so hard for you to get? Giving them what they want and negotiating would still mean the end of everything we have ever known. The lives we had before would be completely gone. I appreciate the ideas, but I would have to disagree with you. What we *can* do is make sure we try to be a step ahead of the Demons. If we could know *when* they plan on attacking, *we* could catch them off guard by being ready and attacking first." Big Mike said looking around at everyone. *Smooth, he's trying to plant the seed for the traitor to hopefully expose themselves.* I thought, feeling smug.

"That may be, but I still think we should find this kid. We might be able to use them to bait the Demons. Then they would attack on our terms." Kirk piped in with a squeaky voice. I wished Chaos were over here to sniff these people and find out which ones were a child of Dionysus. *Maybe the traitor is sitting next to us. Damn this situation to Hades.* I thought eyeing everyone down.

"Sacrificing a kid to the Demons is pretty sick. Training hard and fighting back is better than throwing a kid to the wolves and lying down without a fight. I didn't think you guys were quitters. It's a shame to know that. You guys fought like hell when you jumped us behind the stables. I didn't know you guys would go running with your tails between your legs at the first sign of a real fight worth fighting… seems pretty *cowardly* in my opinion." Zach said glaring at Luke. Luke went to jump out of his seat and launch himself at Zach but the Twins stopped him. After a little scuffling around, Luke stood up with a huff and stormed out the front doors. The Twins followed him out in silence. Those two didn't speak the whole time, which made me *almost* like them.

"Well, I guess that's all we have to discuss then. I hope you all change your minds, I have a feeling this will be an ugly wake up call for all of us and then you will see, that we are right." Lindsay said getting up from her seat.

"Then for now we agree to disagree." I said meeting her eyes. She gave me a curt nod and left with Kirk behind her and Maddie taking her sweet time to follow. Maddie met my eyes again giving me an odd look like she wanted to say something. Instead she gave me a short awkward bow and followed her friends out the main doors. I didn't know what to make of that weird move from Maddie. Maddie and I had never spoken other than when she shouted insults at me when I passed by her between classes before this whole Demigod thing. The whole thing had my instincts buzzing but I wasn't sure what they were trying to tell me.

Chapter Twenty-five

"That was exciting. I'm really glad we talked this time instead of fighting. The last thing any of us need is crap from them in front of everyone else. Good call Cam, by the way, I wish she would have kept being stupid so we could lock her ass up." Zach said with a half smile. Cam chuckled leaning back in his chair.

"I don't even know if we have holding cells for people who cross the line. I'll have to bring that up to Joe tomorrow. We should probably have a holding cell or two, just in case the Demons brand more people like they did with your dad Miles. I don't want to kill any one when they are under the influence of the Spirit Tattoos… that would just be… wrong." Cam said his face turning serious.

"Good idea, I wouldn't want to hurt anyone who doesn't know what their doing. That's so messed up. Well…should we call it a night?" Big Mike said looking around at all of us. Our little chat with Lindsay seemed to be the end of our *normal teenager* fun. Everyone nodded around the table looking grim.

"You guys are a bunch of weenies. This is our one night of freedom and you all want to go to bed? Skye…I'm ashamed of you. Normally you would be up in arms over everyone punking out right now." Zach said looking around at everyone.

"Oh Gods…I've corrupted you. You're supposed to be the

one who talks us out of making bad choices! What have I done?" I said faking shock. Everyone chuckled around the table. Zach gave me a sinister grin and faked a really bad Dracula accent.

"Tis Halloveen my vittle bag of blood...Muhaha! Ve shall vatch a scary movie and play hide and seek... Muhaha!" Zach said making everyone laugh around the table. For the first time in a long time I was cracking up and overly excited to play hide-and-seek like a little kid. I hopped up from my seat right away grinning like a fool.

"Come on then! Everyone to my room!" I said grabbing Josh's hand as we all scrambled out of our seats. I raced over to the dessert table and stuffed everything that would fit into the to-go containers the kitchen staff always kept on a shelf under the table behind the table cloths. The others followed my lead and we grabbed up snacks and sweets greedily. All of us raced out of the Dining Hall and onto the grounds giggling like a bunch of little kids.

When we reached my room we crammed inside laughing like we had just done something naughty and got away with it. Zach started getting the movie ready while Miles, Cam and Kayla went to her room next door to grab pillows and blankets for us to pile on the floor as extra seating. Carla helped me move my random clutter and Miles's girly makeup off the desk and bed, neatly putting it all away. Josh and Big Mike were putting our snacks on the desk and storing perishables neatly in the mini fridge in the back of my closet. Cam, Miles and Kayla returned with blankets and pillows and even Miles's mattress from her bed.

They cleared the floor and made a pile like a fluffy pillow mountain. We all found spots and sat down together still in our gowns and the boys in their tuxes. They had taken off their masks and loosened their ties, but we still looked like the nicest dressed bunch at a slumber party. Zach shut off the lights and hit play on the really old 1970's movie. He then swan dived into everyone on the blanket pile on the floor causing a lot of squealing and groaning. I snuggled into Josh's chest on my bed with Cam and Kayla snuggled up at our feet at the end of the bed. Miles, Zach, Big Mike and Carla lay cuddled up in the blanket heap on the floor.

"The acting in this movie is *terrible*." Kayla said laughing. Cam chuckled and tried to scare her at one of the lame creepy scenes. Kayla pretended to be scared by Cam's lame attempt and hit him with a pillow when he wasn't looking. They broke into a full blown pillow fight. Big Mike and Miles joined in and soon pillows were flying around my room.

"Dude not the face!" Josh said whacking the two of them with a pillow as he took my pillow right to the nose. I laughed like a diabolical villain and went after Zach. He dodged my pillow and threw me like a rag doll on the bed. I landed on top of Josh causing him to let out a very un-manly yelp.

"Sorry! It's all Zach's fault! Are you okay?" I asked worried that I hit his man parts or something. Josh flipped me around on his lap and started kissing me. Not the sexy kind but the kiss-monster attack kind. I cringed and giggled trying to escape his kissing.

Eventually everyone finally calmed down and started getting comfortable again. I looked around at all the girls feeling impressed because not one of us had smeared off our masks painted across our faces. Zach skipped back a couple scenes that we missed during our epic pillow fight and we focused on the movie again.

We all laughed and made fun of the terrible graphics of the old film. We screamed at the wrong parts and made predictions about what was going to happen before it did. I was having a blast. Carla was actually really funny and cool to hang out with. She was acting out the movie pretending to be the villain but saying all the lines in French. It was entertaining. Apparently my face wasn't used to smiling so much and by the end of the movie my cheeks hurt. Zach flipped on the lights and stopped the rolling credits.

"Hide and Seek time! Where do we want to play?" Zach announced looking around at all of us.

"We should probably change out of our dresses no?" Carla asked as she stood up. I looked at all of us still in our gowns. We probably wouldn't get to wear them again.

"Hell no... I have sweatshirts to keep us warm, but I want to stay in mine. When are we ever going to get to wear them again?" I said looking around at the girls. Miles grinned at me and stood up too.

"Let's go in the training arena. That way we don't freak out the night guards or freeze our butts off." Miles said looking excited. We piled out of my room and down the secret side stairs. It was past midnight now and we all were trying to be quiet without much luck. None of us could seem to stop laughing or joking. I held hands with Zach as we wandered towards the Training Arena.

"So are you having fun?" I asked looking up at Zach as we walked through the moonlit grounds together. He smiled down at me and glanced back at Miles who rode piggy back on Big Mike's back.

"Yeah, this is really great. It's so much fun to just be normal and hang out with our friends. It's been so long since we have hung out with anyone who's real and not stupid. I couldn't be happier right now. I love these people. Are you having fun?" He asked draping his arm over my bare shoulders. I leaned into him as we walked with perfect rhythm, our steps matching.

"Yeah, I like this. I love these people too. They're like family now. I couldn't imagine life without them. It's crazy that it took a war to make friends." I said feeling like I was floating on a cloud with joy.

"Who would have thought *we* would have our own group... it is crazy. I guess that's what it takes sometimes though, a three sixty of your whole life and suddenly we're best friends with perfect strangers." Zach said with a smile that lit up his electric green eyes in the moonlight. We fell into silence again and I rode piggy back on Zach's back like Miles and Big Mike.

We reached the training arena without meeting anyone along the way. I felt a little nervous for some reason I couldn't quite figure out. The arena was locked, but Kayla saved the day by picking the lock with one of her hairpins. We crept inside finding the lights off and eerie silence filling the normally noisy arena. A chill ran up my spine. *This is how horror movies start.* I thought as I looked around waiting for a Demon to jump out from behind the rock climbing wall or something. Zach put an arm around me and gave me a squeeze.

"Scared little mouse?" He whispered leaning down to my ear. I instantly felt my body relax, but the nagging feeling of *something* still lingered in my stomach.

"Something feels…off. Didn't you find it strange that we didn't even see a guard on the way here? They were all over the place earlier and I know they run late night shifts. Is this dumb luck that we didn't see a guard or did that feel weird to you?" I asked looking up to his eyes. Concern flooded his features as he thought about it.

"I guess I didn't notice. I think it's just dumb luck that we missed guards. We are here to have fun remember? Relax… this is our only night and I'm feeling a little reckless. Join me?" Zach said with a mischievous grin. I played with the key necklace from Hades I always wore, slowly pushing down the nerves forcing myself to ignore them.

"Wow…I *have* ruined you. It's like we switched places. Alright *mister reckless* I say *you're it!*" I said whacking him on the arm as I took off running. The others scattered like spilled marbles all taking off in different directions looking for places to hide. Josh kissed me on the cheek mid-run making my heart flutter. I watched as Josh sprinted towards the rock wall. Zach covered his eyes and stared to count down from 50 yelling out the numbers so we could all hear.

"Stay on this main level! Don't go to the basement or in the locker rooms! Catwalk, War Room and Ranges are fair game!" Zach yelled before we could all get to far away.

I scrambled towards the Archery Range. I figured I could probably fit inside one of the cabinets where the long bows were stored. Nobody else went the way that I was going. I sprinted over training mats, feeling glad I had my combat boots on instead of high heels. I found the room unlocked and hurried inside silently shutting the door behind me. I crept into one of the tall black cabinets and let the door close casting me into the pitch black. I faintly heard Zach count down the last few numbers.

"Ready or not, here I come!" Zach bellowed from the arena. I waited feeling like I might be able to win this round. *I would really win if I were a cheater and shadowed.* I thought. The thought of shadowing and standing in plain sight right behind Zach made me let out a giggle. I threw my hand over my mouth to stifle the noise. Demigod hearing could give me away in a second if I didn't keep it together. I shut my eyes and focused so I could listen to the goings on outside my hiding spot. At first everything sounded muffled and then I could hear Zach's voice, though it was still slightly distant.

"Come out, come out where ever you are… Gotcha!" Zach said as Miles let out a squeal. I knew it was her right away by her distinct giggle.

"I thought this was such a good spot! Ah man!" Miles said laughing. I heard the two of them find Josh, Big Mike, Kayla and then the whole group finally find Cam. Only Carla and me were left. My excitement grew, I might actually win. I felt anxious now, knowing that I had been hiding in the cabinet for a long time. I was ready to get out of the cramped little space. I was starting to get bored standing in a dark cabinet alone. I listened as the others talked about finding me and where they should look. I couldn't hear the direction they headed because they all fell silent. My legs were starting to feel stiff and I was about to just give up when I heard the door to the range open. I shut my eyes again just in case they were glowing from using my hearing. I held my breath waiting silently in the cabinet.

I didn't hear anything except an odd shuffling and weird breathing sounds. The little hairs all over my body stood straight up making me want to shudder. Something felt *wrong*. The whole group was searching together for Carla and me, this sounded like one person. I hadn't heard them say anything about splitting up. I strained my ears over the creepy shuffling sound. I heard the others' laughter from outside the Archery Range back in the arena. *That means someone else is in this room with me while I'm crammed into a dark cabinet in a freaking ball gown.* I thought as my heart rate picked up. I slowly let out a breath and sniffed the air. I could faintly smell sulfur and rot, causing panic to race through my veins. I wished I could call Chaos to me with my mind like I could in the Underworld. He was too far away, probably hunting with Blaze in the woods. I realized I wasn't ready to face a Demon yet. I had been to the Underworld and faced danger, but the panic at facing a Demon alone sent my heart into a frenzy of freaking out.

Please…please don't be a Demon. I thought feeling slightly sick. The *thing* stood in front of the cabinet. My heart thudded, trying to leap out of my chest. I screamed for the shadows to hide me with my mind. The cool caress covered my skin as I felt the shadows creep over me and hide me. One painstakingly slow silent inch at a time I pulled up my gown reaching my thigh holster and unsheathing my dagger. I waited as the shadow beyond my door shuffled again. Who or whatever it was let out a weird gurgling sound like screaming underwater. I couldn't remember ever hearing the Demons make that kind of noise before. I sniffed the air again, still faintly smelling the foul Demon stench. *A Demon would smell so bad it would make me gag.*

This isn't a Demon. I thought feeling confused. The *something* shuffled past my hiding spot, stumbled and fell to the floor with a thud. I couldn't take it anymore. Slowly I opened the door of my cabinet. Ice flooded my veins as fear and pain tore through my heart. The shadows flew from my body with a rush of freezing air across my skin.

Face down on the floor in a small pool of crimson, lay an Angel in a pale blue ball gown. I wanted to cover my ears as the Archery Range filled with the sounds of screaming. The Angel was having trouble breathing. She was still alive. If the screaming sounds would stop I could probably help the Angel.

Suddenly the doors flew open as my friends rushed in with weapons drawn and looks of rage on their faces. The looks of rage turned to terror. I wanted the screaming to stop. Josh rushed over and shook my shoulders, his lips were moving but I couldn't hear any words. The screaming stopped suddenly. I didn't want to believe it but the pain in my throat meant that the screaming was coming from me. The blood on my dress and hands meant that I was putting pressure on the three stab wounds through the Angel's torso.

I blinked feeling the shock fade out as my instincts took over showing me what I was really looking at. Carla, the beauty from France, the Angel at the ball, lay dying on the floor in my arms. I had turned her over with her head in my lap as I tried to stop the bleeding. The wounds went all the way through her body staining her blue gown. Someone ran through her three times with a long sword. Carla sucked in a breath of air making a wet rattling sound from her chest. She let out a little cough and a bubble of blood seeped out the corner of her mouth. Her eyes fluttered shut and open again, as she struggled to look up at me and stay awake. I didn't know what to do as I looked down at her. The Demon smell had been coming from Carla. I looked down at her hands, she had fought back, Demon flesh and black thick blood stained her hands and a small knife that lay by her side.

Cam leaned down over the Carla's torso, his hands glowing with warm light. Miles sat across from him using her knife to tear off the corset top of the gown. Kayla and Zach were missing. I felt hands on the bare skin of my shoulders as fire and ice ripped across my skin telling me Josh sat behind me. Big Mike stood there in still silence with tears flowing freely down his face. I felt my heart break for him, tearing a hole through the middle of my body.

Chapter Twenty-six

"Skye, I need you to help me get this off her." Miles said as she finished cutting the corset off the lovely blue gown. Miles's mask makeup had smeared down her cheeks and her skin was pale with shock. I nodded slowly, trying to make myself move and be useful. Miles cut gently but her hands shook with the knife. The fabric of the dress had imbedded into the stab wounds. Miles had cut open the top down the middle in between Carla's breasts and along her waist where the top connected to the billowing skirts. I took a deep breath and forced myself to be calm. I couldn't let her die because of my failure to get my crap together. I nodded to Miles and gently began pulling the fabric out of the deep gashes while Cam followed behind me with his healing powers. The healing light Cam used was physically draining him and moving very slowly. Each wound went all the way through her body and he had to heal her ripped up insides before he could heal the outsides. Carla gurgled and more blood spilled out of her mouth onto my dress as she rested in my lap. I couldn't believe she was still alive.

Finally Miles and I got the corset out of the wounds and opened it up exposing her torso and breasts. Big Mike tore off a sleeve from his tux shirt and laid it over her breasts giving her some dignity. I didn't think it really mattered much in the current situation but the sweet gesture hurt my heart again. Josh stood up from sitting behind me and approached Big Mike patting his shoulder.

"We need to find it. Zach and Kayla went for help, Cam and the girls will take care of her. You and I need to find the Demon before it hurts anyone else. For all we know the Demon's are attacking right now. Come on, she's in good hands, let's go kill the bastard." Josh said grabbing a cross bow from the nearby cabinet. Big Mike looked like he wanted to argue but sniffled hard and wiped his face on his remaining sleeve.

"Get me to an ax." Big Mike said as his face turned hard with rage making him look downright frightening. He nodded to me and met my eyes making me feel afraid of what he and Josh might do.

"Do *not* let her die. She will not meet Hades tonight. She belongs with me." Big Mike said as his storm cloud grey eyes bored into my soul.

"I will do everything I can Mike. I promise." I said trying to sound sure and strong. Josh met my eyes and gave me a quick nod and the two of them left the room.

"I don't know if I can do this. I've only healed one of her wounds and I'm losing energy fast. I fixed her lung but this one is through her liver and the other is through part of her spleen and spine. I need *help*." Cam said in a strained voice. His skin seemed pale and he had sweat on his forehead. Carla's breathing was shallow and her skin looked ashy grey. I tried to wipe away the blood from her mouth but smeared it with the thick wet blood from my hands. I held back a shudder at the amount of blood pooled around all of us.

"Can you pull energy from us?" I asked wishing that I could give him the adrenaline racing through my veins.

"Not that I know of. He would need another child of Apollo to share the light. I could probably help though. Athena said I have some ability to heal…maybe I can try to use it? We need to try anything we can. She's dying." Miles said in a shaky voice. Miles lay her hand over the wound that went through Carla's liver and closed her eyes. Nothing happened as her face scrunched up in concentration. I reached out and grabbed Miles's free hand and shut my own eyes trying to will anything of my powers to Miles. My hand felt hot like it might catch fire. I opened my eyes and looked down at Carla who had stopped breathing entirely. I panicked and grabbed one of Cam's hands too forcing myself to focus. Both my hands got hot like fire. I pushed the heat into Miles and Cam hoping with all my heart that it was my energy and not the fires of death or something.

Cam gasped out loud as his hand over the wound to Carla's spine burned brighter. Miles let out a squeak as her hand lit up too with white hot light. She held her hand like Cam, just above the wound and focused. I felt my own heart rate speed up and then slow down. I pushed harder. Whatever we were doing was working. I watched through bleary eyes as the wounds began to heal, but very slowly. I felt myself growing faint, as my heart slowed way down. I was going to pass out soon if I didn't stop. I gave one last push and dropped Miles and Cam's hands. Good thing I did because the room started spinning and my heart seemed to be beating wrong. My breathing became more difficult. I was ready to tip over and let the spots behind my vision take over when the door to the range burst open. Kayla and Zach came bursting into the room with Nurse Lane and my mother behind them.

"Skye...what did you do?" Cam asked, his voice sounding far away, as Nurse Lane took over for Miles.

"I don't know. I wanted to help and I just wished I could give you my strength. I felt like I held fire in my hands and forced it towards you two... I don't think it worked though." I said feeling like I would pass out soon as my words slurred out of my mouth.

"It *did* work. I was able to heal the organs with your...whatever that was... and Miles was able to use her own healing powers, which she never had before now." Cam said looking at me with wide eyes. I had no idea what to say or do so I looked down at Carla. She still wasn't breathing. I wearily lifted my arm and felt for a pulse on Carla's neck. Nothing. I felt tears leak out of my eyes as my mother rushed over to me and forced a bottle of water at me. She made me take a sip. Instantly I felt my head clear and my breathing improve while the spots behind my eyes faded out.

"Miles, Cam, please take a sip. This is Nectar mixed with a lot of water. You guys did well." My mother said passing the water around. I kept crying, knowing that I may have failed Big Mike. Kayla stood in the corner with Zach her hand gripping his tightly and her eyes wide. Zach looked like he was torn between getting mad and crying.

"Mom...she's dead... we couldn't save her." I said feeling my heart grow heavy with loss. Nurse Lane was checking our healing job, adding her own finishing touches. It didn't take her very long as she checked each wound.

"She's alive, but barley. She's lost a lot of blood and is in full shock. I need to get her to the Infirmary with the others." Nurse Lane said as she checked Carla's pulse again.

"She's alive? We saved her?" Cam asked sounding exhausted and full of hope.

"Yes. We have to move her now, before the shock and blood loss kills her." Nurse Lane said sternly. Zach and Cam moved together and ripped off the legs of a heavy looking wooden table from the corner of the room. They set the table top next to Carla and together with my mom's help gently shifted Carla onto the homemade stretcher. Miles and I stood up as the boys each lifted an end of the table. We looked like we had come from a massacre. Blood covered the whole front of my dress and my hands up to my elbows. Miles looked the same with blood smeared across her face where she had touched it. Cam's tux shirt had blood all over it and his hands were stained red. He even had a blood streak through his blonde hair from running a hand through it. Miles looked like she was exhausted and deep in thought. She stopped in her tracks once we got out into the open arena and turned to face me, her face drained of the color the Nectar had brought back.

"She said *others*." Miles said with wide eyes. Confusion fuddled my brain at her odd statement.

"What? Who said that and what are you talking about?" I said feeling the Nectar kick in making me want to do jumping jacks and scream. Miles began to pace while the others carried Carla out the side doors of the arena leaving Miles and I alone.

"Nurse Lane said to get Carla to the Infirmary with the *others*…that means other people were attacked tonight Skye!" Miles said grabbing my arms as fear crept into her eyes. *Damn her memory to Hades. I just want this night to be over.* I thought getting worried.

"Let's get to the Infirmary then." I said heading towards the doors dragging Miles behind me by her hand. I reached the door when not one but two bright flashes of light lit up the entire arena mixed with the scent of the forest and wood smoke. I covered my eyes with my bloody hand. The light passed and I opened my eyes finding Artemis and Hades himself standing in front of the doors. Somehow through my shock at seeing them both I managed a half hearted bow. Miles bowed too looking stunned.

"Hello daughter. I see we have been a busy bee." Hades said in his low voice. He wore his battle armor from when I last spotted him in the Underworld, though this time he was normal height and not covered in Demon goo. Artemis looked like she may have gotten in a fight, Demon blood stained her pants.

"Hi dad…what's going on? Did the Demons take the Palace? I really wanted to help but everyone told me to stay out of it…I'm sorry I should have helped you." I blurted out feeling stupid. All I really wanted was a hug and a shower. Hades looked grim making my heart sink.

"Calm down my feisty one. No, they didn't get the Palace, I would never let that happen and it's insulting that you think I would." He said and held up a hand to silence me before I could argue with him. I clamped my mouth shut.

"I came here to warn you. Oceanus will reach the West Coast within the next twenty four hours, which means the Gods fight will be in your back yard. Tonight's attack was a small one. The rouge Demigod figured out that my child is here running around with your group of friends but is unsure of whom it is. They let a couple Demon scouts in past the guards somehow, probably with the help of the Spirit Tattoos. The Demons outside of my realm are re-grouping as we speak. My realm is safe enough but I will be sending Kirra back here to be under the protection of Artemis. She will return to human form within the hour. Zeus will be sending the Harpies to the forests outside the grounds. Harpies are dangerous cursed women with human faces, bodies of a bird and raging tempers. They get pissed off pretty easily so don't go messing with them. They are under strict orders to only go after Demons but they tend to ignore orders sometimes. I will be unleashing some of my army to the surface to help you Heroes and the Military Demigods. Help will be here shortly. My army will only follow the orders given by Charlie, understood?" Hades said making my head spin. That was so much information I didn't even know what to say.

"My dad is coming back?" Miles said in awe. Like he heard her, a puff of black smoke filled the space next to Hades and disappeared leaving a grinning Charlie standing there. Miles burst into tears and ran into her father's arms. Charlie hugged her tightly and kissed the top of her head.

"I've missed you Mi, you look beautiful in your

costume...don't worry I peeked in at you when you weren't covered in blood. You did really good tonight saving that girl. I'm proud of you Mi." Charlie said as he held Miles. Hades cleared his throat impatiently earning him a slap on the arm from Artemis.

"Don't be rude Uncle." Artemis said in a stern voice. Hades winked at me.

"Easy little Niece I might have to light you on fire like I did over that little debate we had in the Bahamas." He said trying to glare at her without smiling and failing at it. Artemis rolled her eyes at him but stayed silent. I didn't know what that meant but their exchange was slightly amusing.

"Told you she was my favorite...cheeky little thing, just like you kid." Hades said giving me a hard pat on the shoulder.

"Dad...what happened tonight when I helped Miles and Cam?" I blurted out. I needed to know what the heck that was and if I would be safe for me to do it again just in case of another emergency. Hades narrowed his fiery eyes at me and the flames went wild.

"You need to be more careful with that daughter. You tapped into your ability to raise the dead. If you had tried that alone, the daughter of Aphrodite would have died and you would have raised her soul from the Underworld, killing yourself in the process, leaving her soul wandering around without a home. You were able to use that gift, but pass it through to the healing gifts of the son of Apollo and daughter of Athena. It enhanced their own abilities, but drained your life force. I'm glad your mother was there in time with the Nectar. Do *not* do that again. You might not be so lucky the next time." Hades said making me feel small under his stern gaze.

"I'm sorry dad...I didn't know." I said feeling annoyed that he just expected me to know that without anyone telling me.

"I understand your need to help and save everyone, you get that from your mother. Understand kid, all Demigods who die get a one way, free pass to Elysium, unless they turn against the Gods. You have seen Elysium and know that *living* does not truly end when we pass from the Earth. Do not try and change the fate of those who are bound for death." Hades said gently resting his calloused hand on my shoulder again. He let go and turned to Charlie and Miles.

"Well, best get to it then. Charlie, report to me using War as we discussed. The army is outside waiting on your orders. Thanatos will check in tomorrow night. As far as we know we still may have a week before the Demons attack, but I wouldn't trust that knowledge anymore. The rouge Demigod knows you're here now, which means they know for sure you hold the Prophecy and the key to unleashing Typhon. Be on your guard and be ready for the attack any day." Hades said and left us with a flash of light and the lingering smell of wood smoke.

"You two are to go get cleaned up and rested right now. The others will be moved to the rooms on your floor so you will all be in the same place where we can keep watch on you Skye. Kirra will be staying with your mother and Melinda in their apartment. I will give you updates on Carla's health as soon as I know anything. Get moving and do not argue. Charlie you're with me." Artemis said in an unusually stern voice. I chose not to argue with a Goddess this time. Miles hugged her dad and we walked out the doors as Charlie and Artemis headed into the War Room deep in conversation.

Miles and I reached the stables when Chaos and War showed up to greet us. I dropped to my knees and buried my face in Chaos's thick fur as I hugged his neck. He let out a whimper.

I'm sorry I wasn't there tonight. Blaze and I managed to rip apart one of the Demons. We were coming back from hunting when it came through the woods alone. Those things run like the wind. A couple of the Military guards saw us in our true form. They know there is Hellhounds here now. Chaos said. I ran my fingers through his coat and sat back on my butt in the grass.

"They know the child of Hades is here anyways. It's okay big guy, it was bound to happen sooner or later. The rouge Demigod assumes I'm here and they let the scouts for the Demons in tonight. The only thing we got going for us is they don't know exactly which one of us is the child of Hades. Artemis is having all of us move to my floor in the dorms so we are all in the same place together too. My guess is she wants to make it seem like it could be any of us. Let's go, I want to wash tonight off me." I said to Chaos and Miles. Miles nodded and we headed to the dorms. I hoped the others would be there too so I could find out what happened to Carla without breaking Artemis's orders.

I opened the door to my room finding Zach standing there staring out the window. I raced over and hugged him tightly. The blood all over me had started to dry, making my dress stiff and skin sticky. He pulled away looking drained and tired. Chaos hopped up on my bed and lay down watching us.

"Carla is doing okay now, she's sleeping so we won't know for a while what really happened. Nurse Lane gave her some Nectar and Kayla and Big Mike donated some blood. You guys saved her Skye; she'll be fine… eventually. This is my fault. I shouldn't have talked everyone into hide and seek." Zach said sadly, plopping himself on my bed. I let out a sigh of relief and looked around my room. Someone had removed the extra mattress and blankets and made my bed. A vase of fresh lavender and a small plate of chocolate chip cookies sat on my nightstand telling me it had been my mother. The gesture made my heart ache and stomach rumble with hunger. I went to snatch up two cookies, but stopped at the sight of my blood covered hand and plopped back down next to Zach. Chaos sat up, licked Zach's face and then rested his head in Zach's lap.

"It's not your fault and I *never* want to hear you say that again. None of us could have known that would happen. We knew something like this was coming we just didn't know *when*. We were all ready for a night of normal, Zach. We got it for the most part…just ended messed up. Carla is strong… she has to be or she would have never pulled through. I'm the one they were really after…you aren't the only one who feels guilty, you know." I said feeling my stomach turn again with guilt and fear. Zach's eyes widened and he grabbed my bloodied hand squeezing it tight.

"I'm sorry I'm being selfish. You didn't ask for this Skye. You didn't ask to be the child of Hades or the Hero of the new age. You were dealt a crappy hand and you're still in the game. I *know* you can do this. You're strong and brave. If anyone can handle this it's you. Don't you ever feel guilty for what happened or what happens later. People are going to die. We can't stop it but we can do whatever it takes to avenge them and try to protect anyone we can. You did that tonight." Zach said meeting my eyes.

"I know…I'm trying to get my head wrapped around this still. Just don't beat yourself up for wanting to be normal again. We all wanted it and took the risk together." I said wanting to change the subject. Zach tried to speak but I put a finger over his lips.

"I love you, more than anything. I'm ready to take a shower and wash all this…*everything* off me. We can talk later about how miserable we both are. Get outta here and go kiss Miles, make sure she knows Carla is going to be okay. You better tell her how much you love her too." I said sternly as I pointed to the cookies by my bed.

"Eat one of these, go change into pajama's and if you want, come back in here so we can sleep. Tomorrow the hardcore training begins." I said and headed into the bathroom after kissing Zach on the forehead.

"I love you little mouse… Always." Zach said gently as he got up glancing at me before he left, shutting the door behind him. *So much has changed*…. I thought as I shut the bathroom door.

I turned on the hot water and got into the shower still in my blood soaked gown. I scrubbed and scrubbed the dress, peeled it off and threw it over the shower curtain rod. I used all the soaps and scrubby things I owned on my arms and body. Anywhere blood had soaked onto the dress, it soaked through to my skin, staining it red. The water was cold by the time I felt like I was clean enough. Hairpins and glitter covered the drain mixed in with blood. I used toilet paper to grab it up and throw it all in the trash. Then I washed my hands in the sink over and over again until my skin burned. The blood stains were still there but unless I burnt off my own flesh, only time would take away the stains. I came out of the bathroom in a big fluffy towel finding Josh petting Chaos sitting on my bed instead of Zach. I nearly dropped the towel in surprise which would have probably been a bad idea.

"Sorry…I just let myself in. The Dean moved my room to the one at the other end of the hall…well… I just really wanted to check in on you. I'll step out so you can get dressed." Josh said a little awkwardly as he got up and left the room shutting the door behind him. I quickly threw on some clothes and threw my towel in the bathroom hamper. I opened my door letting him back into the room and pulled him in a hug.

"We were able to kill the other Demon. I heard Chaos and Blaze got one. The Dean thinks there was only two but we're not sure. They tattooed three guards with the Spirit markings to make them let the Demons pass by without sounding any kind of alarm. Those three guards are in the Infirmary being healed. Nurse Lane figured out that certain tattoos can be cut off from the person's body and the curse will break. Lucky for those guards these ones weren't like what Charlie had. The traitor Demigod *has* to be one of my old friends. I find it way too suspicious that Lindsay wants to talk about giving up the child of Hades and in the same night the Demon scouts show up knowing right where we all were. I told the Dean what happened and he said he would look into it." Josh said pulling out of the hug and pacing the room deep in thought. I stopped his mad pacing and gently kissed him feeling him relax. I pulled out of the kiss and held the sides of his face as I looked into his eyes.

"We'll worry about that later. For tonight I just need to sleep, now that I know you're okay and Carla will live, I'm exhausted. You need to sleep too. I don't think Zach is coming back so please lay down." I said feeling my eyes get heavy. I pulled a pair of Zach's old sweat pants out of my closet and tossed them to Josh. He caught them and quickly changed out of his tux, not bothering to turn around. I felt like I was being a creeper watching him change, so I turned around instead.

"Zach is passed out with Miles. I went there first to check on her. They're both out like lights. Cam is with Kayla doing things that require locking the door and Big Mike is sleeping in the Infirmary tonight to watch over Carla. He said that I should tell you, thank you and he will talk to you tomorrow." Josh said as he came up behind me and gently made me turn back around. He had the sweats on without a shirt, showing off his chiseled chest and stomach. I wanted to touch him, but felt too tired to lift my arms that high. *Damn it all to Hades. At least for a little while I got to experience a ball and kissing a boy that I might be falling in love with.* I thought as I shut my eyes and let out a sigh, letting the exhaustion fully take over. I felt his hands on my waist and he walked me over to the bed helping me under the covers. He crawled over me and snuggled in behind me by the wall, pulling me into his chest. Chaos curled up on our legs and I was asleep in a second.

Chapter Twenty-seven

I woke up a few hours later feeling pretty good considering I only actually slept for maybe four hours. The nightmare had come again but this time I found that I was not afraid of it anymore. I decided I would use it to help me get used to the Demons. Thunder rumbled the sky waking up Josh. He bolted up with a start, causing a still sleeping Chaos to let out a growl. Alke sat perched in my window sill watching the storm with intelligent eyes.

"Oceanus has reached the coast." Josh said quietly, getting out of bed and walking to the window.

"How do you know that?" I asked sitting up. Josh picked up his discarded clothes and changed back into his tux pants putting the sweats on my bed.

"I can tell by the thunder. I know when Zeus is the cause of a storm and this time it's not him. It's one of my gifts, I can read the storms and know what they will do before it happens. I can't read this one, so I know it's caused by a Titan. I'm going to get ready for training. I want you in the arena and in your gear in one hour." Josh said sternly. He went from snuggly boyfriend to drill sergeant in less than a minute.

"Yes sir…one hour." I said with a salute. Josh smiled and walked over and kissed me gently.

"I mean it Skye. One hour…I'm going to get dressed and check on Big Mike. See you soon; be ready to work your cute little butt off." Josh said as he kissed me one last time and headed out the door with Alke on his bare shoulder.

I dressed in my combat gear quickly, then Chaos and I headed out into the hall. I went to everyone's rooms to wake them up. Well really, I only had to go into *two* rooms. The Dean probably didn't think this arrangement through very well, considering we were all *seriously* breaking the school rules and sleeping together. The most awkward was Kayla and Cam, I saw more of both of them than I needed. Apparently they had a *very* good night and didn't believe in using a blanket to sleep under. I left the room with my cheeks on fire.

You humans…you mate in strange ways. Chaos said with a snuff as we headed down the side steps into the storm outside.

"Oh Gods Chaos…I do not want to have this conversation with you…like *ever.* This is that moment when we just let the weird stuff that humans do in their bedrooms, stay in the bedrooms." I said feeling my cheeks heat up again.

Alright fine. But you have to stop feeling all embarrassed and flushed over there. I can feel it too and I don't like it much. Let's just get some food and check on Carla. We need to get the training started. Chaos said and started running through the harsh cold rain towards the Castle.

I choked down a breakfast sandwich and gave Chaos a handful of bacon and sausage. Not many people were at breakfast. Things had changed drastically, Military guys ate in groups hunched over their plates and the few students who were there, ate in silence. The rest were probably sleeping or in training already. The decorations hung sadly from the ball last night, as nobody had bothered to clean them up yet. News of the Demons little attack had spread already.

Maddie came out of the Library, catching my eye as I rounded the grand staircase, headed to the Infirmary. I stopped and waited for her to pass, watching her as she headed in my direction. She kept looking around, making me feel suspicious of what she could be up to. She slowed her pace turning as if she was simply passing me by and gave a small nod towards the Infirmary. Up close she looked worse for wear, bags shadowed her purple hued eyes, her mousy brown hair was still up from last night but looked messy and her skin looked grey. I felt really confused now and was about to say something, when she spoke first.

"Not here Skye... we need to talk. Follow me." Maddie said in a whisper as she passed by me without stopping or looking at me. I waited a moment, feeding more bacon to Chaos and then followed her towards the Infirmary. She passed by the door to the Infirmary to a closet, for cleaning supplies by the staircase. She went inside and I followed checking to be sure we weren't followed or watched. Chaos sniffed her once we were inside and I shut the door to the small room as Maddie flicked on the light.

She's a child of Dionysus. I don't know if she is the rouge Demigod but she is definitely one of his children. Check her for markings before you talk at all. Chaos said letting out a little growl and pulling back his ears. Maddie took a step back from him, looking a little startled. I pulled out one of my daggers and held it towards her throat.

"Before you say anything I need you to take off your shirt." I said realizing how awkward that sounded. Maddie let the awkward request slide without comment and pulled her long sleeve grey shirt over her head. She stood before me in her black bra and raised her arms spinning in a slow circle. My mouth dropped open. Angry jagged red scars of all sizes covered her torso and back. She must have used makeup to wear the open back dress she had on last night. I didn't need to see her legs to know there was probably a few there too.

"What are those scars from?" I asked feeling like I already knew the answer as I lowered my dagger, but didn't sheath it yet.

"Tattoos... I had to remove them myself. I know you're looking for a child of Dionysus who is giving information to the Demons. I also know who you are Skye. The Demons used me to get more information because their spy wasn't doing a very good job...one of my brothers or sisters is working with them. I don't know which one but I know for a fact they have gotten to Luke, Kirk, Ed and Will. Lindsay is following the others just because she doesn't know any better or at least I *hope* that's what's going on with her." Maddie said in a rush looking around like we might be over heard at any moment. She pulled her shirt back on and looked scared.

"Who are Will and Ed?" I asked trying to believe her. I just didn't trust her, she had never given me any reason to like her or trust her at all.

"The Twins that run around with me, Will is the one with the full facial hair and Ed is more, clean shaven." Maddie said sounding frustrated. I took a deep breath and tried to process what she was telling me.

"Okay so maybe you know what I am...have you felt the need to share that information with anyone other than me? Were you involved in what happened last night?" I asked trying to feel out this situation. I couldn't ever tell what Maddie was thinking before and I felt like she was trying to lay it all out for me but I was still missing something.

"I haven't *told* anybody it's you. I didn't know until I saw you coming back from your scouting mission or wherever you went. Something about your eyes... there was more...fire in them... and then there's your dog. I could tell he was a Hellhound but I wasn't sure until you came back with another one. I wanted to be a veterinarian before this mess so I know a lot about animals. He's no husky breed. I had nothing to do with last night. Only the spy knew about last night… I didn't even know it happened until this morning. Look Skye…I don't really like you and I know that you don't like me. But you are our commander or leader or whatever… and you need to know what you're getting into. The Demons have the Spirit Tattoos and *a lot* of spies. They *will* attack soon and I will do what I can to find out when and how. I'm on the *inside* and if I keep playing like I'm still under their control I can get what you need and keep them off your ass. If they capture you or Professor Kirra… it's over and we all die. I can't let anything happen like what happened to Carla…not to *anyone*… especially when I might be able to stop it. I wouldn't be able to live with myself." Maddie said looking frantic, with tears in her eyes.

I took in her words and really wanted to believe her with all my heart, but it was hard. My instincts kept telling me I was missing something. I figured my only option was to let her be our spy and *hope* she wouldn't betray us.

"How do *you* know about Kirra?" I asked narrowing my eyes at her. She took a small step back from me looking worried.

"The Demons…know she is the keeper of the Prophecy and know that you went to the Underworld to hear it…they just don't know *when* you went because I never told them…even though I knew. I swear Skye, they don't know what the Prophecy says, they just know it's about them and a child of Hades…and they know you're the key to letting Typhon out. Without the Prophecy they don't know how to get to you or who else might be involved in helping you fight. They don't want to make a move unless they are sure they can get you or Kirra." Maddie said looking grave. I huffed out a breath feeling shocked and scared. I still wasn't sure I wanted to trust her.

"So, they don't know who I am for sure and they don't know the core of the Prophecy or where Kirra is…right?" I asked and

Maddie nodded, making me feel slightly better that they didn't know everything yet.

"Alright. You will pretend we never spoke about this and so will I. Find out what you can and report it back to me and *only* me. I can't risk exposure and neither can you or we both get killed. You're right by the way… I don't like you very much, mostly because you've never given me a reason to. So how about we try to get over that and stay on the same side of the battle. I hate to say this… but if you betray me or my friends I'll send your soul to Hades so fast you won't even remember your name." I said in a low voice. Maddie visibly shuddered and nodded.

"I know you would. I agree with you, we'll pretend we still can't stand each other and I'll pretend to be with the Demons still. I'll try to find out who the spy is. The Demons are really smart about that though. Most of us under the Spirit Tattoo influence don't know who else is under the influence. The Demons are smart and speak to everyone individually and only allow one or two of us in on the plans. I don't know what made me different but the Tattoos didn't work on me. They worked for a little while and then it's like one day I woke up out of a haze. I knew I could still be tracked with the Tattoos so I cut them all off. It took forever for them to heal, even with the Nectar… I'm going to do whatever I can, Carla is my best friend and it's my fault she was attacked because I never said anything to anyone. She's the only one that stayed out of joining the Demons. They chose us and for some reason they didn't want her and now I'm glad they didn't…they are pure evil Skye and I wouldn't ever want to see Carla doing the things they are making their Tattooed ones do…We better get out of here before anyone notices us together. Thank you Skye…for trying to trust me." Maddie said with a grateful look. I gave her a curt nod and left the cleaning closet first.

I don't know how I feel about this. I want to believe her but she seems… off. Maybe she still has a Tattoo that we didn't see? Chaos said as I opened the door to the Infirmary.

"Maybe…we better keep this to ourselves for a while. At least until I figure out if I can trust her or not. Maybe I'll only talk to Artemis about it. She might know more than the others." I whispered to Chaos as we walked into Carla's room.

Carla lay in a bed with an IV attached to her arm looking pale. Her hair had been braided to the side, very messily held in place with a rubber band. The room was empty so I figured Big Mike was in training. I needed to hurry up and get there too before Josh came looking for me. Carla was awake and stared out the window. I shut the door behind me and she turned at the sound and smiled at me.

"I am glad you haf come to see me." Carla said in a raspy voice. She seemed okay but very tired and weak still.

"I wanted to check on you. How are you feeling?" I asked sitting in a chair by the bed. She sighed heavily and shut her eyes.

"I am alive. I would not be here if you had not saved me, you and your wonderful friends. I am luckeee to be living. I know you will ask if I remember who wounded me. I only know it vas a Demon. I do not know how they got in the arena. I remember I wanted to go hide in zee War Room but zee door vas locked, then… I wanted to try zee Archery Range…that is when I smelled zee Demon. I haf never smelled or seen one. It made me so afraid and then eet stabbed me and zee world went darkness. I theenk I hit and kicked it back but I am not sure. Zat is what happened Skyee… why did zis happen to me?" Carla said with tears in her beautiful eyes. My breath caught in my throat. I couldn't even tell her why they attacked her. They were looking for a child of Hades in my group of friends and found a child of Aphrodite instead. Guilt ripped through my chest as I told her the truth without telling her too much.

"They were looking for a child of Hades…like what Lindsay

said at the dance. They think the child of Hades is running around with my group of friends. They want to capture the child of Hades and use the child's power to raise the dead and pull precious metals from the Earth. This power will allow them to raise Typhon, the other Titans and an army of the dead being punished in the Underworld. We cannot let them get this power or we lose the war before it even starts. I'm so sorry Carla. This shouldn't have happened to you." I said trying to keep my guilt locked in my chest. Carla was smart and would probably see right through my lies if I didn't play it cool.

"It is okay Skyee. Ze Demons made a mistake by attacking me, which means zey cannot tell which of the Gods our parents are. That might be a good thing to keep zis child safe. Once I am better I will help you fight. I will not be in zis bed for more than anuzzer day, so I can help with ze fight and ze training. I will be with you all ze way to ze end." Carla said holding my hand. The tears leaked out of her eyes and I wanted to rip out my own heart as guilt of not being fully honest with her made me feel sick. I gave her hand a squeeze and held back my own tears of every emotion that wanted to pour out of me.

"I expect you healed and ready to go by tomorrow then. Thank you Carla for being so strong." I said with a smile and I kissed the top of her head and left the room.

I walked to training so deep in thought I was in the building before I even knew it. Josh was practicing on a mat alone, while most of the students were working in their units. I must have passed Zach without even seeing him at the stables with Shake and his unit. I made my way over to Josh's mat and caught his attention.

"You're late. I guess I shouldn't be surprised. You're also soaking wet…walking around in the rain again little Phoenix?" Josh teased. I hadn't even realized it was raining during my walk over. I managed a small smile and plopped down and stretched out my legs.

I pulled my weapons out of their holsters and lay them off to the side for now. Once my body felt loosened up, Josh and I began with hand-to-hand combat. My focus seemed much better than it had the last time. I was able to hear his instruction and stay on my feet much longer than before. We sparred for hours until finally I couldn't focus anymore from hunger. My mother hand delivered lunch right as I hit the mat hard on my back.

"You won't win a war on your back Skyelaa." My mom said as she handed a lunch bag to Josh and plopped the other on the mat next to me. I let out a groan and rolled onto my stomach.

"Nice mom...way to be supportive." I grumbled. Mom let out a chuckle.

"Sarcasm looks terrible on you missy. Hello Joshua, you are doing very well teaching her. Is she learning anything?" Mom asked looking up at Josh.

"Yes ma'am, she catches on pretty fast, when she stays focused. She's an excellent fighter...needs more weapons training but she's very good with hand-to-hand...most of the time." Josh said. I could tell based on his voice he had a giant smile on his face.

"I'm still here you know!" I said with my face still against the mat.

"Oh relax Skyelaa; it's all in good fun. With everything that's going on these days a little bit of humor is needed. Sit up like a lady and eat your lunch." Mom scolded as she opened her own sack lunch.

"Yes mama...thank you for bringing us food. I was starting to worry that I would die of starvation." I said digging into the bag finding more of mom's cookies and a huge turkey sandwich. We ate in silence for a minute and my mother made sure to break the ice with Josh right away.

"So, Joshua…as an instructor at this school you *are* aware of the fact that you are not allowed to date students?" mom said eyeing Josh suspiciously. I was mid drink of my water and spat it right out of my mouth all over my own lap. Josh actually blushed.

"*Mom!*" I managed to choke out after coughing my head off from trying to drown myself.

"Uh…yes ma'am I am aware. I'm not an instructor yet, I'm still an intern to Sergeant Scott. I won't be an instructor until next fall…well if everything goes well with our current situation of course." Josh said bravely meeting my mother's eyes. Mom smiled at him and passed him one of her famous cookies.

"Of course you will Joshua. You will make an excellent instructor; I have never seen Skyelaa work so hard and able to keep her focus until today." Mom said glancing at me. I rolled my eyes and let out a grunt with my mouth full of turkey sandwich.

"Thank you ma'am." Josh said trying not to laugh at my sullen display.

"You may call me Lila, Joshua. You don't have to call me *ma'am*…it makes me feel kind of old." Mom said and Josh let out a chuckle.

"You're not old at all, I'll try to remember that I can call you Lila. My mother is from the south originally and taught me to speak to women with respect at all times. She also taught me to ask permission to date a girl if I feel serious about our relationship. If I have your permission I would like to continue dating your daughter." Josh said calmly meeting my mother's eyes again. My face turned red right away. Damn him and his manners to Hades. To my surprise mom smiled at him.

"Of course you can. Thank you for asking. You two better get back to work soon, I have to get back to my class. I still have to speak with the Dean before then too. Look after her Joshua, she can be a handful." Mom said giving him a wink. I threw up my hands in mock frustration.

"I'm *still* here! Gods…you guys act like I can't hear a darn thing! So rude." I said with a giant eye roll. Josh openly laughed at me. Mom playfully poked my side and kissed me on the cheek.

"Love you honey, listen to Joshua and behave yourself please." Mom said as I hugged her. She kissed me again and headed to the War Room, leaving Josh and I to finish eating alone.

"I think I like your Mom. She's funnier than she lets on in classes." Josh said with a huge smile plastered to his face.

"Thanks, she's actually where I get my *astounding* sense of humor. She thinks I get all my great use of sarcasm from my dad, when *really* she's my mentor. Mom is a really positive thinker and always looks on the bright side of everything. I tend to be…more doom and gloom about things. She helps me look for the brighter side when I can't seem to see it for myself." I said realizing I was rambling. I shoved the last bite of sandwich in my mouth to shut myself up.

"Well…I like her. I think your right about the *doom and gloom* though. You can really be downright miserable to be around." He said looking sideways at me, I wacked him on the arm with an irritated huff.

"Rude! Alright *Mister observant*, get your butt back on that mat so I can kick the crap out of it." I said trying not to laugh. Josh stood up and moved gracefully to the mat. We faced off and started to fight, Josh shouting directions at me as we went.

Chapter Twenty-eight

Four days of hardcore training had my muscles screaming in protest at every little movement. I lay in bed going over the previous day's weapons drills. Woken up by my usual nightmare of the supposed Demon attack, I realized the dream was probably not going to happen that way at all. In the dream I was sitting in my mother's class when the alarms went off. *I haven't been in her classroom to learn anything in nearly two weeks. I'm exempt from all classes until further notice, so the dream can't happen.* I thought hoping I was right.

The other students still had to attend classes, but from what I had been told, the classes focused on Greek History, Field Medic Healing and Battle Strategy and stuff like that. I hadn't really talked to anyone besides Chaos in days either. Part of me worried that I might lose part of my humanity by only talking to an animal. If he wasn't part of who I am as a Demigod, I would lock myself up in a loony bin just for human interaction. Sometimes Chaos would go into way too much detail about his last meal, making me feel both intrigued and grossed out. I was starting to think I needed to speak to a human being about random human things soon before I started hearing actual voices.

Joe spent all her time in the War Room with Charlie, Miles, the Dean and Artemis going over plans and maps and communicating with the Gods. I hadn't even gotten to tell Artemis about Maddie and our weird closet conversation. Maddie had stayed true to her word and not spoken to me at all. Lindsay's whole crew had pretty much avoided all of us since our conversation at the Ball.

Josh and I hadn't even had time to spend a minute alone since our lunch break days ago. All we did together was train and when we were done Sergeant Scott would drag him away to help train other Demigods. I learned a hell of a lot from Josh during our training together. My Demigod senses were top notch and I could move as fast as light now. The hardest part was seeing Zach everyday and never getting to talk to him. He was so busy with his unit and training the horses he had made up a bed in the tack room of the stables and slept there. I missed him. I needed him to remind me how to smile.

I went over the days that had gone by and thought about where we were at in our timeline. It was day five of our second week window, waiting for the Demon attack. So far all everyone did was train, eat and sleep. The rest of the students seemed to be getting restless. Random scuffles were breaking out all over the place. Adrenaline was running high and tempers too. Everyone wanted to fight, but they were also really scared to actually have to fight anything other than a stupid fist fight where nobody died. The staff had been squabbling with each other too. They were pulling serious overtime; teaching, guard duty and training with us. All the staff members trained side by side with the students and Military guys. We were turning into a real live army. I still hadn't been assigned a unit like the others, which suited me just fine. I could be a student, but I have no patience to be a teacher.

Finally I rolled out of bed and got in the shower, feeling slightly jumpy. By the time I got out and got dressed, the storm outside had turned extremely violent, making me think my jitters were from the storm. Oceanus was, for the moment, still being contained by the Gods on the edge of the west coast. Oceanus had not been able to fully reach land, thanks to the Gods effort. That didn't matter much when it came to the weather though. Most of the weather came from the coastline anyways and boy did we have it bad thanks to the severely pissed off Titan. November had been downright miserable. We had already had two feet of snow, sideways rain, hail the size of baseballs and today looked like thunder and more snow. I woke Chaos up and the two of us left my room to breakfast in the Castle.

Cam was standing in front of my door when I opened it, catching me off guard. His little fox, Orion, hopped onto Chaos's back and nibbled his ear. I watched as Chaos and Orion played around the hallway. I looked up at Cam smiling and noticed he had a strange look on his face and looked exhausted.

"Cam…what's the matter?" I asked feeling edgy. I woke up feeling off anyways and looking at Cam was making me think I wasn't alone in that. His had stubble on his normally clean shaven chin and purple bags under his silver eyes.

"I pulled guard duty last night and didn't get in until about four this morning. I took out a Demon scout that I caught wandering behind the Gym. I wanted to tell you, *something* is going on out there. Have your dreams changed at all? There hasn't been a scout since the night Carla was attacked and all of a sudden I spot one and some of the others on duty last night took some more out. There were only about five Demons total that we killed…I feel like it's a distraction. Something feels…off about today. Do you feel it too?" Cam asked looking serious.

"Yeah I feel *something* I thought I was just being weird today. I don't know what's going on… nothing has changed, my dream is the same. I've even been trying to pay more attention to the details and I haven't noticed anything. Something has me feeling…I don't know like I had too much caffeine or sugar…I don't like it." I said feeling jittery. We headed for the stairs following slowly behind Chaos and

Orion. Cam ran his hands across his pants to wipe sweat off his palms on his black combat gear.

"I think they've found a way to block themselves. Kirra can't see a thing and we all know she is the keeper of the Prophecy and can see nearly everything. I visit her sometimes while she's locked up at your mom's place. Melinda stays there most of the time to guard Kirra and keep her company too. Kirra thinks they might have figured out a way to manipulate the Veil...I don't know what it is... I know I sound kind of crazy...I just feel...off today." Cam said sounding frustrated. I nodded as we opened our secret side door and headed out into the wind.

We reached the training arena a short time later. It had been nice having Cam for company. Nobody else showed up from our group to eat breakfast in the Castle, so we decided to head over to the arena and start the day. Training was in full swing once we wrestled the doors open from the raging wind. This time, all of Zach's unit was inside training with weapons and hand-to-hand. I caught Zach's eye and he waved at me from the mats. I walked over to him and Josh who were talking about something probably important. Both of them were deep in conversation and looking very serious. They stopped talking when I walked up, making my jitters really bad now.

"Hey...what's up guys? You both look really serious today." I said trying to calm my jitters. Josh gave me a kiss on the cheek but kept silent, which I didn't like.

"Josh was telling me he felt a little off today...do you feel weird today?" Zach asked looking at me like he does when he knows I'm about to tell a lie. I let out a sigh of irritation and nodded.

"Okay...yeah something's...not right in the world today and I can feel it or something. Cam feels the same way. He told me about what happened last night with the Demon scouts. I need to talk to

Artemis. Let's all go talk to her…if anyone knows, maybe it's the Goddess." I said and headed for the War Room with the boys trailing behind me.

Artemis was sitting in a chair deep in conversation with Miles's owl War about something that made her look upset. Miles was pouring over a map and some notes not even noticing me and the boys come in. Cam came in a moment later with Kayla, Big Mike and Joe. Joe had a hard look on her face that she seemed to never lose anymore. I missed her smile. Joe gave me a curt nod and we all bowed to Artemis, who had finally finished telling War her message to my dad. War flew out of the room with a little hoot and Zach shut the door. Artemis dipped her head and we all sat around the table.

"It would appear you have something to tell me Skye." Artemis said gently, as she rested her chin in her hands. I nodded feeling slightly stupid for calling a war meeting over some jitters.

"Yes Goddess. I feel…off today…uh well, we all do…I think. I just think something is wrong about…something." I said feeling my face turn beet red. I wanted to crawl in a hole and hide with how stupid that sounded. Miles saved me in a second.

"Oh thank the Gods. I thought it was just me being crazy. Goddess, I feel extremely unsettled today. I've been having the same dream about the Demon attack but I thought it would have changed given the circumstances. It's like watching a movie on repeat. Nothing has changed even though it should have. What's going on? Have you heard anything from the Gods?" Miles asked, looking like she wanted to scream in frustration.

"I feel it too. Something isn't right at all and I can't figure it out." Big Mike piped in while the others nodded. Joe huffed out a breath and ran her hands over her shaved head.

"I'm glad you called a meeting about this Skye. I visited Kirra today and she seemed really agitated. She kept pacing around the room talking about random visions being blurry or off kilter. I thought maybe it was cabin fever from being stuck in hiding for the past few days, now I know it's something else." Joe said looking around at everyone with a look of concern. Artemis sighed and closed her eyes for a second. We waited with bated breath for her to do something crazy Goddess like, but she sat back in her chair with a look of annoyance on her face.

"The Veil has been tampered with. I don't know how, but the Demons have figured out a way to make it affect you Demigods more than before. Your gifts of foresight have been basically taken away. Kirra, it would seem, can still See but not as well as before. I would assume the *off* feeling you're all having is the Veil attempting to cloud your minds, while your instincts are working against it. The Underworld is being attacked again as well. The Demons have reached The Fields of Punishment and are near Tartarus. If they reach the Tartarus they will try to release the Titans. We have to be on guard even more than before. I believe the Demons are going to try to release the Titans all at the same time. I think they know their plans have been overheard now and have hatched a new plan. Their spy has been doing well gathering information about what we know. Their tampering with the Veil tells me that we know too much about what they plan to do. I feel like we do not know nearly enough." Artemis said eyeing me down. *Damn her to Hades…she knows I know something*. I thought feeling my face redden. I let out a sigh and told them all about Maddie and what we talked about in the closet.

"She's on the inside with the Demons. I still don't know if I can trust her, but Luke, Kirk, Lindsay and the Twins are on team Demon. I'm pretty sure they are Tattooed but it's hard to say. Maddie cut hers off, I saw the scars myself and so did Chaos. Maddie is a child of Dionysus and is looking to find the Spy. I'll contact her in secret and find out what's going on…I'm sorry I didn't say anything sooner. I just didn't know if I could trust her. I guess we need to chance it anyways." I said as I stood up and bowed again to Artemis.

"I understand why you didn't want to say anything yet. Go talk to her. The rest of you will carry on and act like you do not know this information about her. She may be risking her life to feed us information. Even if the information is false, her life is still at risk because we will kill her for being a traitor to the Gods. Go train and be ready. I'm pretty sure something is coming." Artemis said with glowing eyes. I found it hard to swallow when she talked about killing Maddie for being a traitor.

I didn't even make it to the door when it burst open and Carla came bolting through it with her crossbow in her hands and a full quiver on her hip. She had healed up really well but still had to drink Nectar each day to help her keep from tiring easily. She was babbling in French and Big Mike had to calm her down enough to get her to speak English.

"Zee mountain! It is clouding!" Carla said and grabbed my hand trying to make me follow. Artemis flashed out of the room in a second blinding all of us. I looked at the others in confusion as we all rushed out the doors through the arena and out into the storm. Carla held tight to my hand as we raced past the stables through the sleet and wind to the open field. I couldn't understand what the hell she meant by *clouding,* until I looked up at Mt. Rainier or *Mt. Etna.*

My stomach lurched at the sight. All I could think of was all the volcano movies I had ever seen. Thick black smoke billowed out of the top of the snow covered mountain, so thick it was pushing the dark storm clouds up higher into the sky. The ground rumbled under our feet as thunder echoed around the valley. Flames licked the sky through the billowing black ash and smoke spewing from the enraged mountain. I wanted to run for cover and hide as far away as possible. Other Demigods were outside with us in the empty pasture watching the mountain with fear etched on their faces. Soon the entire courtyard and field was full with everyone staring at the mountains rage.

Someone tapped me on the shoulder drawing me out of my stupor. I turned to find Maddie standing behind me facing the mountain, not even glancing my way. I realized she was pale and looked slightly ill. I stepped back a step to stand beside her and waited for her to speak first.

"This is just the beginning. They know you're here for sure now. They also know Kirra is no longer in the Underworld. The Spirits are using the Veil so you can't see anything the Demons are planning. Luke, Kirk, Will and Ed have left to join the Demons. Lindsay stayed to keep an eye on things here with me. You have maybe ten minutes...*they are coming.*" Maddie said in a whisper. My hair on my neck stood on end.

"If you're lying to me...understand that you will be killed." I said meeting her eyes, which widened in fear. She nodded and I made to decision to trust her, praying to the Gods I wasn't wrong about her.

I raced to the front of the growing crowd of dumbfounded Demigods and Military guys, watching the mountain spew black ash and fire. Ash fell mixed with snowflakes from the black sky as the ash and clouds blocked out the sunlight, casting us into darkness.

I reached the front of the crowd with fear set like stone in my stomach. I took a deep breath and turned off my emotions. I pulled a match from my pocket and struck it against my belt. It was time to reveal myself to my army and hope to the Gods that I wouldn't be killed right away by the rouge Demigod. I took the little flame in my hand, made it into a large ball and held it over my head to make me visible in front of the growing crowd of my fellow Demigods. Chaos was at my side along with Blaze, both of them grew to full Hellhound size and barked at the same time causing the Demigods to draw their eyes to me, some of them screamed, many drew weapons. I climbed up onto Chaos's back, still holding the flames and unsheathed my double ended blade sending the flames to the sword. I raised the fiery sword over my head as my friends raced forward from the crowd and flanked me as we faced our army, most of them appearing ready to kill me.

"The Battle begins now! The Demons are coming! All units to your commanders immediately! We are to defend the mountain and this school from those who wish to destroy humanity and the Gods! I am the Daughter of Hades and I will fight with my life and my honor against those who try to take it from me! Will you stand and fight with me! Will you defend what is yours from those who wish to take it from you! Will you protect the weak from pain and death! Will you fight with me!" I screamed to the stunned looking Demigods, staff members and Military men. Kayla climbed up onto Blaze's back and thrust her ax into the air.

"I!" she shouted. Zach, Cam, Miles, Big Mike, Josh and Carla all rushed to the front of the crowd and yelled *I!* at the same time with their weapons raised. After a silent second, to my surprise, the rest of my army raised their weapons over their heads, yelling a resounding *I* and stomping their feet with a huge earth shaking roar. My heart filled with pride and everyone split to their units to prep for battle. I rode on Chaos's back to the arena to grab my other weapons and find my courage.

Chapter Twenty-nine

The earth rumbled again as Chaos and I reached the training arena. People were running around everywhere getting everything ready. It wasn't even mid-day yet but the ash cloud from the mountain made it feel like the middle of the night. Torches were lit, weapons were being stock piled, tents were going up around the courtyard and full blown battle armor was being strapped onto every living being. Joe and her unit of weapons masters had outdone themselves. Everyone's breast and back plates were custom made to fit each person like a second skin. All the weapons and holsters were sharp and gleaming.

Zach was shouting orders to his unit and strapping bronze armor on Shake's broad chest. Zach looked unrecognizable with his sandy blonde hair a mess and his bronze armor strapped to his chest. I passed him and Shake, dismounted Chaos and bolted into the locker room of the arena.

The locker room was full of girls putting on armor and grabbing up anything they might need from the weapons cage. A couple girls were sitting on the benches alone crying silently. I wanted to say something to make them feel better but I knew I wouldn't be helping anything. Instead I just passed them by and gently pat them on the shoulder. I took a deep breath as I opened my locker and got out my armor, feeling a heavy weight settle in my heart. I strapped on my armor, uniquely made just for me. The breast plate was black with bronze flames etched into the metal. All my holsters had skeleton keys and flames carved into the black leather. Each knife and arrow tip was carved with flames. My 9mm hand guns were loaded with bronze ammo. The guns were black with bronze keys plated into the handles. My armor represented me better than anything. *I am the daughter of the God of fire, I am the one who can harness the flame, I am the Phoenix.* I kept telling myself as I pushed down my sense of fear.

Miles had her armor strapped on, decked out in bronze with silver olive trees etched into the metal across the breast and back plates. Kayla's had black anvils and fire etched onto hers. Carla's was form fitted with lilies carved into the metal and a traditional leather clad skirt.

I had just strapped on my quiver when a flash of light made all of the girls in the room let out yelps of shock. The smell of wood smoke filled the locker room. I turned and found myself facing Hades, dressed in his full black armor and a foot taller than he was the last time we talked. His glowing tattoos swirled like dragon fire under his flesh.

Kayla bowed along with Miles and Carla. Carla looked scared but kept silent. The other girls slowly bowed looking confused. Hades looked around at everyone with scowl on his face. Some of the girls were mid-change, covering themselves up and backing away from him as if he might attack them. Hades smirked for a moment and turned it into a menacing glare.

"I am Hades. I wish to speak to my daughter alone." He said in a deep rumbling voice. The girls grabbed up their stuff and all bolted out of the locker room in a hurry.

"You three, stay here." He rumbled again pointing to Kayla, Miles and Carla. The three of them stopped in their tracks and turned around bowing again. Carla looked torn between excitement and pure terror. Artemis was scary enough but not nearly as frightening as Hades looked now, so I could understand Carla's reaction. Once the locker room was clear he shrunk down to human size and Chaos and Blaze bounded over licking his face and whining like puppies. Hades let out a deep booming laugh, petting them both.

"Hi dad…uh how's things?" I asked feeling like he should be more serious right now, given the current situation. He stopped petting the Hellhounds and stood up meeting my eyes.

"You did well kiddo. Way to get the army pumped up. Ares would *kill* to be intelligent enough to come up with a speech like that. Did you practice that one?" he asked smiling under his thick beard.

"Uh…I came up with it on the fly…thank you. Uh…dad…shouldn't you be in the Underworld, fighting the Demons?" I asked hoping with all my might that I hadn't made a mistake trusting Maddie. Hades nodded and his face turned grave.

"Zeus, my dear loving brother and mister big-shot King of Olympus, *insisted* that I come up here to help. Oceanus has reached land. That's why Mount Etna is erupting. Typhon can sense his brother's presence and is *very* pissed off. He's in there throwing an exceedingly large tantrum right now. I am headed there now, to meet Hephaestus and Apollo. Artemis is already there, getting the Automatons moving. Thanatos is in the Underworld with my wife, trying to hold the Demons back from Tartarus. I just came to tell you the update and to tell you I'm proud of you. You're my daughter. Trust your instincts, fight hard and remember, if you try to bring back the dead…you will die. People *will* die today, the human side of you will try to save them. Do not do so. Let them rest in peace and travel to Elysium where they belong." Hades said meeting my eyes, looking serious. My heart leapt up to my throat making me feel sick.

"I'm *scared* dad. I don't want people to die." I said sounding like a baby. The fire in his eyes turned to golden orange and he rested a hand on my shoulder.

"You'll be okay kiddo. Remember the beauty of Elysium and know that any Demigod who dies while defending the Gods will forever rest there. You must survive tonight or the Prophecy will never be fulfilled and the Demons will win. Stay strong and live daughter. We better go, the Demons have probably reached the boarders of the grounds by now. You three…keep an eye on her please and remember your strengths, you will need them. Trust your gifts and keep an eye on each other's backs." Hades said and with a blinding ball of white hot flames he was gone again. Where he stood was a black drawstring bag the size of a pillow case. I picked it up and found it packed with a bunch of vials of Nectar. The bag gave me some hope that many could be saved if they should fall injured at the hands of the Demons. I also realized that Hades is a good man and I was proud to be his daughter. I passed one to each girl and stuffed one for me into my boot.

We raced out of the locker rooms, Miles going to meet up with her unit, Carla headed to the Infirmary to meet up with Nurse Lane, while Kayla and I ran to the stables. Blaze and Chaos reached full size once outside again and we strapped on their custom armor from the tack room. Each of them had a tail attachment covered in bronze spikes and a single bronze plate that protected their bellies, but didn't prevent them from movement. Leather saddles strapped to the plate holding everything in its place as well as Kayla and me.

Once the Hellhounds were saddled, we split up and I headed to meet up with Josh. I handed a vial of Nectar to each person I passed. Every person I handed a vial to bowed to me or gave me words of encouragement. One girl I didn't even know said she would follow me to death. Her words made it hard to breathe. I was just glad I didn't have to keep explaining what I was handing them, I was having trouble talking from my nerves. With their classes they all knew what to do with the Nectar and not to drink too much.

I found Josh at the stables with Zach lining up the ranks of horses who were awaiting their riders. The earth rumbled again making the horses start and stamp the ash and snow covered ground. I walked over to the only two men I have ever felt like I could count on with a pain in my heart. The lines of the Prophecy were whirling around my thoughts.

One will pass through darkness whole
To emerge with scars upon their soul
One will fall to enemy hands
Returning broken, with their plans
One will watch the others fall
Finding power to save them all
One will face the enemy alone
To save the world, both sky and below

Between Miles, Cam, Zach and myself…the thought of any one of us doing these things made me want to throw up. I looked up at Josh, his golden eyes were hard and fierce ready for another battle. He kissed me gently and looked to Zach.

"I'll leave you to it. Skye you're on second line with Zach and his unit. I'll be helping Big Mike with the front line. We ride out in two." Josh said, his voice gruff and his face set. I nodded wishing I could tell him that I might love him and I didn't want him anywhere near the front line. Instead I fought to keep the lump in my throat down. I met Zach's cobalt blue eyes. Cobalt meant he was mad. I pulled him into a hug and felt how tense he really was, he hardly even hugged me back.

"Zach I…I got your back okay." I said feeling lame. I didn't know what to even say. He sighed and pulled out of the hug looking torn between screaming and punching something. I shuddered, hating the look on his face.

"If anything happens to me little mouse, know it's not your fault. Take care of Miles for me and my mom. And…know that I love you more than you could ever know. Get saddled up with everyone else. We ride out now." Zach said, in a hard voice. He kissed my forehead and walked away without even a hint of a smile. My heart ached as he walked away from me. Then the world shook as an explosion of fire lit up the blackened sky. The mountain spewed more black ash mixed with flame as Typhon raged inside his prison.

We all mounted up and headed to the courtyard in front of the Castle. In the past ten minutes, medic and rest tents had gone up, the War Room had moved to the front steps of the Castle under a massive tent, instant forges like giant barbeques for mending weapons burned in front of the dorms under black tents. Our army stood in the middle and awaited orders. We were massive, filling the space between the Castle and the Gym and the grazing fields on both sides of the Gym.

I looked for my friends. The only friend I could see was Zach's back as he guided Shake in front of our line, barking orders to his unit of two hundred Demigods and Military on horseback. Josh and Big Mike were somewhere in the front line ahead of us on foot with bronze shields as our first line of defense. Miles was off somewhere in the back by the War tent, sending out her stealth trappers and archers. Kayla was manning the forges and prepping the third line of foot soldiers behind my line of horseman. Cam was by the woods with his archers, who will be our last line of defense and our eyes from above in the treetops, as well as our medics for the fallen. Charlie had his army of dead in the outer fields marching towards the mountain already. There must have been about two thousand of us plus one thousand who were dead or an Automaton.

The US Army had been sending us more Military guys every day over the past week and now that they were all out in the open I felt grateful that we had more than just the students. Our army was larger than I had originally thought but possibly too small to fight a mass of Demons and two Titans.

We all stood lined up awaiting our orders from Joe and the Dean. Joe appeared on the Gym steps with the Dean and everyone fell silent, the only sounds were the rumblings of the mountain.

"Today is the day we have waited and trained for. Our outer guards have announced the Demons are coming from all sides and their numbers are large. Front Line to the surrounding areas of the grounds! Second Line, ride to the valley and guard the front of Mount Etna! Third Line, remain here and guard the school! Archers to the trees and rooftops in all areas! Medics split to each line and provide aid! The Dead Army of Hades is defending the mountain as we speak with Sergeant Scott's men. Do not let them down! Remember, you have been chosen. You have been chosen by the Gods because you are the greatest Heroes of this new age. Do not fear the Demons. Trust your instincts and your gifts, trust the man standing next to you. Defend humanity, the mountain and this Castle against the enemy at all costs! Front Line Move Out!" Joe shouted over the roaring mountain. In unison the entire army shouted *I* and stomped their feet causing the earth to rumble from the sounds of courage and hope.

Here we go Skye. Stay on my back no matter what and remember the Demons are looking to capture you. Kill them without hesitation and do not get separated from me or any of the others. We are not only defending the world but defending you. If they get to you, they will have the power to release the Titan. Remember that Skye... and for once, stay out of trouble. Chaos said as we moved toward the front to ride with Zach and Shake.

"Yes *dad*. I know the danger and the price if I'm captured. Just keep yourself safe okay. I need you because I love you Chaos." I said feeling the need to run around telling everyone that I loved them, just in case. Chaos yipped and raced to the front and we rode next to Zach and Shake. I pulled my bow and notched an arrow while my heart pounded into my ribcage like a battle drum. I pushed down my fear. *You can do this. Remember everything you were taught and how important this is for the world.* I told myself feeling my adrenaline fill my veins.

As we approached the hill behind the Gym, I caught sight of the tree Josh and I once sat in. I wished I would have been brave enough to have told him I loved him before I let him walk away and head to the front lines. At the top of the hill I looked down into the valley, the sight before us made me want to scream and run back. Balls of flame flew from the top of the mountain illuminating the pure madness below. Demons…thousands of them fought against the Military guys and the army of the dead. They moved fast in small groups slashing down anyone in their path. The Demons were too close to the hillside for comfort. We were supposed to be defending the mountain, but the Demons had infiltrated the valley before we could even get close to the raging Titan prison. The Demons had moved faster into the valley than we could have imagined. I looked at Zach feeling my heart clench in fear. His face hardened and he turned around facing his unit and raised his sword into the air.

"For the Gods!" Zach shouted as he whipped Shake around and we all charged down the hillside behind him yelling battle cries with our weapons raised.

Chapter Thirty

We met the Demons head on, the smell that they carried with them, like a thick cloud of death, assaulting my nose and mouth. All around me, bronze and steel metal blade met Demon silver serrated blade with sounds like ringing lightening strikes. Massive bronze Automatons were amongst the Military men across the river from us, the dead soldiers and Demigods on horseback, swiping at groups of Demons. The Automatons were fifteen feet tall with human looking bodies made of bronze and silver, with faces of different animals and sharp red eyes. None of the Demons they faced stood a chance. They swiped at the Demons with huge swords, cutting two and three at a time in half with a single blow.

Fires burned from molten lava rocks dropped from the enraged mountain and the ground rumbled under our feet. Chaos ripped apart any Demon we passed with his teeth and swiped at them with his armored tail. I drew back my arrows one by one and let them fly. Each bronze tipped arrow met the rotting grey flesh of a snarling, disgusting Demon, causing them to drop to the earth and melt into a putrid mess of black blood and a charred skeleton.

Zach cut them down with his swords from Shake's back without hesitation, dropping them left and right leaving a trail of skeletons in his wake. More arrows flew from the surrounding tree tops dropping Demons in front of us. My heart surged with courage knowing that

Cam was in those trees helping us destroy the monsters with each arrow. Demigods all around me cut down Demons with blades and spears. I drew my dual bladed sword and felt for the first time like I was truly strong enough to do this.

A Demon caught sight of me and charged me from the oncoming horde. His mouth gaped, showing all the shark-like teeth that would rip my flesh to shreds. I urged Chaos to charge the Demon. We met the Demon head on. The Demon dodged Chaos's fierce bite as he jumped over the top of us, catching my long ponytail and ripping me off the back of my Hellhound. I hit the ground hard on my back, all the air rushed from my body. Terror gripped my chest at my situation. *Chaos said not to leave his back.* My mind screamed at me.

The Demon was suddenly on me, I blocked his serrated sword with my own as it came down towards my face. I rolled to the side as the Demon missed and struck the ground where I had been. I rolled again finally feeling air fill my lungs, causing me to pant. Using the skills Josh had taught me, I leapt to my feet and blocked another blow from the Demon blade, the force making my teeth rattle. The Demon snarled spraying me with black smelly goo. On and on it went, with me blocking each blow as fast as the Demon could give them. I felt the Veil trying to hold back my instincts, making me slower and barley able to see each move from the Demon before it happened. I pushed through it with all my willpower, fighting against the Veils hold over me was like fighting mental sludge, slow and thick in my mind. The Demon suddenly came into better focus, making it possible for me to better see his moves before he could dish them out. I blocked a blow and with a twist of my blade, forced him to drop his sword and I sliced off his hand. In the same motion I drew one of my knives and drove it deep into the Demon's chest. He screamed like a dying animal and with a gurgle, sank down into a sick puddle of black mess and his bones dropped to the earth.

I felt elated. I had just killed my first Demon at hand-to-hand weapons combat. I found Chaos trying to reach me only to be attacked by a pack of Demons. They crawled over his back and tried to stab him while he thrashed and bit any he could get his teeth into. Rage bubbled hot and sticky in my veins.

Nobody hurts my dog. I thought, my own voice growling in my head. I attacked with full force cutting down every Demon that got in my way. I spun and ducked avoiding attacks from Demons as I made my way back to Chaos. I stabbed anything that had grey flesh with my knife and sliced at any part of every Demon with my sword. Chaos whipped his tail around to keep them off his back. With deep growls and snarling he ripped apart any Demon that passed near his head. Between Chaos and I, we managed to take out quite a few of them. I leaped back onto Chaos's back and the two of us burst into the horde of Demons, killing all that crossed our path.

A fellow Demigod riding a chestnut horse next to me fought with vigor, striking down Demons with a thick handled ax. We fought side by side, when suddenly a cry of pain shook my soul and he was cut down off his chestnut stallion by two Demons, making my heart stop. My tunnel vision left me and reality hit me in the face like a brick wall as I saw what the battle *really* looked like around me. The Demigods were fighting hard, many of them injured or fallen, I looked to the Demigod who not a moment ago fought next to me. *No! Get up!* I screamed in my head as I jumped off Chaos's back and bolted to the fallen Demigod.

I cut down another Demon as I approached the injured Demigod. It was a guy I had maybe seen once at school and I didn't know his name. He had dark hair and a thin face with freckles splashed across his small nose. Chaos stood over us as I tried to find a pulse in the fallen Demigod's thin neck. He had to barely be sixteen years old and he was bleeding out all over the ash covered grass from a jagged wound that went from his right shoulder, through his core to his hip bone. He had nearly been cut in half from one strike. I choked back the taste of bile as he sucked in a wet breath and a spurt of blood hit my armor from a severed artery somewhere in the mess that was his chest. I felt myself start to panic at what I was witnessing. *He can't die on me I have to save him.* I thought as memories of Carla's attack clouded my vision. I felt the chill of death settle around us, as I watched the freckle faced kid fading away. I pulled my vile of Nectar out with shaking hands, getting ready to give it to the kid that lay bleeding on the ground.

"Don't Skye…he's gone. Let him go to Elysium in peace." Zach said from above me and Chaos. I looked up from under Chaos's belly and saw Zach firing his crossbow at oncoming Demons. The freckle faced Demigod gurgled once more and then his pale blue eyes went vacant as his soul left his body. I choked back a sob and closed the kid's eyes, placing his ax across his chest. Zach took out a Demon, headed to attack me from behind. I whipped out one of my guns and dropped two more, who were attacking the chestnut horse of the fallen rider. I looked up at Zach, feeling relieved that he was alive. I scrambled up, remembering we were still in the middle of a battle and climbed back onto Chaos's back, feeling a lump in my throat for the ones that will be lost today.

Shake moved closer to us and I got a better look at Zach, who looked battle worn and fierce. He had a deep gash across his cheek and Demon goo all over him staining his bronze and silver armor in places. Black ash lay thick in his hair making it look as dark as Josh's. I looked around seeing horses lying wounded on the ground and Demigods being treated by our medics, while others struck down Demons who were trying to attack the venerable wounded. Anger at their cheap shots against the injured set my adrenaline screaming through my veins again.

Another wave of Demon's came at us out of nowhere. Zach and I fought side by side with our unit of Demigods on horseback, pushing the Demon's back towards the river that ran across the valley. I didn't hold anything back as I slashed and struck down as many Demons as I could. More arrows fell from the tree tops dropping a couple Demons as they came towards me. The Demons had arrows of their own and were firing at the Demigods in the trees.

Zach and I regrouped our troops forming a tighter line, really pushing the Demons with everything we had. The Demons reached the river bank and we kept pushing until they were right on the river's edge. I didn't know what the plan was, but placing the Demons in front of a body of water with a Son of Poseidon around, seemed like a trap to me. I was sure him and Miles had come up with this, as I watched Zach close his eyes. Behind the line of over a hundred Demons, the river waters thrashed within their banks. I fired arrows at the Demons line trying to take out their archers. The river thrashed more violently as Zach thrust his sword in the air and let out a deep booming shout, causing the waters to rise from the river bank, up fifty feet into the air. I caught sight of Zach's eyes as he opened them, feeling stunned and frightened. His eyes looked like a Gods, the true Son of Poseidon, deep green and brilliant blue swirled around like a thrashing ocean storm. The river's dark blue waters reflected the fires of the mountain and crashed over the stunned looking Demons with a deafening roar dragging them into the angry waters. In an instant over a hundred Demons were washed away down the valley drowning in the raging waters.

I looked around and realized Zach had washed away most of the Demons on our side of the river and we were alone now, with only a few Military men who were on foot. The dead army, the rest of the Military and the Automatons were on the other side of the river still fighting and making good progress. Zach rode across our line doing a head count.

"We lost thirty to death or injury, the medics are handling that now. We need to head up to the Castle and see if they need help.

The Demons hit from all angles and the front line is struggling."
Zach said to me quietly. I looked up to him feeling confused as to
how he knew that. His eyes still had a shadow of ocean rage coursing
through them, making him look incredibly fierce.

"How do you know that?" I asked trying to fight down the
fear I felt at the news and the fact that we lost *thirty*, possibly to
death. Zach turned his head to the side showing a black ear bud.

"The Dean has messengers running from location to location
gathering news and passing it through this to the leaders." He said
with a still serious look on his face. I wish that he would smile or
look like himself again just for a minute. He did just wipe out a
hundred Demons with one wave, he could at least gloat for a second.
I looked at his ear bud again and I felt slightly stung that I didn't get
one, so I could at least know what was happening with everyone. I
didn't have long to feel stung though, Zach shouted the order to
everyone and we re-formed ranks and bolted up the hillside again to
the school grounds.

We reached the grounds of the school and the feeling of
being sick crossed my mind again. The Gym burned, flames bursting
out of the windows and licking the stone sides of the building.
Everywhere there were Demons fighting Demigods and Military guys
on foot. These Demons had guns, swords and crossbows and they
were striking down anyone they could find. I caught sight of Kayla
astride Blaze, hacking down Demons with her axes. I looked around
for the others in the spare moment I had during our ride into another
battle. Other than Kayla I was unable to see anyone.

I held tight to Chaos as we met another line of Demons,
battling our hardest. I lost track of how many I was able to strike
down. Chaos bounded over the fallen bodies of the Demons and I
found myself fighting next to Kayla and Blaze. With the help of our
Hellhounds we were killing machines. No Demon could pass us
when we worked together with the work of dual blades, dual axes and

sharp teeth.

The Demons fell left and right at our hands. They must have caught on to the fact that we both rode Hellhounds signifying that one of us might be the child of Hades. At least forty Demons charged us, backing us into our own dorm building. I hopped off Chaos's back and stood next to him, throwing myself against the oncoming horde of Demons. Kayla ended up with her back to mine as we battled together, taking down as many Demons as we could. I felt myself getting tired, each Demon blade making my muscles scream out in protest. Kayla must have been feeling tired too because I felt her faltering and trembling against my back. We were alone in this particular fight. I heard a loud yip and threw my attention to our Hellhounds.

A group of Demons were stabbing and slashing any exposed fur on Chaos. Blaze frantically tried to defend him, biting and ripping through any Demon she could get in her jaws. They attacked him from all angles like a swarm of angry bees. The Demons moved fast and Chaos couldn't keep up with how many were on him. One Demon pulled out a gun, firing a shot at the back of Chaos's head, the bullet nicking his ear. I pulled one of my own guns and dropped three more Demons that were trying to get to my Hellhound. I emptied a clip into another Demon as it charged me. Kayla and I fought back to back, trying to get closer to our Hellhounds, but the Demons put up a good fight, keeping us back. It was starting to make me angry.

Chaos let out another heart wrenching whine as ten Demons stabbed at him from all sides, blood pooling on the ground at his feet from where they stabbed him. He took another jagged Demon sword to his side and toppled over to the ground, unmoving as Blaze let out a terrified howl. Time slowed as my heart thumped in my ears, my body filled with pure rage as my heartbeat took over every other sound. *I have had enough!* I screamed in my own head. I felt my anger surge like fire through my veins. The rage and frustration tore through my heart so intensely I thought I might explode. Heat seared my whole body as a scream of pure rage tore through my throat. I let the rage take over and engulf my mind and body in the fires of my own wrath.

Suddenly, white hot bluish flames burst from my hands forcing my sword and gun from my grasp. I screamed again and the burning hot flames engulfed my entire body. Somewhere in the back of my rage filled mind, I *knew* I could kill the Demons with the fire. I forced the fire to burn so hot I felt my blood boil. I threw out my hands thinking only of killing the Demons. With the sound of a freight train I pushed out the rage and the fire tore out of my body engulfing every Demon near me. I screamed so violently my throat felt like it tore. The fires burst to the Demons with white hot energy, scorching everything in its path. Demons caught in the path of the deadly flame were incinerated in a split second. My body shook with scorching fury all the way to my very soul as I let out a final scream.

The fire left me entirely and I looked around, feeling dizzy and exhausted. The forty Demons around us were reduced to little piles of ash mixing with the ash from the mountain. The remaining Demons fighting in the courtyard, retreated towards the woods and erupting mountain, leaving the Demigod army stunned. Zach and his horseman chased the Demons off towards the woods. Unfortunately, I had shown every Demon around *exactly* who they were looking for. I sighed knowing at least the grounds were safe for now and raced over to my bleeding Hellhound. Once I got close enough to see the damage, hot tears began choking me at the sight of him. I reached out to him with shaking hands as I looked him over.

Bright red blood soaked his side and haunches from stab wounds all over. Some were deep and some were mere scratches. I started sobbing and crawled on my hands and knees to his big head. My whole body shook from the use of power I had just displayed, making me dizzy and unsteady even on all fours crawling like an animal. I leaned close to Chaos's head, listening. He was still breathing but it sounded wet, like they had punctured a lung.

"Please big guy...*please* don't leave me...I need you." I whispered as I pulled his big head into my lap. He let out a quiet pitiful whine and sucked in another wet breath. I listened hard for his soothing voice but he didn't speak. I knew he was dying. As a daughter of Hades I knew by instinct, when the soul was trying to leave the body. Like with the freckled faced Demigod who died by the river, I could feel it, but didn't know what I was feeling. I knew the feeling now, I felt the chill of the presence of death as it came closer to my Hellhound. Chaos's soul was nearly gone from his broken form lying in my lap. Hot tears cascaded down my cheeks. Blaze whimpered and crawled over to us with something large in her mouth drawing my attention to her. She set the mass on the ground gently and rolled it over.

Kayla! My mind screamed. Kayla lay there next to Chaos with a stab wound through her chest.

"Medic!! I need a Medic!" I screamed at the top of my lungs, my voice coming out raspy and deep. I twisted off the cap on my bottle of Nectar, from my boot and with shaking bloody hands, I poured some drops into the cap and opened Kayla's mouth letting the drops fall onto her lolling tongue. I held my hand over the wound in her chest trying to stop the bleeding, knowing it was pointless.

"Please! I need Help! Medic! Medic!" I screamed feeling my voice crack.

I turned my attention back to Chaos who was having trouble breathing. I couldn't give him anymore Nectar because we gave him some in the Underworld. If I tried to give him *any* he would die. I cried so hard it hurt. My heart felt like it might burst from my chest and break on the ground into a million pieces. Cam came rushing over from across the burning courtyard with tree branches stuck in his hair. He let out a yelp at the sight of Kayla lying on the ash covered grass, bleeding out.

"Cam…I gave her some Nectar. I…*I don't know what to do…* I don't know if the Nectar will work, but I tried. *Please* can you help Chaos too? Please…he's dying and I *can't* heal him with Nectar." I said frantically. Cam checked Kayla, finding a pulse and checking her chest wound. It appeared to have stopped bleeding. He leaned down, kissed her head and crawled over to me and Chaos. Chaos let out a gurgle and a pitiful cry, making me cry harder and bury my face in his matted fur. Cam called the healing light to his hands, hovering them over every wound he could find. The light from his hands burned bright and blinding over the deep wound on Chaos's side that punctured his lung. Hot tears burned trails down my cheeks as I watched. Cam was growing tired before my eyes. Chaos sucked in a breath of air that finally sounded clear. I grabbed Cam's hands and stopped him.

"Hellhounds can heal themselves of most wounds. You got the worst, he can do the rest. Thank you Cam…what about Kayla?" I asked wiping my filthy hands across my cheeks to wipe off the tears as I felt the chill of death fade away from us. Cam sighed and crawled over to Kayla right as Orion came bounding over from the courtyard, jumping on Blaze licking her face.

"She's going to live thanks to you… if you had been *even a second* later with that Nectar and she would be dead…thank *you* Skye. You saved her life." Cam said looking exhausted. I poured more Nectar into the little cap and forced Cam to take a sip and then took one myself. We needed to get the wounded rounded up and regroup. The Demons would be back for me and would bring a lot more of them to the party. I leaned down and kissed Chaos on his big head and he huffed at me.

You just can't let me die can you. That's twice you have saved my life now. I think I'm failing as a guardian, I'm supposed to be protecting you, not the other way around. Chaos's said in his wonderful deep dog voice. I let out a choked laugh and buried my face in his fur again.

"You save me all the time, you wretched beast. I love you. You're not allowed to die on me *ever*. Blaze will you carry Kayla to the medic tent. She needs to rest and let the Nectar do it's work." I said sitting up and looking at Blaze. She licked my face and I helped Cam get Kayla on Blaze's back. I helped Chaos stand up and he shook a little on his feet.

"You go with them. I need you healed as soon as possible. Go lie down, eat and drink some water and don't argue." I said and Chaos snuffed at me. He followed behind Blaze to the tent set up near the Castle for the wounded.

Chapter Thirty-one

Everything I have read on historic battles and seen in movies, could not have prepared me for what is left behind once the battle ends. The fight lasted us about four hours, but the aftermath looked like it had been days. All around the courtyard of the Castle, Demigods both students and Military, lay dead or wounded. The stink of Demon's and blood, mixed with the smell of fire and ash making the air hot and sticky. It should be wintery and cold but instead it felt like being in the Underworld near the fires of the Fields of Punishment. The worst part about it was this was only the first battle, I knew we had more coming and soon.

I walked towards the Castle to the War Tent feeling numb inside. Each fallen Demigod I came across, I gave a few drops of Nectar, while thanking the medics as they helped the fallen. Thank the Gods I had given the large bag of Nectar to Carla to take to Nurse Lane, we were going to need it. I whispered a prayer of thanks to Hades for what he did for us, his actions will prevent a lot of death, which is ironic considering he is the king of the dead.

As I passed by the middle of the courtyard I came across Maddie lying in a puddle of her own blood with her spear and crossbow at her side. Her left arm was nearly severed off at the elbow. Tendons and muscles lay exposed on the filthy ground. I fought back a gag and pulled out my mini-med kit and used string to stop the bleeding, tying it just below her armpit. I used alcohol wipes to clean off my hands and got to work. I gently lined up the cut inner parts of her arm back in their proper place and put her arm back where it's supposed to be. I figured she may have a chance to not lose it if I could get it in place for the Nectar to work. I was just glad she was still out and unfeeling to what I was doing. I pushed her dark curls off her forehead, looking at the girl who gave us the time we needed.

"Maddie…Maddie can you hear me?" I said gently as I crouched over her leaning near her ear. She was still alive, breathing slowly and in deep shock. She let out a moan and slowly opened her eyes. I searched her pockets, careful not to hurt her wound further. In her right sleeve pocket I found her vial of Nectar, my own vial was now empty. I poured a few drops into the cap and tilted her head up, making her drink. She let out a sigh as the Nectar hit her system and looked up at me with tears in her eyes. Once I was sure the Nectar was in her system I untied the string from her arm to let the Nectar work its way down to the wound.

"You did really good Maddie. Without you we would have been caught off guard. You gave us the time we needed to get ready. Thank you. I know you have been risking your life for us and you have my deepest gratitude." I said trying to keep her attention off her arm. I watched as the wound slowly stitched itself back together from the Nectar. Maddie took a deep breath blinking as some color returned to her face.

"I tried to save everyone. The Demons are stronger and smarter than we thought. This is just the beginning Skye. They will come for you and soon. They will use anyone they can to get to you. The leader of the Demon army…I think he knows who you are anyways. I think this was just a test to see how strong our army really is. He wants you to release Typhon and the rest of the Titans. Unless they can find the secret way in to Mount Etna they can't set him free.

Only you and Hades can find the entrance. The whole mountain is made of bronze underneath the rock. All except *one* spot. There's one spot that is made of gold. With your powers you can find it and remove the gold and open the door. Bronze is the blessed metal so neither you or Hades can remove it, you can only remove the gold. You can also raise the dead, which means you can release the dead from the Fields of Punishment, making the Demon army stronger with soldiers that can't die." Maddie said in a weak voice. Her knowledge of this made my stomach churn with nerves.

"I know Maddie...but how do you know?" I said feeling worried.

"The Demon leader...he knows all of this because he's not really a Demon. He's a powerful Demigod. Skye...it's Lindsay's father...Marcus Campbell... I didn't know until the day after the dance...after we talked. I couldn't tell you because Lindsay never left me alone... I think her bird... that cockatoo, follows people around and gets information. I was there when her dad showed up and she sent me away... I followed them into the woods, Luke was there waiting for them. I heard what they were talking about... Lindsay thought it was you or Kayla that could be the child of Hades... she just sold out her best friend... Lindsay's dad was pissed...because the spy failed to find out fast enough who the child of Hades was and he had to come out himself to find out...I think the spy is dead...but I don't know. I just know Marcus Campbell is coming for you and Kirra and all my friends are in on it...I thought Lindsay was just caught up in following around Luke...I was wrong." She said looking miserable. I felt my insides grow cold with fear. *Now the Demons know it's me.* I thought feeling angry.

I realized with a jolt, that the whole battle was to draw out the child of Hades, forcing me to fully expose myself. I felt stupid and enraged with them and myself. I knew I would have to expose myself once a battle started but I thought the attack itself would be because the Demons were trying to wipe out the people who would defend the mountain, not a battle used simply to find me.

"Now they know for sure it's me. I used my power over fire to wipe out a bunch of Demons that were trying to kill me and Kayla. They nearly killed Chaos and Kayla, it made me get pissed and I lost my mind and killed all of them instead. That's why they retreated back after I did that... I was hoping I had just freaked them out or something, but it was because they got what they needed... Damn me and my temper to Hades!" I said more to myself than her. I ran my fingers through my messy hair in frustration and took a deep breath. I checked her arm and saw that it was back in one piece though there was still an angry red scar. I slowly helped her to her feet and together in silence we walked to the nearest medic tent. I helped her into a bed and marched over to the War tent, flinging open the door.

Joe, the Dean, Zach and Big Mike turned to me. I raced over and hugged Big Mike making him chuckle. Then I hugged Joe and Zach and even the Dean. They all looked battle worn, covered in dirt, ash and blood stains, but they were all alive.

"I have news and you're *not* going to like any of it. Call the others here right away. Except Kayla, she needs to heal...Cam can fill her in later." I said trying to sound commanding and failing at it. My voice was horse from all the screaming I had done today so I sounded like I was whining. Joe nodded and got on a hand held radio commanding the leaders to come to the War tent right away. I grabbed an ear bud like Zach's from a box sitting on the table and stuck it in my ear. I decided I was going to need one from now on.

In the ear bud I could hear Charlie and Sergeant Scott talking to each other. Saying the Demon's had retreated back behind the mountain and into the woods. *Good, that gives us time to regroup and get a plan going.* I thought. We waited for about five minutes when Kirra, Miles, Cam and to my surprise Carla, helping a slow moving Kayla, came into the War tent. Kayla walked over to me and pulled me into a hug.

"I owe you my life Skye." Kayla said pulling out of the hug and sitting slowly into a chair. Carla checked Kayla's bandages again and looked up at me.

"She *eensisted* on coming in here. I hope et is good I am here too?" Carla asked. I nodded to her and passed her an ear bud too. In my eyes Carla deserved to know everything after what had happened to her. *No more secrets.* I thought as I looked around at everyone feeling a deep hole form in my heart at who wasn't there.

"Where's my mom…Melinda and Josh?" I asked looking around, feeling my panic flutter in my chest. I looked to Kirra, who had an odd look on her face, like she had in the Underworld when she told us the Prophecy. The scar from her own attack shone bright white on her face as her skin paled and her eyes turned black. After a silent moment her eyes returned from black to their normal teal and she sighed.

"He's okay… he's helping the wounded over behind the stables. I can see him now. your mother and Melinda are helping with the wounded in the Infirmary… I think the Demons have lost their hold over the Veil, because I can finally *See* easily now." Kirra said. I let out a sigh of relief. That was good news, my mom was okay, Melinda was safe and Josh was alive. I couldn't have hoped for more. I began to pace the tent as I told them about Lindsay's father and how they planned to use me. We had suspected this from the beginning but now it was confirmed. I told them how this attack was simply to make me expose myself as the child of Hades and not to weaken our defenses like we had originally thought, which made my guilt of the lives lost tear into my heart. I told them what Lindsay had said at the dance and what I had discussed with Maddie the day after again. When I was done the room was silent. The only sounds were the sounds of the eruptions from the mountain.

"So we had a *group* of traitors instead of the possibility of just one or two. Well I can't say I didn't see that one coming. The biggest shock is that the leader of the Demon army is one of our own. That's a huge blow. Marcus Campbell is a very powerful man in the human world and ours. This means he has more power than we could have ever imagined. He has outsmarted the Gods, which means he is working with a God or a lower Titan. This is *bad*." The Dean said putting his head in his hands. Joe stood in the corner facing the door looking out into the courtyard in silence. She popped her neck and turned to us with a hardened look on her already tough looking face.

"Okay, now we know. Right now we need to collect our wounded and bury our dead. Everyone get to it, I need all hands on deck. Kayla, little sister, you stay in the forges tent and oversee weapons maintenance and inventory so you can stay still and heal. Carla go with her and keep her on her ass. I need her well enough for another battle. Gods know there will be another one. Zach round up the horses and tend to them with your unit. The rest of you spread out with small groups and cover the battle zones. I will take the river bank area where I will meet up with Sergeant Scott and Charlie. Get going guys. As soon as you're done, eat and take turns resting up. That's an order." Joe said and walked out the door. The rest of us followed behind her and split up.

Zach kissed Miles and held her for a minute outside the tent. I milled around and waited for them to be done with their much needed moment. Zach walked over to me and hugged me tightly.

"I'll need you to help with the guys at the stables. You rode with them and they trust you. Just stay away from the horses... you still spook them." Zach said and kissed the top of my head as he headed out. I walked over to Miles who was looking out at the courtyard with sad, glassy eyes. I stood next to her for a silent moment and looked out over the grounds, feeling numb and slightly broken inside. The medics were helping the wounded, the fire at the

Gym had been put out, but smoke still came from the windows. Ash still fell thickly from the sky, though the mountain had calmed down a little and finally stopped throwing balls of fire. Small fires still burned in the grass of the courtyard and piles and piles of Demon bones lay all over the place. I pulled Miles into a hug and held her tightly. My sweet little Miles, who had once been so fragile, looked at me with determination in her eyes instead of fear.

"We'll kill them for this. They will *never* get to you or any of us again. You're my family and I won't let them have you. They tried to take my dad from me and I won't let them take anyone else…ever again. I *promise* Skye." Miles said with a hard look. Big Mike walked up behind her and put his giant arm around her small shoulders.

"We all do. We all owe you that…*Phoenix*." Big Mike said giving me a wink. I smiled at him thinking of my ball gown that started his nickname for me.

"I promise to protect you. I give my word… Let's go take care of our own." I said feeling my heart ache at our next task. I headed out to the stables alone, while the others walked out onto the grounds.

I reached the stables in a daze, finding Military guys and Demigods running around everywhere helping the wounded and caring for the horses. A cry from an eagle made me look up. Alke was flying over my head, so I followed him to the front of the Training Arena. Josh had a small girl over his shoulder in a fireman's carry and gently laid her in the grass in front of the arena. He rested a hand over her forehead, said a murmured prayer and stood up looking along the line of bodies. The fire from the torches cast flickering light across his strong jaw line, which was tightly clenched with anger. There were at least thirty bodies resting in the grass along the front wall of the training arena. I felt a lump in my throat as I walked over to Josh. When he turned and saw me his eyes lit up just a little. The usual brightness of his golden eyes seemed muted down with sadness. He pulled me against his armored chest and buried his face in my neck. He didn't cry but he took a couple deep breaths. He pulled away from me and cupped my face in his hands, looking down at me.

"I was terrified that I would have to lay you next to the others. I've had Alke searching for you. He told me what you did with the fire. You pulled flame from nowhere and killed the Demons and made the rest retreat. I'm so proud of you." He said looking hard at me like he was memorizing my face. I looked down at my feet feeling guilty again. I told him everything that had happened and why in hurried whispers. He sucked in a breath when I told him who the leader of the Demon's was and why they even attacked us. He went to give me the whole speech about how I shouldn't feel guilty, but I kissed him to shut him up. It was a deep gentle kiss, sending the feeling of molten lava up my legs and arms. I pulled out of the kiss and looked at him again.

"I love you. I'm *in* love with you, Son of Zeus." I said looking into those eyes I had fallen madly in love with. He smiled and kissed my nose gently.

"It's about time you admit it. I love you, Daughter of Hades. I have loved you since the day we first sat in that tree... *You and me against the world*...always." He said in a deep soothing voice and kissed me again. The kiss didn't last very long because we had more pressing matters than making out in front of everyone.

Chapter Thirty-two

Josh and I worked as a team, cleaning up piles of Demon bones, laying our dead in front of the Training Arena and helping the medics treat wounded. The sky was still blacked out from the ash cloud which continued to swirl around the mountain. I had no idea if it was truly still day or if it was night. The ash stopped falling from the sky but remained a thick layer on the ground and all of the buildings like black snow. Joe ordered us to return to the Castle for food and to rest after a couple hours of helping clean up the mess left behind. Joe had informed Artemis and the other Gods about Lindsay's father. Lindsay's father was missing now. The Gods were absolutely raging pissed about one of their own high powered Demigods turning against them. The Gods were even more pissed because they were unable to find him anywhere, probably thanks to a set of his own Spirit Tattoos.

Josh and I rallied up the entire horseman unit and medics from the stable area and forced them to go to the Castle with us. Everyone was exhausted, filthy and starving. We reached the Castle to find most of the damage cleared from the courtyard. A giant pile of burning Demon bones lay in the middle of the grassy courtyard sending smoke up into the sky. Josh, Zach and I walked through the doors of the Castle seeing the main floor packed with people. There was so many of us, people were sitting on the floor, up the staircase and out on the patio, eating sandwiches. The mood was subdued and sad, even though we had won this particular battle, nobody celebrated or smiled, they were all too exhausted to even speak in more than dull murmurs.

The Infirmary was bustling with movement of medics and wounded. Most of the wounded that had been treated in the medic tents, had been sent to their dorms to sleep. The more serious wounded were in the Infirmary, some of their screams carried out into the main Castle. My mom came out of the Infirmary doors looking exhausted. She had blood down the front of her blue scrub shirt and her hair was a mess. I raced over and flung my arms around her. She hugged me back tightly and took a couple deep breaths. Zach passed us by and went into the Infirmary to see his mom.

"I'm so glad you're alright. I was terrified that the medics would bring you in here next. Is everyone else okay?" she asked looking me over for any wounds.

"We almost lost Kayla…but I was able to give her Nectar in time…if I hadn't been there…I almost lost Chaos too…Cam saved him though. I couldn't have done it without him. Mom…they know it's me…the Demons know who I am. They will try to get to me and I want you to stay here and don't take any chances. I would die if they hurt you to get to me." I said as my stomach filled with worry. My mom shook her head.

"Skyelaa…I can't just sit back and hide…your all I have." She said giving me a stern look. I let out a sigh and nodded.

"Fine, but please try to… for me?" I asked. She looked like she wanted to argue but just nodded. I knew she did it just to keep me happy and I appreciated it. She gave me one last hug and kissed me before heading back into the Infirmary. Zach met her at the door and hugged her, before heading over to the Dining Hall. He kissed the top of my head as he passed me by in silence. I stared at the doors for a minute, listening to the screams of the wounded feeling my heart fill with guilt. I shoved it down trying to ignore it as I looked around the Dining Hall. I found everyone sitting on the back staircase talking quietly. I grabbed a paper bag filled with sandwiches, crackers, a water bottle and an apple and joined them.

Chaos, Blaze and Orion were lounging on the floor at the bottom of the steps with plates of meat in front of them. War perched with Alke on the handrail of the steps, both of them watching over us. I sat on the floor with the animals and leaned against the wall.

"I'm glad you're doing okay big guy." I said petting Chaos on his head gently.

Blaze has been watching over me. I'm pretty much healed up now, just sore and dirty. Thanks to Cam and you, I'll be perfect and ready to fight again by tomorrow. Chaos said wagging his tail, which was still armored, so it thumped loudly against the stone floor. Chaos and Blaze were still full Hellhound size which I knew was more comfortable for them and easier for them to heal. Nobody seemed afraid of their size anymore, after all we didn't need to hide what they were, everyone knew now anyways.

"Thank you Blaze. I'm glad you're here with us. We couldn't have done as well as we did without you." I said reaching out and scratching her muzzle. She licked my hand and then licked the side of Chaos's face.

I looked at my group of companions feeling full and comfortable noticing that a couple of them were missing.

"Where's Kayla and Miles?" I asked feeling stupid for not noticing their absence before. Big Mike leaned forward and stretched.

"Kayla was finally wrestled into her bed by Carla, she's

sleeping so she can heal up and let the Nectar do it's work. Miles is with her dad and Joe getting things ready for our next round with the Demons and setting traps. She insisted on getting it done before she went to bed. She's a determined little thing." Big Mike said as he stood up.

"You can say that again. She told me she wouldn't stop tonight until she was sure we could all sleep with a warning system to wake us up. I'll head out and take food to her and hopefully drag her to bed." Zach said standing up too, trying to stifle a yawn. I felt my eyes growing heavy and stood up too.

"We should call it a night. I know I won't be able to sleep very long but I know I need to try. Let's find out if Joe needs us to do anything else and go sleep for a couple hours. We'll need to bury our dead soon too…I want to be there for that…to show my respect." I said feeling guilt tear through my heart again. Everyone stood and we walked to the War tent in front of the Castle together.

Joe was sitting at a table inside the War tent alone with her head in her hands when we walked in. She looked up wearily, showing how tired she was for the first time all day.

"The dead are all in front of the Training Arena, seventy two losses total, twenty seven of which were students. We lost twelve horses as well. We've all eaten and the Demon corpses have been burned. What are your orders?" Josh asked with a bow to Joe. We all bowed back to her, my heart heavy at the numbers Josh just spouted out. Joe rubbed her temples with her eyes closed for a moment.

"Sleep…your orders are to go sleep for a few hours. Charlie was just here with more bad news. We can probably expect another attack within a few hours. His scouts on the outer area around the school say the Demon's are regrouping and more are showing up with each passing hour. This time I'm *sure* they will come for you Skye. I also expect them to try to cripple our numbers for when

Oceanus gets here, because he *will* get here. They will be coming straight for you… now they know who you are. Don't worry, we knew this would happen eventually." Joe said giving me a small smile. She sighed and continued.

"The Gods are having more trouble with Oceanus and will not be able to aid us. They're having trouble keeping him away from here. He may reach us in a couple days to try to free his brother from the mountain. The battle in the Underworld is nearly failing as we speak. The Titans within Tartarus may soon be released as well. Hades had to return to the Underworld with the Furies to try and push the Demons back. It's near Midnight now, we send our dead to Elysium at dawn. Go rest and clean up. We have to prepare as soon as possible for the worst. Each of you, take four hours to sleep and report back to me. I have to go wake the Dean, his four hours are up." Joe said looking more exhausted than I had ever seen her. Purple bags lay under her lilac eyes, making her look ill. Her skin was ghost white and lined making her seem much older than she really is.

We all gave her a bow and left the tent in silence heading to the dorm across the dark courtyard. Guilt made me feel like I weighed a million pounds as I drug myself up the stairs to my room. Josh went to his room and grabbed a duffle bag full of weapons, more combat gear and medical supplies. He came in while I was peeling my filthy training gear off. My armor leaned against the wall behind my door waiting to be put on again. I moved everything off my desk and laid my weapons on its surface, ready to grab at a moment's notice. Josh laid out his weapons and armor next to mine and started peeling off his own combat gear. We didn't say anything to each other, both of us too exhausted for words. He went into my bathroom and ran a hot shower for me.

I took a shower first and came out in one of my clean sets of combat gear just in case we had to run out in the middle of our rest. By the time he got out of the shower in a pair of his own combat gear, I was in bed nearly asleep on top the covers. Josh let Chaos in and with a thump he dropped to the floor in full Hellhound form and started snoring. Josh crawled into bed with me and I fell asleep before he even lay all the way down on the pillow.

We awoke to the sounds of someone pounding on my door. I had forgotten Josh had locked the door last night and I bolted up in a full panic grabbing my gun from the bedside table. Josh bounded over me with a gun in his hand and flung the door open. With our guns drawn on him, Zach came flying into the room in a full blown freak out, babbling incoherently. I set my gun down and grabbed his shoulders stopping his mad pacing as my own heart flew up into my throat at the sight of his panic.

"Zach! What happened? Zach calm down! Tell me what's going on!" I said feeling fear creep into my gut.

"I tried but I couldn't! *Miles*! I tried…Skye! I couldn't do it! They took her! They took her and I couldn't stop them! Luke… Miles! She will *die*…they will kill her… I love her Skye!" Zach screamed in my face spraying me with spit.

I tried to make sense of his words as I wiped my hand over my face to clean off his spittle and my hand came away red. *Blood?* I thought feeling confused. Realization of what he was saying hit me and I looked hard at Zach's full form as he kept screaming about Miles. His eyes were wild like a churning ocean currant, he was still in his armor and gear from the battle, thick red blood ran down his arm from a wound on his right shoulder. Zach was panting, each breath sounding more and more wet in his chest. I kept looking for wounds besides his shoulder and a bruise on his cheek, as I let him babble. Then without warning, Zach fell silent and his eyes rolled back in his head and he collapsed, Josh caught him right before he hit the floor. Josh let out a grunt and gently laid him on the hardwood on his back. That's when I saw his side. His right arm was raised above his head as he lay there and between his ribs just below his armpit in the weak spot in his armor, was the hilt of a black dagger.

I screamed. I screamed so loud my throat tore and my heart shattered. I broke. I threw myself at Zach but found I couldn't reach him. I watched him lay there and I couldn't move. I realized I was being held back by something. Josh's strong hands dug into my sides like a vice. I fought against him only looking at my Zach. I saw Josh's face, right in front of me yelling words I couldn't hear over my screaming. It's like I was looking at Carla and Chaos and Kayla and the Demigod with the freckles, all over again but this time, it hurt my *soul*. I screamed again knowing my life would end if my Zach was gone. I felt a hard sting across my cheek and realized Josh slapped me. My ears rang from the silence that followed.

"I need you to hold it together right now Skye! I'm sorry I slapped you, but you were going into a fit. Focus…calm yourself… he *will* die if we don't help him right now!" Josh said holding my shoulders tightly. I should have been mad that he slapped me, but I felt my brain begin to work again. I threw myself over Zach's still form and frantically searched his pockets finding no Nectar. Josh tore through everything in the room and found nothing. He sent Chaos to get help and ran to wake up Cam while I pulled Zach's head into my lap. I surveyed the dagger stuck in his side. Blood dribbled out of the side of his mouth with each ragged breath and ran out of his nose, telling me it had hit his lung and possibly lingered near his heart. If I pulled it out his lung could collapse or I could do more damage. I ran my hand over his beautiful face and cried. He opened his eyes at the sound of my crying. He sucked in a wet breath and whispered my name.

"What *happened* Zach…who did this to you?" I sobbed, knowing, because I am the daughter of the King of the dead, *death* was coming for my Zach. I could feel it like a cold shadow in the room as it waited to take him from me.

"*Luke*…Luke came with a group of Demons and ambushed

us. I was helping Miles…Miles and four members of her unit set traps behind…my old dorm…in the woods. They killed the guys from her unit…they were military special ops…the Demon's struck fast and used guns. Miles and I shot back…. Luke showed up with that Kirk guy…they shot Miles in the leg and she fell…I shot at Luke but I missed him trying to help her. The Demon's pinned me down…five of them. I killed two…then…they took her from me. Luke said if I stopped fighting they wouldn't kill her. So…so I stopped and they threw me to my knees. They took her…tied her up… Before they left…Luke told me to tell you; 'surrender yourself or she dies'…I…tried to grab for a weapon but two Demon's…pinned my arms behind my back and tied me up…and Luke stabbed me and *laughed*… He told me it was because we fought before and I had this coming…and they left, leaving me in the woods. I was able to get untied…the knife I had in my boot…I came here… I tried…I failed…I failed her…Tell…her I love her. And …I… I love you…little mouse. *I love you*. I'm sorry." Zach whispered, his voice wet and raspy. His body shook and he coughed again and again, choking on his own blood.

Fresh tears fell down my cheeks as I watched him choking. I turned his head to the side, feeling my heart wrench in my chest as he threw up a lot of blood onto the floor. He choked and heaved, then thrashed his head around, spattering me with his blood as he drowned in my arms. The cool chill of death surrounded us sending chills across my arms as I clung onto what remained of my breaking heart.

Josh still wasn't back yet with Cam…Zach was going to die if I didn't stop it. The guilt from all the deaths, the attacks, what happened to Kirra, Kayla, Carla and now Zach, made my heart hurt so bad I wanted nothing more than to rip it from my chest. *I have to fix it. I have to make it right*. I thought through the pain in my chest. I was alone and couldn't help him. Zach choked again and I knew his soul was trying to leave his broken body. I could feel death closing in, like a cold frost taking over the air in the room. He closed his ocean eyes and his last breath rattled out of his lungs taking my heart with it.

I screamed for my father. I screamed his name over and over again while holding Zach to my chest as if hanging on to some part of him could heal the ragged wound in my soul. I could bring him back but I didn't know how to actually do it. I would die to save him. I knew if I were dead they would *all* be safe. I screamed for Hades as scalding hot tears ran down my cheeks mixing with Zach's blood.

Bright flames and scents of wood smoke filled the room, right as all my friends, Kirra and Joe came bursting through the door. Not seeing Miles amongst them made the hole in my chest grow. I looked to Hades, my only hope, in his black armor and flaming eyes. He crouched down on the other side of Zach's body with pity for me swimming in his fiery eyes.

"*Save him dad…help me save him.* I can't do this without him. *Please.* Just tell me what I need to do, even if it kills me. Zach *has* to live…he's one of the Four…I'll die without him." I said in little more than a whisper as I choked on my tears. Hades looked down at Zach again and let out a sigh as he looked up and met my eyes. His eyes were full of soft orange flame and pity for me. I watched as the fire under the flesh on his skin danced madly around and brightened like the sun.

"His soul is passing to the Underworld, he has not yet reached Charon to board the Ferry…we can bring him back but there with be a cost. He will return with scars upon his soul, forever changing him. He will be a different man and return with new abilities, some which will be dangerous. Are you willing to do this to him daughter?" Hades said quietly to a dead silent room. I thought of the Prophecy and *knew* it was beginning to be fulfilled. Without the Four Chosen Ones, we would lose this war. Zach and Miles are part of the Four and without them I knew we all would fail. I felt my heart jolt with fear and more pain at what lay ahead for all of us. Zach was going to be the first of the lines of the Prophecy. Guilt tore across my wounded soul for what I was about to do to him. Part of me hoped I would die from the attempt to bring him back. If I died, everyone else would be safe.

I sucked in a breath and made up my mind. I nodded to my father and choked back more tears as I laid Zach gently on the floor, feeling my heart ache as his body left the safety of my arms.

"We have to…or the Demons win. I'm ready…show me the way." I said in a whisper. Hades gave me a sad look and nodded as he placed his hands over Zach's body. The flames under his skin burned bright and thrashed like a wildfire. I followed my father's lead and laid my own shaking hands over my Zach's silent heart.

*

The End of Book One

*

Coming Soon

Book Two

Revenge of the Heroes

The Gods

Zeus- King of all Greek Gods: Ruler of Mount Olympus, the sky and law and order.

Hades- God of the Underworld: Ruler of the dead and all the precious metals of the Earth.

Poseidon- God of the Sea: Ruler of rivers, floods, lakes, earthquakes and creator of horses.

Athena- Goddess of Warfare, strategy and wisdom.

Artemis- Goddess of The Hunt, the moon, animals and wilderness.

Apollo- God of the Sun, light, healing and prophecy.

Ares- God of War, violence and bloodshed.

Hephaestus- God of Fire, crafts and metalworking.

Aphrodite- Goddess of Love, beauty, desire and pleasure.

Hera- Goddess of the Heavens, marriage, empires and wife of Zeus.

Dionysus- God of Wine, parties, madness and drunkenness.

Hermes- God of Travel, communication, trickery, language and messenger of the Gods.

Demeter- Goddess of Harvest, growth and agriculture.

Persephone- Goddess of Springtime, growth and wife of Hades.

Hestia- Goddess of the Hearth, home and chastity.

Thanatos- God of Death and minister of Hades.

Nyx- Goddess of Night.

Important Deities & Titans

Typhon- Titan of Storms, bringer of destruction and chaos.

Oceanus- Titan of the Ocean and waters of the Earth.

Cronus- Leader of all the Titans, bringer of destruction.

Perses- Titan of Destruction.

Gaia- Mother of the Titans and the Mother Earth.

Charon- Ferry Master of the Dead, ferry's the dead to judgment in the Underworld.

Cerberus- Guardian of the gates to the Underworld, three headed dog and pet to Hades.

The Furies- Three sisters of justice. Winged and vicious, punishers for the Gods.

The Demons- Born of Gaia at Typhon's request. Sent to kill Demigods and the Gods.

The Spirits

Bia- Spirit of force, power, compulsion and strength.

Eris- Spirit of rivalry, strife, discord and contention.

Deimos- Spirit of fear, dread and terror.

The Algea- Spirits of pain and suffering.

The Androktasiai- Spirits of battlefield slaughter.

Greek Terms

Demigod- Half Human, Half God. Stronger, faster and able to use elements for power. Longer lifespan than a human and better healing abilities.

Alke- Spirit of courage: name of Josh's Eagle.

Orion- Legendary Huntsman placed in the constellations by Zeus: name of Cam's Fox

Nectar of the Gods- Blossoms blessed by the Gods, used for healing Demigods wounds.

Mount Etna- Mountain prison of the Titan Typhon. Created by Zeus, Hades and Poseidon.

Elysium- Final resting place of the dead whom pass through Judgment.

The River Styx- River of Oaths.

The Lethe- River of Forgetfulness.

The Kokytos- River of Wailing.

The Acheron- River of Pain.

The Phlegethon- River of Fire.

Tartarus- Prison in the Underworld, housing the Titans and the worst evils of mankind.

The Veil- Mist that prevents humans from seeing magic, monsters, Gods and Titans.

Foresight- The ability to glimpse the future through dreams.

Seer- One who can foresee future events and the paths and choices which lead to the event.

ABOUT THE AUTHOR

Sedona grew up in a small town in Washington State out in the middle of the woods, spending her days sharpening her imagination. She always wanted to be an author and share her wild dreams with the literary world. Sedona now lives in a slightly larger town in Washington State with her husband, enjoying the simple life in suburbia, which of course drives her mad, because she misses the woods. Sedona enjoys writing and watching movies, so she can play pretend everyday because she is a child at heart. She has also begun her steps to becoming a crazy cat lady with owning two cats, who both talk a lot. Sedona is proud to finally become a member of the literary community and hopes to remain so, for as long as her imagination is alive.

Made in the USA
Monee, IL
26 September 2022

14705740R00213